LOVE AND HONOR

SHERRYL D. HANCOCK

Published by Vulpine Press in the United Kingdom in 2020

ISBN 978-1-83919-338-5

Cover by Claire Wood

www.vulpine-press.com

Thank you to the fans who read these books and leave reviews!
Thank you to all law enforcement for all you do!

Also in the *MidKnight Blue* series:

CHAPTER 1

Who did the bitch think she was? Some messiah for the masses? Did she really think she could make sweeping changes, huge waves, and not pay for it? What was it with women who assumed everyone wanted what they did? Why couldn't the stupid broad stay in the kitchen where she belonged? She was upsetting the balance. That couldn't be allowed. She had to be stopped. Yes, stopped, that was it. I can stop her; it's what needs to be done. Midnight Chevalier needed to be stopped. I can do it—I'll just kill the bitch…

***

Attorney General Midnight Chevalier-Debenshire picked up the phone in her office. She dialed a very familiar number, smiling as she waited for him to pick up.

"Sinclair," Joe answered, his English accent still clear as a bell even after many years in the States.

"Hey, handsome, you busy?" she asked, her voice a lazy drawl.

"Mmm, not if you're an extremely beautiful blonde…"

"No, it's not your wife," she said, laughing as she did.

"Damn!" he exclaimed, laughing too. "How's it goin', Night?" He leaned back in his chair and smiled.

"It's going," she said, looking out the window of her spacious office that faced San Diego Bay. "Look, do you have time to meet with me?"

"Oh Lord, what have I done now?"

"I don't know. Should I be investigating Mach 3 for something?"

"No! No, no, no," he said, chuckling. "When do you want to meet?"

"Today, lunch?"

"No time like the present, huh?" he asked.

"You know me."

"Indeed I do," he said, his tone dropping an octave. "Way more than your husband would like..."

"I'll let him know you said that," she said with a laugh.

"Shit, you would."

"See you at noon?"

"Of course. Would I ever let you down?"

"Nope," she replied sincerely.

"Nope," he echoed.

At noon, Midnight stood up from her desk, stretching and reaching into her top desk drawer for her holstered gun. Habit made her continue to carry a weapon, although as Attorney General for the state of California, she had the best bodyguards available.

As she walked into the outer office, pulling on her jacket as she did, Kana and Tiny stood up. They were her bodyguards—where she went they went, but not this time.

"Relax, you two," she said. "I'm going to lunch with Joe."

Kana and Tiny looked at each other. Midnight caught the exchange.

"Hey, it's Joe," she said. "You know, the one who runs a bodyguard business? I think he can protect my back, don't you?"

Kana shrugged. "Well, he did do it for a lot of years..." she said with a smile.

"He's getting up there, though. Is he as sharp as he used to be?" Tiny asked.

"I can still kick your ass," came Joe's voice from the doorway.

"Yeah, yeah," Tiny said, smiling as Joe walked into the office.

Joe hugged Kana, then turned to Tiny and shook his hand. "So how's this going?" he asked, referring to Kana and Tiny guarding Midnight.

Kana Sorbinno and Tiny Ako had previously worked for Midnight at San Diego PD, where she'd been Chief of Police. Before that she'd been a captain, a lieutenant, and originally the sergeant of a gang task force. She'd hired both Tiny and Kana over twenty-two years before. They were intensely loyal and very protective of the tiny powerhouse of an Attorney General. Midnight had a way of inspiring loyalty in the people who worked for her; it was just her nature.

Joe took Midnight into his arms, hugging her close. "It's been too long," he said, his tone slightly chiding.

"You've been busy, I've been busy." She smiled up at him as she stood in the circle of his arms.

They'd been partners for many years. Joe had been her second-in-command in the gang task force that had gained Midnight much notoriety. Joe had also been her best friend and, at one point, years before, her lover. She was now married to his best friend, Rick Debenshire, and had been for almost eighteen years. Rick and Midnight were very much in love; everyone knew that. But Joe was best friends with both of them. It was a relationship few could understand or comprehend, but it worked for them.

3

Joe had retired from San Diego PD a year before, starting his own bodyguard business. He kept in close contact with his friends, but his time was eaten up with traveling, networking and spending time with his family. There was his wife, Randy, who he'd recently remarried after being divorced from her for a year and a half. He also had two children, aged nine and ten, who were always keeping him busy.

Joe led Midnight out to his black Cadillac Escalade and opened the passenger door for her, glancing around them as she climbed inside. Midnight watched him as he closed the door and made his way around to the driver's side. He was still as handsome as ever; his dirty-blond hair was shorter now than it had been for many years, but still long by most standards, falling just to his shoulders. His light blue eyes, hidden now by dark Predator Ray-Bans, didn't show even a hint of wrinkles around them. His tall, well built body was still as strong and fit-looking as ever. Midnight knew he spent a lot of time in the gym keeping it that way.

Her ex-partner was a damned handsome man; she could definitely say that for him.

As they drove to lunch, Joe reached for a cigarette, lighting it as he rolled down the window.

Midnight raised an eyebrow. "You're still smoking, huh?"

"Yeah, and don't start on me," he said, narrowing his eyes ominously.

"You don't scare me, Sinclair." She smiled. "That might work on those kids that work for you, but you know it doesn't work on me."

"Don't make me call your husband," he warned.

"Call him," she said confidently. "He'll bitch at you for it too."

"I hear it from Randy enough."

"Obviously not quite enough."

Joe didn't reply, simply grinning at her.

"So, what's up?" he asked, when they'd gotten to the restaurant and had been seated on the deck.

"I need your help."

"You got it," he replied immediately. "With what?"

Midnight smiled. She knew she could always count on her friends, and Joe was one of her very best. He never let her down.

"I have an idea," she said, putting her hands on the table between them. "I want to expand my crime prevention unit."

"Okay…" Joe said, a half-grin on his face. He knew Midnight, and nothing she ever said that sounded simple actually was simple.

"I got the idea from you, actually."

"From me?"

"Yeah, the way that you take on the clients who aren't famous, who couldn't normally afford bodyguards."

Joe nodded. "So what's that got to do with your crime prevention unit?"

"Well, what if there was a unit of Special Agents that did just what you do? Only it wouldn't cost stalking victims, victims of spousal abuse, or what have you, a dime?"

"I think you'd make my business partner very happy," Joe said.

John Machiavelli, the man Joe had started the business with, was the one who handled movie stars, musicians and the like. Joe liked to handle "normal" people. He'd had his taste of dealing with stars and their issues when he'd dated rock star Jordan Tate. She'd just about driven him nuts with her insecurities, tantrums and publicity. Joe had retreated quickly to his nice stable life in law enforcement. While John didn't begrudge Joe the freedom to take the cases he saw fit to, he did mourn the loss of income when the clients were unable to pay.

Midnight laughed at Joe's estimation. "Honestly, Joe, what flaws do you see in it?" she asked, trusting his judgment as always.

Joe thought it over as they ordered their meal. "How would you determine who needs help?" he asked.

"Local PDs will refer them to the unit," Midnight said. "They're the ones who get the domestic disturbance calls. We set criteria for DOJ taking over a case, like when there are reoccurring instances of violence, they send in a case file, and we go from there."

"But will these agents work at making a case on the suspect at the same time?"

"Yeah," Midnight said, "they'd have to. I can't assign agents to people indefinitely."

Joe smiled, knowing Midnight would have thought all of this out before coming to him.

"What about liability?"

"The victims would have to sign a waiver releasing us of liability for the service."

"What about the agents?"

Midnight shrugged. "They assume the threat of violence every time they put on a badge."

"True," Joe agreed.

"And if you're talking about any harm done to the suspect in apprehending, it would be no different than standard law enforcement in handling domestic disturbance complaints."

"Oh, I know you, Night," Joe said. "You'll have those people trained to within an inch of their lives on when to use force. They'll know better."

"So, any other problems with the idea?" she asked after a few minutes, when their food had arrived.

Joe thought about it. "What about funding?"

"I'll get the funding," Midnight assured him.

Joe smiled. Midnight was a pit bull when it came to getting funding for a program she wanted. She'd garnered millions of dollars in grants for San Diego PD.

"So what do you need from me?" Joe asked.

Being her sounding board had long ago become the responsibility of her husband. Joe knew she had asked for his opinion to have another angle on it.

"I need you to give me some kind of idea how much it's going to cost me to start and run."

"Okay, that shouldn't be a problem. When do you need it?"

"Yesterday?" she asked, her smile broad.

"Always a rush with you, isn't it?"

"You know how I am…" She didn't look too sorry about it.

"Yes, love, I know," Joe said, smiling.

Midnight was a woman who had made a huge difference in the world around her. In her law enforcement career, she'd made changes, policies and plans to improve the lives of both officers and citizens in the city of San Diego. Now she was taking it up a notch to include the citizens of the state of California.

On the way back to the office, Joe and Midnight talked what they considered "family" business.

"I heard about Donovan," Midnight said, her tone worried. "How's he doing?"

"Well, he's feelin' damned lucky to be alive," Joe said seriously.

"I can imagine."

"I think he's gonna come work for me for a while."

"That would be good," Midnight said, nodding.

"Any word on when Kana and Palani are getting married?" Joe asked.

"Not yet." Midnight rolled her eyes. "I swear I'll kick Kana's ass if she gets cold feet now."

"She's the last one of us to get married," Joe said, grinning.

Midnight laughed. "I know, and I want it done!"

"Tiny still too chicken to get Jess pregnant?" Joe sounded amused.

"Oh yeah," Midnight said. "The big guy's terrified that the baby will be as big as he and his brothers were."

"How big?"

"In the neighborhood of ten pounds eight ounces."

"Holy shit!" Joe said, shocked.

"Tell me about it!" Midnight replied.

She'd only ever had one child, but it had almost killed her, and Mikeyla had only been seven pounds five ounces. The doctors had told her she just wasn't built for having babies. She and Rick had ended up adopting a five-year-old boy, years before, when his mother had been killed. Mikeyla had turned eighteen two months ago. Midnight was feeling old.

"So how are JT and Kat doing in school?" Midnight asked. "Last time I talked to Randy she said that Kat was becoming quite the artist."

"Oh yeah," Joe said. "She decided to paint her room last week."

"Uh-oh. What color?"

"Some horrific green," he said, rolling his eyes. "It looks like a re-enactment of *The Exorcist*. But Randy wants her to have what she wants."

"So it's pea-soup green?" Midnight asked, wrinkling her nose.

"Yeah." Joe grinned. "JT said he wants to paint his room black."

"Is Randy going for that?"

"Uh, no." He rolled his eyes again. "I'm the one not going for that. He can think of something else to 'express himself' with."

Midnight smiled. She knew that Joe frequently had hour-long debates with his wife over what was and was not acceptable for the kids' "expression." Having a PhD in child psychology, Randy wanted the kids to be able to give life to their innermost feelings. Joe was always having to put boundaries on that. Midnight found it endlessly amusing.

They arrived back at the office. Joe walked Midnight to the front door of the building. Taking her in his arms again, he kissed her on the temple. It was a show of affection that he often displayed with her. Naturally, a camera crew was nearby, reporting on the latest developments out of the Attorney General's office. Seeing the two embrace, they rushed over, eager to gain some gossip on the Attorney General.

They quickly recognized Joe Sinclair, the man who'd been linked with rock star Jordan Tate not too long ago. The seasoned reporter also knew that Joe and Midnight had been in a relationship years ago. He wondered if something was beginning anew.

"Mr. Sinclair, are you working for the Attorney General now?" the reporter asked slyly.

Joe turned to look at the guy, then glanced at Midnight, winking at her.

"No, we're secretly meeting behind her husband's back, with news cameras rolling," he said, his smile sardonic.

The reporter laughed. Joe Sinclair was nailing him for what he'd just been thinking.

"So are you planning on coming out of retirement?" the reporter asked doggedly.

"He's working on a special project for me," Midnight put in, "a new program."

"A new program?" the reporter asked, his interest piqued as usual when it came to the ever dynamic Attorney General. "Are you getting ready to shake things up again, Madam Attorney General?"

"I hope so," she said, with an engaging grin.

The reported flashed his famous smile. "Can you give me a hint?"

"Now, Dan, would that be fair?" Midnight asked, her gold-green eyes glittering with humor.

"Sure," the reporter replied. "It's called an exclusive," he whispered.

Midnight laughed, shaking her head. "Once I have everything in place, I'll hold a press conference. But I promise you'll be in the front row and have the first question. How's that?"

"That would be fantastic," the reporter replied gratefully.

Midnight walked inside, flipping Joe a final wave.

Dan Oliver stared after Midnight for a minute. She was definitely nothing like the people who had held the office of Attorney General previously. She gave a whole new meaning to the phrase "mover and shaker."

***

"What?" Christian snarled into the phone as he picked it up in the middle of the night; he glanced at the clock and noted that it was 2 a.m.

"Christian?" said an unfamiliar English-accented voice.

Christian sat up, hearing Stevie groan next to him. Rubbing his light blue eyes, he tried to get his bearings.

"Who is this?" Christian asked.

There was silence on the other end of the line.

"Hello?" Christian queried again. If this was a crank, they were good—there was static on the line, like it was from overseas, and they knew his name.

"Christian, this is your father," was the hurried reply.

Christian's features hardened instantly. "I don't have a father."

Stevie sat up, having heard his icy tone. Christian glanced at her and could see the concern in her green eyes.

"Christian, I know we haven't ever got to know each other—"

"Don't call me that," Christian snapped. "That's your name, not mine."

"It's your given name, Christian," his father said, his tone very proper. "That's actually why I'm calling…"

"To take back your name?" Christian's lips quirked in a sarcastic smile.

"No," his father replied reproachfully, "to tell you that I'd like to officially recognize you as my son."

"And why would you want to do that after all these years?"

"I need to leave an heir, Christian," his father said succinctly.

"Yeah?" Christian asked, his voice still icy. "Well, I don't want nothin' from ya, so don't bother." He hung up the phone.

Stevie looked at him questioningly. "And what was that all about?"

"My father," Christian said, lying back down.

Stevie lay down with him, putting her head on his shoulder as he pulled her close to him. In truth, he was reeling from the call, even if he was outwardly calm. Stevie knew him well enough to know how he was really feeling, so she smoothed her hand over his chest in an effort to soothe his inner turmoil.

"What did he want?" Stevie asked.

"To recognize me as his son."

"Why?" Stevie knew the story about his father.

Lord Christian Jeremy Sinclair, Christian's father, had gotten his Spanish maid pregnant. When she'd told him about the pregnancy, he'd fired her from his house. Josephine Collins had raised Christian by herself, working day and night to keep him fed, clothed and with a roof over his head. Christian had learned to hate his father over the years, culminating in a night when Christian had gone to his father's estate to kill him. "Not close" was an understatement.

"He needs to leave an heir," Christian said wryly.

"Oh."

Stevie knew her husband very well. If he didn't want to talk about this, he wouldn't. She knew exactly when to push him, and when not to. This was not the time.

The following night, when they got another late-night phone call, the stakes rose a bit.

"This better be good," Christian growled into the receiver.

"Christian Joseph Collins, have I taught you no manners at all?" his mother's pert English-accented voice said.

"God, sorry, Mum," he said as he sat up.

"Mm-hmm," she replied, sounding unconvinced. "I understand you were equally rude to your father last night."

Christian's mouth dropped open, then his eyes narrowed as realization hit. "You gave him my number."

"Indeed I did, young man," Josephine replied. "It's about time he decided to recognize you as his son."

"Mother," Christian began sternly, "I don't want a bloody thing from him."

"Do not get mouthy with me, Christian Joseph Collins," Josephine warned. "I'll box your ears, don't think I won't."

Christian rolled his eyes, feeling ten again. Stevie had turned over and was watching him with a smile.

"Fine, fine," Christian said. "But truthfully, Mum, you could have warned me."

"What good would that have done?" Josephine said. "You'd only have had more time to think of your sarcastic rejoinders to his good-will."

"Goodwill?" Christian said disbelievingly. "You've got to be fucking kidding me!" His temper was simmering.

"Christian!" his mother exclaimed.

Christian sighed, knowing he was getting mad at her unfairly. His mother had only ever wanted the best for him. The problem was, she never seemed to understand why he hated the father that had never been there for him. Nor did she understand how deep that hate went.

"I'm sorry, Mum," he said, his voice defeated.

"Will you consider his offer then?" Josephine asked hopefully.

"I don't know."

"If not for yourself, Christian, think of your children. It's a legacy for them."

"I don't have any children," Christian said dully.

"You will someday, won't you?" Josephine asked in alarm.

Christian glanced over at Stevie. "I don't honestly know, Mum. It's not something we've discussed."

"Well, it's something you need to," Josephine insisted. "And you need to think about your father's offer, Christian. It would do my heart so much good to see you accepted in society as the wonderful man that you are."

Christian closed his eyes. She'd just lowered the boom. If he wouldn't do it for his father, would he do it for her? Damn...

After a long pause, Christian sighed. "I'll think about it, Mum," he said. He wasn't willing to totally commit to it yet.

After he hung up, Stevie sat, looking down at him.

"She got you, didn't she?" she asked wisely.

"Nailed me good."

"What did she say?"

"Well, she said that I should think of my future children, that it would be a legacy to leave them…" He trailed off as he saw her grimace. "Then she out-and-out blackmailed me by saying it would do her heart good if I'd do it."

"Ouch," Stevie said, wincing.

"Tell me about it."

"So what are you going to do?"

Christian looked at his wife. "I have no idea."

Stevie nodded slowly, one red curl falling over her bare shoulder as she did. Christian had to admit that even after being married to Stevie for going on three years now, things were never dull with her. The fiery woman who'd taken on the mob to avenge her brother-in-law's death. The woman who'd basically kicked him out of her life when she was sure he loved someone else. And the only woman who'd ever left him for another man, his cousin, Joe.

She was beautiful, with red hair, emerald-green eyes and a body most men would kill over. She was smart, top of her class in the academy and in college. She was tough, surviving being shot three times with an AK-47 assault rifle. There was no one in the world like Stevie, and Christian was extremely happy to be the one married to her.

Not that he was a slouch in the desirable department. At six foot two, with broad shoulders and the body to go with them, jet-black hair, olive skin tone and devastating light blue eyes, he was movie-star handsome. Christian had been impossible for women to catch for years. Stevie had caught him, and she was holding onto him with both hands. It was a mutually passionate marriage.

"Okay, let's look at your options here," Stevie said, placing her hand on his chest. "The way I see it you have two motives."

"Motives?" He raised a jet-black eyebrow.

"Yeah," she said, smiling. "Either you don't do it to piss your father off, or you do it to make your mother happy."

Christian smiled at how easily she'd pared it down to the bottom line.

"Okay, true," he said.

"So, you go with what's more important to you," she said, shrugging a bare shoulder.

He glowered at her. "And you know what's more important."

Stevie nodded, moving to lie over him, her eyes connecting with his. "I think you have your answer, babe."

"Too easy, huh?" he asked, reaching up to smooth her hair back, his other hand already caressing her waist.

"Way too easy," she said, leaning down to kiss him.

He pulled her closer, deepening the kiss. She groaned against his lips, her hands grasping his shoulders. They were making love moments later, phone calls forgotten.

***

Sebastian Bach was sitting with his partner, Kashena Windwalker-Marshal, in her car, a 1996 Chevy Impala. They were heading back to work after having lunch. She was about to start the car when her head suddenly jerked backward. Sebastian recognized the look on her face—her eyes were unfocused, and her hand gripped the steering

15

wheel tightly. He knew when his friend was having one of her "visions." It didn't happen often, but when it did, Sebastian knew something was about to change. He watched as she relaxed, breathing in and out slowly and closing her eyes. She'd explained to him long ago that she got visions that flashed in her head; they seemed to have been a gift from her maternal grandmother, who'd had the gift. Kashena was half Ojibwa Indian on her mother's side.

He looked over at her. "Another one?"

Kashena took a deep breath through her nose and blew it out through her mouth, nodding slowly.

"They look like they hurt now."

"They never feel good," Kashena said, making a face as she reached for a cigar.

"Oh good. You smoke, and I get to smoke." Sebastian grinned as he took his cigarettes from his pocket.

"I thought you quit, Army Ranger," Kashena said, giving him a pointed look.

"Too much work," he said airily as he lit his cigarette and held the lighter out to her to light her small cigar.

Kashena laughed, shaking her head. "No discipline," she said in a disgusted tone.

"And Marines have discipline?" he said with a raised eyebrow.

"Oo-rah," Kashena said, making the sound that all Marines made to show full agreement.

"Bite me."

"Not an option," she replied automatically.

"So was this the vision that told you I'm about to become a millionaire?" Sebastian asked with a smirk.

Kashena laughed. "You wish."

Sebastian had known about her visions since they'd become friends in the military. They'd met during "police actions" in the Middle East. Their companies had run into each other during an operation. Words had been exchanged between her men and his. Kashena had taken charge of her platoon, indicating that Sebastian should do the same with his.

"You telling me what to do, Marine?" he'd asked her wryly.

"And then some, Ranger," had been Kashena's curt reply.

Ocean-green eyes had narrowed. "What's a broad doing leading a company?"

"Same thing a pansy-ass Ranger's doing leading one," Kashena shot back.

The "oohhs" started then.

"I know you're not insulting the Rangers," Sebastian said, "and since you're a woman I won't beat the shit out of you for the implication."

Kashena's dark blue eyes glittered in amusement. "If you're feeling froggy, jump."

Sebastian was taken aback by her words and her stance—she fully expected to fight him.

"Marines are the frogs, right, Cappy?" one of his men said.

"Better than jumping out of perfectly good airplanes," one of Kashena's men countered.

"Afraid you'd hurt yourself?" came the reply.

"Only afraid I'd have to do clean-up when you hit the ground," the Marine snapped back.

"Cut it!" Kashena commanded.

Her men stepped back, as did Sebastian's. It left Kashena and Sebastian standing in the center facing each other. Kashena looked at Sebastian, her eyes never leaving his.

"You throwing, or going home?" she said, knowing she was pushing him.

"You don't want me to hit you, girl," Sebastian growled.

"Then I guess I'll do the hitting." Kashena leveled a punch at his midsection, surprising him with her speed and strength.

Sebastian came back with a jab, which she dodged. Then the fight was on. In the end, it was a draw. They were both bloody, sore and exhausted. They became friends over a bottle of Jack Daniels. Sebastian was actually quite disappointed to find out that she was gay. He got over it, and they became closer than either of them had ever been to anyone in their lives.

During that time, Kashena had confided in him about the visions she had. Rather than being horrified, Sebastian had been intrigued. It had become an ongoing joke between them that she'd see his future "ex-wife" or when he became a millionaire.

When they'd gotten out of the military, they'd joined Sacramento Police Department together. They covered each other's backs in the academy and managed to get assigned as partners once their training time was up. Two years later, when Kashena had gotten fed up with Sacramento PD's habit of not promoting women, she applied to the Department of Insurance as a special investigator. Sebastian had done the same, not willing to lose his partner. They'd gotten hired by the Department of Insurance, and had shortly afterward been handpicked to act as personal security for the commissioner.

Things had been great for three years. Then a new commissioner had been elected. They'd been kept on as his security detail. Unfortunately, the new commissioner, Lyle Condermen, was a devout Southern Baptist. Gays and "philanderers," as Sebastian was dedicated to being, weren't something Lyle Condermen had tolerance for.

It had taken approximately three months for Lyle Condermen to realize that Kashena—who wasn't married with children, as Lyle felt a thirty-four-year-old woman should be—was gay. He'd also determined that Sebastian Bach, also not married at the age of thirty-six, was indeed a philander in the worst way. It didn't sit well with the commissioner, so he was bent on changing their ways—"saving them," as it were.

Sebastian and Kashena spent a great deal of their off time contemplating one hundred and one ways to kill the commissioner and get away with it.

"Wait, let me guess," Sebastian said, "you saw us in handcuffs after we shot the commish, right?"

Kashena shook her head. "But it might have something to do with our next move."

"Move?" he asked, giving her a dour look. "We're changing jobs again?"

"You want to stay with the commish from hell?"

"Point taken," Sebastian replied. "So?"

"I don't know yet," she said. "I have to sort out the pictures and figure out what they mean. You know it's never that simple," she told him, giving him a dirty look.

"Well, next time you order a sixth sense from your ancestors, tell them to send it with captions, will ya?" Sebastian grinned.

"I'll do that," she said, grinning back.

Two days after her vision, Kashena had the answer for Sebastian.

"The AG's office," she said one morning as she got into his black H2 Hummer, which she frequently referred to as his "mid-life crisis car."

"The huh?" He glanced over at her, a cigarette hanging from his lips.

"The Attorney General's office."

"Explain," he said, putting the H2 in gear and pulling out of her driveway.

"That's where we need to apply."

"That's our next move?"

"Yep," Kashena said.

"And you got to this one how?" He took a long drag of his cigarette and blew the smoke out the window.

"I saw fire, an eagle, and a symbol for justice," she explained. "I also saw a flash of a dark-haired woman with very proud features."

"Proud features?" Sebastian queried cynically.

Kashena scowled at him. "It means I could see she was a strong woman, okay? That's the sense I got from it too."

"Okay, and what do you know about the AG's office?"

"I know that I like Midnight Chevalier-Debenshire's style—her politics aren't political, and she's a cop's cop," Kashena said. "And she's family friendly," she added with a smile.

"Okay, that's why you're applying," he said. "What's my motivation?"

"Having to break in a new partner when I leave," she replied, giving him a wink.

"You win." He grinned. "Get me an application too."

Kashena smiled. "I've got it on good authority that Midnight and her security detail will be in town next week. I'm going to see if I can hand-deliver our applications to the woman in charge of security for the AG."

"And that's who?" Sebastian asked, knowing Kashena would have done her homework before bringing this idea to him.

"Kana Sorbinno." Kashena watched to see if Sebastian knew who that was.

Sebastian looked over at Kashena. "Is that the gay cop who was shot down in San Diego? The one who was outed publicly by the jerk running against Chevalier?"

"That's the one."

Sebastian gave a low whistle. "And now I know why you want to hand-deliver our applications," he said with a lecherous wink.

Kashena rolled her eyes. "Up yours, Ranger. I just want to meet her, okay? That's all."

Sebastian nodded, looking unconvinced.

"Seriously," Kashena said. "I would like to work for her, though. I mean, it's gotta be good karma to work for someone who should for all intents and purposes have died when she got hit."

"You don't usually recover from a shotgun blast at close range," Sebastian agreed.

"But she did," Kashena said, "and that's amazing. So I want to meet her, okay? Call it the need to touch God, if you will."

Sebastian smirked. "Gonna get struck down for that one."

"Yeah, yeah," Kashena said, waving her hand in dismissal.

***

A week later, Kashena got off the elevator on the seventeenth floor of the Attorney General's office. She walked over to the receptionist's cubicle, glancing out at the panoramic view of the Sacramento Valley and the mountains just to the east.

"Can I help you?" asked the receptionist, seeing Kashena's badge clipped prominently to her belt.

21

"Yes, is Special Agent in Charge Kana Sorbinno available for a moment?" Kashena knew she should have made an appointment, but today was the final filing date for the security team, and she didn't want to miss it.

"I'm sorry, ma'am," the receptionist said. "You just missed her."

"Damn," Kashena said, shaking her head.

The receptionist looked at the woman standing in front of her; she could see she was holding an envelope with SAC Sorbinno's name on it.

"If you hurry you might be able to catch her," the receptionist said. "She's down in the parking garage waiting for the Attorney General."

"I owe you," Kashena said, smiling broadly.

"Take the elevator to the lobby, then grab the parking garage elevator around the corner to the second floor. When you get off the parking garage elevator, just go around to your right. It's the black Navigator."

"Thanks!" Kashena said, heading for the elevator.

"You're welcome!" the girl called after her.

When Kashena made it to the parking garage, she spotted Kana Sorbinno leaning against the black Navigator, smoking a cigarette. Kashena noted how much more muscular Kana Sorbinno was than herself. And she was very definitely the woman Kashena had seen in her vision, her jawline strong and proud even in profile. Kana's black hair was pulled back from her face in a long braid. She wore all black, including black boots with a two-inch heel on them, and a black leather jacket that fell to mid-thigh. She made an imposing picture. Kashena took a deep breath and approached her.

"SAC Sorbinno?" she queried, although she knew this was Kana.

Kana's head snapped around, her dark eyes taking in the blond woman standing at the entrance to what was referred to as the "bat cave" due to its location and secret entrance to the building inside. Kana quickly assessed the woman, her eyes taking in the professional attire and the badge clipped to her belt in a matter of seconds. Finally, Kana inclined her head as she dropped her cigarette and stubbed it out with a booted foot.

Kashena approached Kana, scanning the other woman's features. Kana was very definitely beautiful, with dark eyes, smooth dark skin and high cheekbones. She had a very strong, impelling presence as well. Kashena felt nervous for the first time in years. Kana's look was direct, and Kashena knew she'd better talk fast or she'd be in danger of making a bad impression.

"The receptionist on seventeen said I might be able to catch up with you down here," Kashena said, smiling warmly, her eyes not wavering from Kana's direct gaze. "I was hoping to meet you and hand-deliver these applications for your security detail here."

Kana's eyes indicated mild surprise at Kashena's approach, but she said nothing to the effect. Her gaze dropped to the envelope Kashena held out to her. Kana took the envelope, her eyes meeting Kashena's again.

"Which position?" Kana asked, speaking for the first time. Her voice had a deep rich timbre, with a very definite command in it.

"Special Agent Supervisor," Kashena said. "And there are actually two applications in there, mine and my partner's."

Again Kana's eyes flickered with mild surprise. "She didn't want to deliver it herself too?"

"He," Kashena corrected with a smile. "And no, he let me handle it, since I'm the one that suggested we apply here."

"So why here?" Kana asked, leaning back against the Navigator again, putting her booted foot against the tire, her look assessing once more.

Kashena was silent a moment. "I like Midnight Chevalier-Debenshire's style; she's someone I want to work for." Her eyes met Kana's. "And so are you."

Kana's surprise was quite evident this time—her mouth opened slightly, then her eyes narrowed.

"What do you think you know about me?" Kana asked.

Kashena's gaze didn't waver. "I know that you've been a cop for over twenty years, I know that you understand the concept of faithfulness for a cause and," she said, smiling at last, "I think you have damned good karma."

Kana's expression went from bewildered to downright shocked. "Karma?"

Kashena took a deep breath, knowing she was risking sounding like a nut now. "I read about you being shot over a year ago. From what I read about your proximity to the shotgun blast, you should have been dead. Anyone else would have been, but you weren't. That's good karma if I've ever heard of it."

Kana surprised Kashena by throwing back her head and laughing. "My fifteen minutes of fame come back to haunt me," she said wryly.

Kashena relaxed, knowing she'd taken the right tack. Kana Sorbinno didn't strike Kashena as the type to be warmed by platitudes. She seemed to appreciate people who told it like they saw it. Kana glanced at the envelope in her hand.

"I'll look these over with interest," she told Kashena.

"Thank you, ma'am." Kashena smiled and inclined her head respectfully.

Just then, Midnight Chevalier-Debenshire and her second body-guard, a huge Samoan man, rounded the corner into the garage. Kana straightened, her eyes scanning the area behind Midnight and the man. Midnight's eyes, however, were on Kashena, as were the man's. Kashena's chin came up slightly. She met the man's eyes, then took in her first long sight of the petite powerhouse that was the California Attorney General.

Midnight Chevalier-Debenshire was far from what anyone expected. She'd grown up on the mean streets of San Ysidro, California, leading a street gang. When her younger brother had been killed in a gang fight, Midnight had changed her life. She'd become a cop and gotten a law degree. Then she'd done what she was famous for—she'd started a gang task force made up of ex-gang leaders and members. She'd used gang tactics to take down the gangs in San Diego.

Her idea, her perseverance in the face of impossible odds, and her burning desire to improve the world around her had made her famous. In her twenty-four-year career she'd gone from a patrol officer to the first female Attorney General for the state of California. And she wasn't done making waves yet, not by a long shot.

The woman herself was a deceiving sight. Kashena knew from what she'd read that Midnight was a only a few months from turning forty-three, yet she looked nowhere near her age. She looked more like Kashena's age, thirty-four. Midnight had long curly copper-blond hair, and cat-like gold-green eyes. She was only five foot five tall, although she frequently wore boots that made her two inches taller. She also weighed all of one hundred and twenty-five pounds. She was petite, but far from frail. Kashena had read about this tiny powerhouse, who was an expert in hand-to-hand combat and marksmanship as well as an out-and-out street fighter.

Only a few years before, there had been a highly publicized fight with a much younger woman who'd attacked Midnight, then still at the San Diego Police Department. The story stated that the younger woman, a disgruntled gang member, had pulled a knife on the tiny police chief in front of thirty of her officers. Midnight had waved off her officers' instant response and ordered them all to secure their weapons, saying that she would "handle" the situation. And she had—she'd beaten the young woman in what had been described as a good old-fashioned street fight.

Kashena was impressed with Midnight, and seeing her now only deepened that sense of awe.

"Ma'am," Kashena murmured, inclining her head to the Attorney General, her eyes lowered.

She didn't see Midnight grin or glance at Kana.

"This is…" Kana realized that she didn't know the other woman's name.

"Special Investigator Kashena Marshal, ma'am," Kashena said, raising her eyes to look at Midnight.

"She's applying for your detail," Kana put in, knowing Midnight would want to meet this woman.

"Really?" Midnight took in the taller woman as she extended her hand.

Kashena took Midnight's outstretched hand and shook it firmly, her eyes staring directly into Midnight's. "Yes, ma'am," she answered.

Midnight glanced at Kana. "Well, you've met Kana," she said, then glanced over her left shoulder at the big man with her. "This is Nathan Ako. We call him Tiny."

"Good to meet you, sir," Kashena said.

Tiny raised an eyebrow at Kana, then nodded at Kashena. "You too, Investigator."

Midnight exchanged looks with Kana and received a nod of approval from the other woman. It was a good sign for Kashena Marshal if Kana already liked her.

"So what agency do you work for now, Investigator Marshal?" Midnight asked.

"Department of Insurance," Kashena answered. "My partner and I are the commissioner's security detail."

"And how long has that been?" Midnight asked.

"Three and a half years, ma'am."

"And before that?"

"Sacramento PD for two years."

Midnight nodded. "Where were you before that?"

"United States Navy for ten years, eight years as a Marine, ma'am," Kashena said, a note of pride in her voice.

Midnight looked impressed. "Excellent," she said. "We'll definitely read over your application tonight. Does your partner have qualifications as good as yours?"

"Better, ma'am," Kashena answered immediately.

Again, Midnight looked impressed. "Well, it was good to meet you, Investigator Marshal. Hopefully we'll be seeing you around here again soon."

"Thank you, ma'am," Kashena replied crisply, secretly thrilled beyond words that Midnight Chevalier seemed to like her.

Kashena shook hands with Kana, then extended her hand to Tiny. He shook it, smiling this time.

Kashena left the garage floor feeling a sense of unreality. Midnight Chevalier was a celebrity in the law enforcement community, and Kashena couldn't believe she'd not only just met the woman, but actually seemed to have impressed her too. Sebastian would kill himself when he heard he'd missed the chance to meet the AG in person.

Back in the Navigator, Kana lit another cigarette, rolling down the window as she headed for the garage exit. Midnight sat in the passenger seat, with Tiny behind her in the back seat. Midnight had opened the envelope Kashena had given them and was looking over the applications.

"Impressive," Midnight murmured.

"What?" Kana asked, glancing over at the application in Midnight's hand.

"She's done a lot," Midnight said. "She has a master's degree in American History with a minor in American Indian Studies. She was promoted to second lieutenant in the Marines and led her own platoon for six years. She's got letters of commendation in here the likes of which I haven't ever seen."

"Interesting…" Kana said, her voice trailing off in thought.

Midnight shuffled to the other application.

"Sebastian Bach," Midnight read, glancing at Kana. "Her partner is male?"

"What's wrong with that?" Kana asked. "Our partners have always been male."

"True," Midnight said with a smile, continuing to read. "Wait a minute… Didn't she say two years at Sac PD?"

"Yeah," Kana said.

"Bach was two years at the PD too," Midnight said, reading on. "And transferred to the Department of Insurance the same day she did…" Midnight raised an eyebrow. "Think they're more than just partners?"

"You mean romantically?"

"Wouldn't be the first time." Midnight grinned; both she and Tiny were married to people they worked with.

"I seriously doubt it is this time, though," Kana said, smiling.

"And you know that how?"

"Because she's gay."

Midnight's mouth dropped open in surprise. "You think so?"

"I know so," Kana replied.

"How?"

"Great gaydar," Kana said, winking.

Midnight chuckled. "So they're just friends, you think?"

"Probably good friends," Kana said with a shrug.

"Think he's gay too?"

"Nah," Kana said. "Gay men and women rarely have anything in common, except their predilection for the same sex."

"Guess you'd know, huh?"

"Guess I would," Kana said, smiling.

"Says here Bach was an Army Ranger captain. He was Army for twelve years."

"That's what she meant when she said he had better qualifications, I'd bet," Tiny put in from the back seat.

"Probably," Kana said.

"Hmmm…" Midnight said, reading over a part of Bach's file.

"What?" Kana said seriously. Midnight's brow was furrowed.

"Bach has a juvenile record," Midnight said. She didn't sound too concerned.

"Don't we all?" Tiny said.

"Yeah." Midnight smiled. "But I'd like to know what this is about."

"Doesn't say?" Kana asked.

"No, just says 'note of juvenile record.' Usually juvenile records are confidential if there are no further offenses."

"Spoken like a true lawyer," Kana murmured.

"Fuck you," Midnight said, making a face at Kana.

"Spoken like the Midnight we know and love," Tiny said.

Kana laughed.

"Anyway, might be something to ask Bach about," Midnight said.

"You want me to check it out through our channels?" Kana asked.

"No, just ask him about it. I'm curious how he'll answer."

Kana nodded. Midnight liked people who were willing to be honest with her regardless of the cost. It was an important factor in who protected her. Kana's focus was always on who was best able to protect Midnight. She and the petite Attorney General had been friends for over twenty-two years, and Kana had vowed to protect Midnight at all costs. She took that vow very seriously, as did Tiny.

"So, you're definitely interviewing these two, yes?" Midnight asked, already knowing the answer.

"You have to ask?"

"Not really, no."

Kana smiled.

CHAPTER 2

Disgusting, filthy, immoral! How could someone in such an important position have employed such a bane of society? A lesbian! And her protection, no less? It only proved how stupid women were. They were "friends"—sure they were. Disgusting! She needed to go too. Couldn't let those immoral creatures, "lesbians," think they could hold a position like Kana Sorbinno did while not paying for their revolting ideals. She'd have to pay too. Time to work on the plan, get everything ready. Their judgment day was coming.

***

Kana had to admit she was impressed with Kashena Marshal. The woman didn't seem to know the meaning of quit. She'd been in the Marines; before that, her record in the Navy was exemplary. She had a master's degree in American History, receiving top scores in all her courses. She'd graduated at the top of her class in the Marine Corps officers' training. Commissioned as one of the few women to make second lieutenant as a Marine Corps officer, she'd commanded her own platoon of twelve men. After the Marine Corps she'd gone to the Sacramento Police Academy, beating out almost every man in her class for top honors. She was highly skilled in hand-to-hand combat and firearms, receiving a marksmanship award. In her time with the PD she'd been commended twice for service above and beyond the call of duty, once in a hostage situation, another in the backup of her partner.

Since changing over to the Department of Insurance, Kashena had been recognized for outstanding professionalism and "grace under pressure," as it had been described by the previous commissioner. There had been no notations made to Kashena's record by the current commissioner. Kana was curious about that.

"Your record is quite impressive, Investigator Marshal," Kana said. "I see a lot of write-ups in here from previous supervisors, even the previous Insurance commissioner."

Kashena nodded, waiting for the question.

Doesn't pat herself on the back too much, does she? Kana thought.

"So, I'm curious," Kana said, putting her elbows on the table in front of her, steepling her fingers together. "Why isn't there anything in here from the current commissioner?"

Kashena looked back at Kana for a long moment. "I'd say the commissioner lives by the rule that if you don't have anything nice to say…" Kashena's tone was even, but her dark blue eyes communicated a whole other story.

Kana canted her head, surprised at the statement but sensing that it had everything to do with a personality conflict, rather than a performance issue. It was something Kana intended to look into. She glanced at Midnight; Midnight raised an eyebrow, nodding.

"Is this range score accurate?" Tiny asked, reading her record. "A perfect 300?"

Kashena nodded.

"Joe'll be happy 'bout that," Tiny said, grinning at Midnight.

Midnight rolled her eyes. "Joe Sinclair, he's our unofficial range-master. He's a perfect-300 scorer too."

"I promise not to outshoot him, ma'am," Kashena said.

Midnight laughed at that, as did Kana and Tiny. "Actually, I'd love to see you do just that, Investigator Marshal," Midnight said warmly.

"Joe'd just say he's getting old," Kana put in.

"He is," Tiny said.

"Hey!" Midnight shot Tiny a scowl. "We're not that far apart in age!"

"Women are ageless, ma'am," Kashena said, with a straight face but a humorous glint in her eyes.

Kana liked her in that moment. Kashena was quick—she knew when to play it straight and when to lighten up.

"Oh, you are so hired," Midnight said with a laugh.

Kashena inclined her head with a grin. Kana knew that Kashena Marshal wasn't taking Midnight seriously, but Midnight was in fact serious. As long as nothing untoward cropped up in her background, Kashena Marshal was indeed hired.

***

"Investigator Bach, your record is very impressive," Kana said, glancing up at the man sitting in front of her, Midnight, and Tiny. They'd already covered the standard questions and were winding down the interview.

"Thank you, ma'am," he replied, his look direct, but respectful.

"How long have you known Investigator Marshal?" Midnight asked, curious about how they'd met—she assumed at the Police Department.

"Eight years, ma'am."

Midnight tilted her head to the side. "So you met while you were both still in the military?"

"Yes, ma'am," Sebastian said, grinning engagingly. The man was dangerously handsome. "She just about kicked my ass the first time we met."

"Really?" Midnight sounded intrigued, even as Sebastian winced at his use of profanity in an interview.

"I mean that she nearly prevailed in a hand-to-hand combat situation, ma'am." Sebastian's green eyes danced in amusement at the more politically correct version of his statement.

Midnight smiled at his revision. She liked him already. He was all cop, not an ass-kisser, like most of the men she was used to working around.

"We're all casual here, Bach," Midnight said. "You don't have to be politically correct."

"There is a God," Sebastian replied, relaxing visibly.

"Investigator," Kana said with a pointed look, "I'd like to ask about your juvenile record. Would you care to tell us what that's about?"

"You're in no way compelled to," Tiny added, wanting to make sure they were covered in terms of Bach's right to privacy.

Sebastian surprised them by shrugging. "It's not a national secret. When I was a kid my father regularly beat me and my mom. So when I was fifteen I started earning money to get us away. I was seventeen when I finally had enough to get us away from him. Unfortunately, he figured out where I'd hidden it, and took it." The muscles in his jaw jumped as he gritted his teeth at the memory of his father's leer as he waved the bills in Sebastian's face. "I pulled a knife on him and told him I'd slit his throat if he didn't give it back. He called the cops on me and had me arrested for armed robbery."

Midnight grimaced, as did Kana and Tiny. All three of them had been members of gangs, or had led one. They'd dealt with the violent side of life in their youth, as Bach apparently had. They could all relate.

"And you had no way to prove it was your money…" Tiny shook his head.

"Nope," Sebastian said. "My only break was that the arresting officer knew what a dirtbag my father was. He strongly suggested that I'd be better off in the military. In the end he was right—I managed to get my mother and little sister away from him and into military housing with me shortly after boot camp."

Midnight realized this man was very definitely honorable. Kana had already had reports from her connections at Sacramento PD that Sebastian Bach was a ladies' man, but no one, not even the women he'd dated, had a bad thing to say about him. He also had a fairly thick file of commendations, many of them from his military service.

As far as Midnight was concerned, she liked this man. He reminded her of a more regimented version of Christian Collins, a young man who'd worked for her at San Diego PD. Collins was a reformed ladies' man and bad boy. With his rakish good looks, easy, unrepentant nature and engaging grin, Sebastian Bach was definitely cut from the same cloth. She'd never had a problem with bad boys.

She told Kana after the interview that she wanted both Bach and Marshal. Kana agreed.

Two hours later, Kana not only wanted to hire Kashena Marshal and Sebastian Bach, she also wanted to shoot the prick that was their current boss.

Minutes into the phone call to Commissioner Lyle Condermen in regard to a reference for Sebastian Bach, he informed Kana that Investigator Bach was a "wild card."

"A wild card, sir?" Kana asked, unsure what he meant.

"He's a philanderer, Special Agent Sorbinno," the commissioner said. "It's hard to know from one day to the next what kind of situation he'll have himself in."

"Does it interfere with his ability to do his job?" Kana asked, wondering if Condermen was jealous.

"It hasn't yet, but it's only a matter of time. Considering the close nature of personal security, I would assume a playboy wouldn't be suitable for a female executive."

"Oh, I assure you, this particular executive can take care of herself in any situation," Kana said, feeling the need to assert the fact that Midnight was no ordinary "executive." "But I digress—you're saying that Investigator Bach would in some way embarrass the Attorney General?"

"It's possible. One never does know with a man like that," Condermen said ominously.

"Yet he's the lead investigator in charge of your security detail," Kana murmured.

"Excuse me?"

"Never mind," Kana sighed. She was wasting her time asking this man anything. "Let's discuss Investigator Kashena Marshal. What can you tell me about her?"

"Oh," the commissioner said cautiously. "Well, she is one of those," he said in a conspiratorial tone.

"One of *those*, sir?" Kana controlled the anger rising in her. She already knew what the commissioner was making reference to.

"You know," the commissioner said, sounding mildly disgusted. "She's gay."

"And you feel that would be a reason not to hire her?" Kana asked, baiting him.

"I think it's something you should be aware of."

"Has it posed a problem in the past?" Kana gritted her teeth to keep from coming unglued at the hateful little man.

"No, but then again, I'm not a woman. I do believe the Attorney General is."

"Yes, she is," Kana said. "She's also married and very straight. Are you suggesting that Attorney General Chevalier-Debenshire would be in some kind of danger if she were protected by a gay woman?"

"You know how that type can be..."

"Yes, I do," Kana said, finally allowing her ire to color her voice, "considering I myself am a gay woman. And last time I checked, Commissioner Condermen, it's illegal to discriminate against people for their sexual preference. Perhaps you should recall that next time you're speaking to someone you don't know, especially when you decide to denigrate a certain class of people." With that Kana hung up the phone.

Tiny glanced over at Kana, a dark eyebrow raised. "Good reference?" he asked brightly.

"Better than that," Kana said, scowling at her longtime partner. "He confirmed that she's gay and that Bach's a player. Now I'll hire her twice as fast."

Tiny chuckled. "What about her partner?"

"Sebastian Bach," she said, picking up the application packet. "He's impressive too. I'm just not sure I want the playboy type around Midnight, you know?"

Tiny raised an eyebrow again. "You wouldn't be discriminating against him because he's straight and good looking, would you?"

"Fuck you, Ako," Kana spat. "You're right—he has a helluva sheet, and his interview was stellar."

"Like Marshal's," Tiny said. "And they're partners. You know Midnight prefers people who work well together."

"I know," Kana said. "I'm calling Marshal. I want her take on her partner."

"You don't think you'll get a biased opinion there?"

"Of course I will," Kana said, "but I think I'll get an honest one too."

Kashena answered on the third ring. "Marshal," she said smoothly.

"Investigator Marshal, this is Kana Sorbinno with DOJ," Kana said, her tone warm.

"SAC Sorbinno," Kashena said. "How are you?"

"Good. Knee deep in applications, but otherwise, good."

"The life of a law enforcement officer is measured in the number of trees decimated in our wake," Kashena replied, grinning on her end.

Kana chuckled, agreeing wholeheartedly. "Indeed it is," she said. "I'd like to get your opinion on something, Investigator Marshal."

"Ma'am?"

"Tell me honestly, Marshal," Kana said in a conspiring tone, "is Investigator Bach the lead in your team because he's good, or because he's male?"

"He's good, ma'am," Kashena answered without hesitation. "His being male not withstanding," she added.

Kana laughed outright at that. She liked Kashena's sense of humor; it was wry and intelligent.

"Is he better than you?"

"Two years better, ma'am," Kashena answered crisply.

Kana knew that Kashena was referring to Sebastian Bach's military service. It said a lot about her respect for her partner.

"Do you think there'd be any personal conflict with his protecting the AG?" Kana asked pointedly.

"Investigator Bach knows his limits, ma'am," Kashena said. "He also knows off limits when he sees it."

Kana smiled. Anyone who watched the news knew about Midnight's love affair with her husband of eighteen years. No one could touch it.

"That's good to know," Kana said.

Kashena was silent.

"Investigator Marshal?" Kana asked.

"Yes, ma'am?"

Kana smiled. "Welcome to the Department of Justice. When can you start?"

It took Kashena a few moments to catch up. "Ma'am?" she said, her voice unsteady for the first time. "Did you say…"

"You're hired, Kashena," Kana said. "So's Bach, but I'll call him separately. When can you start?"

"I…" Kashena tried to regain her wits. She was beyond overjoyed at hearing she'd gotten the job. "As soon as you want me, ma'am," she said , not caring if she gave less than two weeks' notice at the commissioner's office.

"Next week too soon?" Kana was well aware of how fast Kashena was likely to want out of her current assignment.

"No, ma'am." Kashena smiled brightly; it was already Wednesday.

"Then report to the Sacramento office at I Street on Monday at eight. I'll meet you there."

"I'll be there ma'am," Kashena said. "And ma'am?"

"Yes?" Kana was going to have to get Kashena out of the habit of calling her "ma'am."

"Thank you for this opportunity. I promise you won't regret it," Kashena said, her voice finally betraying the exuberance she was feeling.

"I know I won't," Kana said. "And Kashena?"

"Yes, ma'am?"

"Call me Kana."

"Yes, ma'am," Kashena responded automatically, then heard Kana's low chuckle.

"I'm going to have the same problem with Bach, aren't I?" Kana asked.

"It's a military thing, ma'am." Kashena winced as she used the word again.

Kana laughed. "I'll give you both some leeway then."

"Thank you," Kashena said, still smiling from ear to ear when she hung up.

Sebastian, who had his headphones on, glanced over on seeing her smile. He took off his headphones, and rock music blared from them. He narrowed his ocean-green eyes at her.

"You got it, didn't you?" he asked, his grin starting.

Kashena's smile broadened. "I got it."

Sebastian nodded, looking pleased for her.

Kashena canted her head to the side. "Not going to ask if you got hired?"

"Should I bother?" he asked, his tone blasé.

Kashena knew it mattered to him, even if he was pretending like it didn't. She also knew that if she called him on it, he'd just deny it. They knew each other well enough to avoid calling each other's bluffs when it would serve no purpose.

"Your phone should be ringing soon," she told him.

He raised an eyebrow. "Do I have you to thank for that?"

"No, you have you to thank for that, Baz. You have the experience, the knowledge and the right attitude for the job."

"And a friend who already got hired."

"Stow it, Ranger," Kashena said. "You got it in spite of me, not because of me."

"Bullshit," he said, the beginnings of a grin on his lips.

"Could you just be happy for five minutes?" she said. "I know they run that gene right out of you at Ranger school, but rediscover it just for me, okay?"

"When I get the call, I'll be happy."

His phone rang.

"Be happy," Kashena mouthed at him.

He winked at her and smiled.

"Investigator Bach," he answered.

"Investigator Bach, this is Kana Sorbinno with DOJ," Kana said, sure she was about to tell him something he already knew.

"SAC Sorbinno, what a pleasant surprise," Sebastian said smoothly.

"She told you, right?" Kana said, not one to be fooled.

"What would that be, SAC Sorbinno?" Sebastian replied, his grin evident in his voice.

"That you have a new job." Kana found his tone infectious and smiled too.

"Ah, would that be chief bottle washer?"

"Only if the AG needs bottles washing."

Sebastian laughed. "Then I accept, happily so," he said. "In all seriousness, ma'am, thank you."

"You're welcome, Investigator Bach."

"I won't let you down."

"I already know that, Bach," Kana replied with a smile.

41

She already liked these two. They were both confident, yet sincerely pleased to have been selected. Kana felt that spoke volumes about their personalities. She knew she'd made a good selection.

***

Donovan was still reeling. He'd been made! He wasn't sure how it had happened, but his cover had been blown and there was no going back, at least not for a while. An undercover narcotics officer for six years, he found it hard to believe he wasn't going to be able to do it again. Somehow, some way, his duplicity had been discovered, and the discovery had almost cost him his life.

Santiago, the dealer he was trying to take down, had pulled a gun on him and stuck it to his head. Donovan remembered it vividly.

"You're a fucking pig," Santiago had spat, "and you're trying to set me up."

Donovan had remained calm. Dave Dibbins had taught him that much.

"What are you talking about?" Donovan asked.

"A cop, a pig, a narc."

"I don't know who's feeding you bullshit, Santiago," Donovan drawled calmly, "but you better get that fucking gun outta my face before we blow this whole deal."

Santiago was taken aback; it was obvious by the look on his face. Donovan waited, using every ounce of his self-control not to draw his weapon and kill the man. But Santiago had people all around him, and they were all armed. Donovan knew that even if he managed to kill Santiago, one of his people would kill him next.

In the end, Santiago put away his gun. They were talking a million-dollar deal here. Donovan got through the rest of the day, and went in to report the incident to Dave Dibbins, his lieutenant. Dave Dibbins was considered one of the best narcs in the country. He'd finally gotten out of the field when his wife, Susan, had had a baby the year before. Dave had been promoted to lieutenant by the new Chief of Police and was now supervising Donovan's team, Rogue Squadron, and another narcotics unit called the X-Strike team.

Dave decided that Donovan couldn't risk going any further with his case. It was Dave's belief that Donovan's cover had been blown, and until they figured out how that had happened and who knew that Donovan was a cop, Donovan was safer out of the field.

Donovan's wife, Jeanie, hadn't been able to agree more.

"Look, you can still do police work," she had reasoned. "You're just out of the narcotics game for a while."

"Yeah, man," Christian Collins had put in. "Besides, we need a secretary around here."

That had gotten him elbowed by his wife, Stevie, who was also on the team.

Donovan flipped Christian off, grinning. Christian and Donovan had a long-standing love–hate relationship. Christian always needled Donovan, and Donovan did the same.

"Isn't your brother-in-law always looking for good cops to go work for him?" Catalina Roché asked, her blue eyes sincere.

"Yeah. I already talked to Joe," Donovan said in a lackluster voice.

"Hey, I'm going to handle that one case for him," Kevin "Mace" Elmasian said. "It's good money, and it's basically babysitting."

Donovan grinned again. "Great, narc to babysitter inside a week."

The rest of the group laughed.

"You'll be back to being a narc, Pony," Stevie said, using Donovan's nickname. "We just have to make sure you're safe."

"I know," Donovan said. "The sooner you can do that, Stevie, the better, huh?"

"Ten-four," Stevie said, winking at him.

"See, I knew I liked your wife for a reason." Donovan gave Christian a chiding look.

"She's beautiful, sexy and smarter than you," Christian said. "What's not to like?"

"The fact that she got stuck with a loser like you," Donovan shot back.

"Easy you two," Jeanie said. "We don't need anymore incident reports around here."

"I wouldn't kick his ass in the office, Jay," Christian said to Jeanie, using the nickname Donovan had given his wife when they'd first met. "I'll take him out back."

Stevie narrowed her eyes at her husband. "You know, let's not bring up bad memories here…"

"Oh…" he said, grimacing.

Stevie remembered well the fight between Christian and his cousin, Joe Sinclair, "out back" in the motor pool. Christian had returned from a trip to Seattle to find that his girlfriend had taken up with his cousin. He was furious. He'd gone to Joe's office, when he was still a captain at San Diego PD. They'd gone out to the motor pool, and a vicious fight had ensued. It had made Stevie sick to see the man she loved, Christian, fighting his own cousin. She had known seeing Joe was the wrong thing to do. But she hadn't expected Christian, who was usually so calm and unaffected, to actually want to kill Joe for the betrayal. There still lingered an edge about the affair, even after three years of their being married. It was something Stevie still regretted doing.

There was a moment or two of uncomfortable silence, since just about everyone in the group knew what Stevie was referring to. Dave broke it by suggesting they get on with finding out how compromised Donovan's cover really was.

Everyone went back to work.

***

Christian called his father back and stunned him by accepting his acknowledgment of Christian as his son. There was much more to it than that, however. Lord Sinclair informed his son that there was to be a "celebration" in his honor, and that was when Lord Sinclair would officially name Christian the heir to his title.

"You'll need to come to England," Lord Sinclair decreed.

Christian rolled his light blue eyes at the command in his father's voice. "Yeah, no thanks. Either you just do whatever you need to do, or we don't. I don't really care."

"Well, this is highly irregular," Lord Sinclair sniffed.

"Yeah, I don't care."

"My recognition of you needs to be official."

"So make it official. I don't need a party," Christian said. "Believe it or not, I work for a living. So does my wife. We don't have time to come to London."

"Wife?" Lord Sinclair replied.

"Yeah," Christian said, his lips twisting in a sardonic smirk. "I got married three years ago."

"I see."

"Problem?" Christian honestly hoped there was a problem; then he could get out of all of this nonsense.

45

Lord Sinclair was quiet for a few seconds, obviously debating his options.

Christian waited, refusing to say another word.

Finally, there was a sigh on the other end of the line. "Alright then, I'll speak with my barrister and have the papers sent over for your signature. This is certainly not the appropriate way of things."

"Well, we both know I've never been appropriate," Christian told him coolly.

"What was all that about?" Stevie asked.

"Oh, he wanted a whole party and crap. Thanks but no."

"He wanted us to come there?"

"Yeah, for a 'celebration.'" Christian used air quotes for the word.

"Oh well, that sounds like it was going to be awful."

"Exactly!"

"So what's happening instead?" Stevie pulled out a couple of glasses and handed Christian a bottle of wine to open.

"He's going to have his barrister draw up the papers and send them for me to sign." Christian pulled out the bottle opener and opened the wine, pouring them each a glass.

"Barrister?" Stevie took a sip of wine and walked toward their back patio; Christian followed.

"It's the English name for a lawyer," Christian informed her as they sat down.

"Got it." Stevie leaned back in her chair. "So what will this make you?"

Christian contemplated that answer, then shook his head. "I'm not changing my name."

"But him giving you his name doesn't mean you'll be a lord too, or something?"

"Nope, it just means I inherit his holdings when he dies."

"But not the title?"

Christian's brow wrinkled as he thought about what she'd just said. "Well, yeah, I guess I become a 'lord' then." He waved his hand in dismissal. "Don't care. It only means something in England, and even then, not much these days." He winked at her. "But when he dies, you do become a titled 'lady'…" He gave her an evil smirk.

"Oh, hell no!" Stevie laughed. Christian joined her as they clinked glasses.

***

Kashena and Sebastian were officially in charge of the security of the AG's Sacramento office. They were introduced to the current security team and told to decide what else was needed to flesh out the team. Kana let them know that there would be only rare occasions on which they had to protect the AG, only in the event that Tiny or Kana couldn't make the trip with Midnight.

Kashena wasn't sure if she was disappointed or relieved by that bit of information. Sebastian had his hands full with scheduling the security team for updated training. Midnight wanted every member of the security team POST trained, meaning they had a full police academy training. Many of the officers on the current team only had PC 832 training, which meant they'd had the bare minimum to work security and carry a weapon on duty only.

Sebastian and Kashena had their work cut out for them.

On top of that, two months into their time at the Attorney General's office, Kana contacted Sebastian requesting that he handle personal security for one of the environmental law section's lawyers.

"She's received death threats on this case she's been working," Kana said. "Midnight wants to make sure she's kept safe."

Sebastian made a face on his end of the phone. "I'll take care of it, ma'am."

"Baz, Jesus, call me Kana already!"

Sebastian laughed. "Yes, Kana, ma'am."

"I swear…" Kana began ominously.

"Don't swear, ma'am. It's not professional," Sebastian said, grinning.

"You win," she said, giving up.

"I always do, ma'am."

Sebastian definitely liked his new boss, compared to the ultra-religious commissioner. Kana Sorbinno was top notch, and he already had respect for her.

Hanging up his phone, he glanced over at Kashena.

"What?"

"I have a personal detail," he said, looking anything but pleased.

"And?" Kashena asked.

"And it's a damned liberal tree-hugging attorney."

Kashena laughed. "I wouldn't use that as your opening line, if I were you."

Sebastian narrowed his eyes at her. "Why not?"

Kashena shook her head and grinned. "When do you start?"

Sebastian sighed. "Guess I'll head over and introduce myself now," he said, sounding highly unenthusiastic.

After walking out of the stairwell door, Sebastian paused to get his bearings. Then he strode down the hall toward the civil division's offices. He asked the blond receptionist, who was busy filing her nails, where he could find Samantha Cobb.

"She's through that door," the girl said, snapping her gum and checking out the handsome man standing in front of her, "and three offices down on the right."

"Thanks," Sebastian said, smiling at the girl.

When he got down the hall, he found that Blondie the receptionist apparently couldn't count.

"Can I help you find someone?" a female voice asked from behind him.

Sebastian turned, smiling. "Yes, as a matter of fact, you can. I'm looking for Samantha Cobb."

The young woman smiled back. "Lucky her," she murmured. "She's in a meeting."

"I don't suppose you know when she'll be out?"

"No, but I can have her come see you when she's back."

"That would be terrific," he said, smiling brilliantly.

"I'm Janice, her secretary." The young woman extended her hand.

"Sebastian Bach," he replied. "I've been assigned as her bodyguard for the time being."

"Double lucky her," Janice said with a wink.

Sebastian grinned. This girl wasn't shy, was she?

"I don't know about that," he said. "She'll have to put up with an ultra-right-wing Republican for a while."

"What makes you think she's not a Republican?"

"Environmental law?"

"Enough said," Janice agreed. "Well, I'll have her come see you, Special Agent Bach. It is Special Agent, isn't it?" she asked coyly.

"Special Agent Supervisor, but who's counting?" he replied with a wink of his own. "I'm on the twelfth floor, room 1210."

Janice flashed a pearly-white smile. "I'll let her know."

"I'll appreciate you all week," Sebastian replied with another wink.

Turning, he left the area. Janice watched him go. Man, he was gorgeous! Why did the attorneys always get lucky? She knew her straightlaced, uptight boss wouldn't appreciate a good-looking man like that. Hell, look at the wormy little creature she was married to. Some environmentalist with a whiny voice, sweaty palms and the palest skin Janice had ever seen. He was short and skinny and going bald. There was nothing at all attractive about Jeffrey Cobb.

Janice thought someone as pretty as Samantha could have done much better. With her Yale law degree and rich-bitch family, she could have married anyone—why that creature? Samantha was pretty, with a lot of potential. Of course she looked very blah in her dull beige suits, her rich red hair in a bun at the back of her head. She wore little makeup and almost never lipstick. Janice could tell, though, that if Mrs. Jeffrey Cobb ever wanted to she could really be incredibly beautiful.

"Janice," Samantha said, bustling back to her desk after a hectic meeting, "I need those last growth reports, as well as another pull from the latest chemical-level readings."

"Okay, but—"

"I also need another tape transcribing from this meeting—people were talking all at once again, and I know you can decipher them the best."

"Okay, ma'am, no problem, but—"

"Oh, and can you do me a favor? Call Redmon, tell him I need to cancel that meeting tomorrow morning."

"Ma'am," Janice finally said, stopping in front of Samantha.

"Yes?" Samantha said, as if coming out of a trance.

"Agent Bach was here to see you. He said he's been assigned as your bodyguard, ma'am. I told him you'd go down to his office to meet him."

"I don't have time for that now, Janice." Samantha waved her hand dismissively. "He can wait. I have far too much happening before I leave for New York."

"I'll call him and ask him to come back up here, ma'am," Janice said.

"I told you, I don't have time for that right now," Samantha said, rolling her eyes.

"Yes, ma'am."

Two days later, Sebastian hadn't managed to connect with Ms. Cobb. His patience was wearing thin. Janice had done everything to facilitate their sitting down to talk, but Ms. Cobb was always "too busy." As far as Sebastian was concerned, if the woman didn't want his protection that was fine with him.

Kana called on the third morning. "I understand you're having a rough time connecting with Ms. Cobb," she said without preamble.

"She's too busy to meet with me."

"She'll be free this afternoon," Kana said seriously.

"Ma'am, yes ma'am," Sebastian replied, grinning.

An hour later, Samantha Cobb's line rang. Janice answered, as Samantha was in meetings with EPA representatives in her office.

"Samantha Cobb's office," she said efficiently.

"Yes, this is Attorney General Chevalier. I need to speak with Deputy Attorney General Cobb."

"I—yes, yes, ma'am," Janice stammered. "I'll get her."

Janice put the phone on hold and hurried to Samantha's door. Knocking lightly, she didn't wait for the bid to come in.

Samantha's head snapped up at the intrusion.

"Janice, I told you…" she began, her voice scolding.

"I know," Janice said, "but this is an important call. You need to take it."

Samantha shot Janice an angry look, then got up, walked over to her desk and picked up her phone.

"I do hope this is important," she said into the phone.

"It is, I assure you," Midnight Chevalier said smoothly, her tone indicating the narrowed gold-green eyes on the other end.

"Oh. Oh, ma'am, I'm… so sorry… I was in a meeting, and I just didn't realize…"

"Yes, that's been the problem," Midnight said briskly. "You haven't managed to meet with the agent I assigned to protect you, and that's just not acceptable."

"I… Yes, ma'am, I understand," Samantha said.

"You need to understand, Mrs. Cobb, that these safety measures are for your own protection," Midnight explained patiently. "Agent Bach can't do his job if you don't cooperate with him."

"I do understand, Madam Attorney General. I promise you that I'll meet with Agent Bach today."

"Perfect," Midnight said, smiling. "Thank you."

Samantha hung up the phone and sighed. *Lovely. The first time I talk to the Attorney General, and it's so I can get disciplined,* she thought crossly.

Later that day, Sebastian was sitting in his chair, working on the monthly schedule for the security teams. He had Linkin Park on the stereo in his and Kashena's office, and it was fairly loud. He didn't hear Samantha come in, and he didn't notice her standing behind him. The song playing had a very definite rap flair to it; it was called "Hit The Floor." Samantha watched as Sebastian sang the words with enthusiasm. The line he sang talked about being on top one minute and then the next you weren't. Samantha took it personally, especially when his eyes connected with hers and he sang the words with verve. Samantha was immediately sure he knew that Midnight Chevalier had called her. It irritated her. He reached for the remote and turned the stereo down. His ocean-green eyes twinkled with subdued humor. In his mind he was embarrassed at being caught rocking out by an attorney. In her mind he was making fun of her.

"You must be the elusive Samantha Cobb," he said, his voice a deep baritone.

Samantha was still recovering from the surprise of seeing him for the first time. There was no denying how handsome he was. He was tall, at least six foot three, with broad shoulders, but nothing about him indicated that he was fat. His forearms, exposed as the sleeves of his dress shirt were rolled up, looked tan and muscular. His blond hair, combined with rich gray-green eyes, a very strong jawline, and the smooth tan skin of his face, was breathtaking. Sebastian Bach positively screamed machismo. Samantha had to remind herself quickly that she didn't like that type of man.

She also remembered quickly that Sebastian Bach was probably the reason she'd received the call she had from the Attorney General.

Narrowing sky-blue eyes, Samantha resembled the lawyer that she was. "Yes, apparently you found it necessary to report to the Attorney General that I was being difficult in meeting with you," she said in an accusatory tone.

"Hold on there, Ms. Cobb. I think you're overestimating my connections here." Sebastian sounded anything but apologetic.

"You're saying you didn't tell her?" Samantha said sharply.

"I was contacted by my supervisor, Special Agent in Charge Sorbinno, who asked me if I'd gotten your schedule squared away. When

I told her I hadn't met with you yet, I'm sure it was her who told the Attorney General. They're close, you know," he said with a smile.

Samantha stared back at him. "Well, thanks to your lack of patience, I got a call from the Attorney General herself," she snapped.

Sebastian sat back in his chair, steepling his fingers. "Lack of planning on your part, Deputy Attorney General Cobb, does not constitute fault on mine."

Samantha's mouth dropped open in shock. "Who do you think you are?" she said, her voice oozing superiority.

Sebastian gave her a sardonic grin. "I'm the guy who's going to keep you alive, provided you don't irritate me too much."

"How dare you?" she exclaimed, shocked that he'd had the nerve to not only berate her, but was he suggesting blackmail too?

Sebastian said nothing in reply; he merely looked back at her calmly.

"This is unacceptable." She shook her head. "I will not be protected by you."

"You don't have much of a choice," he told her, his tone not wavering in the slightest.

"Oh, I have a choice, I assure you," Samantha said, her eyes blazing.

Sebastian noticed she was much more attractive when she was mad, but he decided this wouldn't be the time to tell her that. Instead he simply spread his hands, the look on his face confident.

"I'm it, babe—take it or leave it."

"Babe?" Samantha echoed, aghast. "Did you just call me babe?"

Sebastian nodded, knowing it had been a mistake. It had slipped out.

"You…" she began in disgust, her eyes scanning him from head to toe. "You horrible excuse for authority."

"Horrible excuse for authority?" he repeated, grinning lazily. "Come on, babe, you can do better than that."

Again, Samantha's eyes narrowed. "You ill-mannered, foul-mouthed, goose-stepping Nazi!" she yelled, turning and slamming out of the room.

Sebastian sat back, smiling widely. The woman could really get riled easily, couldn't she?

He waited for the call he knew he'd get. Kashena had suggested repeatedly that he go up and apologize for his slip, but Sebastian had refused.

"Look," he told Kashena, "I made a mistake, but she's got to realize that she was acting like a child too. Accusing me of calling the boss on her. Give me a break. I can't help it if her majesty was too busy to worry about her own safety."

"Her majesty," Kashena said with a smirk. "Another one you shouldn't use on her, Baz."

"Yeah, yeah," he said, waving dismissively.

His phone rang then.

"Bach," he answered, already knowing who he'd be talking to. He was wrong.

"Agent Bach," Midnight Chevalier said smoothly. "I understand we have a problem."

Sebastian grimaced. "Yes, ma'am," he replied, suddenly sorry he'd allowed himself to get riled.

"What is it that you called Deputy Attorney General Cobb that has her in such a snit?" Midnight asked, sounding suspiciously amused.

"I, uh, called her babe."

"Babe?" Midnight echoed. "She called me about being called babe?" she asked disbelievingly.

"Yes, ma'am."

"Oh, Jesus Christ!" Midnight exclaimed. "You'd think you'd called her… well, something a lot worse." She sighed. "I need you on this case, Bach. I think you're the best I have to protect her, short of hiring a private bodyguard for her. With the budget the way it is, I just can't see me doing that when I have someone so capable that can handle it… Can you handle it, Bach?"

Sebastian sighed inwardly. He was happy that she wasn't mad at him, and yes, he could handle this, probably.

"I can try, ma'am," he said. "But don't be surprised if I kill her myself."

Midnight chuckled. "I understand, Bach. Thank you. If she gives you too much crap, call Kana. She'll let me know, okay?"

"Yes, ma'am," Sebastian said. "Thank you. One other thing, ma'am."

"What's that, Bach?"

"Can I get authorization to use my POV?"

"Your own vehicle?" Midnight queried. "We're not talking a sports car that's going to be highly uncomfortable, are we?"

"Hummer," Sebastian said. "I'm just much more comfortable in it than any State car."

Midnight smiled. "Understandable."

She'd refused her own State vehicle in favor of her classic Corvette. Midnight's husband, Rick, had also purchased a Lincoln Navigator for Midnight to use as her transport vehicle. Rick felt that Midnight should have the best, and since he wanted that for her, he had paid for it. Midnight had felt that the state couldn't afford to buy her such a luxury so had allowed Rick to do just that.

56

"So, is it okay?" Sebastian asked.

"Yes, Bach, your request is approved."

Midnight thought that DAG Cobb would be safer in a Hummer than in anything else. Besides the fact that it wasn't something criminals would expect a Deputy Attorney General for the state to travel in, it was also a very sturdy, safe vehicle.

CHAPTER 3

Kevin Elmasian sat in a small bedroom in a house in Orange County, working diligently on his latest poster. The radio in the room was on, Disturbed playing, and he was singing along with the music. The top of his long brown hair was pulled back, exposing the earrings in his ears. He wore a black tank, having removed his cover shirt to reveal the tattoos on his upper arms. One arm displayed a dragon with its tail curled around an Iron Cross; the other arm had a wolf with a guitar in its mouth. His arms were also cut with muscle. He was rugged and dangerous looking. That's how he liked it.

Chad Reiger stood in the doorway to the extra bedroom, watching the man who his mother said was there to protect them. He looked scary to Chad, but his mother had said that this man was a police officer. Walking forward, Chad craned his neck to try to see what the man was working on.

Kevin looked up. Seeing the young boy, he smiled. He turned the poster around so the boy could see it. Chad's eyes widened in awe. Kevin smiled.

"Chad," Jennifer Reiger said from the doorway, "don't bother Mr. Elmasian."

Kevin picked up the remote and turned down the stereo. "It's okay," he said. "My son is just about his age."

"You have a son?" Chad asked, looking surprised.

"And a daughter."

"Really?" Chad asked in wonder.

Kevin smiled, nodding.

Jennifer leaned against the doorjamb. "How old is your son?"

"He's nine," Kevin said.

"And your daughter?"

"She's nine too."

"Twins?" Jennifer asked.

"No," Kevin said. "My son is actually my wife's boy, and my daughter is mine from another relationship."

"Ohh," Jennifer said. "Are they okay with you doing this?"

"They're supportive no matter what I do," he said, a fond look on his face.

Jennifer was very surprised by this man. When she'd first met him, earlier that day, she'd been shocked. He didn't look like any police officer she'd ever met. He had long hair, earrings, and he looked more like a drug dealer than a cop. At first, she wasn't altogether sure she wanted this man in her home and around her son.

Standing in the doorway and looking at him now, she began to see a different person.

Kevin Elmasian was far from what he appeared to be. Most people never saw past the carefully constructed facade. That's how Kevin wanted it. Only his wife, Erin, saw everything.

He was lying in bed, the radio still on, when his cell phone rang.

"Mace," he answered, using his nickname.

"How did I know you wouldn't be asleep yet?" Erin said, her voice warm.

"'Cause you have to lie next to me most nights, dealing with me tossing and turning."

"You never stay in bed next to me when you're not sleeping, Kevin," Erin chided gently.

He grinned. "I like my wife to be able get a good night's sleep; sue me."

"Mr. Elmasian," she said sternly, "I married you knowing all about your little quirks."

"Quirks? You call ADD and being a recovering alcoholic quirky?"

"Sure," she said. "I never refill the ice trays and I'm always losing my keys. You live with my quirks; I live with yours."

Kevin chuckled. "Yeah, you're pretty hard to live with too, Mrs. Elmasian."

Erin sighed. "I know. But you love me."

"Yeah, I love you," he said, smiling warmly.

It was impossible to believe how good she made him feel. In his past, women had never loved him like Erin did. She stuck with him, no matter what. Kevin had never been loved like that, and it felt like a gift he never intended to give up.

"Are you going to try and get some sleep, hon?" Erin asked, concern in her voice.

"I'll try, babe."

"Promise me?"

Kevin dropped his head back on the pillow, knowing he couldn't get away with not promising her.

"Kevin…"

"I promise, honey. I promise," he said, smiling.

She always worried about him. He loved that about her.

They hung up a few minutes later. He got up and walked through the house; he'd seen that the small house had a back deck. Walking out onto the deck, he pulled out a thin cigar and his lighter. He lit it, then took a long drag. He blew a stream out of smoke, just as his sixth sense started tingling.

He tossed away the cigar, drawing his gun and spinning around in a single motion. He yanked the muzzle up just as quickly when he realized the person sitting on the deck was Jennifer. Her eyes were wide at his action, but she also found that it was comforting to see how fast he could be if the need called for it.

"Sorry," he muttered, sitting on the end of the deck and lighting another cigar.

"You're very fast," Jennifer said, moving to sit next to him.

"In the business I'm in, you have to be," Kevin said, taking a long drag of his cigar.

"That's not a cigarette, is it?" Jennifer asked, smelling the slightly sweet scent of the smoke he blew out.

"No. I smoke cigars."

"Robert, my ex, smokes cigarettes," she said, making a face. "I have to say I hate the smell of them now."

Kevin turned to look at her. "Do you want to tell me a bit about him? It might make it easier to protect you and make a case on the guy."

Jennifer nodded, looking more subdued suddenly. "We met when we were in high school. He was the class bad boy. I should have known then," she said, curling her lips in self-disgust, "but I went out with him anyway, and he seemed so nice... I thought I was the one that could change him. We got together, and things were good for a while. Then after we graduated we moved in together. Robert was always out of work, but I got a job at a grocery store, and it helped us make it. Then I got pregnant."

She picked at invisible lint on her pants as she talked, her expression haunted.

"That was the first time he hit me. When I told him I was pregnant. He told me I was a stupid cunt for screwing us up like that."

"You got pregnant all by yourself?" he asked wryly.

"Must be a first, huh?" she said with a smile.

"Call Jerry Springer!"

Jennifer laughed. "Well, he apologized later, saying he was just shocked and stuff, but I never should have believed him. After that, every time things went wrong he'd hit me. I finally got tired of it, and when he hit Chad the first time, I was done."

"How long ago did you two break up?"

"A year and a half ago," she said. "But every time I get a new guy in my life, Robert appears and starts hassling him. He calls at all hours of the night, threatening me, telling me he'll kill me if I don't get rid of the guy. He thinks he still owns me, and he won't stop."

"Does he stay away from you if you're not seeing anyone?"

"For the most part," she said. "It's like he doesn't want to me have anyone else."

"Well, he doesn't," Kevin said. "You're his territory, and he thinks he's protecting it"

Jennifer nodded unhappily. "So, what do I do?"

"You don't do anything. "That's why I'm here."

"And what are you going to do?" she asked, her tone both worried and defeated.

"Well, I think we need to draw him out. If I witness him threatening you, or I hear any of these calls, I can make a case against him."

"He's gotten really violent a few times with the guys I was dating," Jennifer said, "but none of them were willing to press charges."

"Male pride," Kevin said in a wry tone. "Not a problem."

"So, how do we handle this?"

"I think our best bet is to let him think I'm the new guy in your life."

"Really?" she said uncertainly.

"He reacts to men in your life," he said. "If I ever hope to make a case on him, he's going to have to make a move on me."

"Isn't that dangerous?"

Kevin grinned. "That's why I do this job."

The following day, while Chad was in school, Jennifer said she needed to go to the store. She looked hesitant when Kevin got up to go with her.

"What?" he asked, seeing her hesitation.

"Robert works there."

Kevin smiled. "Good, then he'll get wind of the new man quickly."

Jennifer's eyes widened, but she didn't say anything.

An hour later, they were in line at the store, waiting to check out. They were, by Kevin's design, one line away from Robert. Kevin sized the guy up. He was strong looking, but short, probably only five foot eight, compared to Kevin's six-foot frame. The difference in their appearances was extreme, however. Robert looked like a clean-cut, clean-shaven accountant, for all that his violent behavior testified the opposite. It was obvious to see that Robert was meticulous about everything being in its place. He looked nowhere near as dangerous as Kevin appeared. Kevin knew that was one of his edges.

"The other guys you dated…" Kevin said quietly.

Jennifer glanced up at him. "Yes?"

"Were they all like him?" Kevin asked, nodding toward Robert, who was already looking in their direction.

"What do you mean?"

"I mean clean cut, all that?"

"Yes, pretty much. Those are the types I like."

Kevin gave her a measured look. "Okay, well, I'm warning you now, I'm probably about to shock the hell out of you."

"How?" she asked, worried.

He smiled. "Relax."

They got to the front of the line, and it was obvious Robert was ready to elbow every other bag boy out of the way to get to bag their groceries. As he did, he glared at Kevin. Kevin simply looked back at Robert, moss-green eyes direct, face impassive.

Robert trailed them out to Kevin's Dodge Durango. Kevin opened the back and stepped aside, gesturing for Robert to do his job and put the groceries in. He turned to Jennifer and started talking to her as if they were continuing a conversation. He brushed a lock of hair off her cheek, and then, leaning down, he kissed her. His hand slid through her hair, pulling her closer.

Jennifer tensed, and he intensified the kiss to get her to forget that Robert was standing there. She moaned softly against his lips, then he felt her hands touch his chest. His arms encircled her, pulling her body closer. Kevin didn't see Robert gaping, but he felt it. While it appeared he was totally focused on kissing Jennifer, he was actually quite focused on the threat.

It was for that reason that when Robert threw a punch, he was stunned when Kevin shoved Jennifer to his side and his hand came up to catch the fist.

"I don't think you want to do that," Kevin said, his voice low and dangerous.

"That's my bitch you're sucking on," Robert said, his face suffused with color.

"That's her choice."

"I'll kick your fuckin' ass," Robert growled.

If you think you can take me, bring it." Kevin dropped his hands to his sides, fingers working.

Robert hesitated; Kevin smiled.

"Not so tough when I'm ready, huh?" Kevin asked, his green eyes reflecting amusement.

Robert glared at him. "If I don't get back in the store, I'll lose my job."

"That's not new for you, is it?"

"Fuck you!" Robert snapped, throwing a punch.

Kevin ducked and slammed his fist into Robert's stomach.

"Now," Kevin said, his breathing totally calm, "I'd suggest you get back to work."

With that, Kevin walked a still stunned Jennifer to the passenger side of the Durango, then walked around the front and got in. He started the vehicle with a roar and noted with satisfaction that Robert jumped out of the way. Pulling out of the space, Kevin flipped Robert a sardonic wave and drove out of the lot.

Halfway back to the house, Jennifer looked over at him.

"Are you crazy?" she asked.

Kevin glanced over at her as he lit a cigar and rolled down the window.

"He'll kill you," she said.

Kevin smirked. "Not even on his best day."

"You don't think so?"

"Jenn," Kevin said patiently, "guys like that are really tough against women and little boys. They aren't shit compared to men. Trust me, he has no idea who or what he's fucking with."

Jennifer wasn't sure how much she believed him, but she sincerely hoped he was right. Part of her was still a bit weak from the kiss he'd laid on her. It had been a long time since she'd been kissed like that.

She reminded herself that he was her bodyguard, not to mentioned married, and only did that to provoke Robert. Still, her knees had gone weak. Boy, it was time she started dating again!

***

Midnight Chevalier held a press conference to announce her new program. It was called VOS, Victim Outreach Services.

"Isn't the state taking on a lot of responsibility?" Dan Oliver asked.

"Yes, we are," Midnight said, "but I believe it's important to make sure that the citizens of the state of California feel safe in their own homes."

"How will reporting work?" another reporter asked.

"Citizens can make a complaint via the public inquiry unit, or the local departments can make a request directly to the VOS offices."

"Citizens can't make direct complaints?" the same reporter queried.

"No," Midnight said. "It is necessary to keep staff time down to a minimum. There will be investigations conducted into allegations made by citizens, but only local PDs and the VOS team can determine the true need for protection."

"You're relying heavily on the locals' judgment," said a reporter from the *San Diego Tribune*, his tone indicating his distaste for law enforcement.

Midnight pinned the man with a look. "These people risk their lives every day to protect your way of life. They make judgment calls every minute they're on the job, and lot of times off the job as well. So I think I can trust them with this."

The reporter looked appropriately chastised and didn't ask another question.

"Will Joe Sinclair be helping you with this program?" asked another reporter.

"Yes," Midnight said, smiling and winking at Joe, who stood to the side of the room. "He'll be helping me get it off the ground."

"How much is the state paying him for consulting fees?" the *Tribune* reporter asked, his eyebrow raised.

Midnight looked at the man, wondering if he'd ever learn not to challenge her. Then she looked at Joe; his lips curled into a smile as he inclined his head to her. It was her go-ahead to disclose his "consulting fee."

"Joe is waiving payment for his assistance," Midnight said, her eyes narrowed at the reporter.

"Why would he do that?"

Not learning too quickly, is he? Midnight thought.

Joe strode to the podium, his light blue eyes on the man. Midnight stepped back, gesturing for Joe to step up to the microphone. He did, adjusting it for his six-foot-two, versus Midnight's five-foot-five, height.

"Let me make something crystal clear here," he said, his English accent crisp. "Midnight asked for my help, offered to pay me for my time, but since we're friends and I don't need the money, I don't want any. You all have that? 'Cause I don't expect to be reading any crap in the paper about Midnight and I having an affair, stealing from the state or entertaining goddamned space aliens in the corner office. Got it?"

His tone was no nonsense, and his sharp gaze touched on each one of them pointedly. Midnight looked back at Rick, who was hiding his laughter behind his hand. Yet another score for the Chevalier-

Debenshire bid to turn the state on its ear when it came to business as usual.

With that said, Joe stepped aside and readjusted the mic to Midnight's height again. She stepped back up to the microphone, noting a number of grins in the audience as she did. The *Tribune* reporter was sufficiently cowed this time. The press conference proceeded without further incident.

"Nice speech," Rick said to Joe as the reporters filed out of the room.

"Fuck you," Joe muttered.

Rick smiled. Midnight walked over to them, Tiny and Kana flanking her.

"Nice speech," Midnight said, not realizing Rick had just said the same thing.

Joe looked unrepentant. "The guy was annoying me."

"Me too," she said.

"Then thank me," Joe said.

Midnight laughed. "Okay, you win. Thank you."

"Much better," Joe said, leading the way out of the conference room.

***

Sierra Youngblood hung up her office phone, a chill running through her. The voicemail she'd just listened to was the fourth one this week. It was always the same: Ben Gillam, his voice cheerful, with just an undercurrent of something akin to mania—"Hi Sierra, Ben again, I just thought I'd try to catch you. I was hoping I could see you…" On and on he talked, and it made Sierra's skin crawl every time. She knew she needed to do something. Who knew if he could figure out where she lived? Couldn't you find anything on the internet now? She had Colby to think of. She glanced at the picture of her son on her desk, his dark eyes shining as he smiled up at Sierra next to him in the picture.

Sierra had been with the Attorney General's office for eight years; prior to that she'd been a prosecutor with the District Attorney's office. Ben had been the brother of a murder victim. At first he'd said that he just wanted to help "get" the guy who had killed his sister. It hadn't taken long for it to become something else. Fortunately, she'd left the DA's office not too long after that case, and she hadn't heard from Ben since then. Until recently. Recently he'd been calling, leaving messages with her secretary, then somehow he'd managed to get her direct number. The first time he'd called that number, Sierra had answered, not knowing who it was. He suggested that they meet for coffee; Sierra said no. He got pushy and told her she should just give in. When she refused again and told him to stop calling, he started to yell. She hung up on him. Then her house had been broken into. She'd called the police, and they'd taken fingerprints, but nothing had come back, likely because Ben didn't have a police record.

Sierra debated what she should do, scared but not wanting to overreact. She'd been promoted to Chief Deputy Attorney General over the criminal division by the new Attorney General. Midnight Chevalier had seen the value in Sierra's work, which the previous AG had completely ignored. Sierra wasn't sure if it would be appropriate to go to Midnight Chevalier herself about the matter. Would that make her seem like she was taking advantage? Was she, after all, just overreacting? After a few minutes of indecision, she contacted Midnight's secretary to see if Midnight even had time to talk, figuring the answer would be no. To her shock, Chris Isenagle gave her an appointment for that very afternoon.

"Ma'am, your two o'clock is here," Chris told Midnight.

Midnight looked up from the paperwork she'd been reading. Glancing at the clock above the door, she was surprised to see it was two o'clock already. She could never figure out where her day went. "Thanks, Chris. Send her in."

When Sierra Youngblood walked in, Midnight couldn't help but notice how classic her American Indian features were. Long, silky black hair, perfectly sculpted cheekbones, dusky skin tone, and dark eyes—the woman was beautiful.

"Thank you for seeing me, ma'am." Sierra extended her hand to Midnight as Midnight stood.

"It's Midnight, please," Midnight told the other woman. "I'm not much for formality."

Sierra smiled as Midnight gestured for her to have a seat. Midnight came around her desk and sat in the chair opposite Sierra.

"I know you're really busy, though, so I appreciate you taking the time."

Midnight waved away Sierra's concern. "I'm always here when one of my people needs me. So what's happening?" Midnight wanted to cut to the chase.

"I just wanted… Well, I wanted to talk to you about an incident with the brother of a victim from a case I previously prosecuted when I was with the District Attorney's office."

Midnight nodded. "What's going on?"

"Well, he was one of those people who wanted to be in on every aspect of the case. He wanted to talk to me constantly, to 'find out what was happening,'" Sierra said, quirking her fingers to indicate she was quoting the man. "The problem was, he'd taken an interest in more than just the case." Sierra's look was pointed, and Midnight's chin lifted slightly as she caught Sierra's meaning.

"He was interested in you."

"Yes." Sierra grimaced. "I explained to him that I was married, but he didn't really seem to care about that. He just kept coming around, and it really scared me. Once the case was through and he didn't have an excuse to come see me, he started calling to ask me out. I avoided him for a long time, and eventually, with the assistance of a few visits from a police officer friend of mine, he stopped."

"But…" Midnight prompted when Sierra hesitated.

"But he's started again." Sierra sighed. "My husband is a Marine, but he's overseas right now. It's just me and my son, and I have to say I'm scared. Last week, when he called me directly the first time, not going through my secretary as he had been… well, he got really angry when I wouldn't go out with him. That night my house was broken into. I don't know if it was just a coincidence, but…"

"But probably not," Midnight said succinctly. "I've got just the person for this." With that, Midnight had Chris call Kana to her office.

When Kana arrived, Midnight explained the situation and asked Kana to help "secure" Chief Deputy Attorney General Youngblood. Sierra was shocked by Midnight's quick action, but she also felt a lot safer right away.

In the end, Kana escorted Sierra home, which Sierra hoped would put Ben off if he was actually watching her. On the way, they discussed that Sierra had always been more comfortable around women. Kana got the distinct impression that Sierra Youngblood actually preferred women, and when they chatted, it was confirmed. Kana also established that Sierra more or less put up with her husband, and having him overseas was no true hardship.

As Kana drove away from Sierra's house that night, her heart broke a little for the woman. She knew it was hard to pretend to be something you weren't; it was downright heartbreaking.

CHAPTER 4

What did the bitch think she was doing? Who said women needed protection? It was a man's job to protect his woman, or beat her as he saw fit. Where did Midnight Chevalier get off trying to govern that? She was pushing it too far. The plans were almost complete. I can take her out any time I want. *She thought she was so safe. Well, she wasn't safe. Not safe at all.*

***

Sebastian stood waiting for Samantha outside her home. He had his stereo on, his driver's side window down, and a cigarette in his hand. Smoking as he waited, he was leaning against his vehicle. It was raining lightly, so he was wearing a long black duster jacket over his black slacks and moss-green dress shirt. The man made a striking picture, one Samantha endeavored to push out of her mind as she walked up to the vehicle.

He turned his head, seeing her approaching. Turning, he walked around to the passenger's side and opened the door for her. He stood watching, amused, as she tried to climb into the Hummer, which was higher than a standard vehicle. Finally, Sebastian tossed his cigarette aside and put an arm to her elbow to help her. She threw him a vile glance, even as she accepted his assistance.

Once he was in the driver's seat, he started the engine with a deep rumble. Samantha wrinkled up her nose at the smell of cigarette smoke.

"It's against policy to smoke in a State vehicle," she said pertly.

"One, I wasn't smoking in the vehicle, and two, this isn't a State vehicle."

"It's not?" she asked, her tone sharp.

"You think the state can afford an H2?"

"I wouldn't have a clue how much they cost," Samantha said condescendingly.

"More than the state can afford, trust me. This is my POV."

"POV?" she repeated in a snide voice.

"Privately owned vehicle, ma'am."

She gestured around the interior. "So this is yours?"

"Ma'am, yes ma'am," he answered, military style.

Samantha huffed in obvious dissatisfaction.

Sebastian smiled, saying nothing. *Let her stew.*

It was another ten minutes before she spoke again.

"Did you receive authorization to drive your own vehicle?"

"Yes."

"From whom?"

Sebastian looked across at her, his expression telling her that she was annoying him now. "The Attorney General."

"Oh," she said, her tone colorless.

Again she was silent. Sebastian drove, turning up the radio up slightly. He had the soundtrack to *Tomb Raider* in; the Davey Brothers were singing "Heart Go Faster." Samantha looked out the window, pretending not to be listening to the music. But the very beginning of the song had her intrigued. They talked about knowing what she was searching for and needing. It felt like he was reading her mind. She had the nagging feeling that she should be reevaluating her life lately.

She had a great job, protecting the environment against people who didn't care about the damage they were doing in their need to industrialize everything. Married since college to the man she'd met there. Jeffrey Cobb had been the reason she'd switched from criminal law to environmental law back in her last year of college. He'd shown her how important protecting the environment was.

Samantha couldn't even recall how many nights they'd talked and talked about the wonders of nature. How a plant could regenerate every year, how animals knew their one true mate on sight. There were so many things they agreed on. At least she'd thought they did. In recent years, she'd begun to wonder if Jeffrey had been the one to shape her opinions. She'd met him when he was a senior at Stanford University and she was only a freshman.

Jeffrey had been involved—he organized protests for everything from the burning of the rain forest to the contamination of San Francisco Bay. He loved nature and everything about it. When they first met, he took her camping in the hills above San Francisco. Samantha had been very sheltered growing up—her parents had sent her to a Swiss boarding school—so the idea of being out in the "wild" was an adventure to her. Jeffrey taught her about living off the land. How killing animals for food was a crime. She'd never really thought about her food having a "face" before, but Jeffrey showed her pictures and movies about how the animals were mistreated and slaughtered. She gave up meat because Jeffrey said it was humane to do so.

She did everything because Jeffrey thought it was a good idea. But sometimes it didn't really make a lot of sense to her. Jeffrey was always able to show her the reasons behind his ideals. He loved her; he told her she was the ying to his yang. She believed him, and married him right after graduation.

They'd been married for seven years. She'd been an environmental law attorney for four years, transferring to the Attorney General's office a year ago. She was currently working on a case between the Department of Fish and Game and the citizens of a small town who were suing the state.

There had been a spill of chemicals when a train derailed. The chemicals had reportedly spilled into their lake and contaminated the water supply. It was Samantha's job to represent the state, who'd cleaned up the spill, and Fish and Game, who'd assured local townsfolk that everything was fine. She'd been getting threats from an unknown source. Tempers were high because there was a lot of money and land at stake.

What bothered Samantha the most was that Jeffrey was on the other side this time. He was opposing counsel. They had discussed her getting off the case, but Jeffrey had told her that they would just not discuss the case outside the courtroom. Somehow it bothered her that Jeffrey hadn't offered to get off the case. He had three partners at his firm, and he chose to stay on as counsel. Part of her wondered if he felt he could easily beat her. She was still fairly unsure of herself in court.

Samantha and Sebastian arrived at the office ten minutes later without further incident. Sebastian escorted her to her office, telling her to page him when she was ready to leave for the night.

By the time he reached the offices he shared with Kashena, he was ready for another strong cup of coffee. Kashena looked like she could use one too.

"Coffee?" he asked.

Kashena nodded, standing up and running her hand through her hair—a sure sign she was agitated. Sebastian waited until they had their coffee and were seated at the far corner of the cafeteria.

"So what's up?" he asked, leaning back and stretching his legs out in front of him.

"What's up with you?" she countered. "Didn't you already have your cup of jet fuel this morning?" she asked, referring to the ultra-strong coffee he drank.

"Yeah," he said, "but that was before I had to deal with the tree-hugging liberal pain in the ass this morning."

"Ah," Kashena said. "The ever charming Deputy AG Cobb."

Sebastian rolled his eyes. "I may have to kill her myself."

"Probably not a very good career move, Baz," Kashena said, grinning.

"And?" he asked with a raised eyebrow.

Kashena chuckled, shaking her head.

"So what's up with you?" he asked again.

He knew something was going on. She was definitely agitated, tapping the Marine ring on her right ring finger on her coffee cup.

"You're not going to like it," she told him.

He gave her a baleful look. "Tell me you didn't…" Kashena's train wreck of an ex-girlfriend had recently resurfaced, much to Sebastian's dismay. Even though Kashena had sworn she wouldn't be taken in by the woman again, Sebastian had been sure she wasn't that strong, and now he knew that he was right.

"Can't," Kashena said.

"Damn it!" he exclaimed, shocking people around him.

"Baz, don't start," Kashena warned.

"You told me you weren't going to see the twit."

"I didn't expect to."

"So, why did you?"

"She came to see me."

"And you couldn't escort her to the front door?" he asked.

"Baz…" Kashena said. "I know this is going to come as a shock to you, but it is my life." She was trying to sidestep the nasty argument that was likely to occur, but she knew it would never be that easy.

"Yeah," he said, "and you're my best friend, and I'm sick of that bitch turning you inside out."

"She won't this time. I'm not stupid enough to believe her anymore."

Sebastian didn't say anything, his look cynical.

"Look," Kashena said, "I have to deal with all four thousand of your women. You can deal with me dating a psychotic every now and then."

Sebastian laughed in spite of himself. "Well, at least you finally have her pegged right."

"I have her in perspective, Baz," Kashena assured him.

She honestly felt like she did. Linda still had an effect on her, but she didn't believe it when Linda claimed that she was back to stay this time. She knew better. Linda was a former drug addict and a serious party girl, and she always had spelled trouble for Kashena in the past. Sebastian was right to hate the woman, but that never seemed to matter when Linda came around. Kashena could never totally resist. She did, however, think that she had a handle on it this time.

They stayed downstairs for another ten minutes, then headed back to their offices to handle the day's issues. Trying to manage the security team, as well as various side jobs, handling things Kana would call and ask them to deal with, kept them busy.

Later that day, Sebastian was back at Samantha Cobb's office to take her home. Stepping into her doorway, he saw that she was on the phone. He stepped back, politely waiting outside her office until she was ready to go. He could hear her side of the conversation.

"No, I don't understand it," she was saying, her voice tense. "If McClusky offered to take it, why didn't you let him?" A pause. "Because I don't want to try a case against you, that's why. I don't see why you can't understand this, Jeffrey, I really can't. No, no, I don't want to calm down. I want this trial over. That's what I want." There was another long pause, and she finally sighed. "Someone is waiting for me. I need to go." She hung up.

Sebastian stayed outside her office waiting for her. She walked out a few minutes later.

"Thank you for waiting," she said, her voice approaching polite.

Sebastian merely nodded and gestured for her to precede him. He followed her out to the elevator lobby. They were both silent on the way down to the garage. In the car, Sebastian automatically reached for his cigarettes. Samantha's eyebrow lifted.

Glancing at her, Sebastian held up the pack. "Do you mind?" he asked, sounding not quite civil.

"Would it matter?" she asked sharply.

Sebastian focused stormy green eyes on her. "Yes, it would," he said in a low voice.

Samantha looked back at him, shocked at his tone as well as his words. Eventually she shook her head. "I don't mind," she said quietly.

He shook a cigarette out of the pack, put it in his mouth and grabbed his lighter. Flipping the lighter open and cupping his hand in front of the flame, he lowered his head to light the cigarette. He took a long drag and pointedly blew the smoke out the window.

He drove out of the garage, waving at the security officer standing outside the parking garage. At the next intersection, they encountered protestors on every corner holding up traffic. The protestors were holding up signs painted with black and red letters.

"No blood for oil!" the signs proclaimed, and "No more police actions!" There were a number of other signs with similar messages. Sebastian curled his lips in disgust. Quickly finishing the first cigarette, he reached for another.

"Fucking idiots," he growled under his breath.

"You don't agree with people's right to protest?"

"Right to blather whatever comes to mind?" he said. "No, I don't have problem with it."

"But they're idiots?"

"They don't get it," he replied, driving quickly away from the intersection.

"What is it you feel they don't get?" Samantha asked.

"First of all, doing this won't change anything. We're committed to what we're doing in the Middle East; it's too late to pull out now."

"And second?"

"The last thing our boys over there need to see is idiots like that protesting the war."

"But as Americans that's our right," Samantha said, shocked by what he was saying.

"Oh, trust me, babe, I know that," he said angrily. "And what you *Americans* don't get is that it's guys like me that gave you the right to protest. It was bought with my blood, my sweat, my tears."

"You were in the military?" she asked, not sure why she was surprised.

"Army Ranger, ma'am," he said in a sarcastic tone.

"Well, I don't feel that their protest denigrates what the military men and women are doing over there."

"No?" he said. "'No blood for oil'? Is that what you people really think this is about? That it's just about money? They're trying to help those people escape a life of tyranny, and they're dying over there. No blood for oil—that's a slap in the face of every military person over there."

Samantha looked back at him, her eyes wide. She could tell that a nerve had been hit. And she really couldn't argue with him. It was true; she'd felt that the war in Iraq was more about proving something than any other reason. Another smoke screen sent up by the Republicans to justify massive spending. That's what Jeffrey had said. But was he right this time? And were people right to protest something, when America's men and women were still over there fighting and dying? It was reminiscent of the Vietnam War in a way. Certainly not on as big a scale, but with a definite flavor to it. Hadn't America learned anything from that?

It wasn't big, but it was a tiny chink in the armor of righteousness Samantha had built around herself with her beliefs. Maybe everything she believed wasn't always true or right. It bothered her somehow. She tried to talk to Jeffrey about it that night. His response was lukewarm.

"Why are you listening to some rent-a-cop?" he asked her. "What's his education level?"

"What does that matter?" she asked, surprised by Jeffrey's attitude.

"Certainly you realize that there's a reason he's protecting a lawyer rather than having become one," he told her, his tone chiding.

"That doesn't mean his opinions have no value, Jeffrey."

Jeffrey merely shrugged. "Believe what you'd like to, Samantha. But please don't expect me to defer to the opinions of a man who probably never finished high school."

Samantha found herself appalled by her husband for the first time in their marriage. He sounded like such a snob. She'd always thought that his beliefs were based in an understanding of nature and its balances. In this instance, he sounded like an overeducated, stuck-up bore, and she wanted nothing to do with that kind of attitude.

Oddly, Jeffrey's attitude softened hers toward Sebastian. He noticed it instantly the next morning.

Walking out of her house, she smiled at him and said a soft "good morning."

"Morning," he said, looking perplexed as he opened the door for her and put his hand to her elbow to help her into the vehicle.

They were silent on the ride in, but there was less tension that morning. Sebastian wasn't sure what to make of her change in attitude, but he figured he'd get the tree-hugging liberal pain in the ass back eventually. They were due to leave for New York two days later. He was hoping whatever truce she'd called would last through that trip at least.

**

The next time Kevin ran into Robert, he was alone, and Robert wasn't. Robert had three friends with him. Words were exchanged, and Robert threw a punch, which Kevin ducked. His friends got involved then. While Kevin fought back fiercely, the odds were just too overwhelming.

Jennifer was shocked when he got back to the house. His clothes were dirty and torn, his mouth was bleeding, and he already had a couple of dark bruises starting on his face. He was breathing heavily, like it hurt to breathe.

"Oh my God!" she said, her eyes wide.

He held up a hand to stave off her concern. "I'm okay," he said, coughing.

Walking out onto the back patio, he dialed Joe's cell phone. Joe answered on the third ring.

"Hey, Joe, it's Mace."

"Hey, man," Joe said, smiling as he drove along the beach to have lunch with his wife. "What's up?"

"Just wanted to let you know I'm going to step things up with this Robert guy," Kevin said, coughing again as he lit a cigar, inhaling deeply and finding that it hurt.

"Okay…" Joe said cautiously. "Do you want to tell me why?"

"'Cause he and three of his friends just jumped me, and I'm pissed right now." Kevin's tone was even, but his eyes narrowed.

"Shit, man, are you okay?" Joe asked, all concern for liability gone, replaced with concern for a fellow officer and a friend.

"Yeah." Kevin winced as he sat down on the deck. "Not too much worse than a regular day in the office."

It was an exaggeration; he rarely lost a fight. Never when it was one on one.

"Call Erin," Joe told him. "You know if she hears about it from me she'll freak."

"You could just not tell her," Kevin suggested mildly.

"I won't," Joe said. "You will."

Kevin nodded at his end, knowing Joe wasn't the type to hide anything from his wife. Not that Kevin was; he just didn't want Erin to worry.

She didn't worry. She sent reinforcements.

The next day, Dave Dibbins, Donovan Curtis and Spider Nguyen showed up at Jennifer's house. Jennifer was shocked by the three men standing at her door. They showed her their badges and asked where "Mace" was. Jennifer led them out to the back deck where Kevin was once again smoking.

"Well, you look like shit," Donovan said from behind Kevin as they walked outside.

Kevin's head snapped around. When he realized who it was, he smiled.

"Let me guess," Kevin said. "My wife?"

"Give the man a cigar," Dave said with a smile.

"We thought we'd even the odds up a bit," Spider said, his eyes sparkling with malice.

Kevin was part of the family that they all belonged to, known as the Gang. Spider and Dave were part of the original gang task force started by Midnight Chevalier. Along with Joe, Kana, Tiny and Rick, they were considered Midnight's extended family. That family extended further to close friends, family and spouses of their family. Donovan was Joe's wife's brother. Kevin had become part of the group by getting together with the woman Donovan had dated before marrying his wife, Jeanie.

Erin had been Donovan's salvation for a while, but true love had won out and Donovan had gotten back together with Jeanie and married her. Kevin had fallen in love with Erin the first night they'd met. They'd married a year later. So Kevin was officially part of the Gang. His family members were there to back him up. Since both Spider and Dave were ex-gang members and longtime cops, their fighting skills were honed to a fine art. Donovan, while looking like a clean-cut All-American football hero, had learned a number of things from his brother-in-law and from Midnight herself while growing up. He was a dangerous commodity when he wanted to be.

"You're all here to help?" Jennifer asked, shocked.

"Yes, ma'am," Spider said, smiling broadly as he extended his hand to her. "I'm Spider. That's Dave and Pony."

"Nice to meet you," Jennifer said, trying to recover her composure.

Spider was an Asian man. He wasn't very tall, only about five foot eight, but he had an air of danger about him. His frame was slight, but she could feel definite strength in his grip. He looked about thirty-five; in truth Spider was forty-three.

She shook hands with Dave next. Dave looked like the consummate laidback California surfer dude, with his sandy-brown hair in a long fade, which fell forward to sweep over his forehead as he nodded to her. He had sky-blue eyes and was taller than Spider at about six foot even. In truth, Dave *was* a surfer and as laidback as they came; he was also considered the best narc in the country.

Then there was Pony, as Kevin had called him. Donovan was tall too, about an inch taller than Dave. He had brown hair and the most incredible teal-blue eyes, which seemed to glow. He also had a great smile that she saw when she shook hands with him. This man looked nothing like the other three. He was clean cut, clean shaven—he looked too innocent to be a cop. In reality he'd been a narcotics officer for years; he just never looked like that. It was his edge.

"Pony?" she queried when she shook hands with Donovan.

"A nickname from high school," Donovan explained with a smile. "My last name is Curtis, and my older brother's name is Darrell, like—"

"*The Outsiders*!" Jennifer exclaimed.

"Yeah…" Donovan smiled; rarely did anyone understand the connection. "I also have a thing for Mustangs—you know the pony on the front?"

"I see," she said.

"So where can we find the asshole this time of day?" Spider asked, ready to get to business.

"Robert usually works on Wednesdays till five," Jennifer said, sensing Spider's restlessness.

Dave checked his watch. "Give us an hour," he said. "Come on, boys. Let's go play."

Kevin stood up. "Let me throw on a shirt and my boots," he said, his look intense.

The other three nodded. After Kevin walked into the house, Jennifer looked at the three men.

"Are you three being paid by Joe Sinclair too?" she asked.

They shook their heads. "We're taking care of our own," Dave told her.

Jennifer looked surprised but nodded slowly. She had no idea how Joe Sinclair afforded to take cases with people who couldn't afford to pay him. He had hired Kevin Elmasian to protect her, so the money Kevin was being paid came out of Joe Sinclair's pocket. Now here, on a weekday, were three San Diego PD officers who'd come up to Orange County to back up their friend in a fight. These people were astounding.

An hour later, Kevin leaned casually against the back of his Dodge Durango, smoking a cigar. He wore sunglasses, even though it was getting dark. The top part of his long hair was pulled into a tail at the back of his head. He wore a black shirt, jeans and black combat-style boots. He looked menacing, and indeed was dangerous to Robert at this point.

86

Not too far from where Kevin was sat a midnight-blue 1970 Dodge Charger, with Dave, Donovan and Spider lounging against it.

Robert walked out of the store, rolling up his work apron, his head down. He bumped into someone coming the other way and started to say something rude, when he looked up. He was truly surprised to see the guy that Jennifer was dating standing in front of him. What was wrong with this idiot? Didn't he know when to quit?

"You back for more?" Robert asked, glancing behind him as his friends, who also worked at the store, walked up. They had been heading out for a celebratory beer, because they were sure they'd run the new guy off. Yet here he stood.

"Well, I was thinking we could handle this just you and me," Kevin said, his tone low.

Robert looked back at him, oozing confidence. "I don't think that's necessary. But I'm sure that my friends will be happy to remind you why you should stay the fuck away from Jennifer."

His friends laughed, each of them making gestures to indicate pounding on Kevin. Robert noticed three men coming toward them; he was surprised when they stopped just behind Kevin.

"Do you need something?" Robert asked in a cocky tone.

"No," Spider said, staring back at Robert.

"Then move on," Robert said. "We're having a conversation here."

The three men didn't move. One of Robert's friends, a burly black man, stepped forward, reaching past Kevin to shove Spider. Quick as a flash, the man was on his knees, his arm twisted up behind him.

"I don't think you want to do that," Spider said, smirking.

"Let the fuck go, man!" the black man yelped.

"Shut up," Spider said, pulling his arm up a hair higher, then he looked over at Robert and his other two friends, calmly waiting.

Robert eyed Spider, then glanced at Kevin, whose lips were curled in a sarcastic grin, his eyes unreadable behind dark sunglasses.

"He said let go," one of the other men said, stepping up.

He moved to grab Spider. Before he knew what hit him, Donovan had him on the ground on his stomach. Donovan had his knee in the man's back and was leaning down over him.

"You guys don't learn too fast, do you?" he said, his smirk evident in his voice.

"Hey!" the third friend said, starting to take a step forward.

Dave lifted his chin, his sky-blue eyes pinning the third man with a look.

"Are you sure you want to try it?" Dave asked, his tone warning, his look confident.

The third man hesitated, then shook his head, stepping back.

Robert didn't look near as confident now.

"Now it's just you and me." Kevin brought his hands up, dropping a foot behind him in a fighter's stance. "Let's go."

Robert hesitated, glancing at his friends who were still on the ground. Then he looked back at Kevin. He'd known he couldn't beat the other man; that's why he'd involved his friends in the first place. But with these other guys around, Robert knew he was in for a beating.

"Nah, man," Robert said finally, shaking his head.

Kevin stared back at him for a long moment, then dropped his hands to his sides and straightened. He reached into his pocket, pulled out his badge and showed it to Robert.

"Good decision."

Glancing at Spider and Donovan, Kevin gave a slight nod. Donovan, Spider and Dave all produced their badges. Robert and the other three men looked suddenly very pale.

"Now," Kevin said evenly, "this is how this is going to go. You're going to stay the hell away from Jennifer and Chad. I'm going to write the report up, the one about assaulting a peace officer," he said, giving them a pointed look, "and I'm going to hold on to it. Jennifer will have my pager and cell phone number, and if I even hear the slightest whisper from her that you've come near her again, I'll have your ass in a San Diego jail so fast it'll make your head spin. Are we clear?"

Robert stared back at him, trying to decide what was going on here. Jennifer was dating a cop from San Diego? What the hell? Either way, jail was not a place he wanted to end up. No broad was worth that, not even Jennifer.

Blowing his breath out, Robert nodded.

"I'll leave her alone," he said seriously.

Kevin glanced at Dave. Dave nodded, agreeing that this was an effective course of action. He looked at Robert's friends; he could see that they were relieved that he wasn't going to arrest them. *Good*, he thought. With that said, Kevin stepped aside, allowing Robert and his friends to walk by.

Dave, Spider and Donovan followed Kevin back to Jennifer's house.

Meanwhile at the house, Jennifer opened the door to Joe Sinclair and a pretty blond woman.

"Hi, Jennifer," Joe said, smiling at her.

She'd met with Joe Sinclair when he'd taken her case. He'd said that he'd been told about her case by an Orange County Sheriff's deputy he'd worked with. She had been shocked and very impressed by Joe Sinclair. She'd also been sure she couldn't afford his fees. When he'd told her it wouldn't cost her a dime, she'd been sure he was joking. It was obvious the man made a lot of money—he was driving a

Cadillac Escalade, and he had on a watch that looked like it cost a fortune. Joe had assured her that he wasn't joking, and he hadn't been. She still didn't understand it.

"What are you doing here?" she asked as she opened the door wider and gestured for him to come in.

"I had a delivery to make." Joe nodded at the woman with him. "Jennifer, this is Erin Elmasian."

Jennifer's eyes widened. "You're his wife," she said, feeling overwhelmed suddenly.

Erin smiled, nodding. "Hi."

Jennifer took Erin's hands in hers. "Your husband has been so great. Thank you so much for letting him do this."

Erin smiled again. "Kevin does what he wants to. I just support him."

"Well, I appreciate you lending him to me all the same," Jennifer said.

Erin laughed at her phrasing. "Well, you're welcome."

Jennifer offered them a seat and something to drink. They both declined anything to drink but sat down in the small living room.

Kevin walked in a few minutes later. He turned to tell Jennifer that her problems with Robert were hopefully over. That's when he caught sight of his wife. Jennifer was sure she'd never seen a man's face light up brighter.

"Babe…" he said, as she stood up.

Kevin walked over to her, taking her into his arms and hugging her. "But how?" He looked down at her, then his eyes went to Joe.

"Joe brought me up," she said, smiling up at him.

"Man…" Kevin put his hand out to Joe, without releasing his wife. "Thank you."

"No problem," Joe said. "Pays to have your own jet."

"Yeah, rough gig," Kevin said, laughing.

"Oh, Kev…" Erin had been looking at the cuts and bruises on his face.

He smoothed his thumb over her cheek. "I'm okay, babe, really."

"No," she said, shaking her head. "You way downplayed how bad you were hurt, Kevin James Elmasian."

He lowered his head like a child being scolded. His lips curled into a grin.

"Don't you dare," she said, already grinning too. "You are going straight to a hospital to get checked out."

"I don't need it, babe. If I've got anything it's a couple of cracked ribs. No big deal."

Erin Elmasian sighed. "Well, then you're at least going to take some time off."

Kevin nodded, then turned to Jennifer. "You shouldn't have any more problems with Robert. He's aware that I could haul his ass into jail right now if I wanted to, so he knows he better stay away from you and Chad."

Jennifer shook her head slowly. "I don't know how to begin to thank you," she said, looking at Kevin, then at Joe.

"No thanks needed," Joe said.

"You've saved my life," Jennifer said, tears in her voice now.

Joe smiled softly, as Jennifer walked forward and hugged him, then turned to Kevin and did the same.

"Thank you," she whispered to Kevin.

He gave her an extra squeeze. "You're welcome." he whispered back.

Erin looked on, a smile on her face and tears in her eyes.

CHAPTER 5

Things were just about ready. Time for a few people to learn that you couldn't change the natural order of things. Midnight Chevalier would learn her place, even if it meant killing her. She was taking far too many liberties with her position. The people of the state of California needed to be shown the right way. That women couldn't handle power, that it gave them too many crazy ideas. She'd learn; she'd learn well. And if those bodyguards of hers got in the way, well, he'd just have to take them out too. He didn't like extraneous killing, but the woman was gay after all, and what kind of self-respecting man protected a woman like Midnight Chevalier? They all needed to learn. The time was coming. Time was coming soon.

***

Linda couldn't believe it. Kashena was saying they couldn't go out that night! Then again, Linda realized she shouldn't be surprised—Kashena was always so staid, so stable. On one hand, that was what she liked about the woman, but now wasn't the time to slow down. Things were fun! They were having fun, right? Linda was sure that all she had to do was threaten Kashena with going out to their local bar without her and that would be all it would take. It was all it had taken before.

When Kashena still didn't rise to the bait, Linda went and dressed, did her make up and hair, and went back to the kitchen. Kashena was sitting at the table, eating dinner and reading a report she'd brought home from work. Linda tried to get her to go out, but there was no budging, so she left the house, but not before grabbing Kashena's car keys and some money out of her wallet too. She'd show Kashena she wasn't one to be told what she could and couldn't do.

***

Things between Sebastian and his charge, Samantha Cobb, had gotten to a simmering level. They'd had a number of debates about politics, religion and life in general. Samantha was surprised to find that he was very well educated, for all that she'd had him pegged as a glorified security guard. He had a master's degree in Political Science with a minor in Sociology; that in and of itself was astounding to her. When they debated politics, it was clear he was better educated in that regard than her, and he was quick to point out Jeffrey's flawed thinking around politicians and their motives.

Samantha found that while he was still quite irritating when it came to his attitude about women—he used them like socks—she had to give him some credit. He'd come from nothing, one of the lowest-income neighborhoods in Sacramento, and he'd made something of himself. He'd gotten an education through the military that many people would envy, and in an arena many extremely intelligent people would avoid. She herself could never grasp politics well and had therefore avoided that whole area of law. Sebastian seemed to take great pleasure in the topic and could debate the merits and shortcomings of every politician since Lincoln.

They flew to New York, having a lively debate all the way about the latest Propositions on the November ballot.

"The problem is," Sebastian was saying, while everyone around them turned around in their seats or stood up and listened in, "the legislature buried it so far under rhetoric that most common voters won't read into it the way they should. Most voters believe what they see on television. And the voters that do read the sample ballot will many times only read the first few lines. The actual tax issue is buried at the bottom of the text on the ballot."

"But that's outrageous!" said one businessman. "How can they lie to voters?"

"It's done quite often, and it's not considered lying, sir. It's merely considered spotlighting the more popular version of the truth."

"There are no versions of the truth," Samantha put in, her tone all lawyer.

Sebastian smiled. "In politics, babe, there are innumerable versions of it."

Samantha narrowed her eyes at the use of the word "babe" as she always did, but she didn't comment on it this time.

"Well, that's just reprehensible," said a woman who'd been eyeing Sebastian since he'd walked onto the plane.

Sebastian inclined his head to indicate he agreed with her. "But what's also reprehensible is that people are given the right to vote and either they don't or they vote irresponsibly."

"Irresponsibly?" Samantha echoed. "You mean by voting Democratic?" she asked, sure that was what he meant from discussions they'd had before about what he'd referred to as "goddamned tree-hugging liberals."

Sebastian's ocean-green eyes glittered mischievously. "No, I mean by not bothering to actually read the ballot and believing what they see on television."

Samantha glared at him, knowing that somehow he'd baited her into making a fool out of herself. Sebastian only looked back at her, widening his eyes slightly as if to say "got ya."

Later on the long flight, Samantha got up to stretch her legs and go to the bathroom. By the time she got back to her seat, Sebastian and the blonde in front of them were engaged in a deep conversation. Sebastian was standing, leaning against the woman's seat and talking animatedly to her.

Samantha took her seat and picked up the book she'd been trying to read earlier. She did her best not to pay attention to her bodyguard and the woman he was chatting up. Unfortunately, in the last week she'd come to realize how women could find a man like him attractive. He was good looking in a He-Man kind of way. When they weren't arguing, he had an easy smile that lit up his face and made his eyes twinkle. It was too much that she'd noticed how handsome he really was. It annoyed her that she thought so.

She could hear him chuckling at something the woman had said, and then whispering something to her that made her laugh as well. Samantha wondered if it pertained to her. Self-consciously, she smoothed the French twist at the back of her head. She continued to read, even if she wasn't registering a word of the book in her hands. Somehow she just knew that he was telling that perfect blond Barbie doll that she was a bitch, that she was cold and nasty and "buttoned up," like he'd called her a few days before.

In truth, Sebastian's conversation had centered somewhat on Samantha, but only in that she was the reason he couldn't see the beautiful blonde while he was in New York.

"I'm working, honey," he said regretfully.

"She has to go to sleep at some point, doesn't she?"

"Who knows what time that'll be," he said, shaking his head.

"I'll wait all night…"

"I wouldn't want you to have to," he said with a smile.

"Such a gentleman." She ran a baby-pink nail along his jawline.

He grinned mischievously. "Only where it counts."

"Ohhhh…" she said, her eyes sparkling with interest.

"I better get back. I'm getting the look."

"She's reading a book," the blonde protested.

"Trust me, I'm getting the look in her head."

The woman sighed. "Okay, if I have to let you go."

"You'll be okay," he said, winking at her. "Every man on the plane is watching you."

"But I want you to watch me," she said in a pouting tone.

"Oh I will, trust me," he said, moving to sit down.

Samantha merely moved her arm off the arm rest as he sat down, but he could feel her ire. He smiled to himself. *A little territorial, are we, DAG Cobb?*

When the plane landed in New York, the blonde handed him a slip of paper.

"My number, in case you get time off for good behavior," she said, loud enough for Samantha to hear.

Sebastian nodded, glancing at Samantha and seeing that she was pointedly looking out the window. He smiled at the blonde.

In the taxi on the way to the hotel, Samantha couldn't resist saying, "I do hope I'm not cramping your style."

Sebastian didn't reply, only chuckling as he looked out the window, his senses ever alert.

That evening they went down to dinner in the hotel. When they were just finishing up, the blonde appeared, smiling at Sebastian. Samantha threw a vile look at him, but he didn't see it; he was busy trying to figure out how the woman knew where to find him. Then he remembered mentioning the hotel's name on the plane. He grimaced, realizing how dangerous that could have been. *Need to tighten it up, Bach.*

"What are you doing here?" he asked the blonde, who he'd found out was named Becky from the handwritten note she'd pressed into his hand on the plane.

"Oh, business, pleasure…" she said, smiling brightly.

Samantha stood up. "I'm going to my room."

Sebastian stood as well, catching the crestfallen look on Becky's face.

"You can stay," Samantha told Sebastian sharply. "I can find my way back to my room."

Sebastian shook his head. "I'll take you," he said, his tone all business.

"I'll be in the bar if you get free," Becky said, undaunted by Samantha's attitude.

Sebastian hesitated. He glanced at Samantha, who was busy gathering up her coat.

"I'll try," he whispered to Becky. "No promises, though."

Becky smiled and headed off toward the bar. Sebastian escorted an oddly quiet Samantha to her room.

"I'll be up in a bit," he told her. "I'll check on you when I get in—leave the adjoining room door unlocked on your side. If you decide to go out for any reason, page me and I'll be right up."

Samantha nodded, not looking at him. "Goodnight, Agent Bach," she said evenly.

"Goodnight," he said, closing her door behind her.

Standing in the hallway, he debated going downstairs. It was obvious what Becky was looking for, and while he wanted to accommodate her in the worst way, he also knew it wasn't a good idea. All the same, he could use a drink. A day of tension with Deputy Attorney General Cobb could make a man sterile.

He pushed off the wall and headed down to the bar. One or two drinks—what could that hurt?

Becky was thrilled to see him walk through the doors to the bar. She beckoned him over to the corner booth she'd chosen, watching him as he walked up. My God, he was handsome, with an air of sexuality about him, and she desperately wanted to find out if he was as good as he looked.

Two hours later she followed him upstairs. He had her wait for him in his room while he checked on his charge. He quietly opened the adjoining room door and stepped inside. Samantha was asleep, the sheet pulled up to her neck. Sebastian stared down at her for a few moments. Her long red hair was pulled back in a braid. Did she ever wear it down? What was the point in having all that hair only to tie it up constantly? He didn't get it.

He checked the room out, making sure the windows and the door to the hallway were secure; he put the latch over to keep anyone from entering even with a key. Then he quietly left the room. He didn't see Samantha watching him from the bed as he did.

Back in his room, Sebastian walked out into the living area. Becky was standing looking out the window. He walked over to her, standing behind her and gazing out at the street far below. Becky felt him behind her. Leaning back slightly, she felt his hands at her waist. She reached behind her and touched him, feeling him grow hard against her. His lips were on her neck in moments.

Ten minutes later, they were making it on the couch in the living area. She rode him hard and fast, crying out over and over again as she came. Afterwards, she got up and got dressed, kissing him lingeringly as she left. He certainly had been everything she'd hoped and more.

"Call me if you get a chance," she told him at the door, running her hand over his bare chest.

"I'll do that," he said, knowing he wouldn't.

He showered and climbed into bed. He wore sweat pants and a tank shirt, just in case he was needed in the middle of the night. He didn't hear Samantha open the door quietly an hour later. She'd heard all the goings-on in the room earlier. As much as she'd wanted to deny it to herself, she'd been curious. He was asleep on his stomach, his arms clasped around a pillow, the muscles on his arms and back standing out.

She watched him for a few minutes, knowing she shouldn't. The fact of the matter was, she'd never seen a man built like he was in person. Sure, she'd seen it in movies, but Jeffrey was the only man she ever saw in the flesh, at least with this amount of clothing on. Sebastian was a whole different type of man. A type she didn't like, she reminded herself.

Finally she went back to bed, sleeping fitfully until the morning. It was seven thirty when he rapped on the adjoining door between their rooms. She opened it to see that he was dressed in a suit of dark olive green, with a crisp white dress shirt and a rich blue silk tie with a tiny olive-green pattern. He looked handsome, she couldn't ignore that, but she refused to think further than that.

"Ready to go?" he asked, scanning her from head to toe.

She wore a beige suit that did absolutely nothing for her figure or her skin tone. She wore almost no makeup, and her hair was pulled up into a bun. Sebastian was consistently tempted to remind her that she *was* a woman.

"Yes, I'm ready," she said, picking up her briefcase.

Sebastian escorted her out of the room, making sure her door was secure. As they got to the elevator, he lifted his jacket aside to pull out his sunglasses, and she saw the shoulder holster he wore. It was brown leather, and his gun hung under his left arm. She shuddered at the thought of a gun. Yet another issue she had with the man—she didn't like guns. They were instruments of violence.

The meeting she had took hours. It was a hearing with the EPA, and Samantha was representing the state of California's position. Sebastian spent a lot of time outside the building, smoking and talking to the security officers from the Marshal's Service.

At two thirty, the meeting finally ended. Sebastian was at the doors to escort Samantha out of the building. She shot him an irritated look; she didn't like him dogging her every step. At one point she stopped in her tracks and turned around to look at him.

"Do you have to follow me so closely?"

"How far away would you like me to be?" he asked her, his tone wry.

"Ten feet or so would be nice," she snapped. "At least some breathing room."

He nodded, his expression telling her he didn't care what she wanted.

"I could do that, Deputy Attorney General Cobb. Then again, I could be a hundred feet away too. Fact of the matter is, if I am, I can't protect you," he said evenly.

Samantha stared him down, feeling the need to assert herself in some way or fashion.

Sebastian stared right back at her, unaffected by her acerbity.

She rolled her eyes. "I think you just like being a thorn in my side," she said irritably.

"Yeah, that's my whole goal in life," he said, a smile at his lips.

Shaking her head, Samantha began walking again.

"Perhaps some lunch will better your disposition?" Sebastian asked as he fell into step behind her again.

"Are you saying there's something wrong with my disposition, Agent Bach?"

"You seem a bit… ah… cranky."

Samantha glowered at him. "Kindly speak to me like I'm an adult, rather than a two-year-old, Agent Bach."

"Well, I decided cranky was better than saying bitchy," Sebastian said, a falsely benevolent smile on his face.

Samantha's mouth dropped open in shock. She couldn't believe he'd just said that to her.

"Of all the miscreant, disrespectful human beings in the Department of Justice… Why did I have to get you for my bodyguard?"

"'Cause I was lucky miscreant of the month," Sebastian countered sourly.

"I didn't mean those things together," she snapped.

Sebastian's eyes twinkled with subdued humor.

With an exasperated sigh, Samantha turned and walked out the doors to the building.

"And yes, I'd like to stop somewhere for lunch," she said, her tone anything but appreciative. "Do you think we can manage that in silence?"

"Anything you say, babe," he replied, giving her a rakish wink.

Samantha narrowed her eyes but was wise enough not to say anything. It seemed that no matter what she said to the man, he had a comeback for it. She always ended up looking like a fool.

They had lunch at a café just down the street from the building the meeting had been held in. Samantha insisted on sitting in their outside seating, which had a rail enclosing the area. The railing was waist high; even so, Sebastian chose to sit with his back against the wall of the restaurant. She didn't understand it, but sat to the side of him. While having lunch, Sebastian kept silent. His eyes were constantly on the street.

Samantha assumed that he was looking at the various women walking past. She was wrong—he was watching the street for any signs of trouble. He'd already pegged a few people he was keeping an eye on. One man, a guy on a bike, was standing with his bike between his legs, his eyes scanning the crowd coming toward him. Sebastian guessed he was probably a rip-off artist looking for someone to catch unawares.

Another man was pacing in front of the café, looking around constantly, then looking at his watch. Chances were he was waiting for someone who was late, but Sebastian had noticed that his eyes also kept sweeping over the people sitting in the outside café. That had Sebastian on his guard.

The third man Sebastian was eyeing was a younger guy, with stringy hair and a seemingly foul disposition. He was eyeing people walking by him with a look that read disapproval. He wore a ski cap, jeans, a black shirt and hiking boots that had seen better days. Sebastian had the guy pegged as a troublemaker. The man continually put his hand in the pocket of his jeans, clenching and unclenching his fist. Sebastian suspected he had a knife in his pocket. He wasn't taking any chances.

By the time they left the café, the man waiting out front had finally met with his party and gone inside. The man on the bike was still lurking, as well as the one with the ski cap. They were on opposite sides of the entrance. As they walked out, Sebastian steered Samantha to the left, putting himself on the side where the guy with the ski cap was.

"Will you stop it?" Samantha raged, having been jostled by Sebastian in his effort to get her to go where he wanted her. In her anger, she stepped around him and stared up at him.

Sebastian stopped, as she had, and looked down at her.

Just then there was movement, and Sebastian caught the flash of metal. Spinning, he shoved Samantha behind him and put himself between her and the unseen assailant. Bringing his forearm up, he blocked the knife the kid was wielding. Samantha screamed. Sparing a glance behind him, Sebastian saw the guy with the bike moving toward them. Punching the kid with the ski cap, Sebastian turned to face the man on the bike. He reached out and grabbed the handlebars of the bike, stopping its forward movement. Grabbing the man by a handful of his jacket, Sebastian lifted him off the bike and took him to the ground.

The kid with the ski mask had recovered and was bringing his knife up again. Keeping his knee in the small of the back of the guy he had down, Sebastian ducked the knife coming at him and punched the kid in the stomach. By that time NYPD was there, and Sebastian was able to check on Samantha. She was pale and shaking.

"Are you okay?" he asked her, trying to assess her visually to see if she'd been injured at all.

Samantha's eyes were wide as she stared at the two men who had attempted to assault them.

"Samantha, look at me," he said, his hands on her shoulders.

She looked at him, but it was obvious she was going into shock. Sebastian looked over at the NYPD officers that were arresting the suspects.

"I need to get her back to the hotel," he said, reaching into his pocket for his wallet and pulling out his business card. "We're at the Courtyard Manhattan on Fifth Avenue. Send someone there and I'll make a statement and give you a report. Okay?"

"Will do, sir," the officer said.

"Thanks," Sebastian said, already looking for a cab.

They got back to the hotel twenty minutes later. Sebastian ushered her up to her room and got on the phone, requesting the staff doctor come up. Within an hour the doctor had given Samantha a mild sedative to help with the shock and checked out the cut on Sebastian's arm.

While Samantha was resting, Sebastian made all the appropriate calls to his office to report the incident, calling Kana first and then Kashena.

Both women were concerned for his wellbeing.

"I'm fine," he told them both. "Just a scratch."

"If you're lying to me, Baz, I'll personally kick your ass," Kashena said, her voice low.

"Would I lie to you?" he said. "You've seen me shot, stabbed, drunk, naked... How much worse could it get?"

"Not much worse than naked," Kashena replied predictably, her grin evident.

"That hurts, Kash, it really does," he said with a chuckle.

"Uh-huh. Just take care of yourself, okay? When are you coming back?"

"Don't know yet," he said. "We were scheduled to be here another day and a half, but she may want to leave soon. She's in a state of shock right now. I seriously doubt she's ever been attacked like that before."

"Most normal people haven't, Baz," Kashena pointed out.

"I know."

"Well, let me know what your status is when you know."

"Roger that."

Sebastian spent the remainder of the afternoon and evening checking on Samantha, reading the paper, preparing the incident report on his laptop, and drinking a few beers he'd ordered from room service.

In the evening he asked her if she wanted anything for dinner. She shook her head. She was lying under the covers, her eyes closed. Sebastian left the room, not wanting to disturb her. He knew the sedative the doctor had given her would make her sleep; he figured she needed to do that at this point.

He'd expected her to sleep through the night. That's why it surprised him when she knocked lightly on the door that adjoined their rooms. He had the door propped open so he could hear her if she called for him. Looking up from the paper he was reading, lying on his bed, he saw her staring uncertainly at him.

"What's up, Samantha?" he asked, his voice much more gentle than it had been with her thus far.

She hesitated in the doorway, her uncertainty evident.

"Come on in," he said, sitting up and setting aside the paper.

She walked into the room. In her night clothes, which she'd changed into after the doctor had given her the sedative, she looked much younger. She wore gray, pink and black flannel pants and a pink cotton top that had spaghetti straps. Her long red hair was in a braid that reached halfway down her back. Sebastian was dressed in his sweat pants and tank shirt, as he had been the night before.

Samantha walked over to the bed, standing next to it and looking down at him.

"What is it?" His eyes searched hers. He wondered if she was still in shock.

"I just…" she began, her voice soft. "I…" It was obvious she was still quite upset by the afternoon's incident.

"Samantha, sit down," he said, his voice soft but commanding, as he touched the bed.

To his surprise she complied without hesitation. She sat Indian style on the bed, her eyes lowered.

"What's wrong?" he asked, knowing it was a dumb question.

"I just wanted to thank you," she said in a rush, her eyes still downcast.

Sebastian looked at her for a long moment. "I was just doing my job, Samantha."

"Risking your life like that?" She finally raised her eyes to his.

"Yeah," he said simply, saving the sarcastic retort pertaining to why he made "the big money" for another time and place.

"If you hadn't been there today… If you hadn't…" She shook her head, as if unable to comprehend what she would have done.

"But I was, Samantha," he said, his voice soothing. "What would have happened doesn't matter, because it didn't. Okay?"

She nodded slowly, still trying to reconcile it in her mind. He'd saved her life. He'd risked his own life to save her, no matter how nasty she'd been to him. Why?

"You said if I made you angry," she began hesitantly, "that you wouldn't protect me…"

"I lied," Sebastian said with a smile.

She looked at him for a few seconds, then realized he was joking with her. She smiled tentatively. "But I've been so awful to you…"

"No worse than I've been to you."

She took a deep breath, accepting what he was saying, and that he was absolving her of her actions.

"Still," she said, looking at him directly, "I'm sorry."

"So am I."

She sighed, obviously relieved they'd cleared that up. They were both silent for a while, and it was clear to him that she didn't want to be alone.

"Do you want to hang out in here with me?" he asked. "You really should eat something."

She grinned at him, looking very young. "Are you going to start guarding my health too now?"

"If I need to," he said, grinning back.

He handed her the room service menu and waited while she picked out something to eat. He ordered her food, and himself another beer and a hamburger.

When the food came, they ate in companionable silence. He turned on the TV, and they sat watching whatever was on. After a while it was apparent she was getting tired, so he gently suggested she try and get some more sleep.

"You have an early meeting tomorrow, counselor, remember?"

She nodded, looking reluctant.

"What is it?" He sensed that she didn't want to go back to her room.

She hesitated for a full minute, then finally sighed.

"I can't sleep."

"You slept earlier," Sebastian pointed out.

"That's because of what the doctor gave me, but it's worn off, and I can't close my eyes without seeing those men again…" She trailed off as she realized this wasn't his problem. She could watch TV in her room instead of his; at least he'd get some sleep then.

But he was nodding his head. "You really need some sleep, though," he told her. She'd only really slept an hour or two earlier, between the tossing and turning and all.

"I can't, Agent Bach. I really can't."

He smiled. "You think you could step up to calling me Sebastian now. I mean, considering I got cut for you and all."

"Oh God!" she exclaimed, just then remembering that he'd been hurt in the attack. "Are you okay? I didn't even ask. I'm so sorry…"

"Don't worry about it." He held up his forearm to show her where the doctor had used butterfly tape to close the cut. "It's minor."

Samantha bit her lip, feeling worse suddenly. He'd risked his life, and she'd only been concerned with herself. What kind of horrible person was she?

Sebastian read her self-castigation on her face.

"Sam, will you relax?" he said gently. "It's okay, I'm okay… you're okay too."

Samantha nodded, trying to convince herself. Sebastian could see she wasn't managing it.

"Okay," he said finally, putting his hand on the bed next to him. "Lie down here."

Samantha looked back at him like he was crazy.

He gave her a stern look. "Give me a break, will ya? I just risked my ass to save yours—you think I'm going to try and jump you now?"

Samantha's eyes widened at his terminology. Then she realized he was right. He was her protector, not an attacker. It wasn't like he was a desperate man, considering that just about every woman who looked at him flirted with him.

Chuckling softly, she lay down next to him. As she did, he extended his arm, putting it under her neck. He brought his thumb to her forehead, smoothing it over her skin.

"Now," he said in a soft voice, "close your eyes."

She did as he said.

"I want you to picture those two men," he said, his voice still soft and soothing. "Do you have a picture of them in your head?"

"I can't get them out."

"Okay. We're going to get them out together, okay?"

She nodded, grimacing slightly.

"Relax," he said. "You need to trust me, Sam, okay? Just listen to what I say, and focus on my thumb moving across your skin. I want you to breathe slowly, in through your nose, out through your mouth. Relax your muscles—just let them relax with each breath. Now, you have the picture of those men in your mind. Imagine my thumb is an eraser. We're just going to erase them little by little" He continued to talk, moving his thumb back and forth until he'd walked her through totally erasing them from the picture in her mind.

"Now," he said, "picture the most beautiful painting you've ever seen. Do you have it?" She nodded slowly, seeming much more relaxed. "Feel the texture of the painting. In your mind's eye, touch it. Run your hand over it... Smell the canvas... the paint..."

Sebastian continued to speak until she relaxed against him. He knew she was asleep then. Smiling to himself, he realized he was stuck with a bed partner for the night. He wasn't sure how she'd react to that in the morning, but he was damned if he was going to wake her up and try to move her. And while the cut on his forearm wasn't major, it hurt like hell, so he didn't intend to pick her up and carry her into the other room. She was dressed; he was dressed—what harm would come of that? They were adults, after all.

Putting his hand to her waist, he closed his eyes and was asleep a few minutes later. During the course of the night she snuggled closer to him. Half asleep, he reached down and pulled the covers up over them. They slept through the night.

***

"You've got to be kidding me," Cassie Roads-Machiavelli said, staring up into teal-blue eyes. "You are kidding me, right?"

"Actually, I wish I was," Donovan said tiredly.

"You're my bodyguard?"

"For this part of the tour, yes," Donovan answered, leaning against the doorjamb.

Cassie pursed her lips, displeased.

"We'll see about that." She turned around and walked into the four-bedroom house she shared with her husband.

Donovan stared after her, wondering why he thought he wanted to do this job for Joe. John Machiavelli himself had warned him that his wife could be "highly strung and a royal pain in the ass." So what was he? Nuts?

After three minutes of standing in the doorway to the home, Donovan finally stepped inside. He closed the door and leaned casually against it as he awaited her return. A few minutes later, Cassie returned, phone in hand. She handed it to Donovan and sat on the stairs at the end of the foyer. She didn't look pleased.

"Hello?"

"Donovan it's Mackie," came John's voice. "Just ignore whatever she says—she's in a mood apparently. She's been told that under no circumstances is she to give you any crap."

Donovan chuckled. "Somehow I doubt that's going to matter."

It was John's turn to chuckle. "Well, no one said bodyguard work would be easy, right?"

"That's true enough," Donovan agreed, "but I'm thinking I prefer drug dealers with guns to my head."

"On the bright side," John said, his grin evident even on the phone, "Cassie won't shoot you. She hates guns with a passion."

"Even yours?"

"She tolerates it."

"Ah." Donovan looked toward Cassie, who was watching him with sharp violet eyes. "Doesn't have a problem with daggers though, does she?"

"As in looking them at you currently?" John asked.

"Yeah."

"Don't worry. Chances are those are for me."

Donovan laughed. "I feel for ya, man."

"Thanks."

Cassie Roads was far from an easy woman to live with. The fortunate thing was that John Machiavelli loved her to distraction. She was a tiny little fireball. At two inches under five feet and weighing a total of ninety-six pounds, she didn't seem like much of a threat. However, she had a way of making a person feel incredibly uncomfortable when they were around her. What she lacked in stature, she made up for in attitude.

Donovan hung up with John a few minutes later, having discussed her schedule with him and gotten his bearings on what he needed to do. Joe had already trained him thoroughly on how best to guard someone, in particular Cassie Roads. His best advice had been "Don't let anything she says get to you. She says things for effect—don't let her affect you."

Looking across the foyer at her, Donovan knew he was going to have a lot of attitude to ignore. He walked over and handed her the house phone, his eyes staring right into hers. The gold wedding band he wore on his left finger caught the light, and her eyes fell on it, rather than looking at him.

"You're married?"

"Yes."

Cassie's lips pressed into a dissatisfied line. She said nothing else. Donovan waited in silence. She glanced at her watch—she had a meeting with BJ Sparks in a half hour; if she didn't leave soon she'd risk being late. BJ Sparks was the last person you wanted to be late to a meeting with.

"Fuck," she said, knowing she was about to lose this round.

Donovan glanced at his watch, then looked back at her, saying nothing. The last thing he intended to do was remind her of her schedule. He knew she knew she was risking being late.

Cassie finally stood and rushed up the stairs to her bedroom. Donovan waited in the foyer for her. When she came down ten minutes later, she wore jeans and a black shirt with flowing sleeves, and a black gothic cross at her neck. Her long black hair flowed around her shoulders. She looked beautiful, and Donovan saw in her what the world saw. A tiny gothic princess, perfect with her porcelain skin, violet eyes and dark mane of hair.

"Well, if you're coming, come," she said as she walked by him, heading for the front door.

Donovan took long strides, making it to the door before she did. He opened it for her with a flourish, a wry smile on his lips. She narrowed her eyes at him but said nothing.

Outside, she started to head for her black Lamborghini. Donovan stepped over to the black Cadillac Escalade that Joe had handed him the keys to earlier that morning. Mach 3 Protection Services used only the best, so Joe had bought a fleet of Escalades for company use.

When Cassie realized Donovan wasn't following her, she looked up, locating him next to the black Escalade he'd driven up in. His arms were crossed over his chest as he leaned casually against the back of the vehicle, regarding her calmly. Cassie stared at him, standing next to her car. It was obvious she was already seething. Donovan merely raised an eyebrow at her and glanced pointedly at his watch.

"Fuck!" she yelled, turning and marching toward the Escalade.

Donovan straightened and opened the rear passenger door for her. She moved past him and opened the front passenger side for herself, climbing in and slamming the door. Donovan grinned as he closed the other door.

The drive to Badlands Records was made in complete silence. She did note, however, that he had Maroon 5 on the stereo. Cassie liked them a lot. She had to give Donovan credit, albeit silently—he had decent taste in music at least.

Donovan kept his silence on the drive, knowing that she was stewing and not willing to poke a sleeping snake. Once at the studios, Donovan got out to open her door, but Cassie already had it open. He put his hand out to help her down. She scowled at him, loath to take his hand. He raised an eyebrow and waited with his hand out. She twitched her lips in disgust that she actually needed help out of the tall vehicle. It wouldn't be very dignified to fall and break her neck just so she didn't have to accept his help.

Taking his hand, she got down out of the Escalade. She dropped his hand immediately. Donovan merely smiled, not looking the least bit put out by her attitude. He was already beginning to remind her of John when he'd become her bodyguard.

John Machiavelli had been unflappable, right up until Cassie, in a fit of depression, had tried to kill herself. She'd scared him to death then, and he'd let her know it. He'd saved her life by performing CPR on her until the paramedics arrived to take her to the hospital. It had been during her stay in the hospital, when John had refused to leave her side, acting as a buffer between her and the whole world, that she'd fallen in love with him. He was the strong, protective force in her life, and she loved him dearly.

"You're looking cheerful," Brenden commented dryly as she walked into his office.

Cassie threw herself down in a chair across from Brenden's desk. "Bite me."

"Hey, Pony," Brenden said, nodding at the other man.

Donovan leaned against the wall near the windows in Brenden's office. "Hey, BJ."

"So, what's up?" Brenden asked Cassie. She'd asked for the meeting.

Cassie picked at a string on the leather chair she was sitting in, her eyes downcast. Her smile was secretive as she raised her violet eyes to look at the man who'd made her a star.

"I'm pregnant."

"You're what?" Brenden said, shocked.

"Having a baby, BJ," she said, laughing.

"Holy shit!" Brenden came around the desk and grabbed her in a bear hug. "Congratulations."

"Thanks," Cassie said, smiling brightly.

"John knows, of course?" Brenden said.

"Of course!" Cassie said. "I just wanted to tell you myself."

"So do you want to postpone your tour, or…"

"No," she said. "In fact this tour is perfectly timed, since I'll be off it before I really show."

"So you just wanted to relate the happy news, huh?"

"Yeah. I figured you should hear it from me."

Brenden smiled at her. He'd been there for her at a time in her life when things were really screwed up. Her boyfriend at the time had beaten her up. Brenden, as the owner of the Badlands label she and her band, Fast Lane, had just been signed to, was her new boss. He had taken her into his home and protected her from the press and from her ex-boyfriend. It had been BJ who'd hired John Machiavelli to protect her after Mike, her ex-boyfriend, had attacked her and left her for dead. Brenden James Sparks held a very special place in her heart; she looked on him as a cross between a father figure and the older brother she'd never had.

"Does Tabbie know?" Brenden asked her. Tabitha was his daughter.

"Nope. I didn't tell her, knowing she'd die trying to keep from telling you."

Brenden laughed. "True enough." He crossed his arms in front of his chest. "So, what do you need from me, Cass?" he asked, his tone sincere.

"Not a thing," Cassie replied, then glanced sharply at Donovan. "My husband has already seen fit to hire me another bodyguard."

Brenden grinned at Donovan. "I feel for ya, man," he said, his eyes sparkling in amusement. "If she gets out of hand, just call her husband. She'll shape up in a hurry."

"BJ!" Cassie swatted him on the leg.

Brenden only laughed, shrugging. "Can't say it's not true, Cass."

"Yes I can," she said, her eyes narrowed.

"Look, don't give Pony heartburn. It's not his fault your husband is overprotective, okay?"

Cassie looked over at Donovan, a little less malevolently this time. If Brenden liked Donovan, Cassie felt like she needed to re-evaluate her attitude toward him. Donovan looked back at her, unmoved. He'd learned to hide his emotions behind a calm facade from Dave Dibbins. He'd been taught by the best, and learned well. No one knew what he was thinking or feeling unless he wanted them to know. It was a valuable tool.

Later, as they drove out of the Badlands parking lot, Cassie looked over at him.

"Why do they call you Pony?" she asked, her voice devoid of attitude for once.

"Because of my last name."

"Which is what?"

"Curtis."

Cassie shook her head. "Sorry, you lost me."

Donovan blew his breath out. "My nickname is Ponyboy, like the character from a movie called *The Outsiders*. His last name was Curtis. His older brother's name was the same as my older brother's name as well."

"Oh." She pressed her lips together, sensing that he was still irritated at her original attitude toward him.

"So it doesn't have anything to do with coke, huh?" she asked mischievously.

"I'm a narc," he replied tightly.

She broke into a smile. "And?"

Donovan glanced over at her and realized she'd been needling him. He could see it in the way her violet eyes sparkled.

"Don't make me shoot you," he said, his tone serious.

Her eyes widened slightly, and it was Donovan's turn to smile.

"I think I'm gonna like you, Pony."

"You really weren't getting an option, Cassie."

"Yes," she said, "but BJ wasn't kidding about giving you heartburn. I really tortured John when he was my bodyguard."

"Yeah, well, I'm betting you'd fit perfectly in my duffle bag. So I wouldn't give me too much shit if I were you."

Cassie laughed. "You've been taking lessons from my husband."

"No," Donovan said. "From his partner."

"You know Joe Sinclair?"

"He's my brother-in-law."

"Really?"

"Yeah, he's been married to my sister since I was about sixteen."

"Oh," Cassie said. "The woman Jordan Tate lost him to, right?"

"Well, he just went back to his wife and kids," Donovan said. "I wouldn't call that losing him to my sister. She was willing to let him go if it made him happy."

Cassie sensed easily that Donovan had very definite loyalties there. She didn't want to push her luck. They'd just gotten on good terms.

"Well, it worked out anyway. Jordan got married a while back and has a baby girl now. So she's doing good now too."

"Everything goes the way it's meant to go," Donovan said.

Cassie nodded, surprised to hear such a sentiment from a man, especially a cop. Cassie had always regarded cops as cold and cynical. John had been an NYPD cop for years, and he did have a cynical streak. He was by no means cold, however. It had taken her a while to get used to the way John handled things. There were times when he was gruff and unyielding about things; that was his "cop side," as she called it. But he loved her like no man had ever loved her, and for that she was willing to make concessions.

When John had become partners with Joe Sinclair, Cassie had met yet another cop that didn't fit the idea she'd had. Now Donovan seemed to be different too. It said a lot about the danger of stereotyping people. If nothing else, it could make a person look quite foolish.

CHAPTER 6

Did she really think it would be so easy? That she could just walk in and make these changes and no one would challenge her? Was the bitch stupid, or just so egotistical that she couldn't see past her own agenda? No, this wasn't how things were meant to go. The time was drawing closer. The winds of change would blow right back into her face, and she'd be sorry she ever stepped into his realm. Very sorry indeed.

***

When Ben stepped up his stalking of Sierra, even following her down to Los Angeles and leaving a rose on the windshield of her rental car, Kana decided the attorney needed full-time protection. When she told Sierra that she would be bringing Kashena Marshal to protect her, she was surprised to find that Sierra already knew Kashena from years before in college.

Her comment was "She rescued me once."

Kana wasn't sure what to make of the look on Sierra's face when she said it, but her sixth sense said there was a lot to that story. Regardless, by the next day, Kashena was assigned as Sierra's personal protection.

***

Sebastian waited at the end of the gangway. He was looking for a dark-haired, butch-looking ex-Army Ranger named Barbara Strauss. She was the only woman he'd ever commanded; she'd been in his unit for the last two years before he'd left the service. The unit had been assigned to the Middle East at the time, and Strauss had been a hard-line butch lesbian. Sebastian had an understanding of lesbians by then, thanks to his friendship with Kashena, so he'd been easily able to handle Barbara's preferences.

He'd had no idea how much she'd appreciated him until the first time she'd written after he'd gotten out of the military. She'd told him repeatedly in her letters that it was his excellent command that had shown her what Army Rangers were made of. They'd stayed in touch in the six years he'd been out. Now she'd been discharged and had told him she was coming to Sacramento. Sebastian had volunteered his home as a place for her to stay and told her he'd be picking her up at the airport.

"Army Rangers take care of their own." It wasn't just a saying to Sebastian; he meant every word. And since she'd been a member of his unit, she was entitled to complete loyalty and any assistance he was able to give. He remembered the tough-looking woman well. She was small, only about five foot four, but she worked out a lot, and her muscles rivaled any man's. She was strong and agile at the same time, small enough to fit into spaces men couldn't, so they'd used her as their mole, which was how she came by her nickname.

She'd had short hair when she was in the military, and Sebastian had never seen her in anything but army fatigues. It was for that reason he was shocked when a woman with long dark brown hair, wearing smartly cut slacks, a definitively feminine blouse and heels stepped off the plane.

120

"Mole?" he said, dumbfounded by her change in appearance.

"Maestro?" she replied with a smile, using his nickname from his time in the military. They'd called him Maestro for the fact that he was named after a famous composer, as well as the fact that he "played" women like music.

"Wow." He smiled at her as she stepped forward to hug him. He hugged her, then pulled back to look at her again. "You don't look anything like the Barbara Strauss I sent into every hole in Iraq."

She laughed. "I had to look butch then, or no one would have accepted me."

He nodded, accepting that answer. Kashena had been the same way, very butch in appearance until she'd gotten out of the military and the Middle East. "Better that I'm mistaken for a guy," Kashena had always told him. "Especially in a country where women have absolutely no rights."

Sebastian led Barbara down to the baggage claim, where she picked up her one piece of luggage, a large military-issue duffle bag with STRAUSS printed on it. Taking the bag from her, Sebastian led her out to his vehicle parked at the curb. The nearby sheriff's officer waved Sebastian on when he saw the badge at Sebastian's waist, as his partner had earlier when Sebastian had driven up.

"Nice," Barbara said, admiring the black H2 Hummer. "Almost like home, huh?"

"Almost," he said as he put her duffle bag in the back and opened her door for her.

"Thank you, sir," she said, smiling at him.

"Don't get used to it, Ranger," he replied, smiling back.

She laughed as she got in, and he shut the door behind her. Five minutes later they were on the freeway headed toward his house in

Natomas. It was a short drive. But long enough for her to shock the hell out of him.

"So what are you planning to do in Sacramento?" he asked her as he lit a cigarette.

"You," she answered simply.

"Huh?" he said, sure either she'd heard the question wrong or he'd heard the answer wrong.

"I plan to do you while I'm in Sacramento."

Sebastian started coughing immediately, having inhaled far too deeply on his cigarette in shock. Barbara watched him, an amused smile on her face.

"You okay, Maestro?"

"I, uh," he said, coughing slightly still, "I didn't think anyone could shock me anymore, but you just did. You wanna explain?"

Barbara dropped her head, a guilty grin still on her lips.

"You are a lesbian still, aren't you?" Sebastian knew that sounded like a really dumb question, but in light of what she'd just said, he didn't feel it was too dumb.

Barbara lifted her head. "I never was a lesbian, strictly. I know I came off as butch, and I really thought I only wanted women, before I met you."

Sebastian looked back at her, still obviously shocked by what she was saying.

She took a deep breath. "My mother is a lesbian. I grew up around it. And when I was with my first guy, I hated it. He was a jerk and he was lousy in bed, so I tried again. After about three really lousy lays that did absolutely nothing for me, I decided I must be gay too. I was with my first woman, and she was fantastic compared to the men I'd been with. So that was it—I was gay. And I was convinced of that until I got into your unit and met you. You were the first man I'd ever wanted on sight."

Sebastian rubbed the bridge of his nose with his forefinger. "There were better-looking guys in the unit."

"Like hell there were. Besides, it wasn't just the looks. It was the way you treated me, the way you acted, the command, the power, everything."

Sebastian exhaled deeply and reached for another cigarette. This was far from the conversation he thought he'd be having with her. He'd expected a lot of talk about the military. That he could handle. This was just too weird for words.

Barbara was silent for a while. Sebastian smoked and turned over what she'd said in his head. She was definitely attractive; that wasn't in question. The way she was now... Hell, she was even wearing makeup. But Jesus, what was she expecting?

"So, let me get this straight..." he said as he turned into his drive-way and parked the vehicle.

"What's to get straight, 'Stro?" she asked. "I want to fuck you— it's as simple as that."

Sebastian shook his head. "Can I at least take you to dinner first?" he asked, his boyish grin warm.

Barbara laughed. "If you insist."

They had dinner at a local steakhouse. Neither of them mentioned the conversation in the car. Barbara wasn't sure if he was planning to take her up on her demand or not. It was her style to be direct, he knew that about her, so she hoped she hadn't been too direct this time. She'd had six years to consider how she wanted to approach him. It had been impossible to do anything until they were both out of the military. But she'd known all along she had to do something about this. So she'd waited and kept in touch with him.

Sebastian had a few drinks, still reeling from the bomb that had been dropped on him. He could almost hear Kashena now, laughing her ass off at him for hesitating. By the time they got back to his house, he still hadn't come up with a way to get out of this gracefully and with his pride intact.

When they walked inside the house, Barbara didn't give him half a chance to back out. Turning to him, she slid her hands up his chest and kissed him hungrily. Caught by surprise and reacting solely on instinct, he wrapped his arms around her, deepening the kiss as he pulled her closer. She moaned against his lips, sliding her hands into his hair, her fingertips grasping at the strands.

Putting his hands to her waist, he lifted her off her feet and felt her wrap her legs around his waist. He continued to kiss her, his tongue sliding between her lips, demanding and sexual. She responded heatedly as he moved toward the kitchen, the closest room. He set her down on the counter and pulled at the blouse she wore, taking it off impatiently as her hands worked at unbuttoning his shirt.

Things were frantic and heated. Sebastian wasn't able to think past the excitement of the situation. He took her the first time on the low counter, eliciting screams of pleasure and a few new scratches on his back. After that, she was insatiable. Reaching between them, she touched him tentatively at first, then with more confidence as his hand came down over hers, guiding her.

He rolled to his back and pulled her over him, guiding her down as she sat astride him. They made love again, his expertise taking over this time, making her come three times before he gave in too. He carried her to his bedroom, where they made love a third time in the shower. It was hours, and many new experiences for her, later when they lay asleep in his bed.

Kashena opened the door to his bedroom, expecting to see him asleep.

"Shit." She turned her face away when she saw that he had a woman with him.

Then it hit her. Didn't he say he was picking up the lesbian that used to be in his unit... Kashena turned her gaze back to them as Sebastian lifted his head and looked at her; the woman too was now looking at her. Kashena recognized her, although she looked very different now, and she was naked in Sebastian's bed!

"Uh..." Barbara glanced worriedly at Sebastian on seeing the shocked look Kashena was sending in their direction.

"Don't worry," Sebastian drawled as he sat up and reached for a cigarette. "You're jamming her gaydar."

Kashena glared at him. "You son of a bitch," she snarled.

Sebastian's response was to laugh as he lit his cigarette. "Good morning to you too, Kashie."

"You... you..." Kashena gestured at the bed and its occupants.

"I fucked a lesbian, yes."

Barbara sat up, holding the sheet over herself. "Should I leave you two alone?"

"No," Sebastian said. "She'll storm out of here in a minute or two."

"If I don't shoot you first," Kashena said. "I'll put some coffee on. You drag your ass out of that bed, Ranger, and come explain."

Sebastian grinned. "Ma'am, yes ma'am."

Kashena spun on her heel and left the room.

"Is she really mad?" Barbara asked, unsure what to make of the scene she'd just witnessed.

"She's shocked." Sebastian got out of bed, stubbed out his cigarette and pulled on his jeans. "She sucks at being shocked."

Barbara nodded, still not sure what to think.

Sebastian buttoned his jeans, leaving the top button undone as he reached for his cigarettes and his lighter.

"I'll be back." He winked at her, then left the room.

When he walked into his kitchen, Kashena whirled on him.

"What the hell are you doing?"

"Smoking a cigarette, and hopefully having coffee with my partner," he said, raising his eyebrow at the coffee pot behind her.

Kashena made a disgusted sound in the back of her throat, then turned back to making coffee. Ten minutes later she brought it out onto his back patio, where he was sitting and smoking.

"You want to tell me what happened?"

"Apparently, she's bi, not a lesbian," Sebastian said.

"And you know this how?"

"She slept with me, didn't she?"

"Apparently," she shot back, making a face.

"Hey," he said, giving her an offended look. "Just because you're not interested in me, let's not get all disparaging here, huh?"

"Sorry," she said, looking contrite. "It's just it was kind of a shock, you know?"

"I know," Sebastian said, "and you suck at shock."

Kashena took a drink of her coffee and grimaced. "How do you drink this shit so strong?"

Sebastian took a sip of his. "Actually it's a little weak for me. You didn't use enough coffee."

"Fuck you."

"Nah. One lesbian a month is my limit."

Kashena's mouth dropped open in shocked offense, then she shook her head and laughed. "Only you, Baz, can take a perfectly respectable lesbian and screw her up."

"Or down, or…"

"Ugh!" Kashena clapped her hands over her ears.

Sebastian threw his head back and laughed. Kashena left a little while later, and Sebastian rejoined Barbara in bed. It was a nice, comfortable day off.

***

Midnight lay on her bed, her head on Rick's stomach. She was drifting in and out of sleep. She felt Rick's hand on her hair, stroking it. Knowing her husband as she did, she knew he was sitting there, reading the paper with one hand, the other on her hair, and a bottle of Corona next to him on the nightstand. True to form, Rick set the paper down next to him, picked up the bottle of beer and took a drink.

"So predictable," Midnight said, smiling.

"You're supposed to be taking a nap."

"I know, I know." She turned over and looked up at him.

God, he was still so handsome after all these years. The only change was that he'd cut his hair. After being married for over eighteen years, Midnight had finally acquiesced to letting him cut his long light-brown curly hair. She'd been shocked when he came home—his hair, which used to fall to two or three inches past his shoulders, was now just above his collar; it was also straight.

"Straight?" she had asked. "How did it get straight?"

Rick had grinned. "Didn't you ever notice that in those pictures my mum showed you, if it was short, it was straight? The curly happens when it gets long."

"You've been lying to me all these years, Richard." She'd narrowed her eyes, then run her hands through his hair. "But you're a damned handsome man even with short hair."

And she'd meant it. He actually looked younger with the short hair, and still so damned sexy it wasn't legal. Englishmen aged well, she guessed. Her best friend, Joe, still looked damned good too. *It must be genetic,* she thought as she smiled up at her husband.

"What?" he asked, still sounding very English after all these years, his deep sapphire-blue eyes sparkling in the sunlight streaming through the window of their bedroom.

Midnight sat up. She took the beer out of his hand, taking a drink and setting it aside.

"I was just thinking what a damned handsome man I'm married to," she said, smiling warmly.

"Who is he? I'll kill him," Rick said darkly, then leaned in to kiss her.

Midnight put her hand to his chest as his arms encircled her, pulling her closer. They kissed for a long while, settling into a comfortable embrace. Their eighteen-year-old daughter was out at the moment, and their nine-year-old son was at a friend's house. They had the house to themselves. They took full advantage of it.

He pulled off the T-shirt of his that she wore, exposing creamy skin, flawed by a few scars, but Rick knew each one and what had caused them. He kissed her shoulder as she pulled at the shirt he was wearing, then he obliged her by taking it off and tossing it aside. She kissed his neck, hearing him groan deep in his throat. Kissing down his chest, she straddled his waist, pulling at the button on his jeans. His hands moved to her hair, caressing as she finished unbuttoning his jeans and pulled them off.

When they were both naked, they took their time exciting each other, knowing the other's most sensitive areas. By the time her body finally slid down over his, they were both more than ready, and cried out together minutes later in their release. Midnight lay over him, her long copper-blond hair spread out over his chest. He stroked her hair as they both tried to catch their breath.

"God, I love you," he whispered, still sounding out of breath.

Midnight kissed his chest. "Mmm, I love you too."

They'd been together nineteen years, yet they could still excite the hell out of each other, and it kept their marriage passionate. There was never a time when she didn't want him. He could still look at her in a certain way and have her stumbling over her words when she gave a speech. Fortunately, the press hadn't figured out this phenomenon yet; God help her when they did. Rick found it endlessly amusing.

"So, you're headed to LA this week?" he asked when she was lying next to him, his arm around her shoulders.

"Yeah. Kana wants to leave tomorrow night to beat some of the traffic."

"Oh sure, what's one more night?" Rick said with a smile.

"You can come with us if you want to…"

"Nah, K hates it when I travel with you. She says it makes her feel she and Tiny are just hangers-on."

Midnight laughed. "Only because she'd rather be home with Palani these days."

"True," he said. "I might come up on Tuesday night after I get everything settled at the office."

"Yeah?" she asked, smiling.

"Yeah."

"Lots to settle these days, Captain?"

"Don't even start with me," he warned. "I never wanted to be a bloody captain and you know it."

"Hey, Kyle lost a few good people in losing Joe, Kana and Tiny in one year. He needed you in that captain's spot."

"He should have promoted Spider."

"He wanted to promote Spider, and still might. He's considering expanding Narcotics again, and if he does that, you'll be heading up IA, Homicide, and Traffic, and Spider will be captain over Vice. So relax."

"Easy for you to say," he said, a grin already forming.

"Oh yeah," Midnight said, not seeing his grin. "So easy to watch my department change without me. Sure, this is great. It's like seeing one of your kids grow up without you there. I don't know what I was thinking leaving. I should have stayed where I was..."

Rick was laughing before she'd even finished her diatribe.

"Oh shut up!" she said, smacking his chest with a grin of her own.

"Poor little Attorney General. Not making enough waves statewide, she wants her little small-potatoes department back too."

"Small potatoes, my ass," she growled.

"Compared to the whole state?" he asked with a raised eyebrow.

Midnight scowled. "Okay, you win."

"As always."

"Bite me, Debenshire."

"I just might," he replied, widening his eyes at her.

Midnight laughed, shaking her head. She loved that they could talk so comfortably now about her going out of town. There had been times when her being gone a lot would have driven him crazy. At one very low point in their marriage, it had actually driven him into the arms of another woman. They'd almost gotten divorced over that error in judgment on his part. Her near death at the hands of a dirty cop had only widened the gap between them, since she'd been unwilling to let him help her. It had sent him running home to England to lick his wounds.

In the end, Joe's disappearance had brought Rick back, and fortunately, he and Midnight had been able to work things out. He'd never looked at another woman since. He'd found out quickly that Midnight was the only woman he ever needed. The love he felt for her was beyond explanation. She was one of a kind, his wife, and he knew it, and he had no intention of ever letting her go again.

Midnight, too, realized what an incredible man she'd married. He'd been through hell a few times because of her. There had been a time when she'd been thought dead, killed in an explosion when a car bomb had been set in her classic Corvette. It had been meant to kill her, and for an agonizing two weeks, everyone believed it had worked. Rick had been devastated. Midnight had seen the footage from her "funeral"—it had been obvious to her and everyone who had seen him that Rick was barely holding it together. It showed Midnight how much he loved her.

There had been other incidents when he'd proven how much he loved her. He'd even stepped in front of a bullet to protect her a year after the incident with the car bomb. Rick was always there to protect her, comfort her, and be the stabilizing force in her life. She loved him more than anything or anyone in the world.

***

Sebastian sat in his Hummer, waiting for Samantha to come out of her house. As usual, he was smoking a cigarette and drinking coffee. When Samantha came out, he tossed out his cigarette and turned the vents up high to blow the smoke out of the cabin. It was a polite gesture; he was in a good mood that morning.

"Good morning, princess," Sebastian said, grinning as she climbed into the vehicle.

She gave him a dirty look, then closed the door.

"Bad morning?" he asked as he backed out of her driveway.

"Oh, the usual rush," she said, airily. "I just never seem to have enough time anymore."

"I can show up later if you'd like me to," Sebastian suggested.

"No, it wouldn't matter," she said, sighing. "I'm hopeless these days with being on time."

Sebastian nodded, staying silent.

"So did your visit with your friend go well?" Samantha asked a little while later.

Sebastian had mentioned not being available during the weekend because he had an ex-Ranger coming to town from his old squad. Samantha had commented about not overdoing the "male bonding." So Sebastian had explained that it wasn't an issue, since the ex-Ranger was a woman. Samantha's answer had been "I see," with a knowing look.

"No, not like that," Sebastian had said. "She's gay."

Samantha had uttered a shocked "oh," and that had ended that conversation.

Now she was asking how the visit had gone. Sebastian couldn't squelch the chagrined look that crossed his features.

Samantha caught his look, then realized what that meant, or at least thought she did.

"Surely you didn't…"

"Didn't what?" he asked, smirking mischievously.

"Oh my Lord! You did!" she exclaimed, her eyes wide.

Sebastian said nothing, only reaching for another cigarette as he rolled down his window.

"But you said she was gay," Samantha said accusingly.

"She is, or was… Hell, I don't know now," he said as he lit a cigarette.

Samantha stared at him open mouthed. "But she was before you got to her?"

"Jesus, now you sound like Kash," he said. "When she was in my unit in Iraq she told everyone she was a lesbian. But apparently, according to her, she wanted me. So that would make her bisexual, rather than a lesbian."

"You know a lot about the alternative lifestyles," Samantha said, her tone amused.

"My best friend is a lesbian, Sam."

"Really?" Samantha was surprised at that.

"Yeah, the other agent I work with, Kashena Marshal? She's a card-carrying member of the lesbian community."

"Oh… I—" she stammered. "I just assumed…"

"You assumed since I'm this macho, ultra-military, goose-stepping Nazi that I wouldn't tolerate gays?"

Samantha pressed her lips together, realizing that was indeed what she'd thought. She looked immediately contrite. She put her hand out and touched his arm.

"I'm sorry, Agent Bach," she said sincerely. "You're right. That wasn't a very fair assumption of me."

"You make a lot of assumptions," he told her, his tone mild.

"Yes, I guess I do."

"I thought attorneys were supposed to be objective."

"Well, mostly judges and journalists are supposed to be objective," she said with a smile, "but I should at least be fair."

"Work on that, will ya?" he said jokingly.

"I'll do that."

CHAPTER 7

Gay marriage now? Gay rights? They had no rights—they chose to do something so vile and disgusting as having sexual relations with someone of the same sex; that gave them no rights. Now they wanted to be recognized as human beings? And Midnight Chevalier was behind the idea? Was she stupid? What kind of person thought that two people of the same sex should be allowed to have the rights reserved for the complete sanctity of marriage? Marriage was a holy union, sanctified by God himself! What they wanted was not only immoral but completely disgusting. It was too much. They needed to be stopped, and they needed to be stopped now.

***

A week after being assigned as Sierra's security, Kashena escorted Sierra to a conference in Los Angeles. She'd already had to argue with Linda, the troublesome ex-girlfriend who was ensconced in her house for the time being. Things hadn't gone well. Linda wanted to invite some of her friends over while Kashena was gone. Kashena soundly vetoed the idea, and when Linda balked at the prohibition, Kashena had simply told her, "Get a new set of friends and we'll discuss it." That hadn't gone over well either. Things had actually almost got physical, and Kashena knew that she really needed to get away from Linda.

She was still thinking about it on the plane down to Los Angeles. She smiled down at Sierra, who had fallen asleep during the short flight. What was funny was that Sierra had ended up with her head on Kashena's shoulder. Kashena considered the other woman, remembering very clearly their meeting back in college. They'd been in an American Indian Studies course, and Sierra had been the other outspoken American Indian in the class. Of course Kashena had noticed the woman—who could ignore her? She was beautiful, and very obviously intelligent. Regardless, Kashena, a Marine who was always in uniform, avoided the other woman. The last thing she wanted was to put either herself or Sierra in the lesbian spotlight on campus.

Sierra attempted to invite her to coffee, but Kashena declined. She managed to avoid Sierra successfully after that. Right up until the night they attended the same party, and Kashena observed Sierra going upstairs with an ardent admirer. Her damned protective streak prompted her to follow the couple upstairs and linger for a few minutes near the closed door. She was about to leave, telling herself that she was insane to feel protective over someone she didn't even know. Then she heard Sierra's raised voice and headed through the door to the dorm room.

Inside, there was a short confrontation between Kashena and the man who'd attempted to push Sierra for more than she was willing to give. It didn't go well for the young man, who ended up on the floor unconscious.

Kashena had escorted a fairly upset Sierra back to her own dorm room. Once there, Sierra had become somewhat hysterical as she realized what could have happened. The two had ended up in an embrace that had led to a kiss. A kiss Kashena hadn't forgotten, even though she hadn't seen Sierra until the day Kana had introduced

135

them, and Sierra hadn't seemed to recognize her. Kashena had decided that it was for the best.

***

Once they were on their way to the hotel in their rental car, Sierra looked over at Kashena.

"Agent Marshal?"

Kashena grinned. "You can call me Kashena, or Kash if you want to."

"Okay, Kashena." Sierra smiled.

Kashena waited in silence, glancing over at Sierra a couple of times.

"You don't remember me, do you?" Sierra blurted out suddenly.

A slow smile spread across Kashena's lips, her deep blue eyes sparkling in the sunlight.

"I remember you," she said softly.

"You do?" Sierra asked, unconvinced.

Kashena nodded. "The University of San Diego, Indian Studies class…" she said, her voice trailing off.

"A particularly foul frat house room," Sierra finished.

Kashena nodded again in agreement.

Sierra narrowed her eyes at Kashena. "So if you remembered me, why didn't you say anything?"

"Why didn't you?" Kashena asked with a smile.

Sierra pressed her lips together. "Good point," she said, laughing softly.

Kashena smiled again.

"I was sure you didn't remember me," Sierra said, grimacing.

"Of course I remember," Kashena said. "You almost cost me my military career."

"What?" Sierra asked with alarm. "How?"

"That whole scene in the frat house."

"Rescuing someone isn't acceptable to the Marines?" Sierra asked, aghast.

"Punching a civilian in the face isn't acceptable to the Marines," Kashena clarified.

"Oh," Sierra said. "What would they have expected you to do?"

"Subdue him through non-violent means."

Sierra canted her head. "And you could have done that?"

"Of course," Kashena said.

"So why didn't you?"

Kashena grinned. "Because he pissed me off."

"You broke his jaw, you know."

"I know," Kashena replied. "I felt it crack."

Sierra's mouth dropped open, her eyes widening. "I'll make a note to myself not to piss you off," she said, smiling.

Kashena laughed at that. "I'm in better control of myself these days."

"Good to know," Sierra said lightly, her smile wide. "So what happened to you after that?" she asked. "I never saw you around school after that semester—after that night, even."

"I shipped out right after that," Kashena said, seeing Sierra's relief and raising an eyebrow at her. "Did you think it was because of you?"

Sierra hesitated, then shrugged. "I didn't know for sure."

Kashena nodded slowly. "Well, now you do."

Sierra dropped her head, smiling. "I just figured I was a really bad kisser or something," she said, surprising herself by bringing that up.

Kashena surprised her further by laughing. "Not that bad, no."

Sierra bit her lip, not daring to look at Kashena, afraid her face would reflect what she was thinking.

They made it to the hotel a little while later. Kashena escorted Sierra to the area where the conference was taking place. At dinner that night, Sierra had a few glasses of wine. By the time they got back to the room it was clear she was drunk.

Sierra decided to take a shower to "clear" her head. Kashena grinned knowingly. By the time Sierra emerged from the shower, Kashena had changed into her comfortable clothes. Sierra wasn't used to seeing Kashena so casual. She also had her hair down, which was a first in Sierra's presence; Sierra found that she was entranced. There was such a draw to this woman, she just couldn't deny it, and the alcohol still in her veins was making it really hard to think clearly. Kashena was on the phone, but when she saw that Sierra was out, she hung up.

"That shower didn't help much, did it?" Kashena asked.

"It helped," Sierra insisted. "I feel really, really good right now."

Kashena pursed her lips as she attempted not to grin.

"I'm not drunk!" Sierra insisted.

"Right..." Kashena nodded, sounding unconvinced.

Sierra narrowed her dark eyes. "You know..." she said in a warning tone.

"No, what?" Kashena asked with an indulgent smile.

Sierra made an impatient noise in the back of her throat, causing Kashena's grin to widen.

"Stop it," Sierra said, her voice a whine now.

"Okay, I'll stop," Kashena said placatingly.

Sierra gave her an assessing look. "Do you have any idea how much more beautiful you are when your hair is down?"

Kashena was caught totally off guard by the comment. Her mouth dropped open, then she started to shake her head.

"And don't think that this is the alcohol talking," Sierra warned. "I thought you were beautiful in college too, only I never saw you with your hair down."

"True," Kashena said. "You only ever saw me in uniform then."

"And with your hair up every time I've seen you recently too," Sierra put in accusingly.

"It's more professional."

"Well, I like it down," Sierra said petulantly.

Kashena nodded, her lips tugging at the corners.

"You're still writing this off to alcohol, aren't you?" Sierra asked.

Kashena slowly expelled a deep breath and nodded again.

"Okay," Sierra said, her tone changing slightly, "how about this? Remember I told you that I remembered that kiss you gave me like it was yesterday?"

"Uh-huh."

"Well, what I didn't tell you is that after you disappeared on me, I went about dating women for the next four years or so."

"You did?" Kashena asked, shocked in spite of herself.

"Yes," Sierra said.

"And apparently you swung back the other way," Kashena replied knowingly.

"Yes," Sierra said, sitting forward, her eyes staring directly into Kashena's. "Because no one made me feel like you did with one kiss."

Kashena stared back at her, unable to think past what she'd just heard. Then reason kicked in.

"How many women did you date?" she asked.

"A lot."

"How many?" Kashena repeated.

"I don't know, maybe ten or so," Sierra said. "That's not the point. The point is that no matter what they did, no matter how hard they tried, how pretty, how butch, how smart they were, none of them did for me what you did."

Kashena pursed her lips, her mind churning. Finally she shrugged, sitting back against the headboard of the bed.

"It was the excitement of the unknown the first time," she said.

"No," Sierra said. "It was you."

Kashena shook her head, unconvinced.

Sierra stared at her for a long moment. Then, without warning, she moved forward, up between Kashena's knees. Bringing her face within an inch of Kashena's, Sierra stared into the other woman's eyes.

"It was you," she repeated, moving to lightly touch her lips to Kashena's.

Kashena pulled back, searching the other woman's eyes, then she moved in again, her lips taking possession of Sierra's. Sierra moaned immediately, her hands moving into Kashena's hair as Kashena cupped her cheek gently, her other hand moving to the back of Sierra's head. The kiss was passionate and excited, and there was no denying the fire that ignited between them, and it was just the beginning as they melted together.

CHAPTER 8

Donovan sat back, watching the rehearsal. He was still fairly awestruck by the fact that he was watching a Grammy-award-winning band from backstage. He'd been traveling with Fast Lane for a week now, and it still didn't seem real.

Tommy Timmerman, the guitarist for the band, had quickly become a constant companion. While Donovan and Tommy had little in common, Tommy a hardcore metalhead and Donovan a clean-cut narc, they'd united over the fact that Cassie was impossible to deal with sometimes.

"I love her to death," Tommy had confided in Donovan, "but I'd actually like to love her *to death* some days."

Donovan had laughed. "You have to admire Mackie for his self-control if nothing else."

Tommy had laughed at that, and they'd been fast friends ever since. Cassie had, however, softened quite a bit toward Donovan. She told him it was the pregnancy hormones; he nodded, accepting that excuse. The fact was, she actually liked Donovan. He seemed like a really good guy, and what she liked more was that he seemed to truly respect her marriage. The fact that he was married too probably had something to do with it as well.

That day, they were in Chicago. It was unseasonably warm, so Donovan was dressed in gray Dockers with a white and light gray patterned shirt over a black tank shirt. His weapon was in a holster at his back. After the rehearsal, he escorted a sweating and cranky Cassie back to the hotel.

"I'm going to take a shower and a nap," she said.

Donovan nodded, opening her door and stepping in behind her, his eyes scanning the room. When he was sure it was secure, he walked through to his room, which adjoined hers.

"I'll be in here if you need me. "Just leave this door open."

"Okay," she said, already stripping off her shirt.

Donovan pointedly walked out of the room. Cassie grinned. He was very proper—she liked that, but she also liked to shock him. She climbed into the shower, turning the water to almost totally cold. Stepping under the cold needles of the shower, she washed her hair and did her best to cool off. She closed her eyes, letting the water wash over her face. She was hit suddenly with a wave of dizziness. Putting her hand out, she steadied herself on the wall, holding onto the bar there. A wave of nausea came over her.

"Lovely…" she growled to herself. She'd already suffered through a month of morning sickness; now it was going to happen in the afternoon too?

She finished her shower hurriedly and climbed out. She toweled herself off, not bothering to dry her hair. After padding into the other room, she pulled on a pair of cotton shorts and a tank top. As she lay down on the bed, she fought another wave of nausea. She fell asleep, doing her best to concentrate on anything but the need to throw up.

Donovan woke her at 5 p.m., letting her know that she needed to be at the arena by 6 p.m.

"I know, I know," she said, irritated. She couldn't believe she'd slept the entire afternoon away.

"Do you want me to go down and pick you up something to eat?"

Cassie's stomach growled in response to the idea of food.

"That would be great," she said, smiling at him and reaching for her wallet.

"I got it," he said. "You want a sandwich or something?"

"Yeah, something like roast beef. I'm feeling carnivorous today."

Donovan chuckled. He left a few minutes later, reminding her not to leave the room without him.

By the time he got back to the room, Cassie was ready to leave. He noticed she looked pale and asked her about that.

"Morning sickness again."

Donovan nodded. He'd heard her throwing up for the last few weeks.

"Are you going to be okay for the show?" he asked her.

"Yeah. I'll be okay. I just need to eat."

On the drive over to the arena she ate the sandwich he'd gotten her and drank some juice.

"Okay?" he asked her when they reached the arena.

"Yeah, I'm okay," she told him, smiling.

He took her to her dressing room, waiting outside until she was ready.

"Hey, Pony," Tommy said as he passed by.

"Hey," Donovan replied.

Tommy glanced at his watch. "She running late?"

"I don't think she's feeling too hot."

"What's up?" Tommy asked, sounding worried.

"Extended morning sickness."

Tommy grimaced. "Glad I don't have to worry about that shit."

"Me too," Donovan said, "but we do have to listen to it from our women when they get pregnant."

"Hey, I'm not even married," Tommy said, holding his hands up. "So no pregnancies in my near future."

Donovan laughed. Tommy was dating and living with Shannon Teary, an up-and-coming movie star in Hollywood. They'd been together for three years.

The show began, and Cassie was dynamic as always. Donovan caught a grimace a few times, however, and wondered if she was still feeling sick. It was for that reason that he stayed backstage, near where Cassie stood most of the time. Fast Lane was in the middle of their latest single when Donovan heard Cassie stumble over the lyrics. That wasn't like her—she was a pro at this. Stepping closer, Donovan watched the tiny lead singer closely. He could see that Tommy was doing the same from the other side of her.

When Cassie suddenly started to fall, there was a screech of feedback as Tommy threw off his guitar and lunged for her. Donovan did the same; he was closer, so he was the one to catch her before she hit the floor. She was out cold. Donovan lifted her limp form into his arms and strode toward the side of the stage. Lying her down, he checked to see if she was breathing. She was.

"Get an ambulance!" he called to the stage hand standing closest to him.

"Is she okay?" Tommy asked.

"She's breathing, but she's out cold."

"Donovan…" Tommy said gravely.

"What?" Donovan asked, glancing up at Tommy.

Tommy's face was sickened, and he was staring down at a spot near Cassie. Donovan followed his line of sight and saw what Tommy had. Blood.

"Shit!" Donovan picked Cassie up and walked toward the doors to the stadium. "Tell them she's bleeding. We need to get her to a hospital now!"

Three hours later, Cassie lay in a hospital bed. She'd nearly died when the hemorrhaging from the miscarriage had evaded control for far too long. Her face was pale, even though she'd had a transfusion.

She stirred, reaching up to rub her eyes and feeling a tug at her hand. Opening her eyes, she saw the IV in her hand. Her violet eyes widened as she looked around her.

Donovan stood up, seeing her stir. He touched her hand gently.

"Mackie'll be here soon," he told her softly.

"What happened?"

"You passed out," he said, not wanting to relate the rest just yet.

She nodded, taking in his stoic look. Fear hit her then, her mind whirling.

"It's gone, isn't it?" she asked in a toneless voice.

Donovan winced, then nodded slowly. "I'm sorry, Cassie…"

Her hands went to her stomach, her fingers splaying out as if she were trying to recapture the baby she'd lost. Her lips trembled.

"Can you leave me alone for a little bit?" she asked quietly.

Donovan didn't want to invade her privacy by staying when she wanted to be by herself, but John Machiavelli had specifically asked Donovan not to leave his wife alone.

"Cassie, John asked me to stay with you," he said gently.

Her violet eyes looked back at him, then she nodded. Closing her eyes, Cassie pressed her lips together, fighting the tears that threatened to overwhelm her. Donovan watched feeling helpless. He prayed that John would get there soon.

Thankfully, John did make it to the hospital fifteen minutes later, having shattered every speeding law known to man between the airport and the hospital. Striding into the room, he nodded to Donovan, who quietly stepped out.

"Cassie…" John said softly, touching her cheek.

Cassie opened her eyes, tears already shining in them. Sobbing, she sat up, and John pulled her into his arms, cradling her on his lap.

"Shhhhh…" he said, his lips at her forehead as he smoothed his hands over her back and hair. "It's okay, little one, it's okay…" His voice was soothing and calm.

In truth, John was reeling from the fact that he'd almost lost his wife that night. The doctor had told him that Cassie's pulse had been lost at one point, that she'd lost a lot of blood.

"It's gone, John," she whispered, her tone haunted. "Our baby is gone…"

"I know, honey, I know," he said. "I'm just glad you're okay."

Cassie clung to him, sobbing uncontrollably for what seemed like hours. Finally she fell into an exhausted sleep. John laid her on the bed, gently, covering her up, his hand lingering on her cheek. Then he went to talk to the doctor.

"I'm sorry, Mr. Machiavelli," the doctor told him ten minutes later. "It is my conclusion that your wife's body is just unable to withstand the trauma of pregnancy."

"What do you mean, unable to withstand it?" John asked. "Ever?"

The doctor shook his head. "I don't believe she will ever be able to carry a child to full term. It's too much stress on her."

John felt a tight knot in his stomach. Cassie wanted a baby more than anything in the world. This was not going to go over well with her.

"I can't what?" Cassie asked hours later when John told her what the doctor had said.

"You can't have a baby," he said gently.

"You mean for a while, right? Because of this," she said, her gesture taking in the hospital around her. "But eventually we can try again, right?"

John shook his head slowly.

"Bullshit!" she screamed. "That doctor is wrong. He's just wrong, that's all."

John put a calming hand out, touching hers, which were clenched in her lap.

"We can get another opinion, honey. But I think the miscarriage is a pretty big indicator."

"No." Cassie shook her head. "It was just something that happened. I can do this, I can."

"Babe…" John said, his hand on hers, "we'll talk to another doctor, okay?"

Cassie nodded, looking placated.

She was not placated a week later when another doctor confirmed the first doctor's diagnosis.

"It's unlikely that you'd ever be able to sustain a pregnancy," the second doctor, a woman, told Cassie and John.

"Unlikely?" Cassie repeated. "But it's possible right?"

"Mrs. Machiavelli," the doctor said, her voice reasoning, "attempting to conceive again could endanger your life. It's impossible to know when or how traumatically another miscarriage could occur. It's inadvisable that you get pregnant again."

Cassie left the doctor's office, her expression stoic. John suspected that she was not done with this fight. She did, however, go back to her tour, saying nothing more about a baby. Not one to be fooled by his wife, John asked Donovan to keep close watch on her.

Donovan agreed to do just that. Over the next couple of weeks, he and Cassie grew closer. She confided in him that she still thought she could get pregnant again. Donovan told her he thought she was risking way too much. She informed him that a baby was worth everything to her. He wasn't sure he liked the sound of that.

***

Midnight Chevalier arrived at the conference in Los Angeles on the second day, escorted, as always, by Kana and Tiny. Kana had just walked in with Midnight ahead of her when she saw Kashena walk into the room from a different entrance, carrying a bagel on a plate and a cup of coffee. Marshal stopped in front of Sierra, setting the items down in front of her. Sierra looked up at Kashena with a brilliant smile and a very private look. Midnight turned to say something to Kana and noticed that Kana was looking elsewhere. Midnight followed her line of sight to Kashena and Sierra. Kana's lips were quirked in an odd expression.

"What?" Midnight asked, seeing the look.

"Nothing," Kana replied, schooling her features.

Midnight narrowed her gold-green eyes at Kana, but everyone had noticed her entrance by that time, so she wasn't able to question the big Samoan any further.

Kana was concerned that Kashena and Sierra had gotten involved, but she couldn't be sure. The intimate look between the two in the conference room had set alarms off in her mind. Ever mindful of how any impropriety would look, Kana was always careful to keep things professional when there were people around. Seeing a possible problem, Kana was intent on finding out.

The day's occurrences certainly brought light to that concern. It started when Kana asked Kashena about the "rescue" Sierra had mentioned to Kana when Kashena was selected as her bodyguard.

Kashena's answer seemed a bit evasive, and it raised Kana's concerns further. Later that morning, when Kashena suffered a suspiciously sudden "migraine", Kana had Tiny take the younger woman upstairs to her room.

"How is she?" Kana asked Tiny when he returned.

Tiny shrugged. "She said she had a migraine."

Kana curled her lips. "That didn't look like a migraine."

"No, it didn't."

When the conference broke for lunch, and Kana told Sierra about Kashena being indisposed and that SAS Ako would be taking over as her detail until Kashena felt better, Sierra insisted that she go up and see Kashena. It was easy to see that Sierra was more concerned about her bodyguard than she should be. It just confirmed Kana's suspicions.

After discussing what had happened to Kashena, Midnight asked Kana to go up and check on Kashena to insure she was okay. Kana knocked on the door to the room; Sierra answered. Kana ended up seeing the sight Tiny had seen—one bed unmade, one bed not slept in.

Midnight was surprised by what she was hearing. "So they're involved?"

"Definitely," Kana said.

Midnight nodded, trying to look at the ramifications objectively. "Think anyone else figured it out?"

"I doubt it," Kana said. "I just happen to know Sierra's story, and I saw how she reacted when I said Kashena was going to protect her."

Midnight nodded again, turning over the possibilities in her mind. It wasn't like she wasn't used to romances on the job. She'd been married to Rick when he worked for her at San Diego PD. Joe had been involved with Randy while she worked there. Hell, half the people she knew were involved with someone they worked with. This wasn't new territory.

"What are you going to do?" Kana asked, her voice even.

Midnight canted her head to the side. "What do you think I should do?"

Kana looked surprised at the question, then shrugged. "I guess that depends on your opinion of the situation."

Midnight knew that Kana was dodging the question and suspected she knew why. "What's yours?"

"Mine doesn't matter," Kana said.

"It does to me," Midnight countered, knowing that Kana was holding Kashena to a different standard because she was gay, and she wanted to know why.

"Why?" Kana's apprehensive look spoke volumes.

"Because, Kana, you understand lesbian relationships better than I do. Do you think it's going to be a problem?"

"Which part?" Kana asked, putting her hand on the table between them. "The part where she's married? To a man? The part where she's a Chief Deputy Attorney General for your criminal division, therefore very high profile? Or the fact that Kashena is her bodyguard and should therefore be objective where her charge is concerned?"

Midnight knew she'd just heard Kana's main concerns, even if they were a bit tainted by her own hardline values.

Midnight glanced over at Tiny. "What about you?"

Tiny looked pensive. "I don't know how much we have a right to interfere."

"They both work for Midnight, Tiny," Kana said.

"True," Tiny said, "but it's their private lives."

"They're conducting it while at a state conference."

"Not in the conference room, they're not," Tiny countered.

Kana narrowed her eyes at him. He narrowed his back at her.

Midnight grinned—they were like two kids sometimes. Many of the people that had worked with her for years tended toward protecting her, whether they were her bodyguard or not.

"I made Sierra my chief deputy because I trust her judgment. I'm just going to have to trust that she'll use good judgment where Agent Marshal is concerned."

Kana nodded, not looking convinced.

***

Sebastian lay on the bed in his hotel room, listening to the radio and searching for a decent rock station. There was a light knock on the adjoining door between his and Samantha's hotel rooms.

"Yeah?"

Samantha opened the door. "You're still up?" she asked politely.

"If I wasn't before, I am now," he said, smiling.

"Oh," she said, looking chagrined.

"Don't worry about it." Sebastian waved dismissively. "What's up, counselor?"

Samantha looked back at him, her face pensive.

"What is it?" he asked encouragingly.

When she didn't answer the second time, he smiled broadly. "Can't sleep?"

She shook her head.

Sebastian held his arm out to the side. "Come here."

She walked over and lay down next to him.

"You probably think I'm crazy," she said in a self-castigating tone.

"No," he said, "just lonely."

She glanced up at him, surprised, then saw his grin. She laughed softly. "I think I'm so used to having someone next to me in bed..."

"Don't worry about it."

She nodded, putting her head against his chest. They were both quiet as Sebastian found a station with rock music.

"You always have to have some kind of noise around you, don't you?" she asked curiously.

"I thrive on chaos," he said with a smile.

"Is that healthy?"

"Probably not," he replied, "but getting shot at isn't either, and I do that for a living."

Samantha shifted against him so she could look up at him easily. "Why did you go into law enforcement?"

He grinned. "For the adventure."

"Adventure?"

"Yeah. How many other jobs can you deal with a drunk one minute, a prostitute the next, and a mad woman with a frying pan minutes after that?"

"A mad woman with a frying pan? One of your ex-girlfriends?" she asked with humor in her voice.

"My exes love me."

"I'm sure," she said wryly.

"Okay, love might not be the right word."

"I think you may have been looking for loathe," she said, quirking a grin.

"Not nice, counselor," he told her, smiling back.

"I learn from the best, Agent."

They spent the rest of the evening chatting, and fell asleep lying facing each other, Sebastian's arms around her. It was the same for the three days they were out of town. Every night she wandered into his room; every night she ended up in his arms, sleeping.

It was the same for the trip after that. Sebastian commented on it one night.

"What's the point in getting two rooms when you always end up in mine?" he asked, his arms around her yet again.

"Propriety."

"So hubby doesn't find out?" he asked, smirking.

"Sebastian, our relationship has been strictly platonic."

"I know that," he said, "but I don't know if Jeffrey would see it that way."

"Jeffrey is a reasonable man. I'm sure he'd understand."

"Is that why you haven't told him about it?" Sebastian asked.

"What makes you think I haven't?" she countered.

"Because you just said he *would* understand, indicating that you haven't told him yet."

"Well, it's not that I'm hiding anything from him," she said.

When they got back to Sacramento, Samantha thought for a long time about what Sebastian had said. Should she tell Jeffrey? Was she somehow cheating on him by lying next to Sebastian when she traveled? It wasn't like they'd had sex. Or did that not matter?

Walking into her house, she noted that everything was exactly where it should be. Her house was never messy. Jeffrey liked everything in its place and had a housekeeper to accomplish just that. She put her briefcase in the entryway closet and took her suitcase upstairs. While she unpacked, she turned on the radio. Suddenly she found herself smiling—Sebastian always had a radio on, and now she was picking up his habit. Although her musical tastes were very different from his. She liked classical music. But she still found it funny that she now felt the need to have music on in the background.

By the time Jeffrey got home two hours later, she'd unpacked and set her suitcase back in the hall closet and was in the kitchen cooking dinner. She had the radio on downstairs as well.

"What's going on?" Jeffrey asked, walking into the kitchen.

"With?" Samantha asked, confused.

"Why do you have the radio on? Are we expecting company?"

"No." She picked up the glass of wine she'd been indulging in. "I just felt like listening to music."

"I see," he said, sounding like he did anything but see. "When will dinner be ready?"

"In about half an hour."

Jeffrey nodded, turning and walking out of the kitchen. Samantha watched him go and wondered idly why he never kissed her hello anymore. Mentally shrugging, she went back to work on dinner.

When they sat down to dinner, they discussed his current case.

"I don't see a problem with the settlement," he said, "since the client is happy."

"But don't you think it's a little excessive?"

"Excessive?" Jeffrey queried

"Well, yes," Samantha said, "considering the defendant was only partially at fault. Your client was aware of the dangers of using that product."

"That isn't the point," Jeffrey said disparagingly. "My client shouldn't have been able to use a product with the strength of that one. The company should have been more careful."

"They're a small business."

"Are you saying I cheated them?" Jeffrey asked incredulously.

"I'm just saying that a settlement like this could put that man out of business," Samantha said. "It seems a bit injurious."

"Injurious?" Jeffrey repeated in a snide voice. "I think you've been working at your plush state job too long, dear. The idea here to is to win a good settlement for your client."

"Regardless of the effect?"

"Ours is not to question the outcome," Jeffrey said self-importantly.

"Jeffrey, you cause the outcome," Samantha said.

"Where is all of this coming from?" he snapped.

"I'm sorry?" she said, surprised at his change in tone.

"Why are you questioning me all of a sudden like some errant schoolboy?"

"I'm not supposed to disagree with you?"

"You're supposed to trust my judgment," he said.

"I don't agree with your judgment in this case," she told him, surprising herself.

She rarely if ever disagreed with Jeffrey. Suddenly she was doing so, and quite often.

"I see," he said tightly.

With that he stood up from the table, politely folding his napkin and setting it down next to his plate. Then he walked out of the room. Samantha just stared open mouthed at the chair he'd sat in moments before.

That night when she came to bed, he turned away from her coldly. She didn't understand it.

"You aren't toeing the line," Sebastian told her the next day when she talked to him about it.

"What?"

"You aren't bowing and scraping, and that sounds like what he's used to from you," Sebastian pointed out.

"That's not true."

"No? When was the last time you disagreed with him?"

"I—" she stammered, realizing that she never really had. "That doesn't mean I've bowed and scraped for him."

"No, but it does mean that he's not used to getting any argument out of you."

Samantha's brows furrowed as she thought about what Sebastian said. "Perhaps he reads it as my saying he's wrong."

"Sounds to me like he is," Sebastian said.

"Why do you say that?"

"Because he's taking money from people when they either can't afford it or shouldn't rightly have to pay it. If you ask me, I think he's just perpetuating the myth about lawyers being sharks."

Samantha laughed at that. "I think Jeffrey would be more in line with a guppy."

"Sounds like a shark to me…"

"Stop it!" she said, laughing in spite of herself.

After a few minutes she looked over at him pensively. "Sebastian?"

"Hmmm?" he asked as he reached for a cigarette.

"Do you think I'm cheating on Jeffrey?"

"With me?"

Samantha nodded.

"Hell no," Sebastian said.

"But you pointed out that I haven't told him about us sleeping in the same bed when we're traveling."

"Yeah," Sebastian said, "but I don't think what we're doing constitutes you cheating on him."

"But isn't omitting the truth, in essence, lying?"

"Only to a lawyer," he replied, grinning.

"Sebastian!" she said with a laugh. "Seriously, though, do you think there's some reason I haven't told him?"

Sebastian assessed her. "Are you afraid that if you tell him he'll be mad?"

Samantha considered the question. She shrugged. "I'm not sure how he'd react."

Sebastian raised an eyebrow slightly. "Are you sure about that?"

Samantha looked back at him, surprised. "I…" She shook her head slowly. "I'm worried that he'd think there was more going on than that."

"And since there's not, there's no need to worry the guy."

"Right," Samantha said, relieved that he thought the same way.

"Right," he echoed, smiling.

Sebastian was ever astounded at his level of control where Samantha was concerned. Regardless of the way she dressed, she had a great body under there, and he'd thus far done nothing to find out just how great. He knew that she was kidding herself about "maybe" Jeffrey would think more was going on. Jeffrey would likely try to have him fired for what they were doing and/or not doing. Sebastian wondered if Samantha had even thought about that, or if that was why she wasn't telling Jeffrey.

CHAPTER 9

The test had been conducted. Now he had to see what happened. Would it work? It needed to work. If she died, then it had worked. One less disgusting, immoral creature in the world. As long as it worked, that was all that mattered. Once he knew the results, and he knew he'd see it on the news if that was the case, he could move forward with his plan. It wouldn't be too long now. Soon judgment day would come for them all.

***

The minute Sable Sands laid eyes on Catalina Roché she was intrigued. She'd been contacted by the San Diego PD Chief, Kyle Masterson, who'd heard that Sable's bodyguard had been shot in downtown San Diego. Chief Masterson had invited her to come down to the department to meet with him. Once Chief Masterson had talked to Sable, he'd made a phone call.

"You wanted to see a narc, Chief?" asked the beautiful blonde that walked into Chief Masterson's office. The blonde's eyes went to Sable and widened ever so slightly; she inclined her head, and then looked back over at the Chief.

Sable gave the woman her world-famous smile. Sable, a very popular rock star, had been in the charts for many years. She was consistently compared to Melissa Etheridge, not just for her hard-edged style, but for the fact that she was openly gay. Sable had tailored her look to fit her name perfectly, with her rich mane of chestnut-brown hair, warm chocolate-brown eyes and richly tanned skin.

"Ms. Sands," Kyle said, "this is Sergeant Catalina Roché. She works in one of the narcotics units."

Sable extended her hand to Cat, making a point of staring directly into Cat's eyes as she did. It was a test: if a woman she was interested in stared back at her for more than three seconds, Sable was convinced the woman was gay. Catalina Roché stared back at her for four seconds. Sable was immediately elated.

"Narcs don't look like they used to," Sable breathed as Cat took her extended hand.

"Well, we still have some that look like they used to," Cat said, smiling, "but it's not only a boys' game anymore."

Sable didn't reply. She was thinking what a beautiful woman Catalina was, and Catalina was still staring back at her. When Sable finally started to feel somewhat uncomfortable, she broke her stare and looked back at Kyle. She knew that she might be pushing her luck and edging on the inappropriate—even Sable Sands knew when to back off a bit. Chief Masterson definitely seemed to notice the exchange, but he didn't comment; instead he gestured for Catalina to sit down.

"Ms. Sands had an incident late last night," Kyle said, looking from Sable over to Cat. "And I'm tending to think it was drug related."

"Is this the shooting I heard about?" Cat asked.

"Probably," Kyle said, nodding. "Ms. Sands' bodyguard was shot. It's believed that they interrupted a drug deal."

"Believed?" Cat replied. Sable could hear suspicion in the other woman's voice.

"We drove up on it," Sable clarified hastily.

Sable noticed that Cat didn't seem to believe that statement; she wasn't sure why. Regardless, she didn't comment.

"Cat, I'd like you to go with Ms. Sands to the scene and see what you can come up with from there."

"You got it," Cat said.

Ten minutes later, Sable followed Cat to a dark blue Chevy Blazer. Once in the car, Cat reached for a cigarette. "Do you mind?"

"No," Sable answered. "As long as you don't mind if I smoke too."

"Not a problem," Cat replied.

As Cat started the Blazer, Linkin Park blared from the stereo speakers. Cat reached over, turning down the stereo.

"Linkin Park?" Sable was surprised. Catalina didn't seem that hard core.

"Yeah," Cat affirmed. "My partner got me into them."

"Partner?" Sable asked hopefully.

"Yeah, you know—narc, cop stuff," Cat said with a knowing grin. "He loves this stuff."

Sable nodded, feeling disappointment settle on her. She didn't see the glance Cat directed her way.

"Besides," Cat added, "my girlfriend doesn't like the hard stuff."

"Girlfriend?" Sable felt hope stirring again, although the realization that Cat was involved with someone wasn't happy news either.

"Uh-huh." Cat smirked.

"So you are gay?" Sable stated.

"Uh-huh."

"But you have a girlfriend." Sable shook her head ruefully.

"At this point." Cat sounded irritated.

"Really?" Sable asked. "Problems?"

"Enough," Cat said wryly. "So," she said, signaling a change in topic, "where did this happen?"

160

Sable was once again disappointed; she'd been hoping to discover more about the blond narcotics officer and this mystery issue with her girlfriend.

"Downtown, at the corner of Broadway and Market."

Cat nodded, driving out of the lot and heading toward downtown.

"So tell me what happened," Cat enjoined.

"We got turned around when we left the Sports Arena last night," Sable said. "We were trying to get back to the Intercontinental. We had just stopped at a light when my bodyguard noticed two men hassling another man. He told the driver to hold on and got out to see what he could do. When he got out, one of the men turned and shot him."

Sable's voice was tremulous as she remembered the horror of watching her longtime friend and bodyguard gunned down. Cat reached over to touch her hand in empathy.

Sable nodded, doing her best to regain her composure.

"What did the two men look like?" Cat asked.

"They were black, both of them tall."

"What were they wearing?"

"Both of them had on jeans and dark shirts, T-shirts."

"Any colors?" Cat asked.

"Colors?"

"Yeah, you know, bandanas, wrist bands, something," Cat replied.

"Yes," Sable said. "They both had red bandanas—one had it sticking out of his pocket, the other had his under a baseball cap."

"Shit..." Cat muttered under her breath.

"What?" Sable asked, realizing that it meant something to Cat.

"We've been hearing noise about the Bloods trying to move in on some of the drug business here, but this is the first proof."

Sable nodded, having heard about the Bloods over the years. The Bloods were a street gang of notoriety; they were dangerous and violent. Sable realized suddenly that things could have gone much worse for her and Jake.

Cat looked over at her, her expression assessing. "You weren't the one making the deal, were you?"

"No," Sable answered, shocked by what Cat was asking.

"You aren't lying to me?" Cat's voice held a slightly accusatory tone.

Sable looked at Cat, her rich brown eyes steady. "Sergeant, if I get any narcotics, I don't buy them myself, nor do I go to street-level dealers."

Cat chuckled. "This narc didn't just hear the part about 'if you get narcotics.'"

"Good," Sable replied, widening her eyes but smiling all the same.

They drove to the spot where the shooting took place. Cat parked the Blazer and got out, telling Sable to stay in the vehicle. Cat checked out the area and talked to a few people nearby. Sable found herself watching Cat's every move, fascinated. Cat was wearing jeans that fit perfectly on her petite shape, and a cropped navy blue camisole top. She also wore brown dress boots with a two-inch heel, and a brown belt that matched. On the belt at her hip sat a brown leather holster, with a nasty-looking gun in it. Something about the power a woman with a gun presented intrigued Sable no end. Cat walked back to the Blazer and got in.

"Everything okay?" Sable asked.

Cat nodded, reaching for another cigarette as she started the Blazer again. "I'll tap a few of my sources and see what I can come up with."

Sable sighed in relief, then she looked over at Cat.

"I don't suppose I can take you to lunch?"

Cat considered for a moment. "I'm not really supposed to accept gratuities."

"I want to take a hot-looking cop to lunch," Sable said, her smile unrepentant. "That's a crime?"

"No…" Cat said.

"Then let me take you to lunch."

Lunch ended up being in Sable's hotel room, since Sable was certain her bodyguard would kick her ass for being out about in public without him. They discussed a few topics, and Sable got to learn more about Catalina's girlfriend. In the end, Sable couldn't help but ask the intriguing blonde about San Diego's nightlife.

When Cat hesitated, Sable added, "Strictly platonic." Something she absolutely did not mean, but she desperately wanted to see this woman again, and she wasn't about to take no for answer. They decided to go out the next night.

The following evening, Cat picked Sable up. Sable insisted on taking Catalina out to dinner, before they went to Hillcrest. It was a whole other experience for Sable, and she definitely got to see a couple of different sides to Catalina.

One side was all cop, when fans at the club they went to tried to get a bit pushy with the superstar.

At first Cat stood back, letting Sable work the crowd. However, when a taller butch woman with short dark hair was insistent that

Sable have a drink with her, her hand on Sable's arm, Cat intervened, and the woman backed off.

"You're handy to have around," Sable said, her hand on the small of Cat's back.

"Uh-huh," Cat said, feeling Sable's hand but not mentioning it.

Sable lowered her head slightly, her lips right next to Cat's ear. "Are you always so forceful?" she asked, her voice husky.

Cat felt the involuntary shiver go through her; it was a natural reaction to the feeling of such a sexy woman so close to her. Turning her head, Cat looked directly into Sable's eyes.

"Always," she replied, her lips quirking.

"Mmm…" Sable murmured, feeling her pulse quicken.

It wasn't the last time that night. There was a definite connection there, and Sable was never one to ignore a connection.

***

"What's this from?" Linda asked, her fingers brushing over a red mark on Kashena's upper arm.

Kashena lifted her arm listlessly, glancing at the mark Linda was touching. Then she shrugged. "I don't know, caught it on something in the airport."

She'd been feeling lousy since returning home from Los Angeles; the last thing she wanted to do was play Twenty Questions with Linda. She just wanted to sleep, and Linda was being a pain. The fact was, Linda was mad that Kashena was pulling away from her. They'd had a confrontation about Sierra, who'd answered the phone in the hotel room when Linda had called. Linda had confronted Kashena about it and made the accusation. Kashena hadn't denied it, but she had also told Linda that she knew about the man who'd obviously been in their bedroom while she'd been in Los Angeles. Linda had promptly dropped the matter.

Over the next three days, Kashena felt worse and worse. Sebastian was worried when she called off shift for the fourth day in a row. He decided he'd better check on her.

"What are you doing here?" Linda was annoyed to have to deal with Sebastian; she'd avoided him so far during her time with Kashena. How dare he just show up?

"Checking on my partner," he said, his storm-green eyes narrowed.

"She's sick," Linda said, shrugging. Duh, why didn't the man just go away?

"I know, she called me," Sebastian said. "Now get out of my way so I can go see her." He pushed past her.

Linda wasn't about to be pushed aside. She followed him into the bedroom, ready to bawl him out for being an asshole. The look on his face when he looked at Kashena worried her immediately though.

"What?" she asked, her gaze sliding from him to Kashena then back again.

Sebastian didn't answer, striding over to the bed and putting his hand to Kashena's cheek.

"She's burning up," he said sharply. "Didn't she take anything?"

Linda gave him a wry look. He was supposed to be her best friend? "You know Kash doesn't take medication."

"Did you think to call the healer?" Sebastian snapped.

Linda felt guilty instantly. She hadn't thought of that. Kashena took care of herself—she didn't need Linda's help, right?.

"Why doesn't that surprise me?" he raged.

Straightening, he opened Kashena's bedside drawer, pulled out her address book, and tossed it to Linda. "It's under H."

"For healer?" Linda asked.

"For Hilea," he replied with a denigrating look.

As Linda was looking in the book, she noticed that Sebastian was taking off his jacket and shirt.

"What the hell are you doing?" she snapped.

"Relax, babe," he said snidely. "We need to get this fever down, and the best way to do that is adding body heat to hers so it'll break. And the longer you stand there gaping at me like an idiot, the longer I'll have to do this, so could you get your ass on the phone?"

"Why aren't I doing that and you making the call?" Linda asked suspiciously.

As soon as Sebastian wrapped his body around Kashena's and she felt his heat surrounding her, she tried to jerk away from him. Fastening arms of steel around Kashena as she fought against him, he looked up at Linda.

"Think you're strong enough to handle her, sweetheart?" he asked sarcastically.

Linda curled her lip in disgust at him, knowing he was right. Kashena was damned strong, and it was obvious she didn't want Sebastian's heat anywhere near her.

"I hope she manages to nail you in the balls," Linda spat angrily.

"Wouldn't be the first time, honey," he said with a wink. "Now make the goddamned call, will you?"

Linda called the healer, and Sebastian worked on trying bring Kashena's fever down. When the healer arrived, she further annoyed Linda by talking to Sebastian and ignoring her. During his attempt to break the fever, Sebastian was rewarded with a vicious elbow to the ribs from Kashena.

"Fuck!" he yelled as he grabbed her arms tightly again, doing his best to protect his now aching rib.

In the end it took four full days for her to get over whatever was making her sick. Eventually Linda got tired of not being the center of attention and made the excuse that a friend had invited her to stay with him, so she left.

As soon as he heard that Linda had gone, Sebastian made a phone call.

Sierra was sitting in her office when her phone rang.

"Attorney General's office," she answered automatically, her mind on the brief she was reading over.

"Chief Deputy Youngblood?" asked a male voice.

"Yes?"

"This is Agent Bach," Sebastian said in a businesslike voice. "I thought you'd want to know that Agent Marshal is doing better now."

Sierra sighed softly. "Wonderful," she said, smiling.

There was a slight pause on the other end of the line.

"I also thought you might want to know that her girlfriend has left her alone for the weekend," Sebastian said then, his tone still informational, as if reading off a script.

Sierra arrived at Kashena's house not too long after and took care of the other woman until she was feeling better. Sebastian was glad that his partner seemed to have found someone who cared about her more than she cared about herself. Linda never did anything that didn't serve her own needs; Sebastian knew that and hated her for it. He wanted the best for Kashena. Linda was definitely not that.

CHAPTER 10

Nothing! He couldn't believe it—nothing! It hadn't worked. The test had failed. The woman hadn't died. Damn it! He'd even confirmed it by calling her office. She'd answered the phone! He was infuriated, so much so that he'd ripped the phone out of the wall and thrown it across the room. What had he done wrong? It wasn't strong enough; he'd have to make it stronger. He didn't want them to know what had really hit them until it was far too late to do anything. Let them think he was inept; that was part of the plan... He'd show them all.

***

"Are you okay?" Samantha asked as they boarded the plane.

She'd noticed how gingerly Sebastian was moving and wondered about it.

"Yeah," he said, smiling. "Just a cracked rib."

"A what?" she exclaimed, stopping in the middle of the gangway.

"Keep moving, counselor," he said, glancing over his shoulder. "The idea of pre-boarding is to get on before the other people on the flight do."

"How did you get a cracked rib?" she asked when they were in their seats.

"My partner," Sebastian said. "She gets really nasty sometimes."

Samantha looked horrified, then Sebastian smiled.

"I'm kidding," he said.

"About which part?"

Sebastian laughed, a deep baritone sound that had the flight attendant turning to look at him, her eyes alight with interest.

"Kash was sick," Sebastian explained, not noticing the other woman's attention. "I was trying to hold on to her to sweat out her fever. In trying to get away from me, she whacked me in the ribs."

"Wait, wait." Samantha held up her hand. "You were trying to sweat her fever out? Haven't you Army Rangers ever heard of modern medicine?"

Sebastian nodded. "But Kash is very limited on how non-traditional she'll go."

"Non-traditional?"

"She's half Ojibwa Indian, the very stubborn half."

Samantha glanced at the stewardess, who was making a point of walking by a lot. "So she won't take medicine?"

"Only if she's dying, bleeding profusely, or it comes from a tribe healer."

"So you were trying to do what, exactly?"

"I was using my body heat to try and sweat the fever out of her," Sebastian said, knowing exactly what Samantha would think next. "And yes, she's still a lesbian," he told her with a wink.

Samantha narrowed her eyes at him and saw his ocean-green ones twinkle with mischief. "I assumed that's why she cracked your rib."

"Nah, she cracked my rib because I made the mistake of letting her get an arm loose when she was trying to get away from my body heat."

"She's that strong?"

"Strong?" Sebastian said. "Kash is deadly. If she'd been cognizant and in actual danger, she could have driven her elbow through my rib cage, breaking off a rib and sending it into my heart or at the very least my lungs."

"Charming girl, is she?" Samantha asked.

"She doesn't mess around when it comes to protecting herself or others."

"Are you equally dangerous?"

"And then some," he replied, winking at her again. "They make Rangers almost impossible to stop."

Samantha smiled. "Good to know."

They were both silent for a few minutes. Sebastian gazed out the window, watching the luggage being loaded.

The flight attendant walked by once again, leaning down close to Sebastian, letting him catch a whiff of the musk perfume she wore and a fairly nice eyeful of cleavage.

"Sir, you need to put your seatbelt on," she told him, her voice breathy, her hand trailing over his thigh suggestively.

Sebastian looked up at her, taking in the dark hair and blue eyes. *Probably contacts,* he thought.

"Thank you," he said with an engaging smile.

The flight attendant, whose name tag read "Sandee," winked at him, then smiled and walked away.

"Does every woman you meet come on to you?" Samantha asked before she could stop herself.

"Nope," Sebastian replied. "You haven't come on to me yet."

Samantha's mouth dropped open at the use of "yet." Then she caught the twinkle in his eyes.

"Don't hold your breath."

He laughed. "I never do with you."

The short flight to San Francisco was uneventful. The flight attendant, however, found it necessary to take extra good care of the "officer" on board.

"We feel so safe with you here," she told him, her hand on his arm.

Sebastian nodded, not responding to her flirtation. He had long ago sensed Samantha's tension whenever he flirted with women while protecting her. Since he'd grown quite fond of the uptight Deputy Attorney General he protected, he didn't want her exposed to his dalliances. So, in deference to her obvious disapproval of the action, he waited until he was off duty to do his flirting. The relationship with the ex-Ranger, Barbara, had ended with them being friends and occasional lovers. She'd moved into her own apartment a few weeks before. Sebastian wasn't really into being with one woman all the time; it wasn't his style.

When they arrived in San Francisco, the flight attendant pressed her cell phone number into Sebastian's hand as he left the plane. As he escorted Samantha through the terminal, he dropped the paper into a trash can.

"What was that?" Samantha asked.

He shrugged. "Her phone number."

"Not going to call that one?" Samantha asked, surprised to feel a prickle of envy yet again.

"I'm workin'," he replied, not catching the flash of jealousy in her eyes.

"I see."

They made it to the hotel within an hour and a half—not before Sebastian had insisted on upgrading the rental vehicle to an SUV.

"Should've just driven," he grumbled to himself.

At the hotel, they settled in. Samantha felt tired, so she didn't want to go out to get dinner. Sebastian suggested that he go and get them something and bring it back. Samantha instantly felt guilty. Part of the reason she didn't want to go out was so she didn't have to sit and watch women throw themselves at Sebastian. His height, obvious virility and rugged good looks, combined with the confidence that practically oozed out of every pore, drew women to him like bees to honey.

Knowing she was being unaccountably jealous, Samantha changed her mind about going out to get dinner. She noticed that as they walked to the restaurant near the hotel, Sebastian kept himself between her and the street. His eyes also constantly scanned the sidewalk in front of them. She could tell by his tension that he was on his guard. She asked him about it at dinner, where he insisted that he sit with his back to the wall.

"Isn't it tiring, being so guarded all the time?" she asked him as they were brought their drinks.

"It's the job."

"Yes, but isn't it difficult?" she went on doggedly.

Sebastian looked at her for a moment. "It definitely has its drawbacks."

"I guess it would be much more difficult if you had a family at home."

"Who says I don't have any family?" he asked with a raised eyebrow.

"Well, you've never spoken of any," she said. "I just assumed."

"Never assume."

"So what family do you have in Sacramento?"

"My mother and my sister." He was already thinking he was sorry he'd said anything. For some reason it was starting to bother him that she chalked him up as an irresponsible, carefree player.

"What about your father?" she asked.

"Don't know, don't care."

"Did you ever know where he was?" Samantha realized too late how rude that sounded.

"Yeah, up until I joined the military," he answered. "When I moved my mother and sister to military housing with me, he disappeared."

"You moved them to military housing, without your father?"

"Yeah," he said, his expression darkening. "Right after I told him that if he ever set one foot in my house, I'd personally kill him as a trespasser."

"Oh my..." Samantha breathed. "So I take it the two of you weren't close?"

"That's a safe assumption," he said, grinning in spite of himself.

"What about you?" he asked her after they'd ordered. "Where's your family?"

"Back East. My family is from Boston."

"You went to Yale, right?"

"How did you know?" she asked.

"Noticed it in your office."

"Pays to be observant in your line of work, doesn't it?"

"Always," he said. "So you grew up in Boston?"

"Yes."

"What kind of childhood did you have?"

"I'd have to say it was rather clichéd," she said. "I was sent to the best schools, took riding lessons, ballet, piano, all the right things for a young woman to learn."

Sebastian smirked. "I rode a number of Hummers, does that count?"

"I'm sure it does," she said, smiling.

"So, you were a ballerina?" he asked, picturing her as a child in a pink tutu.

Samantha rolled her eyes. "I was terrible."

"Fell over a lot?"

"Fell over, fell down, fell on my best friend…"

Sebastian laughed out loud at that picture. "I'm sure she appreciated that."

"She did, actually—it got us both out of class for the day."

Sebastian watched her for a few moments. "You had a very sheltered upbringing, didn't you?"

"What makes you say that?"

"Just some of the things you've said during some of our more intricate debates," he said unaccusingly. "You seem to have had some of your opinions formed for you."

"What do you mean by that?" she asked, curious about his opinion of her.

"I mean that sometimes you say things, but you really don't have the conviction to back it up at all. It's like, you parrot what you've been told is right, and you don't know why it's supposedly right."

She frowned. "I don't think I like the term 'parrot.'"

"I'm not trying to be mean, Sam," he said. "I'm just making an observation."

She nodded, thinking about what he'd said. The thing was, he was right. Many of her "opinions" came from Jeffrey's opinions. He'd said certain things so many times that she'd come to believe them as fact. It bothered her no end that as intelligent as she really was, her opinions had made her seem witless somehow.

"What are you thinking about?" he asked when she'd been silent for a long time.

Samantha sighed. "I'm thinking that you're right about me, and it really bothers me."

"I didn't say it to upset you."

"I know," she assured him, "but it does bother me to think that I come across as so shallow."

"I didn't say that, Sam."

"I know you didn't," she said, putting her hand over his on the table, "but it's true. If I spout opinions I can't support, simply because someone spouted them to me, it makes me a fool."

Sebastian winced at her term. "I think you're way too damned hard on yourself."

"Or not hard enough."

Sebastian spent the rest of dinner wishing he had kept his mouth shut. Where did he get off judging her? He was the victim of a jaded childhood, even adulthood. Being in the Rangers had only further served to make him more opinionated, less flexible, and more likely to put down anything or anyone that didn't hold with his beliefs. Now he'd put that on Samantha and made her doubt herself, and there was no way out of that. He felt like a jerk.

**

"She's what?" Dave asked, sure he hadn't heard correctly.

"Gone, Dave. Cat's gone," Kevin told him, sounding stressed.

"Wait, wait." Dave held up his hand and got out of his chair, his sky-blue eyes on the younger man. "Gone as in took off, or gone as in taken?"

"I don't know," Kevin said. "I can't get ahold of Elizabeth. Does your wife know where her sister is?"

"Let me check," Dave said, reaching for his phone and dialing Susan's cell phone number.

She answered on the second ring. "Yes?" she said, her English accent still as sophisticated as ever.

"Hey, honey, it's me," Dave said, unable to keep from smiling.

"David? What is it, what's wrong?" she asked, knowing that he rarely had time to call her in the middle of the day.

"It sucks that you know something's wrong when I call you, doesn't it?" he said, his tone only half joking.

"You know I always worry about you."

"Well, this isn't about me this time, honey," he said. "Do you know where Liz is?"

There was a moment of silence. "She didn't say anything to me about going away... Is it about Cat?"

Dave's lips twitched. He knew this was just going to worry his wife more. "Yes, Cat's gone, and we're not sure if it was voluntary or if we should worry."

"Things have been strained between them," Susan said thoughtfully, "but I can't imagine Cat would just disappear without a word to you at least."

"That's what I'm afraid of," Dave said, his voice serious.

"Do you want me to check the apartment?" Susan asked.

"Are the kids still in school?" Dave asked, referring to Kat and JT Sinclair, who Susan was a nanny for.

"Yes."

"Well, I'll have Mace come over and get you. I want you to take DJ to Marie, or even over to Randy, and you let Mace check the place before you go in, okay?"

Dave wanted his wife to take their one-year-old son, David Jr.—a name Susan had insisted on—to either the Debenshire's nanny or to Randy's center for safety. He didn't even want Susan there, but he knew that it was appropriate to have Elizabeth's sister open the door for Kevin to check the apartment.

"I'll do that," Susan said, knowing what Dave's thoughts were.

She always did everything she could to lessen the stress on her husband. Dave was sixteen years her senior, and in the very stressful position of being a lieutenant over two very successful narcotics teams. Spider, now captain over Vice, was talking about giving him yet another team. Dave was ready to kill his best friend of years. Spider and he had previously been partners in Narcotics. Spider had become a lieutenant, whereas Dave had opted for staying in the field where he felt more comfortable. Having David Jr. had changed his mind. He wanted to be home for his wife and son. Susan knew that his job caused him a lot of stress, so she tried to be the peace he came home to, and she was, every time. They'd been married over four years now and had yet to have an argument. They fit together perfectly, soul mates. He loved her beyond all reason, and she loved him equally so.

"Be careful," he said softly.

"I will, David, I promise."

"I love you."

"And I love you," she replied, smiling at her end. "I'll wait here for Kevin."

"Perfect. Thanks, honey."

They hung up a few moments later. He looked over at Kevin.

"Go get my wife—she'll let you into Cat and Elizabeth's apartment. Don't let Susan in there until you're sure it's secure."

"I like my head on my shoulders." Kevin grinned, knowing Dave would remove his head from his body if something happened to his wife. "I'll make sure she's safe."

"Report to me as soon as you have an idea of what's going on," Dave said, his tone official even as he smiled at Kevin's reference to the violence he'd be dealt for allowing anything to happen to Susan.

Two hours later, Dave got a call from Kevin.

"There's a message on the answering machine from Liz, saying she had to make a run to San Francisco," Kevin reported. "Supposedly for supplies." His tone indicated that he didn't believe that for a second. "It was from yesterday afternoon; it hadn't been picked up. Cat's vehicle isn't here, but nothing seems to be missing from the apartment, like clothes or anything to indicate that Cat packed and left. I'm getting a really bad feeling, Dave…"

Dave nodded silently in agreement. "I'm starting to think you're right," he said. "Alright, tell Susan to see if she can find out where Elizabeth ran off to, and with who. I'll put an all-points bulletin out on Cat's Blazer. I'll get the team in here too."

"Okay, I'll take Susan back to your place, then I'll be back in," Kevin said.

The team was mobilized. Dave contacted Joe, who'd just gotten back from England a few days before. Joe contacted Midnight. Midnight was in Washington but said she'd come home immediately.

"Could just be that she took off with Liz," Joe pointed out, "or got pissed that Liz took off and did the same…"

"Would you be calling me if you believed that?" Midnight asked, already motioning to Kana to get them a flight back to San Diego.

"No," Joe said. "Mace has got a bad feeling about it, and he's about the closest to her these days."

"I'll be home as soon as I can," Midnight said. "Call me if you need anything I can provide."

"Will do," Joe said, smiling.

Midnight may not be the Chief of Police of San Diego PD anymore, but she still considered them all family. Cat, of course, was close to actually being family to Midnight, considering she was currently dating Midnight's niece.

A lot of people, even in the Gang, had been shocked by Elizabeth's getting together with the newest member of the family, Catalina Roché. Catalina, openly bisexual to anyone who asked or cared to pay attention, had come to the department from the Sheriff's office. Christian had recruited her when she'd ended up on the same narcotics case as him. She'd been a good addition to the department, the team, and to the family.

Cat had been responsible for the resurrection of Kana's love life, when Kana and Palani's breakup had threatened to shut Kana down emotionally forever. Everyone had been very grateful to Cat for that. During that time, Cat had also secretly taken on Elizabeth's drug problem and helped her get clean. That had earned her both Midnight's and Rick's eternal gratitude. Neither of them were happy that Elizabeth and Cat were having problems. And they were very much aware that it was Elizabeth's inability to stick with things that was at the heart of the conflict.

"So, where is Elizabeth?" was the first thing Midnight asked Joe when he picked her, Kana and Tiny up at the airport that afternoon.

"In San Francisco, apparently," Joe said, clearly irritated about it.

"With who?" Midnight asked. She knew Joe wouldn't be displeased for just any reason.

Joe curled his lip in disgust. "Apparently with the bartender from Cat's Bet. She took him with her on the 'restocking' trip."

Midnight shook her head and glanced at Kana, seeing the big woman's eyes darken dangerously.

"Let's find Cat first, K," Midnight said to her old friend. "Then we'll kick Elizabeth's ass."

"I get first shot," Kana said, her tone serious.

Midnight nodded.

Kana still had a very soft spot in her heart for Catalina. When Cat and Kana had been together for that short time, Cat had done everything she could to make Kana happy. Unfortunately, since Kana had still been deeply in love with Palani, it was a losing battle for Cat. It had hurt Cat immeasurably to feel so inadequate for Kana. It was Kana's belief that she still owed a great debt to Cat, and she intended to see that Cat wasn't hurt by anyone. And Elizabeth was risking Kana's wrath at this point, which was never wise when dealing with a five-foot-ten, 220-pound, body-of-pure-muscle, hardcore Samoan woman.

It took another twenty-four hours to find Cat's Blazer. Midnight, Joe, Kana and Tiny were first on the scene.

"Joe!" Tiny called from the passenger side of the Blazer, which was on the side of a remote freeway exit.

Joe walked around to the other side of the truck. Tiny held both hands up to him.

"Fuck," Joe said, his voice low.

"What?" Midnight asked, walking over to where he and Tiny stood. "Shit…" she muttered as Kana came around too.

Kana saw what Tiny was holding and closed her eyes, shaking her head.

In one hand he held Cat's badge; on the other hand was blood.

"We have to find her," Kana said.

"We will," Joe assured her.

180

As they walked back to Joe's Escalade, Midnight got on her cell phone. Kana looked back, watching the tow truck hooking up the Blazer to take it to the lab for further examination. There had been an obvious struggle, and it worried Kana no end. Cat was tough, but she was small, and if she'd gotten to the point of pulling her badge, things must have been bad. The fact that the badge had been in the dirt on the ground with a small pool of blood next to it indicated that whoever had taken Cat hadn't cared that she was a cop. That was not a good sign.

Four hours later, they had a call, a ransom call. They had "the cop," and they wanted money to give her back.

"I want to talk to her," Kyle told the man on the phone. "I need to know she's still alive."

"You'll talk to her when I have the money," the man said in his Mediterranean accent.

"Not good enough," Kyle said. "We found blood at the scene where her vehicle was abandoned, and I want proof she's alive."

"No proof," the man snapped angrily. "Get the money or she's dead."

"Just put her on the phone for a moment," Kyle persisted, glancing at Midnight, who was nodding as she stood behind the agent from the Bureau of Investigation who was trying to trace the call.

There was silence on the other end of the line. Kyle waited anxiously, a knot in his stomach. His wife, Rhiannon, stood behind him, putting her hand on his shoulders to try and ease his tension. He blew his breath out silently, nodding in gratitude for her efforts and presence.

Finally, there was the muffled sound of the phone being held to material, probably the man's shirt, as he took the phone into another room. Then came the sound of breathing.

181

"Cat?" Kyle said, his tone worried. "Cat, is that you? Are you alright?"

"In some sense of the word," she replied in a gravelly voice.

"We'll get you back, don't worry," Kyle said, hoping to get enough time to trace the call.

"10-4," Cat said. "Hate the beach anyway."

The phone was quickly yanked away, and they heard a muffled thud. Kyle and Joe, who was listening in on the tap, grimaced. Cat had just given them a clue, and the suspect knew it. It hadn't been a gunshot they'd heard, thankfully, but it had sounded violent nonetheless.

"You have three hours." The man slammed down the phone.

Kyle looked over at the BI agent; he nodded. "I got a good fix," he said, "and what she said only confirms it—they're in the Ocean Beach area. I can get the street, but I can't pinpoint the house exactly. We're going to have to do a little surveillance."

"We don't have a lot of time," Kyle told the agent.

"Then let's get on it," Kana said, moving off the wall she'd been leaning against.

An hour later they had a National Guard C-26 with infrared up in the air, scanning the houses for anything that might help.

"Third house on the left," the pilot called out. "Person on a bed, arms above their head, could be cuffed or tied. Three others in the house, two with rifles—looks like our house."

Midnight nodded, looking over at Kyle. He picked up his radio. "Hit it," he told the team.

The team was made up of the Gang. They trusted no one else to do this job. Cat was one of their own, and they were getting her back. Even though Kana and Tiny no longer worked for San Diego PD, Kyle had authorized them to be on the team, as well as retired captain

Joe Sinclair. No one took one of his people and got away with it—that was all there was to it.

Joe, Kana, Tiny and Spider hit the back door. Christian, Stevie, Jeanie, Dave and Rick hit the front. There was a crash as Christian kicked in the front door, then a lot of yelling and a few gunshots.

Kana got to Cat first, gritting her teeth at the disheveled state of her friend. Kana pulled out her Spyderco knife and cut the ropes holding Cat's wrists above her head. Wrapping the smaller woman in the sheets under her, Kana lifted Cat in her arms.

Cat moaned softly.

"I've got you, babe, I've got you," Kana said soothingly.

Cat passed out again, dropping her head against Kana's shoulder. Dave and Christian ushered Kana out of the house and down the stairs to the waiting ambulance.

Three hours later, the team was given the update on Cat.

"She's been beaten severely," the female doctor told Midnight and Kyle, while the rest of the team listened in. "She's been cut in a few places, but we were able to stitch those easily. She's got a lot of internal bruising, and we had to stop bleeding into her stomach. It looks as though the men who had her tried to rape her, but she apparently fought back hard enough to keep them at bay. It probably accounts for the bruising on her face."

"Is she going to be okay?" Kana asked from behind Midnight.

The doctor looked at the big woman and nodded. "Her injuries are numerous and in some cases severe, but not life threatening."

The entire group breathed a sigh of relief.

"Okay." Midnight looked over at Dave. "I want someone interrogating those men. Did they know who they were grabbing? And why? And what were they after, because it wasn't money."

Dave had the same feeling himself. The house they'd hit had been a very expensive place. Not the hovel of a common kidnapper.

Palani, Susan, Rhiannon and Erin had joined the group at the hospital. They waited until they could be assured that Cat was resting comfortably. Palani waited with Kana, knowing that Kana was extremely worried about Cat, and even more irritated that Elizabeth still hadn't been located. They'd contacted the hotel Elizabeth usually stayed in while on business trips to San Francisco, but she'd failed to return their call yet. As the hours passed, Kana became more and more restless. She smoked constantly in the atrium area of the hospital, standing outside with Joe half the time, the other half with Kevin.

***

Elizabeth arrived back at the hotel that evening. She knew she was pushing her luck, leaving her cell phone off, but she also knew that her guilty conscience couldn't handle questions from Cat. God help her if Cat found out she'd brought Victor with her to San Francisco. It was a stupid thing to do, even more so to sleep with him, but he'd been flirting with her for months. He was the kind of man that usually turned her on, and that hadn't helped in the least bit. This was stupid, she knew that now, but it was too late—she'd cheated on Cat. Her only hope was that Cat wouldn't find out. She truly had spent the day buying supplies for the restaurant, as she'd said in her message.

The problem was, she'd climbed out of bed with Victor to go and do so, this morning and the morning before. Hiding out from Cat. She planned to say that her phone had been on the blink, and she had called the apartment a couple of times. Her guilt was assuaged a bit by the fact that Cat hadn't answered. *Working again,* Elizabeth had assumed angrily. Cat was always working these days. As if she too was avoiding what was wrong with their relationship.

Stopping by the front desk, she airily asked if there were any messages.

"Yes, ma'am!" the young woman exclaimed, looking worried. "You have a number of messages from the San Diego Police Department, as well as one from the Attorney General herself."

Elizabeth took the stack of messages with a sense of dread. If Midnight was calling, in her official capacity, it meant something was very wrong.

Reading the messages as she hurried to her room, Elizabeth felt sick.

Three hours later she all but ran into the hospital. She knew she was in deep trouble, but her concern for Cat overrode that fear. All Midnight had said on the phone was "Get your ass back here now!" It had been an order. One even Elizabeth wasn't fool enough to ignore.

On her way to the airport, she'd heard a news report that a San Diego PD officer had been abducted, beaten and raped, but found hours later by a team of both San Diego PD officers and agents of the Attorney General. Elizabeth knew she had been in the wrong place at the worst time. Now all she could think of was getting to Cat.

Kana sat next to Cat's bed, waiting for her to come out of the anesthesia they'd given her to repair the damage to her body. Cat stirred, opening her eyes slowly. Kana reached out and touched Cat's hand.

Cat smiled slightly, then she moved her head, looking around the room. Kana knew she was looking for Elizabeth. Cat's blue eyes came back to Kana.

"She's not here," Cat said. It was a statement not a question.

185

Kana took a deep breath, expelling it slowly and shaking her head.

Cat nodded slowly, closing her eyes for a moment. When she opened them again, they were glazed with tears.

"Where is she?" she asked softly.

"Cat…" Kana began, shaking her head.

"I don't want to know, do I?" Cat asked, her voice quiet.

Kana couldn't answer, dropping her eyes from her friend's. Cat closed her eyes. Silent tears slipped down her cheeks. Kana gritted her teeth, doing her best to control the anger welling up in her on seeing Cat hurting so much.

Elizabeth chose that unfortunate moment to open the door to the hospital room.

Looking across the room, Elizabeth saw Kana, then her eyes went to Cat. She gasped at what she saw. Cat's face was black and blue, her lips cut in two places, one eye blackened and swollen. Kana stood up, and Elizabeth's gaze went back to her. She took an involuntary step backward as Kana walked toward her, anger blazing in her dark eyes.

It took every ounce of control Kana had to walk past Elizabeth without striking the girl. She left the room, closing the door behind her.

Cat opened her eyes when she heard the door close. She saw the guilt on Elizabeth's face instantly. Cat looked away, willing herself not to cry anymore, not in front of Elizabeth, not in the face of her betrayal.

Elizabeth walked over to the bed, her eyes searching Cat's face, her look pained.

"Cat…" she began, reaching out to touch Cat's hand.

"Don't," Cat growled, pulling her hand away.

Elizabeth's lips trembled. She knew she was in the wrong, and there wasn't much she could do to change it right now. She just hoped she could make up for it somehow.

"Cat, please…"

"Get out," Cat said, her voice cold and hard.

"Please—"

"Now," Cat said, her voice unchanged.

"If you'll just let me explain—" Elizabeth whispered.

"Get out!" Cat roared, coming half up off the bed in her vehemence. "Now!"

"Catalina, please!" Elizabeth cried, terrified now, knowing she'd screwed up badly this time.

"She said to get out," Kana said from the door, her look immovable. "Get out, now. Or I'd be more than happy to remove you."

The last was said in a low threatening tone, and Elizabeth didn't doubt Kana for a moment. She hurried out of the room past the glaring Samoan. Out in the hallway, Elizabeth encountered her aunt and uncle. There was a closed look on Midnight's face. Glancing at Rick, Elizabeth saw his disapproval clear in his deep blue eyes. She ran from the hospital, unable to handle the overwhelming sense of failure she was feeling.

***

Sebastian lay in his hotel room, staring at the ceiling and listening to Linkin Park; it was turned up loud. All the same, he heard the light knock on the adjoining door. He merely smiled, pulling his arm out from behind his head and holding it out. Samantha lay down next to him and snuggled close. It was a routine for them now.

Sebastian turned the stereo down, and they lay together quietly for a while.

"Is your father the reason you thrive on chaos?" Samantha asked softly.

Sebastian was silent for a few seconds, then nodded. "Probably."

"Was he really horrible?"

"He drank too much and had a habit of taking his drunken temper out on me, my sister and mother."

Samantha winced. Putting her hand to his cheek, she stared up at him. "I'm sorry that happened to you."

His ocean-green eyes met hers, and he shrugged. "It probably made me stronger."

"It's still not exactly an idyllic childhood, like mine was."

Sebastian smiled. "You feel guilty about having a good childhood?"

"I think all children deserve a good childhood," she said softly.

"All children do," Sebastian agreed, "but reality is that many don't get one. I just happen to be one of the many."

Samantha nodded.

"I would think you'd be more in favor of social programs, because of your childhood," she said a few moments later.

"Why?"

"Well, had there been more funding for social programs, ones that can get children out of such environments, it may not have had to be that way."

Sebastian smirked. "I don't think social programs really do all that much, Sam."

"What do you mean?"

"Well, in the end, it was getting arrested and having a cop suggest the military to me that got me out of my situation, my mom and sister too. And Democrats are all for getting rid of more cops, and military too, for that matter."

"I don't think that's true. I think that Democrats just feel that the best defense isn't always a strong offense."

"Right up until someone has a missile pointed at your ass, or flies a planeful of jet fuel into the World Trade Center."

"You feel the military isn't responding to that?"

"I think we'd be a hell of a lot safer in this country if hundreds of bases hadn't been shut down because the Cold War was over."

Samantha had to agree with him there. "But what about community policing? Don't you think that was a good thing?"

"Community policing sounded really good to the public," Sebastian said. "The thing the public didn't understand was that they were taking money and resources away from narcotic enforcement to fund the programs."

"Really?" Samantha asked.

"Yeah," he said "because liberals believe drugs should be legalized, therefore they don't see it as much of a problem. In fact the Democratic drug interdiction plan during the Clinton administration didn't even address stopping drugs at their source."

Samantha looked back at him, amazed that he knew so much. He was always able to support his opinions with factual information. She really loved that about him. Even with his ultra-masculine, tough-guy, military exterior, he was really intelligent. Not some brawn without a brain.

"You're really an amazing man," she said, surprising herself by admitting what she was thinking.

Sebastian looked shocked by the comment too, then he grinned. "How many glasses of wine did you end up having at dinner tonight, babe?"

Samantha's mouth dropped open, then she couldn't help but laugh.

"You are, Sebastian, really. I mean, you know so many things, and you're always ready to defend your beliefs…" She shook her head, a self-deprecating look on her face.

His fingertip on her cheek stopped her.

"I said one stupid thing," he said firmly, "and you're going to hold it against yourself forever. Stop it."

She stared back at him, surprised by what he was saying. Swallowing convulsively, she felt something inside her give, a wall she'd been keeping up, a defense. He saw it instantly, her vulnerability, her need to be loved and accepted as she was, not as she'd been made to be. It was an impossible combination to resist.

His fingertip slid down under her chin, guiding her face up to his. As he leaned down, his lips met hers halfway. The kiss was soft and in a way searching, as if they were both testing how they felt about it. His fingertips splayed over her jawline as his lips continued to move on hers, gently exploring their softness.

Samantha's body was one big riot of sensation and emotion. She wanted this, she knew she did, but her mind was reminding her she was married. Even so, her body was responding to the sheer sexuality of the kiss. She pressed closer to him, already knowing his body well having slept next to him so many times.

It was Sebastian who came to his senses and pulled back, breathing heavily at the effort of stopping.

"Sam, wait," he said, shaking his head as if to clear it. "We can't, I mean… we can't."

Samantha bit her lip, but nodded in agreement. "I know," she said, breathing heavily too.

"It's not that I don't want to," he said, his voice husky still. "I just can't compromise my protection of you like this."

She looked up at him, seeing that he was definitely torn. It assuaged her ego a great deal. "I understand," she said, her voice sounding far from normal too.

Sebastian wrapped his arms around her, hugging her close to him and kissing the top of her head. His body was screaming at him to finish what he'd just started, but he knew it was wrong to do that. He'd lose his objectivity about her, and he needed that to keep her safe. They fell asleep with their bodies still pressed close together, his arms still around her.

Sebastian woke the next morning to feel her body pressed against him. She'd turned over during the course of the night, putting her back to his chest, staying within the circle of his arms. Unfortunately, that also pressed her rear right into a very sensitive spot. He lay there, willing himself not to get excited, although it was already too late for that. Finally, he moved carefully, getting up from the bed and covering her back up.

It took two hours at the hotel gym to get rid of the sexual urge he'd been feeling. When he arrived back at the room, Samantha had awoken and ordered coffee for both of them.

"I'm going to grab a shower," he told her, sweaty from his workout.

"Okay," she said, unsure what to feel about everything at that point.

Within an hour and a half they'd both showered and were ready to leave the hotel. He drove her over to the courthouse, where her meeting with some witnesses was taking place, then waited outside until noon when she broke for lunch. He escorted her down the steps of the courthouse. As he did, a man walked toward them. Sebastian scanned his clothing; the man was wearing a business suit. He was smiling at Samantha.

Turning his head to see if Samantha recognized the man, he didn't see the quick movement of the man bringing up a gun. Samantha did, her eyes widening. Sebastian reacted instantly to that. He pulled his own weapon and lunged in front of Samantha as he heard the gun go off. He felt the impact to his chest as he brought his own gun up and fired. The last thing he saw was the man's surprised look as he fell, then Sebastian hit the stone stairs. He heard Samantha screaming, but he was feeling lightheaded. Then everything went black.

***

Kashena hit the doors to the hospital at a dead run, lifting her jacket aside to show the security guard her badge as she passed him. Inside she ran straight up to the front desk. She pulled her badge off her belt and showed it to the nurse.

"Agent Sebastian Bach was brought into Emergency—I need to know where he is and who can tell me how he is."

The nurse looked startled but responded quickly to the authority in Kashena's voice. She tapped at the keys on the computer in front of her.

"Mr. Bach is in surgery right now. There's a waiting room on the sixth floor. The doctor will find you there when Mr. Bach is out of surgery."

"Thank you," Kashena said crisply, and strode toward the elevators.

When the elevator didn't come fast enough, she located the door to the stairwell and jogged up the six flights of stairs. She was doing her best to work off the tension she was feeling. All she knew was that Sebastian had been shot and had killed his assailant.

She'd contacted Midnight to let her know; Midnight had told her to go to the airfield where the Aviation unit for the Department of Justice was housed. There she'd gotten an immediate flight to San Francisco. An agent from the San Francisco Bureau of Narcotic Enforcement office had met her at the airport and driven her directly to the hospital.

In the waiting room, Kashena saw Deputy Attorney General Samantha Cobb. She was being set upon by reporters asking her what had happened. The attorney looked frantic as she was assailed with questions.

Kashena walked up, pushing her way through the reporters.

"Alright, back up," Kashena said, moving to stand in front of Samantha. "The Attorney General's office has no official statement at this time."

As she pushed the reporters back, Kashena blocked anyone from getting to Samantha again. When the reporters finally retreated, Kashena turned around to look at the much smaller woman.

"DAG Cobb," Kashena said, "are you alright?"

Samantha stared up at the blond woman.

"Who are you?" she asked.

"Special Agent Supervisor Kashena Marshal," Kashena said, pulling her jacket aside to show Samantha her badge. "Are you alright? Were you injured?"

Somehow, knowing that this was Sebastian's best friend, and knowing that she was most likely worried sick about him but asking after her instead, made Samantha lose her composure. Bursting into tears, she shook her head.

Kashena was surprised by the attorney's tears. She knew that Sebastian and this woman had been at odds on a number of things. But she also knew that Sebastian had a soft spot for the headstrong, opinionated attorney. He'd told her about the nightly sleeping arrangements when he and DAG Cobb were out of town. Funny thing was, he didn't seem too put out by the inconvenience of holding the fiery-haired attorney all night long so she could sleep.

Sensing that Samantha Cobb was sincerely upset by the incident, Kashena did her best to comfort the other woman. She was careful to keep her gestures professional, however, considering there were a number of people around them, including the reporters.

Kashena got a call from Kana an hour after she got to the hospital.

"What the hell is going on?" Kana asked sharply.

"Bach's been shot," Kashena replied, shocked at Kana's opening question.

There was silence on the other end of the line, then Kashena heard a sigh.

"I'm sorry," Kana said. "I didn't mean that the way it came out. We just had an officer down here attacked and hospitalized too. Someone I'm fairly close to, so I'm on edge right now. Things are just going incredibly sideways all of a sudden. I'm sorry, Kashena. Have they told you how he is yet?"

"Not yet, ma'am," Kashena answered.

"Call me as soon as you hear anything. I'm sending a message to the San Francisco office to give you whatever help you need."

"Thank you, ma'am," Kashena said. "I hope your friend is okay."

"She will be. Bach will be okay too," Kana assured Kashena.

"I hope so, ma'am."

Kana hung up at her end, shaking her head. Things were getting weird, and she didn't like that they was all happening at the same time.

"Is he okay?" Midnight asked.

Midnight, Rick, Kana, and Rogue Squadron were all still at the hospital in San Diego. Everyone else had gone home, planning to come back the next day to see Cat, although she'd already said she didn't want to see anyone.

"They haven't told Kashena anything yet," Kana said, looking worried.

"You're not thinking these incidents are related?" Midnight said.

Kana shrugged. "Probably not," she said. "But it's too much of a coincidence for my liking."

Midnight nodded. "I know what you mean."

***

Back in San Francisco, Kashena found a private waiting room for herself and Samantha. Sierra called her on her cell phone a few times. Kashena waited until she was safely able to talk before she called Sierra back.

"Is he okay?" Sierra asked first thing.

"I don't know yet," Kashena said, shaking her head, starting to feel the effects of what was happening.

"I wish I could be there with you," Sierra said, her voice soft.

Kashena blew her breath out, closing her eyes. "I wish you could be too."

Sierra was silent for a moment. "Kashena, do you want me to come there?"

Kashena hesitated. Yes, she wanted Sierra there—she knew that Sierra understood what this meant to her, her best friend being shot. She wanted someone to hold her hand and tell her everything was going to be alright. She wanted Sierra to be that person, but she knew it was impossible.

"It's too risky," she said finally. "There are reporters here. If they see you here they might get suspicious."

Sierra was silent at her end. "Okay," she said softly, feeling both disappointed and sad that she couldn't be there when Kashena needed her most, and wishing desperately that things were different.

"I'll call you as soon as I hear something," Kashena said.

"Okay," Sierra answered again, trying her best to hide her feelings.

It was another four hours before the doctors came out to talk to them.

"Agent Marshal?" the doctor said, walking over to Kashena.

"Yes?" Kashena asked, her heart in her throat.

"Mr. Bach is in recovery right now," the doctor said. "We removed a nine-millimeter bullet from his chest wall. He lost a lot of blood, and there was some damage to a corner of his heart, but we've repaired that and feel that his prognosis is good."

Kashena was sure she'd faint from the relief. It was Samantha Cobb who fainted instead. Kashena caught her before she hit the floor. She carried her over to the couch in the room and laid her down, asking the doctor for some smelling salts or something. It took a while, but Samantha came around.

"What happened?" Samantha asked, her voice tremulous.

"You fainted," Kashena said.

"Oh…" Samantha said. "Sebastian is going to be fine, right? That's what the doctor said?"

"Yes," Kashena said, smiling. "Yes, that's what he said."

"Oh, thank God," Samantha said, moving to sit up.

"I think you should stay down, Deputy AG Cobb," Kashena said, as she saw the other woman sway slightly.

"Samantha?" came a voice from behind them.

Samantha opened her eyes and saw her husband, Jeffrey, standing in the doorway to the waiting room. Kashena stood, stepping aside. Jeffrey walked in and stood next to where Samantha lay.

"Are you alright?" he asked, sounding mildly concerned. "Were you hurt in the attack?"

Samantha sat up with an effort. Kashena noted that her husband made no move to help her.

"No, I'm fine," Samantha replied. "I simply fainted a little bit ago."

"Fainted?" Jeffrey queried. "Why?"

"She's been through a bit of a shock, Mr. Cobb," Kashena put in when Samantha couldn't come up with an answer.

Jeffrey looked at Kashena in speculation.

"She watched her bodyguard gunned down in front of her," Kashena said.

"Yes, he did his job well," Jeffrey agreed.

"His job?" Kashena repeated incredulously.

"Jeffrey," Samantha said, putting herself between Kashena and her husband, "I think I need some coffee. Could you get me some, please?"

Jeffrey looked hesitant. He glanced at Kashena, whose look had turned to stone. Finally he nodded, walking out of the waiting room. Samantha immediately turned to Kashena.

"I'm sorry for what my husband just said," she said sincerely. "Jeffrey tends to forget his manners in stressful situations."

197

Kashena raised an eyebrow at the smaller woman. "I see," she answered simply.

Samantha grimaced, knowing that Jeffrey would only stick his foot in his mouth repeatedly where Sebastian was concerned. Kashena, being Sebastian's best friend, was likely to tell Sebastian what Jeffrey had said. The fact was, Jeffrey had never considered Sebastian anything but hired help, nor would he change his mind now. As far as Jeffrey was concerned, Sebastian had served his purpose in keeping Samantha from being hit in the attack.

It showed the polarization of the differences between her husband and Sebastian. Something that had been slowly but surely becoming clearer in the time that she'd known Sebastian Bach. She had no idea how she was going to handle Jeffrey being there. She was worried sick about Sebastian, and now here was her husband. It was going to be difficult no matter what happened.

As Samantha had suspected, the next two hours were extremely tense, with Kashena leaning against the far wall of the waiting room, as far away from Jeffrey as she could get. Unfortunately, it wasn't far enough not to hear repeatedly the comments that Jeffrey made. He had no idea why Samantha didn't want to leave the hospital.

"There's nothing you can do," he said snidely. "You're not a doctor, for God's sake."

Samantha glanced over at Kashena to see if the woman had heard. Indeed she had, because her dark blue eyes narrowed as she stared across the room, pointedly looking away from Jeffrey.

"Jeffrey," Samantha began quietly, "I need to make sure he's okay."

"Why?" Jeffrey asked, his voice louder than necessary.

Kashena turned to look at the man, her lips pursed in consideration. She was evaluating whether or not wiping the floor with him would be construed as assault. Given that he was a lawyer, it might be considered an environmental improvement.

Samantha noticed Kashena's look and hoped the other woman wouldn't say anything. In truth, however, Samantha was getting fed up with her husband's attitude.

"He saved my life, Jeffrey," Samantha said, her voice louder this time in her rush to defend Sebastian. "I think that warrants a great deal of respect and appreciation."

Jeffrey actually had the temerity to give a sarcastic snort.

"He's paid to protect you, Samantha. That's what he did."

Samantha saw Kashena's chin come up slightly and her body tense. She bit her lip, not sure what was going to happen now. She refused to try and run interference for her husband again—he didn't have any sense of propriety or even courtesy at all, and it was making her mad.

"Jeffrey," she said sharply, "go home."

"What?" he asked, sure he hadn't heard her right.

"I said, go home, Jeffrey," Samantha said, standing and gesturing toward the door.

"What are you talking about?" he asked her, standing too, his look perplexed.

"I want you to leave," Samantha clarified.

"Why?"

"Because you're pissing me off, that's why," she snapped. "You're an inconsiderate snob, and I'm tired of listening to it tonight. So just go home."

Jeffrey's mouth dropped open in shock. He glanced at the blond woman standing at the far wall, her lips curling into a smirk. It annoyed him. He turned his gaze to his wife.

"I think you've been keeping far too much company with the lower classes, Samantha," he said condescendingly. "You're starting to talk like them."

"Better them than you," Samantha replied with an angry look.

She turned away, walking over to where Kashena stood and then sitting down in a chair, her arms crossed in front of her chest. Jeffrey stared after her, shocked. He narrowed his eyes at Kashena, a sneer on his lips. Turning on his heel, he strode out of the waiting room.

The room was silent. Samantha sat doing her best to calm down.

"Very nice," Kashena murmured in approval, a grin in place.

Samantha glanced up at the other woman and saw her smile. Laughing softly, she shook her head.

"I'm just sorry you had to listen to him this whole time," she said.

"Fortunately, Marines are known for their self-control," Kashena said, grinning still.

Samantha laughed again.

***

Sebastian woke in the semi-darkness of the hospital room. His chest felt tight, and he felt disoriented. He closed his eyes again, focusing his mind on remembering. He remembered the courthouse, walking down the stairs. Then he remembered the man who'd approached Samantha extending his hand and smiling. The picture of the man pulling a weapon flashed through his head, and the feeling of the impact of the bullet. Shit! The guy had gotten off a shot!

He was yanking cords out of his arm and throwing off the covers instantly. What if Samantha had been shot? Was she okay? He had to know.

He felt a little woozy as he stood up, but he was intent on getting information on his charge. He heard the sound of the alarms going off on the monitors, screeches and beeps going crazy around him. Suddenly there were two nurses in the room, telling him he needed to get back in bed. One nurse actually had the temerity to try and push him back to the bed; one strong arm easily shoved her away. Then the doctor got in his face.

"Sir, you have to lie back down!" the doctor, who was all of about five foot three, yelled.

Sebastian took the time to look down at the doctor, anger making his face a dark angry red. "Move or I'll kill ya," he growled.

Then Kashena was there, pushing her way past the doctors and getting up in his face.

"Baz, calm down," Kashena said as she stood in front of him, keeping him from leaving the room. "Samantha is fine. You need to lie back down."

"She's okay?" Sebastian asked suspiciously.

"She's right there," Kashena said, pointing to the doorway.

"I'm fine, Sebastian," Samantha assured him as she walked into the room. "Please lie back down."

Sebastian looked Samantha over, truly surprised by the fact that she was okay. Reaching out, he touched her cheek; he had to know whether or not he was dreaming. Suddenly, all the fight left him. He felt dizzy, and wavered. He felt Kashena and Samantha helping him into the bed; he was relieved to actually lie down again. The doctor and nurses moved in to reconnect all of the lines and monitors he'd yanked off.

As he began to drift back into unconsciousness, he heard the doctor telling Kashena and Sierra they could stay in the room with him. With that, he let himself sink back into sleep.

It was just breaking dawn when Sebastian stirred again. Opening his eyes, he located Kashena leaning against the wall, a cup of coffee in hand. He also saw Samantha sitting in the chair next to his bed, her hand in his. She was asleep.

Giving her hand a little squeeze, he whispered her name. She woke immediately.

"You're still here?" he asked, surprised that she'd stayed.

"Can't go anywhere without my bodyguard," Samantha said, smiling at him.

"You still have work," he said, worried that she would get herself into trouble over some silly sense of loyalty to him.

"A day or two away isn't going to compromise any of my cases."

"If you say so," he finally replied, but he wasn't truly convinced.

Samantha simply smiled. Kashena walked over and looked down at her partner.

"Still alive?" she asked blithely.

"Currently," he replied with a grin.

"Roger that."

Sebastian chuckled softly. His eyes were already closing again. He was asleep moments later.

"I'll be back," Kashena told Samantha.

Walking outside, Kashena went out to the smoking area. She wasn't inherently a smoker, but she found that smoking the cigars she did calmed her nerves more often than not. Standing in the quad, she leaned against a nearby wall and lit a cigar, staring up at the sky, which was clouded over and looking like rain.

The quad was where Joe found her a few minutes later. His light blue eyes scanned the agent. Midnight hadn't been kidding—Kashena Marshal was beautiful. She also had a definite look about her that would make a person think twice before messing with her.

"Agent Marshal?" he queried, his English accent clear in the quiet quad.

Her head came up, deep blue eyes assessing the man walking toward her purposefully.

"I'm Marshal," she answered, nodding.

Joe extended his hand. "Joe Sinclair," he said, smiling at her.

Kashena took his hand. Not only did he look familiar, his name sounded familiar too, but she didn't know who he was. She waited in silence for him to tell her as she shook his hand.

"Midnight sent me," he said. "She's asked me to take over for Agent Bach while he recovers, at least until we assess any further danger to the Deputy AG."

Kashena nodded, her eyes not giving anything away.

"Can I see your badge?" she asked, her tone and look direct.

Joe grinned, rubbing the bridge of his nose with his index finger.

"That's gonna be tough—it's at home in a redwood shadow box. Perhaps this will help," he said, reaching into his pocket and pulling out a business card as well as his cell phone.

He handed Kashena the card, pulled out his phone, and dialed a number. He then handed the phone to Kashena. Leaning back against the wall, he reached for a cigarette, his light blue eyes on her as he lit it.

The phone was answered on the third ring.

"Chevalier."

"Ah," Kashena stammered, not having expected to be connected with the AG herself. "Attorney General Chevalier?"

203

"Yes," Midnight said, smiling at her end. "Agent Marshal?"

"Yes, ma'am."

"I assume Joe just got there?"

"Yes, ma'am," Kashena answered again.

"I've sent him to keep an eye on Deputy Cobb, until things settle down a bit," Midnight said. "I've also sent one of my people to keep an eye on your charge while you're there with Agent Bach."

"I—" Kashena stammered, suddenly realizing she'd left Sierra without protection in her haste to get to Sebastian. "I'm sorry, ma'am, I—"

"It's okay, Kashena," Midnight said. "I want you to be able to be where you're needed right now. I just want to make sure we cover all our bases while we're at it."

"Yes, ma'am," Kashena said, grimacing still, feeling like she'd let both the AG and Sierra down.

"Kashena," Midnight said, her voice softening. "See the guy standing in front of you?"

"Yes, ma'am."

"He's been my partner for over twenty years. If something happened to him, and it has, I would and have dropped everything to be there for him. So relax, okay? I know where your head is right now. I want to make sure you're able to stay with Bach as long as you need to, while Sierra is protected too."

Kashena blew her breath out, ever amazed at the woman she worked for. Was there no end to the understanding Midnight had? She was very much a cop's cop—of that there was no doubt.

"Thank you, ma'am," Kashena said finally. "I promise to get back on the job as soon as I feel Baz is stable."

"I've assigned Christian Collins to Sierra. Joe can give you his cell number. Just let him know when you're ready to take over again," Midnight said. "And Marshal?"

"Yes, ma'am?"

"Make sure you take care of yourself while you're at it," Midnight said, knowing full well how often she'd failed to eat or take care of herself when one of her people had been in the hospital.

"I'll do my best, ma'am," Kashena said.

"All I can ask for," Midnight replied. "Put Joe on, will you?"

"Yes, ma'am," Kashena said, handing Joe back the phone.

"All clear?" Joe asked into the phone, laughing out loud the next minute. "I figured the direct route was fastest," he said, his eyes on Kashena. "You got it. I'll give you an update once I make contact with DAG Cobb. Let me know what happens down there."

Joe hung up his phone a moment later, pocketing it again as he took a long last drag of his cigarette.

"Any questions you want to ask?" Joe asked her.

"Christian Collins?" Kashena replied.

"My cousin, a narc, and a very good cop," Joe said. "And you can trust him to keep her safe."

Kashena's eyes narrowed slightly. She was wondering if Joe knew the nature of her relationship with Sierra Youngblood. His look gave nothing away, however.

"I hope you understand," Kashena said, gesturing to the cell phone in his pocket. "I had to check."

"I would have been worried if you hadn't," Joe replied. "How is Agent Bach doing?"

"They said he's stable," Kashena said, sounding immensely relieved. "The bullet nicked his heart but didn't do a lot of damage, thankfully."

205

Joe nodded, remembering countless times he'd been relieved to hear a good prognosis on one of his friends. From what Midnight had told him, Kashena and Sebastian Bach were best friends. Much like he and Midnight had been forever. He understood her concern, and her need to be at the hospital at this point. He could also see that she desperately needed some sleep.

"You should seriously considered grabbing some sleep," Joe said, his tone friendly.

"I know," Kashena said, nodding. "The AG already told me I need to take care of myself. I guess you guys have been through this a few times?"

"And just yesterday again," Joe said, grimacing.

"What happened?" Kashena asked, remembering what Kana had said.

"One of our people down south was attacked," Joe said. "She's a close friend of ours and a cop, a narc."

"Damn, is she okay?" Kashena asked, always worried about fellow officers.

"Yeah," Joe said. "At this point, I think her heart is taking a bigger beating."

"Why's that?" Kashena asked.

"Her girlfriend—well, let's just say she was in the wrong place at the wrong time when Cat needed her."

"Girlfriend?" Kashena couldn't help but query.

Joe nodded, his look pained. "Midnight's niece, actually. So needless to say, things are a bit of a mess down there."

Kashena nodded, surprised at having been told such intimate information. Apparently Joe considered her part of the group, since she was a cop. What she didn't know was that Joe considered her part of the group because Midnight had already told him how much she liked the blond agent. Kashena Marshal had proven to be a professional when the chips were down, and that was what mattered to Midnight. Nothing had ever been mentioned by any employees, or by the press, about Agent Marshal and the woman she was protecting. So as far as Midnight was concerned, it wasn't a problem.

"Can you take me into Agent Bach's room and let Samantha Cobb know I'm cleared?" Joe asked with an engaging smile.

Kashena chuckled. "I can do that, yes."

***

While Joe was making contact with Kashena in San Francisco, Christian walked into the AG's offices in Sacramento. He showed his badge to the security officer in the lobby and said he needed to be directed to Chief Deputy Attorney General Sierra Youngblood's office.

"She's on seventeen," the older officer said, handing Christian a temporary building badge.

"Thanks," Christian said as the officer opened the security door for him.

Standing in the lobby, Christian didn't even notice all the women gawking at him. He rarely paid attention anymore. There had been a time when he was always on the lookout for a someone new to sleep with, but those days were over. He had the woman he wanted back in San Diego. No one else would ever do.

Still, his tall frame, jet-black hair and light blue eyes stood out, and he was noticed. The receptionist on the seventeenth floor stumbled over her words trying to direct him to Sierra's office. By the time she'd buzzed him through the door at the end of the elevator lobby, the women were gathered to watch him walk by. Sierra's secretary literally stared up at him dumbfounded for a full minute before she could find her voice.

"I'm sorry, what?" she asked, shaking her head as if to clear it. She'd never seen a more handsome man in person.

"I'm here to see Sierra Youngblood. Attorney General Chevalier sent me," Christian said, used to having to repeat himself.

"I, uh, do you have an appointment?" the girl stammered.

"Attorney General Chevalier sent me," Christian repeated, his tone the same as before.

"I... yes... but..."

Christian sighed. He took out his phone and dialed Midnight's cell number, handing the phone to the secretary. The woman's eyes widened to saucer size when Midnight answered the phone with her usual, "Chevalier."

"I—ma'am," the secretary stammered further. "There's a..."

"Christian Collins," Christian supplied.

"Christian Collins here to see Assistant AG Youngblood. I needed to know—I... oh, yes, alright, I understand completely. Thank you, ma'am. I'm so sorry to have bothered you."

The secretary hung up the phone and handed it back to Christian.

"Sorry," she said as she stood up. "I just wasn't sure."

"I understand," Christian said, an amused glint in his light blue eyes.

The girl walked over to Sierra's door and knocked lightly. When Sierra called, "Come in," the secretary opened the door.

Christian's first impression of Sierra was how small she was. She had long sleek black hair, held back from her face by two braids, the rest hanging down to her waist. She was dark skinned, with wide dark eyes. He saw the expected widening of those eyes when she looked at him. Most women found him attractive to the extreme, at least to begin with. His cocky attitude usually turned them one way or the other—either they loved him or hated him. It was always hard to tell which way they'd go.

He was, however, on his best behavior, under strict orders from Midnight.

"Don't even start shit with Sierra Youngblood, Blue, or you'll deal with me," she said, her cat-like green eyes narrowed at him.

"Ma'am, yes ma'am," he'd answered, an evil smile on his face.

"Please, Blue," she'd responded. "She's one of my best DAGs, and she's already in a stressful situation."

"I won't let you down, Midnight," Christian had told her, and he'd meant it.

Looking at Sierra, Christian felt the temptation to say something, but he didn't. Instead he inclined his head.

"Assistant Attorney General Youngblood, I'm Sergeant Christian Collins. AG Midnight Chevalier asked me to look after you while Agent Marshal is in San Francisco."

Sierra nodded, looking surprised by his statement.

"Is Kashena okay?" she couldn't help but ask.

"She's fine, I'm sure," Christian said. "But AG Chevalier feels that she'll need to be with Agent Bach for a while, and she wants to make sure you're safe in the meantime."

Sierra nodded, looking pensive.

"So, if you can give me an idea of your agenda," Christian said, "I can make plans accordingly."

"I want to go to San Francisco," Sierra blurted out.

"I'm sorry?" Christian queried, surprised by the outburst.

"I want to go to San Francisco," she repeated, feeling more sure about it this time.

She waited in silence to see if he'd question her. To his credit, he merely nodded. "I'll make arrangements. When would you like to leave?"

"As soon as possible."

Christian nodded again, then turned and walked out of the room.

An hour later they were driving to her house to pick up a few things.

"You said 'Sergeant,' didn't you?" Sierra asked, after a few minutes, "You don't work for DOJ, do you?"

"No, ma'am," he said. "I work for San Diego PD."

"Do you do bodyguard work there?" she asked, thinking that didn't sound right.

"Narcotics work," Christian answered, then glanced at her, seeing her perplexed look. "I'm a close friend of Midnight's—she trusts me to do the job right."

Sierra blinked a few times.

Christian smiled. "Midnight's best friends with my cousin, Joe. He's over in San Francisco watching over Agent Bach's girl."

"I see," Sierra said, still trying to understand.

Christian's phone rang. He hit the hands-free.

"Collins," he answered.

"Hey, it's Mace," said a man's voice.

"Hey, man, how's Cat?"

"She's good, man. Doctors say she can go home in a couple of days."

"But what home?" Christian asked, an edge to his voice.

"Kana and Palani's," Kevin answered.

"I was hoping you'd say that," Christian said, breaking into a smile.

"Yeah, you know K. She takes care of her own."

"Indeed she does," Christian replied. "Thanks for the update, man. Did you get anything out of those guys?"

"Nah, not really," Kevin said. "But Cat says that they mentioned Elizabeth."

"Really?" Christian asked, narrowing his eyes. "Family business, then."

"Sounds like it."

Christian nodded, not looking happy in the slightest. "Well, keep me up to date. Keep an eye on Cat when K heads back out with Midnight too, will ya? And check on my girl every so often too, huh?"

"You know I will," Kevin replied. "All for one."

"One for all," Christian replied with a grin.

"Later, man."

"Later," Christian said, then hung up the phone.

The people that surrounded Midnight Chevalier had long been a curiosity of Sierra's. So much had been said about Midnight's "people"—so much, but so little. Sierra remembered the report about Midnight's friend and now bodyguard, Kana Sorbinno, being shot during Midnight's campaign. The subsequent stories about Kana being gay and Midnight being "more involved" than just a friend. Followed closely by Midnight's well worded speech about love knowing no gender, and how anyone that paid attention could see, however, how in love she was with her husband. Since then, many people had been curious about the people who seemed to both shield and stand behind Midnight Chevalier. This was a chance she couldn't pass up.

"So, can I ask who Cat is?" she asked tentatively.

"A member of my team," Christian answered, reaching for his cigarettes and glancing at her. "Do you mind if I smoke?"

"Not at all," she said. "What happened to her?"

"She was attacked, actually the same day Agent Bach was shot."

"Oh my God, is she okay?" Sierra asked.

"Yeah," Christian said. "It sounds, though, like they may have been after Liz, Cat's girlfriend."

"Girlfriend?" Sierra queried in a slightly odd tone.

Christian gave her a measured look. "Yeah, Liz and Cat are dating. Liz is Midnight's niece."

Sierra nodded, surprised by that but knowing she shouldn't be. Midnight Chevalier had already stated quite publicly that she didn't care about things like that. Love knew no gender.

"So that's what you meant by family business?" Sierra ventured. "Because they might have been after the AG's niece?"

"Yeah," Christian said.

"But you're not related to Midnight Chevalier, are you?"

Christian grinned. "Well, no, but neither is ninety-five percent of her family."

"I'm sorry?"

Christian laughed at that. "What Midnight considers her family is a group of us who have become her extended family. Either because they've been with her from the beginning of her law enforcement career, or by family ties with those members, or by being the lovers, wives, girlfriends of the aforementioned."

"And you're a family-tie member?" Sierra asked.

"Yeah," Christian said. "So's my wife, in a few ways."

"A few ways?"

"Long story."

His phone rang again; he answered it.

"Collins."

"What's a good-looking guy like you doing way up in Sacramento?" came the husky reply.

Christian's smile was brilliant. "Talking about my beautiful wife, as it happens."

"Oh shit, what are you saying about me?" Stevie replied, laughing.

"I was just trying to explain to Chief Deputy Youngblood the intricacies of our family."

"Oh God," Stevie replied. "That ought to have her confused for a week or two. No one understands us, babe, you should know that by now."

Christian glanced over at Sierra. "Oh, I dunno. She seemed to be grasping the concept pretty well."

"You get into the whole Donovan, Mace, Erin, Jeanie thing yet? Or the Joe, Rick, and Midnight thing yet? Hmm? Or better still, my sister, Kyle, and Midnight? That's when it gets complicated, babe."

Christian rolled his eyes. "No, I hadn't gotten into all that," he said, glancing at Sierra and seeing her eyes on him expectantly. "But it looks like I'm gonna end up explaining it all now."

"Oops, sorry," Stevie replied, not sounding like she was. "So you obviously got up there okay?"

"Yeah," Christian replied, "and I'm headed to San Francisco on a 2 p.m. flight."

"Huh?"

"Chief Deputy Youngblood wants to go to San Francisco," Christian replied, his eyes staring straight ahead.

"Oh," Stevie replied, sounding perplexed but not questioning further. She knew her husband and that he was purposely not explaining.

"Hey, Mace said that this thing with Cat might have been family related," Christian said, his tone serious now. "Promise me you'll be careful out there."

"I will be, babe, you know that. Dave isn't even sending us out alone right now."

"Mace having to cover both you and J?"

"No, Dave's going out with me. Mace is going out with Jeanie."

Christian nodded, looking comforted. "Good."

"We'll be fine, babe, don't worry."

"Good." Christian said again, his expression serious.

"I'll let you go. I know you're trying to juggle driving, smoking, and talking to me all at the same time."

Christian laughed—his wife knew him well. "You got it."

"You be careful up there, too, okay?" Stevie said, her tone softening.

"Always, love, always."

"I love you," she said seriously.

"And I you," he replied, his smile gentle.

Sierra knew she was seeing a man deeply in love with his wife. It made her heart ache. She missed Kashena desperately. She hoped Kashena wouldn't be too angry with her for showing up in San Francisco, but she just felt she needed to be there. That was the beginning of the realization. She didn't miss Jason at all, and he'd been gone for eight months. Kashena had been gone less than two days, and she missed her presence keenly.

She was risking having Christian Collins report to Midnight Chevalier that one of her Chief Deputy AGs decided to make a run to San Francisco because she missed her girlfriend. To her credit, she'd insisted on using her own credit card to pay for both her plane ticket and Christian's, as well as for the rental car. She had no intention of filing a claim to get the money back either. This trip was personal, not business. She would have done it sooner, but Kashena had warned her to be careful and not travel at all while she was unprotected.

All Sierra knew was that she needed to see Kashena, and she needed to be there when Kashena needed her.

***

Samantha was sitting next to Sebastian's bed, her hand in his. He'd awoken a few times but had said little. It was obvious he was still weak from the surgery he'd had to remove the bullet.

Joe walked in, noting the way the Deputy Attorney General was holding the injured agent's hand. He knew from Midnight that Samantha Cobb was married, and fairly straightlaced from what Midnight had said. To Joe, however, Samantha's continued presence in the hospital spoke volumes about her feelings for Agent Bach.

"Deputy Attorney General Cobb," Joe said quietly as he stepped to her side.

Samantha stood, looking up at him as she did. She glanced at Kashena for reassurance.

"I'm Joe Sinclair." Joe extended his hand to Samantha. "Midnight Chevalier has sent me to look out for you while Agent Bach recovers."

"I—" Samantha's eyes went to Sebastian, then back to Kashena, then back to Joe again. "I'm not ready to leave."

Joe nodded. "That's fine, Mrs. Cobb. I'm here for when you *are* ready to leave."

Samantha pressed her lips together, worried that she was seeming difficult. This handsome Englishman with his light blue eyes and long hair didn't seem irritated at all, however. Sitting back down, Samantha looked over at Sebastian, who was stirring.

Sebastian opened his eyes slowly. He looked at Samantha, then sensed another presence in the room. His eyes turned to Joe and narrowed slightly, but he saw that Kashena was there too, so he relaxed immediately.

"Agent Bach," Joe said, inclining his head to the younger man, "I'm Joe Sinclair. AG Chevalier sent me to look after your charge while you get back on your feet."

Sebastian stared at Joe. "Mach 3?" he asked, naming the company Joe had started with John Machiavelli.

"You've heard of us?" Joe replied, surprised.

"Yeah," Sebastian said. He looked at Samantha. "He's good, Sam, one of the best. You're in good hands."

Samantha bit her lip in hesitation. "I don't want to leave you here," she said quietly, knowing she sounded foolish but not caring.

Sebastian took her hand. "Sam, you have work to do. I'm okay. You have a case to prosecute, save the whales or somethin'," he said with a smile.

Samantha laughed softly. "Or a tree to hug, right?"

"Or that," Sebastian agreed. "How much sleep have you had?"

Samantha averted her eyes from his. "You know I can't sleep in a strange place."

"All the more reason to go home, Sam." Sebastian looked at Joe. "Take her home, will you?"

Joe looked from Sebastian to Samantha, then back to Sebastian. "That's gonna be up to her."

"Uh-uh," Sebastian said. "Sam, you need to go home," he said in a no-nonsense tone. "You're going to make yourself sick sitting here with me. In a few days I'll be out of here and back home."

Samantha looked unhappy but nodded slowly. Joe was surprised. Midnight had told him that Samantha Cobb was an ultra-liberal,

216

tough feminist, and here she was taking orders from a man. Something wasn't jibing, but Joe said nothing.

Later on the two-hour drive back to Sacramento, Joe stumbled onto a few things. Samantha witnessed some surprising phone calls, much like Sierra had back in Sacramento. The first was to Midnight Chevalier herself.

Joe dialed the number using the hands-free, since he was keeping both hands on the wheel. Midnight answered on the second ring.

"Chevalier."

"Hey, Night, it's me," Joe said warmly.

"Everything secure where you are?"

"Ma'am, yes ma'am," Joe replied with a grin. "How's Cat?"

"She's good," Midnight said, "considering. The doctors say she can go home in a couple of days."

"To her and Liz's place?" Joe asked pointedly.

"To K and Palani's place."

"Ah," Joe said. "So that still hasn't been resolved?"

"Resolved?" Midnight said, like Joe was crazy. "Kana's still threatening to kick the shit out of Elizabeth if she comes anywhere near Cat right now."

Joe chuckled, shaking his head. "How does Cat feel about that?"

"Cat's not even close to wanting to see Elizabeth right now. In fact, Liz hasn't been brave enough to come back to the hospital yet."

"She's okay though, right?" Joe asked, his tone changing slightly.

"Don't worry. Rick's got Spider keeping an eye on her."

"Good," Joe said.

"The ranks are closing, just like always, Joe. Nothing to stress about. Kyle's even put black-and-whites with four of his best on Sinclair House and your place while you're gone. They got to us once—it won't happen again. Don't worry."

Joe took a deep breath and expelled it slowly. "Good. Thanks, Night."

"Don't thank me. Just be safe up there," Midnight said, her voice serious.

"I always am," he said, smiling. "I'll check in later."

"Got it. Talk to you soon."

Joe hung up a moment later.

"You're fairly close to the Attorney General," Samantha said. It wasn't a question.

"We've been best friends for almost twenty-two years now."

"A member of your family is in the hospital?"

"Well, sort of," Joe said. "Cat, one of the members of the circle of friends that Midnight and I consider family, was attacked down in San Diego."

"Is Cat a police officer too?"

"Yeah, she's on the same narcotics team as my brother-in-law and cousin." Joe grinned as he realized how that sounded.

"Your brother-in-law?" Samantha asked.

"Yeah, my wife's younger brother."

"And your cousin?"

"Uh-huh," Joe said, smiling.

"You're a rather close group, aren't you?" she asked, not sounding offended by the thought.

Joe laughed. "Oh, you have no idea."

"What do you mean?"

"Well, let's see… Midnight's husband, Rick, works for the department. Rick was my best friend growing up in England. Rick's niece is married to Dave, who is an original member of the gang task force Midnight started. Rick's other niece is, or was, dating Cat, the officer in the hospital. Then there's my brother-in-law Donovan's wife,

Jeanie, who works for the same unit as he does. My cousin's wife, Stevie, also works for that unit. Stevie's sister, Rhiannon, is married to the now police chief, Kyle Masterson. There's Mace, whose wife used to date Donovan. It just goes on and on from there. Most of us are basically either in law enforcement or married or dating someone in law enforcement."

Samantha nodded, looking like she was working at understanding.

"Why is that?" she asked eventually. "I mean, is that kind of thing on purpose?"

Joe thought about the question, then shrugged. "I don't know if it's calculated, but cops tend to drift toward other cops, or people who are like minded."

"Like minded?"

"Well, people who understand why cops do what they do."

"And why do cops do what they do?" Samantha asked, curious as to his take on it.

Joe looked over at her, trying to determine what she was after. Finally he said, "Well, we're all in it for various reasons. Most of us are in it to make a difference."

"A difference?"

"In our lives, in other people's lives, in the world we live in."

"In your lives?" Samantha asked, intrigued by that.

"Many of the people I'm close to got into law enforcement to change our lives, or the course of our lives."

"How so?"

"Well, Midnight herself led a gang when she was eighteen."

Samantha's brow furrowed. "I remember reading something about that during the election. I thought that was just tabloid fodder."

"Nope, it was true," Joe said. "Her younger brother was killed in her gang—that's why she got out and into law enforcement."

"And what about you?" she asked.

"I led a gang back home in London," Joe said. "My parents were killed by a rival gang leader."

"Oh," Samantha said, paling significantly. "I'm so sorry."

"S'okay. It was a long time ago. I've dealt with my guilt in that."

"So you joined law enforcement to get you out of the gang?"

"Well," he said, his tone somber, "actually, in my case, the accident that killed my parents also had me in the hospital for six months. After that I came to America to get away. While I was here, I decided to go into law enforcement as a way of making amends."

Samantha nodded, both surprised and intrigued by what he was saying.

"Police officers are really very different than I believed," she said.

"What did you previously believe?"

Samantha bit her lip, knowing that what she had previously thought wasn't exactly the kind of thing she should tell someone like Joe Sinclair. Nonetheless, he'd asked, and she was going to answer him.

"I tended to believe what I read in the paper and saw on the news, that police officers were out there beating on innocent people, breaking the rules to suit themselves, and basically not doing what they were overpaid to do."

Joe pursed his lips, nodding. He knew that there were a lot of people like her in the world. People who never had any real contact with a police officer, other than in a negative experience. Receiving a parking ticket, a speeding ticket, getting stopped for DUI, or getting arrested or whatever—it was almost always a negative experience. It was something cops faced every day, people hating you because you enforced the law regardless of who those laws applied to. The ones that didn't have actual contact with police officers believed what the media presented, which was almost always negative. Cases like Rodney King were always front page. The countless lives saved by police officers were rarely advertised. It was "good journalism." They wanted dirt, not necessarily the truth.

Finally, when he'd had a chance to digest what she'd said, he looked over at her. "But your opinion has changed?" he asked, a slight edge to his tone.

Samantha caught it and understood it completely, especially considering that one of his fellow peace officers had just about given up his life to protect hers.

"Definitely," she said, "and not just due to the incident in San Francisco. Please don't misunderstand—I'm in complete awe of the fact that Sebastian just risked his own life to protect me. However, before that, he'd changed my opinion of police officers. You see, I'd never really had any long-term contact with a police officer before he began protecting me. At first I had the worst impression of him possible."

"What impression was that?"

"Well, the first time we met I called him a goose-stepping Nazi," Samantha said.

Joe laughed at that. "I don't think I've ever heard that one."

Samantha laughed softly too. "He made me so mad that first day, simply because he was immovable and not very impressed with me. And he called me babe."

"You mean, like I just called the Attorney General a little while ago?"

"I noticed that, yes," Samantha said, smiling. "But you've known her for a long time. Sebastian had just met me."

"And being called babe by someone you don't know is a bit pointed."

"Indeed," Samantha said. "The things is, as I got to know him, I found out that not only was he very intelligent, but he had points of view that were so very different from mine that we may as well have been on different planets."

"And that was okay with you?" Joe asked, sounding perplexed. Usually people liked people to have the same opinion as they did.

"It was difficult at first, but the thing about Sebastian is that he can back up his opinions with actual facts. He doesn't just make sweeping statements about things. I found him to be fascinating, once I got over my own biases."

Joe grinned.

"What?" she asked, seeing his expression.

"I can't say all cops are like Sebastian," Joe said. "Some of us do have opinions formed on experience. A lot of those opinions are jaded because of the element we deal with every day."

"So you admit that cops are flawed?"

"We are human," Joe said. "Everyone has flaws. Cops are no exception to that rule. Although the public seems to expect them to be. It's a very difficult standard to adhere to."

Samantha nodded, noting that she had yet another highly intelligent police officer on her hands.

"So what does your wife do?" she asked after a few minutes. She'd noticed the gold wedding band he wore.

"She runs a center for children."

"What kind of center?"

Joe smiled, knowing he was about to back up everything he'd said. "A center for children displaced from their homes during police actions."

"Explain that," Samantha said, already intrigued.

"Which part?" Joe asked.

"Police actions."

"When the parent or parents are arrested and/or it's in the best interests of the child to be removed from the home," Joe explained.

"Aren't there government programs already in place for that?"

"Yes," Joe said, "but Randy's ideal was for children to have a warm, nurturing and less sterile environment in which to make the adjustment to their new situation."

Samantha looked over at him. "So what does your wife do differently?"

"Well, first of all, the center is located in a house, rather than a government building. Randy has a PhD in child psychology, as do many of the people who work for her. They try to help the child understand what's happening, rather than simply placing them in custody or a foster home. She also works toward finding permanent stable homes for children whose parents forfeit custody of their children."

"Forfeit?" Samantha asked. "Is that a euphemism?"

"No." Joe shook his head. "Sometimes they want to give their kids up. Other times, however, they are legally required to do so."

"Does your wife work with the government programs though? Rather than simply usurping their purpose?"

Joe raised an eyebrow at the term "usurping." "Social Services, as well as Child Protective Services, are overwhelmed on a consistent basis. They not only work with Randy; they welcome her assistance. In fact, she's working toward opening another center."

"Obviously it's a non-profit venture—how does she get funding?"

"Well, originally, I funded it."

"You?" Samantha asked, looking shocked.

"Yeah."

"That must have cost..." Samantha shook her head, unable to fathom it.

"The house the center is in cost two million," Joe said, knowing he was only shocking her more.

"I wasn't aware police officers made that kind of money."

"We don't," he said, "but my family had money, and I inherited it."

"I see," Samantha said. "It's very noble of you to use the money that way."

"Noble?" Joe asked, making a face.

"Yes. You don't think it's noble?"

Joe shrugged. "I don't think of it at all. My wife wanted to do something; I helped her achieve it. Had my father been alive, he would have done the same."

"But you don't like the word noble?"

"I've had it attributed to me too often recently," Joe said.

"Really?" Samantha asked.

Joe's phone rang, saving him from further explanation.

"Sinclair," he answered, hitting the hands-free again.

"Joe, it's me," Christian said, a grin in his voice.

"Hey, what's going on?"

"I'm headed to San Francisco," Christian said.

"Oddly enough, I'm leaving San Francisco."

"That figures," Christian replied. "Midnight wanted me to check in with you. So that's what I'm doing."

"And a bloody good job you're doing, too," Joe said, laughing.

"Yeah, yeah, bite me."

"Stevie's job, not mine," Joe replied. "So, are you driving or flying?"

"Flying and renting a car at the airport."

"Got it. Well, just let me know where you end up," Joe said.

"Will do."

"You talk to Stevie?" Joe asked.

"Yeah."

"You got the latest on Cat then?"

"Yeah, I'm happy to hear she's going to Kana's," Christian said. "Apparently Dave's working with Stevie right now, and Mace is keeping tabs on her for me while I'm up here."

"Yeah," Joe said. "Kyle's doubling everyone up for now that's family. We don't want any more surprises."

"Too right," Christian said, sounding very English. "Anyway, the plane's about to board, so I'll talk to you later tonight."

"Alright, man. Take it easy. Be safe."

"You too."

Joe hung up. He noted that Samantha had listened to the conversation with a quirk to her brow.

"You certainly move in interesting circles, Mr. Sinclair," she observed.

"It's rarely boring."

Samantha chuckled. She liked Joe Sinclair; he was a very interesting man. He wasn't near as gruff and straightforward as Sebastian. It was obvious he had an upper-class upbringing, simply in the way he spoke and carried himself.

Samantha was surprised but pleased that Joe had told her all that he had about what she would consider the inner sanctum of Midnight Chevalier's people. Midnight had both intimidated and confounded Samantha from the first time she'd heard of her. The woman was not a politician, running for an office that quite frequently was highly political. Jeffrey had, of course, written Midnight Chevalier off as someone who'd bought the election, so was, therefore, worthless. Samantha hadn't been too sure, although Midnight Chevalier's connections were rather noteworthy. Her own husband was from a rich English family, and so, apparently, was her best friend. She was friends with rock stars and movie stars. She was also a celebrity in the law enforcement community. Midnight didn't strike Samantha as the kind of person that bought elections.

Since getting into office, Midnight Chevalier had made sweeping changes in the direction of the office. It was her intention to make a difference for the people of the state of California. Her way of handling things was very different than her predecessor's, and many in the department had no idea how to take Midnight. If she wanted something done, it got done, one way or the other. She had no qualms about walking into anyone's office, sitting down and explaining what she wanted and why. Hardy was the soul that countered Midnight Chevalier—few had tried it; fewer had succeeded in swaying her opinion. It was, however, common knowledge that Midnight Chevalier never made anything personal. It was business to her, so she didn't fire a person for having a different opinion, or for telling her that they thought she was wrong. If they managed to convince her she was wrong, she'd change her mind. The problem was, the woman was rarely wrong, or in a position where she had to change her mind.

Samantha had just seen and heard that Midnight was very human—she had very real friends, and they were admirable people from the sounds of it. It changed Samantha's opinion a bit more.

CHAPTER 11

It wasn't enough; they weren't caving like they should have been. It was as if they'd got closer, their ranks growing tighter, rather than making them careless. This wasn't right! One in San Francisco, one in San Diego—why weren't they reacting the way they should? Damn it!

***

Sable Sands arrived back at her hotel in London after a day of promotional interviews for her latest tour. She had just showered and was wrapping a plush robe around herself when there was a knock on the bathroom door.

"Yes?" Sable asked.

"Something you need to see," Jake said from the other side of the door.

Sable walked out of the bathroom, looking quizzically at Jake. He pointed to the TV. The newscast was just coming back from a commercial.

"An American police officer in San Diego, California, who has not been identified, was rescued today by members of the San Diego Police Department. The officer, a female, was abducted a couple of days ago and was injured by her captors—she's seen here being put into an ambulance. San Diego Police Chief Kyle Masterson said they are not releasing information at this time, as this officer serves in an undercover capacity…"

The reporter went on, but Jake pointed out the officer being loaded—she had long blond hair, but her face was blurred, making her unrecognizable.

"Doesn't that look like your lass?" Jake asked.

Sable stared at the image frozen on the screen. She'd immediately thought of Catalina Roché when she'd heard it was a female officer.

"It could be," Sable said, reaching for her cell phone. "I'm going to call Kyle Masterson."

She wasn't able to get ahold of Kyle, his secretary said he was too busy, but she left him a message. It took two days for Kyle to get back to her.

"Ms. Sands, this is Kyle Masterson—you left me a message."

Sable motioned to the band to stop playing; she was in the middle of a sound check. She walked off the stage so she could better hear Kyle. "Was the officer who was hurt Catalina?" she asked without preamble.

Kyle was silent for a moment, not completely surprised by Sable's interest. He'd heard from Kana that Sable and Cat had shared a kiss at the bar back when Cat was investigating Jake's shooting. What he wasn't sure of was whether or not to disclose the information to Sable about Cat's kidnapping.

"Yes," Kyle finally answered, wondering how serious Sable Sands was about his officer.

"Is she going to be okay?" Sable asked, already making plans in her mind.

"She's in for some recovery time, mental and physical."

"Can you give me her number?" Sable motioned to Jake, who stood at the side of the stage.

"I think it would be best if you speak to Kana Sorbinno. I can give you her number."

"Fine, thank you." Sable memorized the number Kyle gave her.

Once she hung up with Kyle, she looked at Jake. "I need you to get ahold of my plane. I need to get to San Diego, in the next few days."

"You have concerts..." Jake trailed off as Sable's eyes flashed in irritation.

"I'll handle that—you handle what I asked for!" she snapped, in a rare show of anger at her bodyguard. She sighed. "I'll talk to BJ about postponing a couple of dates. Please make the arrangements."

Jake nodded, glad he wasn't the one contacting BJ Sparks. He didn't need to get yelled at by two hotheads in one afternoon.

***

After a week at Kana and Palani's, Cat was feeling a bit smothered. The first few days at the house, Kana had been extremely attentive, even coming into the room she was staying in and lying down behind her, holding her. Cat had spent a great deal of time listening to the radio and just lying on the bed, trying to get her mind around everything that had happened. Whenever Kana tried to broach the subject of Elizabeth or the abduction, Cat would avoid the topic, saying she didn't want to talk.

Kana was worried sick about her friend. She knew Catalina wasn't dealing with what happened; she was also making noises about moving to a hotel, to "think" about things. Kana didn't want Cat alone, but she also had to get back out on the road with Midnight.

A solution presented itself two days later. Kana got a call from Sable Sands; she was looking for Cat. Kana happily told the rock star where to find her. It was perfect.

An hour later, Sable walked into the bedroom Cat was staying in. Cat was lying on the bed, wearing gray shorts and a black tank top. Her long blond hair was pulled up into a ponytail, and she wore no makeup. Sable noticed light bruises on Cat's skin and grimaced inwardly, imagining that they'd been much worse the week before.

Cat heard the door open and glanced up. Her eyes widened as she moved to sit.

"What are you doing here?" she asked Sable.

"I was in town and heard about what happened," Sable said, by way of explanation.

"You were in Europe," Cat replied, her tone circumspect.

"And now I'm in town," Sable said smoothly as she walked over to the bed and sat down, her gaze trained on Cat's face.

Sable wanted to touch Cat, and even reached out to do so, but she saw a pained look in Cat's eyes instantly. Nodding, Sable dropped her hand.

Kicking off her sandals, she moved to sit on the bed, putting her back to the headboard.

"This is Evanescence, isn't it?" Sable asked about the song on the radio.

Cat nodded.

"Amy has an incredible voice." Sable had always admired the tiny dynamo from Evanescence.

Again Cat nodded, moving to lean against the headboard too.

They ended up sitting there listening to music for the better part of two hours. "So," Sable said conversationally, "your chief tells me you're on leave for another two weeks or so."

Cat nodded, not looking pleased about the idea.

"Ever been to Europe?" Sable asked, keeping her tone casual.

"Have I what?"

"Been to Europe," Sable repeated, her rich chocolate eyes staring directly into Cat's. "I want to take you there."

Cat's mouth opened as if to say something, then she shook her head, like she didn't understand. "Why?"

Sable shrugged, looking around her. "I think you could use a change of scenery."

Cat looked perplexed. "Why are you doing this?"

"Because I'm an extremely eccentric rock star, haven't you heard?" Sable asked with a wry smile.

Cat looked suspicious, and it exasperated Sable a little bit more.

"Just come with me," Sable said before Cat could level some kind of accusation at her. "No strings, no hassles, I swear."

Three hours later, Cat was on Sable's private Gulfstream jet on her way to Europe. It was a surreal experience to say the least.

***

Back in Sacramento, Samantha arrived home in the afternoon. She busied herself unpacking the few things she'd had with her. Joe checked out the house, then left her, giving her his cell phone number as well as his pager. He told her not to leave the house without contacting him.

"At this point we need to be extra careful," he said seriously.

Samantha nodded. Sebastian had already made a huge sacrifice, and the last thing she wanted was for it to have been for nothing.

When Jeffrey didn't come home that evening, Samantha was relieved. She had dreaded the confrontation they were likely to have. She'd literally told him to leave in San Francisco, and she doubted that the embarrassment of being asked to leave by his own wife in front of what he considered an inferior would sit well with him.

She made herself a light dinner, took a bath, put on her pajamas and curled up in bed to read a book, but not before calling the hospital to check on Sebastian. They put her through to his room. He answered on the third ring.

"Bach," he answered automatically.

Samantha laughed softly. "Are you programmed to answer a phone that way?"

He chuckled. "I guess so."

"How are you feeling?"

"Like I'm swimming underwater with a suit of armor on."

"Well, better that than in pain."

"Yes," he said, "but you can see why I wanted you protected and away from here, right?"

"Protected I understand, but why away from there?" Samantha asked.

"If they want to try for you again, Sam, they'd know where to look at the hospital."

"Oh," she said, sounding shocked—she was.

"Don't worry, Sam," Sebastian said, his tone softening. "Joe Sinclair is one of the best there is. He's been a cop almost longer than you or I have been alive. He'll keep you safe."

Samantha smiled sadly. She still couldn't get over the fact that this man had almost died keeping her from harm. She couldn't begin to think of a way to thank him.

"Sebastian…"

"Hmm?" he murmured, sounding like his thoughts were far away.

Samantha hesitated. She couldn't thank him on the phone. That was far too cold. She needed to wait until he came home; she needed to talk to him in person.

"Nothing," she said. "Just make sure you rest so you can get better."

"Now you sound like a mother," he said, smiling.

"Well, hopefully I also sound like a concerned friend."

"Not a concerned employer?" he asked, his voice tinged with humor.

Samantha knew then that Kashena had told him about what Jeffrey had said in her presence.

"Sebastian, I hope you know I don't think like my husband does, not anymore."

He was quiet for a while, then finally he blew his breath out. "Then getting shot was worth it."

"I changed my opinion about a lot of things before you got yourself shot, Sebastian Bach," she said sternly.

"Ma'am, yes ma'am," he replied, grinning at his end.

Samantha smiled. "Just you remember that, Mr. Ranger."

"It's Army Ranger, ma'am," he corrected.

"Army Ranger," she repeated, smiling.

"You got it."

"I'll let you get some rest," she said after a few moments of silence. "I just wanted to check on you before I went to bed."

"You do have some sleep to catch up on."

"I know," Samantha said. She'd been feeling it all evening.

"At least you have a warm body there to hold you," he said evenly.

"Well, the warm body isn't home yet." She glanced at the clock; it was 7 p.m.

"He will be."

"I suppose," she answered, feeling bereft suddenly. She had the strangest urge to tell Sebastian that she wished it was him who would be holding her that night. The thought hit her like a ton of bricks.

It hit her again that night when Jeffrey crawled into bed behind her. She felt him get into bed; the clock read 11 p.m. His hands snaked around her as he pressed against her from behind. She felt him—he was horny. *Oh God,* was all she could think. Not responding to his futile attempts to caress her, nor the pressure of his hard-on against her, Samantha lay motionless. The memory of waking that last morning in San Francisco, with Sebastian holding her from behind, her body pressed against his was still fresh in her mind. His body had been hard and strong, and the excitement she'd felt from him was much more, both literally and figuratively. With Jeffrey she felt nothing, least of all a desire to have sex with him.

After a while, Jeffrey moved away. Samantha lay thinking about Sebastian. How had she become so attached to a man like him? It was true he was handsome, and he'd proven to be very intelligent. Even so, he was the kind of man she'd always shunned. He had that air of "beefcake" written all over him. Samantha had always written men like that off as absurd. But it was Sebastian's arms she was longing for that night, of that there was no doubt.

***

When Sierra and Christian arrived in San Francisco, Christian had driven her over to the hospital without even asking if that was where she wanted to go. The hospital staff had told them that Agent Marshal had gone down the street to the hotel. Sierra hadn't been sure if Christian knew exactly why she was in San Francisco until they were standing in the hallway in the hotel. He'd managed to get the information out of the hotel staff as to what room Kashena was in, using his badge and his charm to persuade the girl at the front desk. He also managed to get an adjoining room next door in case he was needed.

At the door to Kashena's room, Christian handed her the key and her overnight bag.

"I'll be next door if you need me," he said, his tone casual.

She nodded, appreciating both his discretion as well as his lack of apparent judgment on the situation. He quirked a grin and walked over to his door, opening it and waiting for her to do the same. She walked into the hotel room, closing the door quietly behind her. She immediately saw Kashena lying asleep in the bed in the room. Leaning back against the door, she stared at the woman who'd haunted her every thought for quite a while now.

She set her bag down and kicked off her shoes. Sitting on the bed, she touched Kashena's cheek gently. Kashena was awake immediately, her deep blue eyes widening when she recognized Sierra.

"What? How? Wait, where's Collins?" Kashena's words tumbled out on themselves.

"Relax," Sierra said, smiling, "he's next door. He brought me here."

"What? How? Wait, where's Collins?" Kashena's words tumbled out over themselves.

"Relax," Sierra said, smiling. "He's next door. He brought me here."

"Why?" Kashena asked, looking perplexed.

"Because I asked him to," Sierra answered.

Kashena drew in a breath, her eyes reflecting concern and caution.

Please don't be angry with me," Sierra said, lying down next to Kashena and reaching up to touch her cheek again. "I needed to be here with you."

It said everything Kashena needed to know.

They made love then, and lay together afterwards.

"Kash?" Sierra said softly after a few minutes.

"Hmm?"

Sierra was quiet, hesitating. Maybe this wasn't the time to mention this.

Kashena pulled back, looking down at Sierra in the dim light of the hotel room.

"What's up, babe?" she asked softly.

Sierra raised her head. "I got a letter yesterday," she said cautiously.

Kashena nodded slowly, waiting for the rest.

"Jason got his orders. He's coming home," Sierra said in a rush, as if saying it quickly would lessen the impact.

Things were about to change. Neither of them were sure they were ready for that, but only time would tell.

**

A week later, Sebastian was released from the hospital. Kashena was there to drive him home; she'd even driven back to Sacramento and picked up his Hummer to take him home in, knowing he'd be more comfortable in his own vehicle.

"You just wanted a chance to drive it," he said accusingly, his smile wide.

"Yeah, I didn't get enough of this in the Marines," Kashena said, rolling her eyes.

"I could actually drive home, you know..."

"With all the shit they've got you on? Like hell."

Sebastian laughed. "Fine," he acquiesced, "but you have to listen to my music."

"Oh Lord," Kashena said, rolling her eyes again.

Sebastian grinned evilly. "Just for that..." he said, pulling out his Disturbed CD.

Three hours and four Advil later, Kashena delivered Sebastian to his house. She ordered him to get himself settled in his bedroom and went about making him some lunch. Naturally there was nothing usable in the kitchen, so she grabbed the keys to her Impala off the counter and walked down the hall to his bedroom.

"I'm going to the store. Any special requests?"

"Beer," he said.

"Are you supposed to be drinking while you're on that medication?" She nodded at the bottles of meds on his nightstand.

"You questioning me, Marine?" he asked darkly.

Kashena grinned. "Sir, yes sir," she said, seeing him scowl. "However, I was merely asking because I'll more than likely have to drink with you if that's the case."

Sebastian nodded. "Roger that."

Kashena went to the grocery store and stocked up on food. She also bought a twelve-pack of Heineken and bought herself a six-pack of Corona She knew it wasn't a good idea for Sebastian to drink, but she also knew that he was on edge about being down so long. If having a few beers would help that, she was all for it as long as she was there to keep an eye on him.

In the end, they spent the evening having dinner, which Kashena made him, drinking a few beers and watching movies. The next few days were spent much the same. Kashena slept in bed next to him, her hand usually on his shoulder most of the night. It was her way of reassuring herself he was okay. Sebastian appreciated her help, knowing he wouldn't have been comfortable with anyone else taking care of him.

On the third day he was home, Kashena had just gone to the kitchen to put their plates from lunch in the sink when the doorbell rang. She opened the door and was mildly surprised to see Samantha Cobb standing there.

"Do you think he's up to a visit?" Samantha asked.

"I'm sure he is."

Samantha had called every day since he was home to check on his status, but she'd only talked to Kashena.

"Is he still doing alright?" Samantha asked.

"He's doing great." Kashena stepped back to let Samantha into the house. "Go see for yourself. He's down the hall, last bedroom on the left."

"Thanks," Samantha said, smiling warmly at Kashena.

In the doorway, Samantha paused, drawing in a deep breath. He was sitting up, his attention on the TV. Bare chested, his blond hair tousled, he looked amazingly handsome to her. She realized suddenly that she'd missed him a lot more than she'd thought. Sebastian glanced up at the doorway and saw her there. He grinned boyishly, looking at the clock on his nightstand.

"Isn't it a little early for you to be off work?"

She raised an eyebrow. "Who says this isn't a business meeting?"

"Is it?" he asked, his smile widening.

"No," she said, walking toward him, her blue eyes taking in the still red two-inch scar on his chest. "I think you peace officers call it a welfare check."

Sebastian nodded, his ocean-green eyes staring up at her.

Samantha bit her lip, not sure what was acceptable to do next. As usual, Sebastian solved the problem for her. He patted the bed next to him. She sat down, reaching out to touch the scar gently. He flinched at her touch.

"I'm sorry, did I hurt you?" she asked worriedly.

"No," he said. "It just feels strange right now."

Samantha started to take her hand away, but Sebastian caught it in his and held it to his chest, just to the side of the scar. When she looked up at him, his eyes were searching her face.

"You're not sleeping, are you?" It wasn't really a question; he could see it on her face.

She shook her head, swallowing. For some reason she was suddenly very emotional. The feeling of his hand over hers, the beating of his heart under her hand... He was still alive, but it could have been so different.

Sebastian saw the waves of emotion play across Samantha's face. He pulled her down to lie against him on his right side. It was all she could take; the tears started then. Sebastian held her, realizing that this entire incident had been harder on her than he'd thought. Part of him was pleased that she appreciated the gravity of what had happened, but another part of him felt that he'd simply done his job and that she was worrying about him needlessly.

He held her for a long time, stroking her hair and doing his best to soothe her. When she calmed, she looked up at him, frowning.

"I'm sorry," she said, brushing away tears. "The last thing you need to deal with is a hysterical female."

"It's okay." Sebastian touched her under the chin to tip her face up to his. "So what's goin' on?"

Samantha sighed. "Things are just such a mess right now."

"Well, things have been a bit much lately," he said, brushing a finger over her cheek.

"It's so awful right now…"

"What's going on?" Sebastian sensed this was beyond worrying about him.

"I just…" Samantha shook her head. "Things at home are very strained."

"With Jeffrey?"

Samantha nodded. "Sebastian, he was so awful when you were in the hospital, and since then, I just can't seem to understand him."

"Awful how?"

"He kept saying that you had merely done your job in protecting me, that it was your job…"

"Sam," Sebastian said, his finger stilling her lips, "he's right."

"What?" Samantha asked, shocked.

"Sam, it was my job. I was paid to protect you, and that's what I did."

"Sebastian, it's one thing to say you'd give your life to protect someone; it's something totally different to actually almost die doing so. You almost gave up your life for me, Sebastian. That's not something I'm going to easily forget."

"Okay, Sam." He touched her cheek softly. "But don't let that ruin your life."

"Ruin my life?"

"Yeah," he said, looking concerned. "It's totally normal for things to go awry when something this traumatic happens. What you can't do is let it affect your entire life."

"But, Sebastian, it wasn't just this," she said. "Things with Jeffrey have been getting worse and worse."

"In terms of what?" Sebastian asked.

"He's so conceited. He thinks so little of people who deserve so much more respect…"

"People like who?"

"Like you," she replied, her look direct.

Sebastian closed his eyes, frowning slightly. He'd been afraid of that. Opening his eyes, he looked down at her.

"Sam, I think you're confusing gratitude for something else."

"It's not that, Sebastian," she said, touching his cheek. "You're so different from what I thought. You're just… you're so…"

"I'm exactly what you thought," he told her. "Goose-stepping Nazi, remember?"

Samantha rolled her eyes at him. "I said that when I didn't know you at all."

"I'm the same man I was then, Sam," he said solemnly.

She shook her head, looking into his eyes.

"Besides," he said, "nothing could ever happen between us."

"Why?" she asked, sounding hurt.

"Because you're married, Sam."

"That doesn't seem like something that would ever bother you," she said, wincing at how that sounded. "I mean…"

Sebastian chuckled. "You're right, it usually wouldn't. But somewhere along the way, I developed respect for you. I've also gotten to know you, and I don't think you're the kind of woman that can cheat on her husband."

Samantha sighed in consternation. He did know her too well, didn't he? She'd been wrestling with the idea of actually having an affair, and it was so difficult to overcome her upbringing that she felt totally tormented. It was what kept her up nights—that and missing him so much.

"So what would you suggest?" she asked him.

"Marriage counseling?"

"Jeffrey would never do that," Samantha said. "He doesn't believe in that kind of thing."

He smiled. "A liberal who doesn't believe that talking about your feelings will solve everything?"

"Yes, shocking, isn't it?" She loved that he was so easily able to tease her, and nothing that he ever said bothered her in the slightest now. He'd said it himself—he respected her now, and she knew that.

"In all fairness, though, Sam," he said then, his voice serious, "you might try just talking to him. Tell him how you feel about what's been going on, and see what happens. He's used to you having one opinion, and that's his. You never know, he might welcome the new more independent you..." He rolled his eyes. "Jesus, do I sound like that Dr. Laura broad now?"

"Maybe, right up until you used the word 'broad,'" she said, winking at him.

Sebastian laughed. Samantha dropped her head to his chest again, feeling both comfortable and safe. Sebastian inspired those feelings in her. She felt him tighten his arms around her, and she snuggled closer to him. Within minutes she was asleep.

Sebastian sat holding her against him, reflecting on what they'd just talked about. He knew he'd been right about her not being the kind of woman to cheat on her husband. She just wasn't that type. In truth, he didn't think he'd want her to cheat on her husband with him. Chances were that anything they'd have would be fleeting. They were very different people from very different worlds. He knew that she was putting all her feelings about his saving her life on him. That kind of feeling wore off quickly, and he didn't know if there was anything there to take its place. He definitely didn't want her giving up a seven-year marriage for him.

***

Jason Thorn was happy to be home. Back where there was cold beer, no sand, and good old American food, not that raghead shit or whatever the military slop of the day was. As he pushed the lawn mower over his lawn, he felt a sense of pride. He had this nice house, a hot wife and a kid. Yep, it was the American dream. He was a classic Marine—flat-top blond hair, darkly tanned skin from his time in the desert. He was feeling pretty good about himself with his shirt off, his tattoos on display. He'd noticed the redhead from next door looking at him. She was pretty hot, maybe a little young, but… that kind of thing rarely stopped him. It hadn't in the Middle East, that was for sure.

He noticed the black Suburban drive up, saw a blonde chick with shades on driving; in the passenger seat was his wife. She'd told him that she had a bodyguard. *Who the fuck is she gonna protect anyone from? Skinny bitch…*

Sierra got out of the vehicle after saying something to the blonde, then walked up to the house. She moved past him, but Jason wasn't having that shit—he grabbed her, giving her a hot, crushing kiss.

"Who's the broad?" Jason asked when he let her go.

"That's my bodyguard," Sierra said, her tone all high class.

Jason gave snort of sarcastic laughter. "Some skinny little broad is going to protect you? From what? Flies?"

Sierra looked back at him. "For your information," Sierra she said tightly, "Kashena is an ex-Marine."

"Bullshit!" Jason snapped. *No fucking way!*

"No, not bullshit," Sierra replied. "She was a second lieutenant and led her own platoon."

Jason curled up his lips in disgust. "So she fucked some general and got herself made a second lieuy, so what?"

"I seriously doubt that," Sierra replied scathingly, "since she's a lesbian."

That stunned Jason into silence for a full minute. *A fuckin' dyke? What the fuck?* Lesbos weren't allowed in the Marines! He'd been hearing shit about that excuse for a president Obama looking at getting rid of "Don't Ask, don't Tell," but that meant the dyke had been lying to the Marines. It appalled Jason no end. It took him a full ten minutes to recover from the thoughts running around in his head. When he walked into the house, Sierra was cooking dinner. He leaned on the counter, looking at her.

"So how do you know she's a homo?" he asked crudely.

When she didn't answer, Jason moved to stand behind her. "I asked you a question," Jason said in a tight voice.

"She told me," she said. "Why?" he asked, his tone still a growl. "She hoping to fuck you?"

"Jesus, Jason!" Sierra said, glancing around. "Do you have to use that kind of language? I don't need a call from the school saying that Colby is talking like that now."

"So? Was she hoping to fuck you or not?" Jason asked, ignoring her whining.

"Contrary to popular belief," Sierra said condescendingly, "not all gays are depraved degenerates that will sleep with anything of the same sex."

Jason made a sound in the back of his throat. He didn't believe that shit for a second.

Later that night, he crawled into bed naked next to her, pressing his hard-on against her. He was ready for some action.

"Jason..." she sighed, shaking her head as she tried to read the brief she had in her hands.

"Put that shit down for a few," Jason said, pushing aside the brief and reaching for her hand. He guided it to his hard-on. "Do you know how much I missed fucking you?" He knew it bugged her when he talked like that. All the more reason! She was his wife, his property, and he'd fuck her whenever he wanted. If she didn't like it, too bad.

The next morning, Jason sat at the kitchen counter, reading the paper with his coffee, as Sierra bustled around the kitchen, getting ready and packing Colby's lunch. When Sierra told him she was leaving, Jason followed her out the Suburban now parked next to his driveway. He wanted to size up this fake Marine. The blonde was smoking, the driver's window open. Jason strolled over to the driver's side.

"So you're a bodyguard, huh?" he asked snidely.

"Yes," Kashena answered, flicking her cigar pointedly over his head.

Sierra got into the vehicle and glanced at Kashena, once again sorry she'd told Jason that Kashena was gay, knowing her husband had a big mouth. Naturally that was the next thing he asked.

"Sierra says you're a lesbo," Jason said. "That true?"

"Is that pertinent to my protecting your wife?" Kashena asked, raising an eyebrow at him. "Maybe," Jason replied, defensive because

245

she'd used some million-dollar word. Who did the bitch think she was? "How do I know you're not cruising her for a piece of ass?"

The blonde's look was icy as Jason waited for her response. He was feeling pretty good about his snappy response. *Take that, dyke!* He was, therefore, surprised when she didn't answer him; instead she put the Suburban in gear and turned the wheel, nearly clipping him in the process. He jumped back. He stared at the back of the vehicle as he watched the blonde drive away. *Fucking dyke!* was all he could think.

Having Jason home was proving to be even more hassle than either Kashena or Sierra could have realized. Kashena got to a point where she didn't want to have sex with Sierra if Sierra had been with Jason, so they instituted a forty-eight-hour rule, which meant that Kashena would only make love to Sierra if she hadn't been with Jason for forty-eight hours. Unfortunately that was harder than they'd figured; Jason was constantly pushing for sex. Things between the two women became untenable rather quickly, and Kashena wasn't sure what to do.

When Kashena couldn't take it anymore, she knew what she had to do. After work, she drove down to the river, parking the vehicle and getting out to walk.

Sierra knew that Kashena was fed up. She hadn't been able to avoid having sex with Jason over the last week, and that meant she and Kashena couldn't be together. She had no idea what Kashena was thinking, but she could tell by the look on Kashena's face that she was mad. Sierra stood next to the vehicle, watching Kashena stride down the path, smoking and generally looking pissed off. Sierra was nervous; she could sense things were coming to a head, and she had no idea how to stop them from doing so.

"This isn't going to work," Kashena said as she strode back to the SUV, confirming Sierra's fears. "I can't keep on like this."

"Kashena, please…" Sierra said, her tone pleading. "I know things are really hard right now, but I'm sure things will settle down with Jason soon. He's just… I mean, he was in the Middle East for so long…"

"You think he didn't fuck anything that wore a skirt there?" Kashena snapped.

Sierra felt sick immediately. She hadn't really thought about it, but to be confronted with it the way she just had was shocking. She couldn't think of anything to say in response to that question. Had she thought about that? No, but did it matter?

Before Sierra could formulate a response, though, Kashena shook her head and moved to the driver's side of the vehicle.

"Look," Kashena said then, "I thought I could deal with this, but I can't. So, we need to stop seeing each other."

"But…" Sierra began, getting into the vehicle as Kashena was doing, her mind reeling. She couldn't think—she needed this! "I mean, what about this? The protection part?" she asked, finally, stunned beyond reasoning.

"You don't have to worry about the protection part," she said, her tone icy. "I was going to tell you tonight—it's my understanding that Midnight has finally gotten your stalker picked up for just that. He won't be bothering you anymore. So you have no need of my *services* anymore."

Sierra didn't respond. She had no idea how to keep Kashena from leaving her. She wondered if she really had the right to even ask. After all, she was married; what right did she have to expect Kashena to stay with her? Sierra sat in the passenger seat, her mind churning, feeling a huge sense of loss. Part of her wanted to scream, cry, beg, but the reasonable side of her realized that Kashena had made up her mind.

When they stopped in front of the house, Sierra got out quietly, doing her best not to burst into tears, since Jason was in the front yard once again, beer in hand. Sierra moved past him, going into the house and closing the door softly. Inside, she went upstairs, took off her clothes, went into the bathroom and locked the door. She climbed into the shower. There she cried herself sick for what she'd just lost.

***

That night, Linda came home to find her bags packed. She practically stumbled over them when she walked into Kashena's bedroom.

"What's up with this?" she asked, motioning to the bags.

Kashena, who was sitting on her bed, smoking a cigar, looked back at her for a moment, then shrugged.

"I'm cleaning house today."

"Cleaning house?" Linda said sharply.

"Yeah," Kashena replied, her eyes like ice.

"So, you're leaving me for that lawyer?" Linda surmised.

"Nope," Kashena replied. "I broke it off with her too."

"So why are you doing this?"

"Let's just say I'm tired of being used," Kashena said, her words more telling than her tone, which was stone cold.

Linda couldn't think of a reply to that. She had been using Kashena, especially lately. Things between them had been over when

Kashena refused to marry her. Linda knew she'd lost then. So she'd been biding her time until she could meet up with one of her friends who would take her in. That hadn't happened yet, so this was not the time to let Kashena kick her out.

"Kash..." she said, putting on her best pout.

"Don't bother," Kashena said. "There's two hundred dollars in an envelope in that bag." She pointed to the black bag on top. "Use it and get out."

Linda's mouth dropped open at Kashena's attitude. She couldn't believe this was the same woman she'd had wrapped around her little finger just a year ago. Kashena had changed totally. A thrill went through her at Kashena's renewed strength. This time, Linda didn't want to leave her. Linda wanted her more than anything. It drove her crazy that she'd lost her, to a fucking lawyer, no less. Some married bitch lawyer!

Walking over to Kashena, her look seductive, she touched Kashena's shoulder.

"What if I promised never to stray again?" Linda said. "You're who I want to be with, Kashie, you know that..."

"Well, that's a damned shame for you, Linda," Kashena replied sardonically, "'cause I'm not interested."

Linda curled her hand into a fist. Kashena merely raised an eyebrow at her.

"I wouldn't trust my level of control at this point," Kashena said casually.

"With what? Wanting to hit me or fuck me?" Linda asked, her eyes glittering with excitement, though her look was haughty.

"I was thinking more along the lines of either killing you or just beating you senseless," Kashena replied coolly.

Linda stepped back involuntarily. This was not something she wanted to test. Moving back to the bags, she hastily picked up her things, looping both bags over her shoulders. She turned and looked back at Kashena.

"You're going to regret leaving me," Linda said confidently.

"Don't count on it," Kashena replied. "Oh, and leave my key on the dresser."

Linda did as Kashena told her, her movements angry. She left without another word. Kashena sat on her bed, smoking another cigar and staring at nothing. It was shaping up to be a shitty night.

***

Sebastian was lying on his couch when he heard his doorbell ring. Getting up, he pulled on a shirt and went to the door. He opened it to see Samantha standing there. She looked unhappy. Opening the door wider, he stepped back, allowing her to walk inside.

"What happened?" he asked as he followed her back to the couch.

Samantha shook her head as she sat down.

"Nothing really," she said. "I did ask Jeffrey to go to marriage counseling—he asked what we needed counseling about." She looked up, her eyes searching his face. "I couldn't even think of a decent answer, Sebastian."

"Maybe you can tell him that it's just to deal with things going on in your own head."

"Actually, he suggested that I needed to get a better grip on myself," she said, sounding irritated.

"So he thinks you need counseling, but not him."

"Right."

"Well, maybe it wouldn't hurt to talk to someone." He held his hands up in a defensive gesture when her head snapped up. "I'm just saying, you love the guy. Maybe you need to figure out why you're so unhappy now."

Samantha sighed unhappily. "That's just it, Sebastian. I don't know if I've ever really loved him."

"You married him, didn't you?"

"Yes, but that doesn't mean I ever loved him. Women get married for many reasons."

"Well, you weren't pregnant, right?"

"No," she said, giving him a scathing look.

"Then why did you marry him?"

She was silent for a few moments, then shook her head. "I guess because I honestly believed we had a lot in common. I didn't realize, until recently, that what we had in common was his opinion on everything."

Sebastian grimaced. "That was it?"

"Well, our families were all for the idea. He's from a good family, and my parents always believed in marrying well."

Sebastian curled his lip in distaste at that statement. "Okay, so you didn't love him," he said, shrugging.

"Well, I thought I did." She bit her lip.

"Thought?"

"Until recently," she said, looking more cautious.

"Why?" His tone was as searching as his eyes were.

She touched his arm. "Because I think…"

"Don't say it, Sam," he said sternly.

Her eyes stared up into his. "Why?"

"Because you don't," he said. "You feel a lot right now because of what happened in San Francisco. It's not real, Samantha. It's an illusion. It's a perception of being safe, and that makes you think it's real. It's not."

"How do you know? she asked him, her tone pleading.

"Because I know," Sebastian said. "And I'm not going to have you throwing away your marriage for something that isn't what you think it is, Sam."

"My marriage isn't what I thought it was," she said, her voice settling into what Sebastian would call her "lawyer" tone. "It's for that reason that I'm considering throwing it away. The feelings I have for you are totally separate from that."

"Are they?" Sebastian asked cynically.

"Yes," she answered, her voice sure. "I felt a lot for you before I watched you gunned down before my eyes."

Sebastian raised his chin, a wary look on his face. "But you know the kind of man I am, Samantha. Why would you want to put any kind of hope on me?"

She didn't have a ready answer for that. Yes, she knew he was a man who didn't stay with one woman for long. He toyed with women, in a way that had previously infuriated her. However, now, she wanted that; she wanted his attention. The problem was, could she handle his rejection later, if and when—and it was likely to be *when*, rather than *if*—it came to that? She didn't know, but she knew she wanted to find out. There was too much there not to try.

"I guess I'd have to take my chances like the rest of the women on this continent have." She gave him a mischievous smile.

"The whole continent?" he asked, grinning.

"At least."

He narrowed his eyes at her; she laughed softly. "I'll have you know I've been on other continents, too," he told her, his grin turning devilish.

Her mouth dropped open in amused shock.

That was when he kissed her, his hand cupping her cheek, his lips on hers. She found herself pressing against him immediately. The kiss was soft at first but deepened quickly as she wrapped her arms around his neck, pressing even closer. His hands went to her back, gathering her closer still. She moaned softly as the thumb that had been stroking her cheek touched the corner of her mouth, parting her lips. His tongue slid between her lips, smoothing over her upper lip, then licking at her lower lip, making her shudder at the sheer erotic feel of it.

"Sebastian…" she murmured, wanting so much, all right then.

He moved forward, his hands on her back, and laid her back onto the couch, his body over hers but supported on his elbows. Samantha felt him pressing against her in all the right places, the places that were already aching for him. Her nails slid down his back, eliciting a moan from him, as well as increased pressure against her.

They kissed for a long time; he kept her body at the very peak of excitement. At one point his body left hers, and she literally cried out, thinking that he was changing his mind again. He kneeled next to her, then picked her up in his arms and carried her to his bedroom.

Sebastian was damned if the first time they were together was going to be in as uncomfortable a place as his couch. It nagged in his mind that location had never bothered him before. But Samantha was a bit different to him. He had been her protector; it had ingrained in him the ideal that she was to be treated gently. Even if she had him going crazy with her little moans, sighs and surprised reactions to his touch.

That only got worse when he slowly removed her clothes. Her sense of wonder and awe was written all over her face and in every sound she made. Jesus, how inept was Jeffrey Cobb? Was the man a complete fool? She had the body of a goddess, something he'd been convinced of since the first time he'd seen her in her pajamas. She was slim and petite, but with just enough curves to her to make her soft and feminine. His hands traced the outline of her body repeatedly; his lips followed shortly after that.

Samantha was in complete ecstasy. It all made sense now, all the women who flocked to him. Somehow they knew this about him; somehow they sensed it and craved him, as she was craving him at that moment. Never before had she been touched so much before making love. Jeffrey was very clinical about sex, and she'd only had one other lover before Jeffrey and he'd been as young and inexperienced as she. It felt like Sebastian was revering her, not just making love to her.

There was no denying the exquisite sensations she was experiencing, and she was vocal about them. That fact surprised her—she was never vocal with Jeffrey. Early on in their relationship, Jeffrey had told her that only whores make a lot of noise during sex. She had no idea that her moans, gasps, screams and sighs were playing hell with Sebastian's iron control.

She had no fewer than three orgasms before his body finally claimed her totally.

Sebastian was holding on tightly to his control, but sliding inside her almost made him lose that.

Jesus, Jeffrey really is a pencil dick, isn't he? Samantha was so tight around him that he could barely breathe, that combined with the sounds of pure unadulterated pleasure Samantha was making. It took everything he had not to let go then. Rolling so she was on top of him,

Sebastian guided her hips over him. Within moments she was coming again, and he allowed himself release as well, increasing the intensity of her own orgasm.

Afterwards she lay against him, both of them panting to catch their breath. His hands on her back held her against him. As almost an afterthought, he pulled the hair tie out of the long braid she wore. Sliding his fingers between the sections of the braid, he loosened it, shaking her hair out of its confines. Her fiery hair fell around his body in silken waves. He felt her smile against his shoulder.

"Just had to do that, didn't you?"

"Yep," he replied simply.

They said nothing for a few more minutes, each lost in their own thoughts. Then Samantha lifted her head, looking down at him.

"Should you have been doing this much already?"

Sebastian looked at her for a second, then laughed out loud. "Well, this is a helluva time to think of that, Sam," he said, grinning, "but I'm sure it's fine."

"Didn't the doctor say you were supposed to be taking it easy?"

"This was taking it easy, Sam," he said, his ocean-green eyes twinkling.

Her eyes widened. "You mean…"

"Yeah," he said with a smirk.

"Oh my," she said, sounding both young and proper at the same time. She was silent for a while, obviously thinking about what he'd just said. "So you're at least this good, all the time?"

Sebastian laughed. "I don't know what you consider 'good' but"—he shrugged—"I was actually a little bit out of control this time."

"Out of control?" She was surprised that she'd even started this conversation, but as usual with him, she was comfortable talking about anything.

"Well," he said, putting a fingertip to her lips, "you really tested my self-control."

"I did?" she asked, looking shocked.

He canted his head slightly, trying to decide if her shock was contrived. It didn't look it at all.

"You have no idea what you were doing, do you?"

"I wasn't doing anything," she said. "You were the one doing wondrous things to me that had never been done before."

That left him speechless for a moment.

"I'm guessing Jeffrey isn't, ah, a good lover?"

"I don't really know that what he does could be considered being a lover," she said, surprising herself with her candor.

"Oh." Sebastian's expression indicated his disgust for any man who couldn't hold his own in that department. "The office isn't the only place he uses a pencil either, is it?"

Samantha stared at him, perplexed by his comment. Just then, as if to make his point, she felt him harden inside her again.

"Ohh," she said, closing her eyes as excitement started in her again. "Well, no, no it's not."

They made love again. Sebastian was more "in control" this time, which proved to be a very, very good thing. Samantha didn't think she'd had as many orgasms in her lifetime as she had with him that evening.

Later, as they lay half asleep, their bodies still intertwined, he looked over at her.

"You do realize this means you've cheated on him now—you know that, right?"

"No," she replied simply.

"No, you don't know that?"

"No, I haven't cheated on him."

"Explain," he said.

"I filed for a legal separation today. He should be served tomorrow."

"And you couldn't have told me that earlier?"

Samantha smiled. "I didn't want to push you."

"I see," he said, a smile on his own face too.

They fell asleep much the same as they had many nights before, his body wrapped protectively around hers. Samantha found that sleeping next to him naked was even nicer than with both of them wearing clothes. She smiled as she fell into a deep, sated sleep.

CHAPTER 12

The next phase had taken so much coordination. Would anyone ever appreciate the intricacies of what he'd done for them? Would they understand how difficult it had been to stay silent during such trying times? Would they grasp that what he'd done had taken the intelligence she'd foolishly underestimated? They all underestimated him. Some would be sorry; others might be forgiven—he wasn't sure yet. He perhaps needed some of them to rebuild what she'd destroyed, but maybe once that was done he could seek his revenge. In the end, they'd all be sorry, so sorry. Very soon now, it would begin.

***

"I want you to stay," Sable said, her tone sure.

Cat lifted her head to glance up at the older woman. "Stay?"

"Yes," Sable said, touching her under the chin, stroking her jawline. "Stay here, with me."

Cat lowered her head, kissing Sable's skin. "I can't do that. You know that," she said softly.

"Why?" Sable asked entreatingly. "You don't have to work, Catalina. I can take care of you."

Cat rolled to her back, looking up at Sable as she did.

"I don't need to be taken care of, Sable," Cat said, her voice serious.

They'd been together for weeks at this point. Cat knew she was hiding from her life, and she needed to return to it at some point. The last thing she wanted, however, was to be a groupie for Sable Sands. Cat told Sable that she needed to get back home. Sable rallied, asking Cat to stay with her until the Pride parade in San Francisco in less than two weeks' time.

"San Francisco, huh?" Cat asked.

"Yes," Sable said. "Please come with me. It's a really beautiful city, and I could show you the sights."

"I've seen the sights," Cat said, grinning.

"No, I mean the ones that normal tourists don't see," Sable insisted. "Like the Castro District," she added, naming the biggest gay community in San Francisco.

"I spent my entire childhood in the Castro District, Sable."

"What?" Sable said, shocked.

"I grew up in San Francisco, born and raised there."

"Really?" Sable asked, surprised by this.

"Yep," Cat said. "My mother still lives there."

"In the Castro District?"

"She's a lesbian," Cat explained.

"Really?" Sable asked again.

"Yes, really." Cat chuckled at the look on Sable's face.

"Well, then maybe you can show me around," Sable said, winking.

***

"They want you to what?" Rick asked.

"Speak at the Gay Pride parade in San Francisco," Midnight repeated.

"Oh great," Rick said, rolling his eyes. "I'll never get you back."

Midnight laughed. "I don't think anyone would accost me, Rick. I'm not anyone's type there."

"I wouldn't be too sure," Rick said. "Kana says you're a fantasy of a lot of gay women at this point."

"Yes, well, as much as I love Kana," Midnight said with a smile, "I have this thing for a certain man, so…"

"Let's just keep it that way, huh?" He put his arms around her waist and pulled her to him.

"Oh yes, let's," she said, smiling up at him.

He leaned down to kiss her; her hands were in his hair moments later as the kiss turned passionate.

"Should we leave?" Kana asked from the doorway to Midnight's office.

"Yes," Rick said, his eyes on Midnight.

"No," Midnight said, grinning at her husband.

"Overruled again, Debenshire," Tiny said as he and Kana walked in and sat down.

Rick smiled all the same. "Happens a lot."

"Does not," Midnight said.

Rick kissed her on the lips again. "I'll see you tonight, love."

"Okay," she said with a smile.

"You two," he said, pointing at Kana and Tiny, "keep her safe till then, huh?"

"We'll see what we can do," Tiny said.

Kana grinned. "Maybe."

"Uh-huh," Rick said, grinning back. "Later, you two."

"Bye," Kana and Tiny said together.

After Rick left, Kana turned to Midnight. "So did I hear correctly? You're speaking at the Pride parade?"

"They've asked me to."

"But you haven't answered them yet?" Kana asked.

"No," Midnight said. "I wanted to talk to my security detail about it first."

"Why?" Tiny asked.

"Because I need to know if you two will feel comfortable—"

"Around gays?" Kana asked, raising an eyebrow at Midnight.

"Protecting me around that many people," Midnight continued as if Kana hadn't interrupted. She gave Kana a pointed look. "Are you ever going to have faith in me, K? I accept the gay lifestyle just like any other lifestyle. Why do you keep waiting for me to change my mind?"

Kana let her breath out in a sigh. "I'm sorry, Night, you're right. I just… Palani and I had to deal with a little bit of attitude yesterday in a restaurant. It's not your fault."

"So quit taking it out on her," Tiny put in.

Kana glared at Tiny; he glared back.

"Okay, no fighting, kids," Midnight said with a broad smile. "I need to know your honest thoughts here. Kana, have you ever been to this Pride parade? It's big, isn't it?"

"It's huge in San Francisco," Kana said.

"Will it be safe, me speaking there?"

"That would depend on the security they'll already have in place."

"We could do some checking," Tiny said.

"Great." Midnight smiled. "Do that and get back to me. Can you have an answer for me today? I really need to make a commitment one way or the other soon."

"Will do, boss," Tiny said.

***

"Nothing seemed to help," Rick said, shaking his head.

Midnight rested her head on his shoulder. "You did your best."

They were in bed and talking about their days, as they almost always did when she was home. It was their way of staying connected. It had been difficult for Rick, years before, to have Midnight gone a lot, so Midnight wanted to make sure that they never got disconnected again. They were discussing Elizabeth; Rick had gone to see his niece and tried to talk to her, but it hadn't seemed to do any good.

"I just don't feel like I got anywhere with her," Rick said. "And I'm not exactly the one to talk to her about this anyway."

"Why?"

"She brought up my own mistake in being in the wrong place at the wrong time, with the wrong person." The last was said pointedly.

Midnight stared back at him. Then understanding dawned.

"Jesus, she brought that up?" she asked, stunned.

"Yeah," Rick said, looking contrite.

"Richard," Midnight said softly as she touched his cheek, propping herself up on her elbows to look down at him, "she had no right to pull that on you. What happened between you and me that long ago doesn't excuse what she did. It's not a contest."

"I know," he said. "I think she's just really depressed right now and looking to hurt whoever she can."

Midnight nodded, not pleased that Elizabeth had sought to hurt Rick. He had stood up for Elizabeth time and again with her father. Rick, of all people, deserved Elizabeth's loyalty. It irritated Midnight that in her pain she'd attacked him.

"She thought we were mad at her," Rick said, unaware of the direction of Midnight's thoughts.

"Well, I am now," Midnight said.

"Babe…" Rick pleaded.

"No, Rick, it's bullshit that she wanted to hurt you just because she fucked up her own relationship."

"She didn't really know it would hurt me."

"Bullshit!" Midnight exclaimed. "Everyone who knows you knows how much that part of our lives hurts you. She knew what she was doing, and it wasn't fair of her."

"Okay, I'll give you that," Rick said, "but it doesn't matter, babe. She's hurting, and I'm worried about her."

Midnight nodded, still unwilling to let go of her irritation. "So what do you want to do?"

"I think I'll have Susan go and check on her every so often. She won't see Susan as so much of a threat."

"Yeah, that might work."

Rick knew that Midnight was still angry at his niece, but he couldn't really fault her for that. She loved him, and didn't like anyone who hurt him purposely. It would be the same if anyone hurt Midnight, so it was easy for him to understand.

***

Jason didn't know what the hell was wrong with his wife, but she was being a major bitch all of a sudden, and worse still she was holding out on him. When he turned on his charm, pressing up against her in the kitchen one night, she snapped at him in what he called her high-and-mighty voice.

"Jesus, Jason!" she gasped in a harsh whisper. "Colby is in the other room!"

"So?" he said, not understanding the problem. "I'm leaving for Twentynine Palms in a little while. I'll be gone for two full days… I need something before I go." He found that her resistance was actually turning him on.

But then Sierra turned around, looking him square in the eye. "Stop," she told him.

What the fuck? Who was she kidding?

"And if I don't?" he asked, his tone amused.

"Jason, just—"

"When's dinner ready?" Colby asked as he ran into the room.

Sierra stepped back from Jason, turning to her son.

"Soon, babe," she said, smiling. "In fact, why don't you come here and wash up? Then you can set the table."

"Okay!" Colby said excitedly.

Jason narrowed his eyes at her but said nothing. He went to finish packing, thinking she'd better get with the program. He'd received orders to report to Twentynine Palms, and eventually they'd be moving there permanently. She was going to have to get a job down in Los Angeles. *Probably better anyway,* he thought to himself. *She needs to get away from that Chevalier cunt.* Jason thought that Midnight Chevalier was a mouthy bitch who needed to be put back in her place. If he were her husband, he'd have slapped that twat down by now. Obviously her husband didn't know how to handle uppity bitches.

He knew what he'd do to shut Chevalier up, he thought with a leer.. Thinking of that reminded him that he needed a good servicing from his bitch of a wife too, show her who was boss. In the end though, Sierra avoided him, till it was too late. Jason made a mental note to handle that business when he got back into town.

***

Kashena wasn't sure what she was doing. She'd been going insane at home, so she'd come out to the bar. Unfortunately, that had resulted in running in to Linda, and now Linda was doing her best to seduce her from the dance floor. Right about the time Kashena had decided it was time to leave, Sierra walked in and came straight up to her.

"We need to talk," Sierra said.

"Excuse me," Linda inserted, moving toward Sierra.

Kashena didn't look away from Sierra, only holding her hand up to stop Linda's forward motion. Emotions were running through her—seeing Sierra again was both exciting and, in a way, terrifying. It had taken everything Kashena had not to seek out the other woman; Kashena had spent a lot of time at the gym to avoid doing just that. Now here she was... She looked beautiful, and smelled amazing.

"Let's go outside." Kashena told Sierra, knowing she was losing her iron-clad control.

Outside, Kashena lit a cigar, leaning against the wall, looking for all intents and purposes calm. That didn't last long when Sierra kissed her with so much sweetness that Kashena caved instantly.

When their lips parted, Sierra whispered, "I'm sorry. I love you. Please forgive me."

That ended all of Kashena's pretense of being unaffected. She took Sierra's hand and led her to the Impala.

Minutes later they were at Kashena's house, where they kissed again, and they spent the next two hours exulting in being together again. Afterwards they discussed what had broken them up in the first place. Sierra admitted that the only reason she'd been having sex with Jason was because she didn't want to fight with him. While Kashena agreed about not fighting him, Sierra was determined to prove to Kashena that she didn't want Jason.

***

Jason couldn't believe what was going on. His wife was trying to withhold sex from him! He'd noticed that she was more icy than normal, ever since he'd started commuting to Twentynine Palms, but at least she'd been giving in. Now all of sudden she was too "busy," telling him that she needed to get some report done. Why did he fucking care?

"Well, I need something too," he told her, grabbing at her tits from behind.

She turned her chair around, knocking his arms away with its high back. "I said I'm busy right now," she said, her tone haughty. "You're just going to have to survive without me for a night."

"Bullshit," Jason said, his tone darkening. "Your shit can wait. I've been gone for three days, and I want to fuck. Got it?"

Sierra stood up, not looking at him.

"Is that what I am to you?" she asked him evenly.

"What?" Jason replied, surprised by the question.

"Am I just something to be fucked and used?"

Jason glowered at her. *What the fuck is this shit?*

"You're my wife." he said flatly.

"Yes, but nowhere in the marriage contract does it require me to fuck you whenever you feel like it," she snapped.

"What is this?" he said suspiciously. "You think you're going to start holding out on me now?"

"I think I'm going to start having some say as to when we have sex," Sierra said.

"Tell ya what," he said, taking a menacing step forward and grabbing her wrists. "You can say where we fuck."

"Jason, no!" she yelled, trying to pull away from him, but his grip was like iron around her wrists.

He was going to fuck his wife. She didn't like it, tough shit.

The minute it was over, Jason went off to take a shower. Sierra sat back down in her office chair, shaking as she did her best to straighten her clothes. Something inside of her snapped. She couldn't do this anymore. She grabbed her keys and left the house, crying all the way to Kashena's house.

***

"I'm leaving him tomorrow," Sierra whispered to Kashena.

"I'm coming with you," was Kashena's reply.

Sierra kissed Kashena's neck, then moved her lips to Kashena's ear.

"I love you," she whispered softly.

Kashena kissed Sierra's temple. "I love you too, honey."

They fell asleep, Kashena holding Sierra.

***

Jason was working in his backyard that afternoon. Colby had wanted to help, so Jason showed him how to use the edger. He knew that Sierra would probably bitch at him about it, because she thought everything was too dangerous for their son to do. In Jason's mind, hard work never hurt anyone. His father had taught him how to do yard work when he was a kid, younger than Colby was at ten. Sure, his dad had beaten the crap out of him for screwing up a few times, when the

267

mow lines on the lawn weren't perfect. *At least I don't beat my kid.* Jason figured that made him better than his old man.

They'd finished up and were headed into the house when he noticed the black Suburban was parked in front of the house. Jason curled his lips in irritation. The bitch had disappeared the night before; now he figured he could guess where she'd gone. Walking up the stairs, Jason could barely contain his anger. So she was sleeping with the dyke now? *We'll just see about that.*

Walking into the bedroom, he didn't notice Kashena—his attention was on Sierra and the suitcase she was closing.

"What do you think you're doing?" he snapped.

"Leaving," Sierra said simply, turning to him. "I'm leaving you, leaving this house and leaving this marriage."

Jason was stunned. *What the fuck?* She actually thought she was leaving him? Colby came bounding into the room then.

"Mom!" he said, excitedly, "I got to use the edger thingy and—" He stopped as he saw the suitcase. "Where you going?" he asked, assuming she was going on a business trip.

"We're going," Sierra told Colby. "Why don't you go pack some clothes for the next few days at school, and I'll—"

Oh, fuck no. Jason stepped forward and backhanded Sierra. There was no way she was leaving him and taking his kid!

"Stupid cunt! Think you can take my son, think you can leave me" he yelled, "I'll fucking—" he began as he brought his fist up.

Suddenly, in one move Kashena grabbed his fist and twisted his arm up and behind his back, and then, turning, slammed him into the nearest wall face first.

"You won't do anything else," Kashena said to Jason, glancing down at Sierra.

Colby, who'd screamed when his father hit his mother, was down on the floor next to Sierra, holding on to her in complete terror.

"Let me go, you fucking dyke bitch!" Jason yelled. He was struggling to get a hand free. He'd show the dyke a thing or two. He couldn't believe how strong the woman was; he couldn't break her hold.

"Not gonna happen," Kashena said. "So calm down before I break your arm." Jason felt his arm being lifted. He let out a yell in spite of himself. He stopped moving then, wondering if she really could break his arm.

"Sierra," Kashena was saying, "get on the phone, call 911 and have them send out a black-and-white. Colby, I need you to do what your mom asked you to, okay? It's okay, your mom's okay, but you need to get your things. Can you do that for me?"

Jason couldn't believe it. His son, his baby boy, was listening to the dyke bitch! Colby left the room to do what she'd told him to, and Sierra was making the phone call.

"What the fuck do you think you're gonna do?" Jason taunted. "Think you're gonna arrest me, bitch?"

"No, I think the officers that arrive in the black-and-white are going to arrest you," Kashena said calmly. "I'm just going to tell them what I witnessed, and show them your wife's cut lip and bruised face."

"She won't press charges," Jason said confidently. Sierra wouldn't want to cause a scene, he knew that.

"She doesn't have to, moron," Kashena said. "In this state, the cops only need to see evidence of domestic violence. And I can assure you, considering who your wife is and who she works for, the DA will be happy to take your ass to court for it. You just made a big mistake, pal. A very big mistake."

In desperation, Jason started to struggle again. She couldn't be right! But part of him was terrified that she was. He finally managed to get an arm loose; turning, he grabbed the dyke by the throat, using his superior strength to lift her off the ground. He wanted to kill her. How dare she try to take what was his? Feeling triumphant, he started to squeeze, waiting to feel the crack of her windpipe. So intent on killing the blonde cop, he never expected the knee to the groin. Pain shot through every part of his body; he dropped Kashena and doubled over to protect himself. Her fist slammed into his jaw, he saw stars, and then everything went black

Jason woke slowly. His jaw hurt like hell. He tried to reach up to rub his face; that's when he realized his arms were behind him, and he felt the cold metal of handcuffs around his wrists. Suddenly he realized he was lying on his side on the floor, the rug under his cheek.

He heard people talking, then he heard the blonde cop. "So you've got him for domestic violence," Kashena was telling the officers. Someone hauled him to his feet again, and he could see that Kashena was looking at him. "And you can add assault on a peace officer to that too."

"You fucking bitch!" he screamed in futility. "Fucking dyke bitch. Come into my house, think you can beat me up? I have rights!"

"Yes," Kashena said as they came face to face. "You have the right to remain silent, and if you're fucking smart you will," she said, her voice deep and threatening.

With that the officers took Jason away. It didn't stop him from screaming threats and obscenities all the way to the squad car.

CHAPTER 13

Now, now was the time. He was finally ready; everything was in place. Just a couple more days, then it would all be set in motion. He could barely contain his excitement. Soon that bitch would get what she deserved. She'd learn quickly never to underestimate him. Never underestimate the master, little girl, never.

***

Sable and Cat arrived at San Francisco International Airport the night before the Pride events began. They were met by the paparazzi; Cat did her best to avoid the pictures, not wanting her image appearing in papers and tabloids. That was not an easy feat. It took a while to get through the melee, and Cat was stunned when she found out that Sable had purchased a new SUV, which had been brought to the airport by the dealer.

"Don't tell me you just bought an SUV to drive around San Francisco in," Cat said, as Sable handed the porter the keys so he could load their luggage in the back. "You know they have rental agencies that rent out luxury cars?"

Sable only shrugged, smiling at Cat. Cat rolled her eyes. Even so, she checked out the vehicle, while studiously ignoring the men with the cameras behind her. It was habit now.

The SUV was a Porsche Cayenne, their answer to the sports utility vehicle trend. It was nice, Cat had to say that—Sable had excellent taste. Naturally, Sable had gotten top of the line, the Turbo model, which held a 4.5-liter, 8-cylinder engine that put out 450 horsepower. A very powerful engine indeed. Starting at $90,000, it should be. Sable had chosen the blue with the steel-gray leather interior.

When the porter had finished putting the bags in the vehicle, he went to hand the keys back to Sable. Sable shook her head.

"Give them to my girlfriend, please," she said, handing the man a hundred-dollar bill.

The porter tipped his hat to her, and then walked around the vehicle and handed Cat the keys.

Cat looked around the vehicle at Sable.

"It's your town," Sable said, smiling. "You drive."

Later, in the Castro, the LGBTQ-friendly area of San Francisco, they met Cat's mother, Melanie Roché, who happened to be a huge fan of Sable's. The meeting went well—until, while Cat was in the ladies room, Sable and Melanie made the mistake of discussing what had happened to break Cat and Elizabeth up.

Melanie pointedly changed the subject as she saw Cat heading for the table. "So you're performing at the Pride parade?"

Sable picked up the cue. "Yeah, tomorrow night."

Cat narrowed her eyes at her mother, knowing that she was covering.

"How long ago did this show get booked?" Cat asked, as if just joining the conversation.

"About three months ago, I think," Sable said. "But I'm almost always here for the parade. Why?"

Cat looked at her mother again. "Nice try, Mother. You would have known about Sable being here long before now."

"Why do you say that?" Melanie asked, knowing she was caught.

"Because you're one of her biggest fans, and you know whenever she's going to be in California at all. Remember you called me and begged me to get you tickets to her San Diego show while I was in college? And when I forgot, you wouldn't speak to me for a month."

Melanie rolled her eyes. "I don't think it was a whole month."

"At least a month," Cat said.

"You're exaggerating."

"And you're covering your ass," Cat countered, then looked at Sable. "She asked you what happened with Bet, right?"

Sable didn't say anything, shooting Melanie a glance.

"Well, it was obvious you weren't going to tell me," Melanie said, her tone hurt.

"Because I didn't want to relive it to tell you, Mother," Cat said sharply.

"So," Sable said, putting her hand on Cat's hand, "now she knows and you didn't have to relive it."

Cat looked at Sable, her expression displeased. Sable removed her hand. Turning to the bartender, she ordered another shot. The evening was over shortly thereafter. Cat dropped Sable off at the hotel, telling her that she was going for a drive. Sable didn't look happy about it, but nodded and walked inside. Cat gunned the powerful motor and headed for the Wharf, where she'd spent a lot of time as a child.

***

In the hotel room, Sable paced as Jake sat on the couch watching her. He was surprised by his boss's attachment to Catalina Roché. He personally liked the blond narcotics officer; she was a very definite departure from Sable's usual type. Catalina was smart, strong willed, and certainly not awed by Sable's rock-star status. She also wasn't interested in how much money Sable would spend on her. It was unfortunate, however, that Catalina didn't seem to be swayed by Sable's declarations of commitment. Jake wondered if this was going to be the first time Sable got her heart broken.

The phone in the room rang, and Sable strode over to it, snatching it up off the cradle.

"Cat?" she said breathlessly.

There was silence on the other end of the line, then an English-accented voice said, "Actually, that's who I'm looking for."

Sable knew instantly that this was Elizabeth Endicott, and she couldn't believe the woman's audacity in calling her hotel room. Who did she think she was?

"Well, that's too bad, isn't it?" Sable sneered.

Elizabeth sighed. "Can I just speak to her, please? I'll come up there if I have to."

"She's not here." Sable curled her lips in annoyance on her end, frustrated that she was in this position. Irritated more that Elizabeth Endicott had actually had the nerve to assume that Catalina wanted to see her!

"Where is she?"

"What business is it of yours?" Sable snapped.

"I flew all the way to see her, so I don't believe it's out of the realm of reason that I inquire as to her whereabouts." Elizabeth's aristocratic tone was haughty and infuriating at the same time.

"Well, you came a long way for nothing," Sable said. "And you shouldn't have wasted your time." With that she slammed down the phone and began pacing again, this time much more furiously.

Jake sighed inwardly. It was going to be a long night, apparently.

***

Cat walked into the hotel lobby, intent on talking to Sable about her feelings and trying to get things on a more even keel for them.

Then she saw her. Elizabeth, standing in the lobby, looking straight at her.

"Catalina…" Elizabeth began.

Cat stopped dead in her tracks. This wasn't happening. Why was Elizabeth here? How? Cat didn't want to know. Shaking her head, she turned on her heel and walked out of the hotel and down the street.

"Cat, wait! Please!" Elizabeth called, trying to catch up to Cat.

Catalina just shook her head again, continuing to stride away from Elizabeth. *I'm not ready for this, I'm not ready for this,* she kept telling herself.

She was just about to turn around and tell Elizabeth to leave her the hell alone when she heard her scream. Cat spun around, reaching for the gun at the small of her back. But she was knocked down, her gun clattering to the ground. She hit her head hard on the pavement, but even then she rolled to her side, reaching for her dropped weapon and grabbing it. Glancing back toward the hotel, she saw a man shoving Elizabeth into a van. Cat squinted at the license plate on the van as her vision started to blur and she started feeling lightheaded. Someone was calling her name; it seemed like the voice came from far away. She managed to read four numbers on the license plate on the van before blackness overtook her.

***

275

"It's too friggin' early for this," Tiny growled as they pulled into the San Diego Airport terminal area.

"I know, I know," Midnight said, "but they want me there for the start, and I didn't want to leave last night. I'm sorry, guys."

"Look," Kana said, smacking Tiny on the back of the head, "you made her feel guilty now. Happy?"

"Ouch!" Tiny exclaimed, scowling at Kana.

Kana scowled right back at him.

"Settle down," Midnight said from the back seat, making them both grin.

Minutes later they were in the terminal. Kana was with Midnight, waiting to check their bags and show their gun letters. Tiny was standing to the side with the bags, waiting for them to get up to the front, watchful as always. Kana was looking at their tickets, making sure she had everything together. She always endeavored to make Midnight's travel as easy as possible.

"Couldn't get Sinclair's plane for this one, huh?" Kana asked.

"He's using it," Midnight said with a grin. "He and Randy went to Tahoe for the weekend."

"Lucky them," Kana said, grinning too.

"We'll get some time off soon," Midnight said, knowing they'd been working hard again. After everything had happened with Cat, it had put Midnight off schedule with all she wanted to do, so they'd been traveling almost non-stop since then. It was starting to wear on all of them.

"I know," Kana said, as her cell phone rang. Pulling out her phone, she answered, "Sorbinno." It was obvious she was confused as she listened, holding up her hand. "Rick, Rick, hold up, what are you talking about? She's right here, she's fine… Here," she said, handing Midnight her cell phone.

276

Midnight looked perplexed. Kana shrugged.

Midnight took the phone. "Rick?"

"They said—" Rick began, but the phone cut out and she missed the next few words; the next word she heard was "hospital."

"What?" Midnight asked, confused. "Wait, Rick, I can't hear you. Hold on…" she said as she stepped around the poles that blocked off the lines for check-in. She started walking toward the glass doors that led outside the terminal.

Kana had just gotten to the front of the line. She glanced back to see Midnight walking toward the doors to the terminal, still trying to get a signal.

"Go get her," she told Tiny, but Tiny was already headed in that direction. Kana turned back and caught movement out of the corner of her eye. Then she saw someone reach up in front of her face. Something wet hit her eyes as she pulled her gun and yelled for Tiny.

Tiny, however, didn't hear her, because he was busy running for the door. He'd seen a flash of metal from the window of a car parked in front of the terminal. He saw Midnight pause, dropping the phone, and then lurch as the first bullet hit her in the shoulder. Tiny dove through the doors, trying to get to her, but the second bullet hit her in the midsection. The third hit him as he grabbed Midnight, pulling her to him and covering her body with his.

People were screaming everywhere around them. The car screeched away. Tiny looked up in time to catch the make, model and color of the car, but he barely caught a glimpse of the plate.

Looked around him, he saw airport security running toward him.

"Get an ambulance, now! The AG has been shot!" he bellowed, then looked back toward the terminal and saw Kana slumped on the floor. "Fuck!" he yelled. He couldn't be two places at once—it was his partner or Midnight. "In there!" he shouted at the second officer running up. "Officer down—call it in now!"

It was a nightmare, and Tiny was praying he'd wake up soon, but it didn't end.

***

Two hours later, the chaos was worse, not better. Rick and Mikeyla were missing; no one knew where they were. Midnight had been shot twice, Tiny once, and Kana had been sprayed with something that had knocked her out cold. There'd been an intruder at Dave and Susan's house, one Dave had scared off, fortunately. They were frantically trying to contact Elizabeth—there was obviously a hit out on Midnight's family.

Joe and Randy flew back from Tahoe, and the calls started going out.

***

In Sacramento, Kashena was just getting up, moving to kiss Sierra good morning, when the vision hit. She jerked her head back as if she'd been struck, sucking in her breath sharply as the pictures flashed in and out of her mind.

Sierra watched, her hand on Kashena's leg, her eyes worried. When Kashena relaxed again, lying back on the bed, Sierra looked down at her.

"Are you okay?"

Kashena nodded, breathing shallowly as the headache started. She put her hand to her forehead and rubbed it.

"Was that a vision?" Sierra asked, recognizing the pained look on Kashena's face.

Kashena nodded again.

"Hold on," Sierra said, getting off the bed and going to Kashena's medicine cabinet.

Ten minutes later, she brought Kashena tea laced with the herbs from the healer and sugar. Kashena drank it gratefully.

"I need to call Baz," she said, reaching for the phone.

"Why? Was it about him?"

"No, the AG. Something's wrong," Kashena said.

Sierra handed Kashena the phone as Kashena got up and started pacing.

The story had led the news that morning. Sebastian answered his phone, knowing it was her.

"We need to go to San Diego," he said.

"I know," Kashena said, already heading for her closet to get her suitcase. "I'll meet you at the airport in an hour."

"See you there."

***

When Sebastian and Kashena arrived at the hospital, there was a skirmish over who should be protecting the Attorney General. To Kashena and Sebastian's way of thinking, it was their responsibility, but to Midnight's extended law enforcement family, these two were newcomers and had no place there. Fortunately, Kyle stepped into the fray to defuse the situation.

"I'm Kyle Masterson," he said, extending his hand first to Kashena. "Chief of San Diego PD. And you are?"

"Special Agent Supervisor Kashena Marshal," she said, shaking his hand.

"Special Agent Supervisor Sebastian Bach," Sebastian said, looking calmer.

"Good to meet you both," Kyle said. "Sorry about that reception you got," he said, indicating the four men standing together down the hall. "We're all on edge right now. Midnight, Kana, and Tiny are family to us."

"We're just trying to do our job," Sebastian said.

"I understand that," Kyle said. "But when Midnight's extended family consists of almost nothing but cops, you can believe she's being protected."

Sebastian nodded, looking undaunted.

"Baz!" Kashena said, knowing her partner saw only duty at this point. "Relax, will ya? We're here, and we're going to do what we need to do to make sure she's safe. Okay?"

Sebastian looked at her, his eyes on hers as she gave him a pointed look. Finally he nodded.

"Now," Kashena went on, looking at Kyle. "How are they doing?"

"Fine," Kyle said. "Midnight was hit twice, but neither was serious. Tiny was hit once in the shoulder—he's fine. The problem is that Midnight's husband and daughter are missing, and one of her nieces is too. I've sent people to San Francisco to help locate her."

"Damn…" Kashena said, shaking her head, trying to fathom all that was happening and knowing it was all somehow connected. "Do we know anything about the people who attacked the AG?"

"Not much," Kyle said. "She was hit walking out of the terminal. Tiny was hit trying to cover her. Kana was sprayed with something that knocked her out—she's still out. Tiny got the make, model, and color of the car, but nothing on the plate. The airport police are interviewing as many people as they can, anyone who might have seen something."

Sebastian glanced at Kashena. "Anything there?"

Kashena shook her head. "It was a face, and a word, along with a smoke cloud, probably the gunshot."

"Excuse me?" Kyle asked, looking from Sebastian to Kashena, clearly lost.

Sebastian looked at Kashena, as she did him. He shrugged. "You could try telling him."

"Telling me what?" Kyle asked, sensing something was up here.

Kashena sighed, not sure how her information was going to be received. "I don't know, Baz…"

"If you know something," Kyle said, his tone changing to "chief."

"I don't know anything for certain," Kashena said. "I get, well, I get these visions."

Kyle's eyebrows shot up, telling Kashena that he wasn't one to believe in such things.

"Never mind," she said, reaching for a cigar and glancing around for a place to go smoke it.

"I'll cover you," Sebastian said, nodding toward the courtyard to the right of the corridor.

"Thanks," Kashena said, striding toward the exit and away from the San Diego Chief of Police.

Outside, Kashena got on her cell phone and called Sierra, feeling the need to talk to someone that didn't think she was crazy. Sierra was, as always, supportive, but Kashena explained her frustration.

Something big is going on, Sierra, I can feel it. That vision was vicious—my head is still ringing. This is big, but I can't explain this

281

to them. The Chief of Police is already looking at me like I have two heads."

Sierra was worried about Kashena, not liking that the powers-that-be were skeptical of Kashena's gift. After the phone call, Sierra felt impotent, wanting to help Kashena in any way she could. She started forming a plan of her own.

Kashena went back inside. She wasn't sure what had been said to Kyle Masterson, but Sebastian was leaning against the wall next to the door to Midnight's room, and Kyle Masterson was gone.

"Better?" Sebastian asked.

"Uh-huh," Kashena said.

"We're on our own on the vision thing," Sebastian said, his tone slightly irritated.

Kashena nodded. "Figured as much."

***

Rick woke slowly, feeling very out of it. His first thought was that it had been a dream—a nightmare, really—but as he came fully awake, he realized with a start that he wasn't in his bed. Sitting up quickly, he felt instantly dizzy. He had to clamp down on the desire to throw up. Lying back, he closed his eyes, trying to remember what had happened.

It had been very early when he'd gotten a phone call. Midnight had left an hour before with Kana to pick up Tiny and head to the airport. She was flying to San Francisco for two days. When the phone rang, he assumed it would be Midnight telling him something she'd forgotten, or simply to tell him she loved him. For that reason he'd answered the phone with languor in his voice.

"'lo?" he'd said, smiling to himself already.

"Mr. Debenshire?" said an officious-sounding voice that had the hairs on the back of his neck standing on end.

"Yes, this is he," Rick said, sitting up in bed.

"Mr. Debenshire, I'm sorry to have to call you," the voice said. Rick felt immediately sick to his stomach. "I'm afraid your wife has been shot."

"What?" Rick exclaimed, jumping out of bed and grabbing his boots, the phone under his chin. "Where is she? Is she okay? When did this happen?" he asked, his questions tumbling out on themselves as he pulled on his boots.

"It just happened a few minutes ago. They're taking her to Emergency at Mercy. You need to get here right away—it looks fatal."

"Jesus…" Rick breathed, feeling his entire world spin out of control.

"Mr. Debenshire?"

"Yes?" Rick asked, his mind already reeling.

"You should bring her children, just in case," the man said.

"Oh God…" Rick wanted to throw up. "I'll be right there." He hung up the phone and tossed it away from him.

He steeled himself. He knew he couldn't lose it now. Midnight needed him; he needed to get to the hospital. His mind raced. Mikeyla was home, but Ricardo had stayed with friends the night before. Rick couldn't take the chance of going to get him before going to the hospital. If it was his last chance to… His mind skittered away from the thought that Midnight could be dead. This wasn't happening again, not again. *No!* his mind yelled, and it propelled him into action. He finished getting dressed, then went to Mikeyla's room and banged on her door.

"Keyl, get up, now! There's an emergency!"

He strode back to their room, picked up his gun and placed it at his back, and then put his badge in his pocket. Mikeyla was ready minutes later, and they left the house.

"What's happening?" Mikeyla asked, her voice terrified.

Rick had no idea how to tell her. "Your mother's been hurt. We need to get to the hospital," he said as he threw his Saleen Mustang in reverse and backed up the long driveway to their house.

"Oh my God…" Mikeyla said, seeing the look on her father's face and knowing it was bad.

Rick drove at breakneck speed down the streets of Pacific Beach, racing toward the freeway.

"What about Kana and Tiny? Where were they?" Mikeyla finally thought to ask.

Rick glanced at her. *Yeah, where were they?*

He pulled out his cell phone and dialed Kana's number, while trying to get onto the freeway at the same time. It was relatively quiet; it was only 6 a.m.

Kana picked up on the third ring.

"Kana, it's Rick," he said, his tone harried. "What happened? How the hell did someone get past you and Tiny? How did this happen? How could you let her get shot?"

"Rick, Rick, hold up, what are you talking about? She's right here, she's fine…" Kana had said, then a pause. "Here."

Then the most wonderful sound in the world. Midnight, sounding as normal as humanly possible, said, "Rick?"

He was confused. He started to explain, but she told him the phone was cutting out. She told him to hold on. Then she said, "Okay, now what?"

The next thing Rick heard was the sound of the cell phone clattering to the ground, then he heard gunfire. He heard Tiny's voice yelling for Midnight. What Rick didn't see, until it was too late, was the van pacing him, or the muzzle of the rifle sticking out of the window and shooting out both driver's-side tires. It sent the Mustang into a spin; Rick worked against it, jamming on the brakes and relying on the anti-lock braking system to keep his tires from doing just that. Fortunately, they hadn't gone farther than the slow lane on the freeway, and a park and the Bay were on his right. The car spun off the road, but Rick managed to bring it to a stop before it flipped. Before he'd had a chance to recover or see how Mikeyla was, however, he'd been dragged from the car, and something had slammed into the side of his head, knocking him unconscious.

He hadn't seen the men who'd removed the plates and set the car on fire to make it less easily recognizable.

"Fuck," Rick said out loud, sitting up again. He had no idea if Mikeyla was okay. He looked around him, noticing the sun coming through the tiny window near the ceiling. That told him that he was probably in a basement.

The wave of nausea hit him again, and he saw the man sitting in the corner.

"Who're you?" Rick asked, his English accent thick, his voice gravelly.

"You don't need to know that."

"Where's my daughter?"

The man didn't answer, merely shrugging.

Rick got off the bed and took two menacing steps toward the man. The man produced a gun and pointed it at Rick. He stopped. He'd be no good to Mikeyla dead. Rick didn't, however, retreat, even though his head was screaming at him to lie down.

"Where is she?" he asked again, his tone threatening despite the gun pointed at him.

The man scowled. "Who do you think you are to ask me questions? I am in charge here. I have the gun."

"Big man with a gun," Rick sneered. "Where the fuck is my daughter?"

"Aren't you worried about your wife? Your friends? Your family?"

Rick stared at the man, knowing somehow that this had been the man that had shot Midnight, and he was sure she had been shot. Something in his gut told him that.

"Why don't you put the gun down," Rick growled, "so you and I can have at it properly?"

"You think you scare me?"

"I think you should put the gun down, and let's find out," Rick said, his tone all gang member.

"I think you better shut up if you want to see your daughter again."

Rick was silent for a moment, then his lip curled in disgust.

"Takes a real man to hurt an innocent girl," Rick said derisively.

"She's been raised by you and that stupid bitch of a wife," the man spat, his anger boiling to the surface. "How innocent can she be?"

Rick glared at him. "Tell yourself what you need to," Rick said, "but Mikeyla's done nothing to you. So hurting her only makes you a coward."

"You need to pay," the man said.

"For what?"

"For the damage your wife has wreaked on this state."

"Interfering with your life, is she?" Rick asked with a sardonic smirk. "She does that a lot, especially with scumbags like you."

The man shot him then. Rick wasn't expecting it, but he still wasn't sure why it surprised him quite so much. The bullet slammed into his stomach, knocking him back; he fell and hit the floor. Somewhere he heard Mikeyla scream. He tried to get up, but the man stood over him, his boot on the wound he'd just caused.

"You will all pay," the man said, then kicked Rick in the head, knocking him out again.

***

Kevin was sitting at the hospital when his phone rang.

"Yeah?" he answered, sounding stressed.

"Mace, it's me," Cat said.

"Cat! Where are you?"

"I'm in San Francisco. Look, I don't have time for details—something's happened. I need to talk to Rick or Midnight."

"Well, that's going to be a problem," Kevin said seriously. "Midnight was shot four hours ago. Rick is missing along with Mikeyla."

"Fuck..." Cat breathed. "Mace, Elizabeth has been grabbed. Wait, Midnight was shot? What about Kana and Tiny?"

"Tiny took a round in the shoulder, Kana got knocked out, but they're all three okay—the wounds weren't fatal. But there's an all-out assault out on the Debenshire household, and we're chasing our tails here," Kevin told her, feeling his stress level rise another few notches.

He and Erin had been awoken by a phone call from Dave that morning, telling them what had happened and to get to the hospital right away. When they'd gotten there, they'd been told by Kyle that Rick and Mikeyla were missing too. It was a mess, and now to find out that Elizabeth was kidnaped too? Was it possible it was a coincidence? Kevin didn't think so.

"Okay," Cat said. "What have you got on Midnight's shooter?"

"Almost nothing."

"Okay, well, I have four numbers on a plate up here on the van that they put Elizabeth into. So maybe if we can find them, we can find Midnight's shooters and figure out where Rick and Mikeyla are too."

"Got it," Kevin said, nodding. "I'll talk to the Gang and call you back as soon as we have a plan of attack. I'll be there, partner. You stick tight."

He hung up and immediately walked over to Kyle and Dave.

"We got more problems," Kevin told them.

"Jesus, what now?" Kyle asked.

"I just talked to Cat. She's up in San Francisco, and she says Elizabeth was snatched too."

"San Francisco?" Dave repeated. "What the hell is going on?"

Kevin shook his head, understanding Dave's outburst. "Cat said she got four numbers off the plate on the van that the kidnappers were driving. It might be a clue."

Dave looked at Kyle. "We need to get Rogue Squadron up there now."

Kyle nodded. "I'll make a call."

Within two hours of Cat's call, Rogue Squadron and Susan arrived at Sable's hotel in San Francisco. Joe had agreed with Cat that if they could find Elizabeth with the information Cat had garnered from the plate, it would likely lead to Midnight's shooters as well as Rick and Mikeyla.

Cat introduced everyone from San Diego to Sable and Jake, and the team immediately got to work. They set up in the large hotel suite, pulling out laptops and cables and connecting them to the hotel's internet and phone lines.

"Blue, run up DMV—we need any vans, light in color, either white or beige, and with a California plate with RA69 in it." Cat was pacing, her mind going a mile a minute.

"Got it." Tapping away at the keys, Christian connected to the CLETS system.

"What's that?" Sable asked, looking at the screen over his shoulder.

"It's the California Law Enforcement Telecommunications System. Ironically enough, it's maintained by the California Attorney General's Department of Justice." Christian logged in and set to work defining the criteria for his search.

Meanwhile, Jeanie was on the phone with her former contacts at San Francisco PD, garnering assistance from them. Fortunately, she'd made a few lasting friendships while she'd been with Alcoholic Beverage Control in San Francisco for eight months, years before. Those friends had enough pull to get her what they needed to storm any place they deemed necessary.

"Never thought they'd come in handy," Jeanie said, closing her phone and sighing.

"Never do know," Donovan said.

"Okay, I got thirty-one hits," Christian said.

"In San Francisco?" Cat asked, stunned.

"In California," Christian corrected. "We don't know that they didn't drive it up here from San Diego or wherever—we can't assume they're from here, babe."

"Good point," Cat said.

"Did you get a look at the people who grabbed her?" Donovan asked.

"Not a good one, no," Cat said. "I was walking away when I heard her scream."

"Male?" Kevin queried.

"Yeah."

"Dark hair, light hair?"

"Dark," Cat said.

"Cross-check the license pictures of the registered owners of each of those, weed out the females, and narrow it down to men with dark hair," Donovan told Christian.

Christian nodded, tapping at the keys again. As the system was compiling the information, Christian stretched. He'd been up all night on a case the night before, and chances were he wasn't sleeping any time soon.

"Is there a Starbucks around here?" Stevie asked, seeing her husband's fatigue.

"Can't swing a dead cat in San Francisco without hitting a Starbucks," Cat said, smiling.

"One block away," Jake said in his Irish brogue. "I'm taking orders." He stood up and pulled a pad of paper and a pen out of his jacket pocket.

Sable handed Jake her credit card. He shook his head. "I got this," he said. "Good cause and all."

The group chuckled.

Jake was back twenty minutes later with a box loaded with cups of coffee, lattes, and cappuccinos, as well as a bag of pastries.

"Figured we all needed to eat," he said.

Sable looked at her bodyguard, shocked by his change in personality. Usually a very quiet, reserved man, Jake was an ex-mercenary as well as ex-paramilitary and a martial arts expert. He was rarely social in the year he'd been her bodyguard. Apparently it took this kind of situation to bring it out in him. Or maybe it was the company.

Sable sat down on the couch in the living area of the suite, where the group was gathered. She watched Cat. Cat, too, was very different around her people. There was an air of authority around her now. Sable knew it was that air of authority that had drawn her to Cat in the first place. She'd forgotten that in the crush of wanting to possess the girl. It had been reawakened the night before when she'd seen Cat with her weapon in her hand. Now she was seeing Cat in her element again, and it was very distracting.

"Okay, we're down to ten," Christian said. "Jay, Cat, check these addresses—any thoughts there?"

Jeanie and Cat both moved to look over Christian's shoulder.

"That first one is Nob Hill," Jeanie said. "Not likely there."

"That second one is on Bay, also not likely," Cat said, pointing out the address.

Within minutes they had the list narrowed down to four addresses.

"Okay, mount up. We need to hit these places," Donovan said, pulling out his gear bag as Christian got up.

Cat spread her hands plaintively; Kevin turned and tossed her a gear bag.

"Figured you'd need it," he said, grinning.

"I knew Erin loved you for a reason," she said, winking at him. She put her gear bag on the couch next to where Sable sat and opened it.

Sable watched as Cat pulled black BDU pants on under the miniskirt she wore, pulling the skirt off afterwards. She then took off her shirt, tossed it on the floor and put on a black tank top.

"You're not actually going?" Sable said hesitantly.

"Yeah, I actually am," Cat said as she laced up black boots that looked like army boots.

Cat tossed her bulletproof vest over her head and set to work adjusting the straps. Sable looked around and noted everyone else doing the same thing.

Within minutes they were all dressed.

"I've got two SUVs out front." Jake said, "Both black and nondescript."

Donovan smiled. "Thanks, hadn't covered that part yet."

"No problem," Jake said, inclining his head.

"Jay, call your friends at the PD. Me, Mace and Cat will hit this house," Donovan said to Jeanie, pointing to the screen. "You, Blue and Stevie hit this one. Have the PD send us two teams to meet up at the hits in ten minutes."

"You got it," Jeanie said, pulling out her phone and dialing as Donovan continued to talk.

"Let's make these quick, surgical strikes." Donovan pulled out his gun, checking the ammunition clip and his spares. "Cat, you're not full strength right now, so I'm handing the shotgun off to Mace." He took out a shotgun and handed it to Kevin. Cat nodded, understanding the logic. "Blue, you carry for your team. Let's hit them hard and fast. I don't want any more of us down." Donovan turned to Cat, touching her under the chin so she'd look at him. "I need you to clear your head," he said, his voice dropping. "This isn't Elizabeth we're going in after—it's any other citizen. You're a cop doing her job. Right?"

Cat took a deep breath, then let it out slowly and nodded.

"I refuse to lose one of my best teammates," Donovan said. "So keep your mind on business. Put everything else out."

Cat moved her neck around, stretching her muscles, which were indeed tense. Closing her eyes, she did exactly as he'd told her and cleared her mind of everything but what they needed to do. When she opened them again, all of Rogue Squadron was watching her. They all had determined looks on their faces, and Cat knew that if anyone could get Elizabeth back, it was her team. That gave her confidence the last shot it needed.

"Let's go kick ass and take names," she said, her voice perfectly calm.

"Yeah!" the rest of the team agreed.

Three hours later, they'd checked out every house that they'd pinpointed, and nothing. They'd found a good deal of illegal activity—San Francisco PD was having a field day—but not what they were looking for.

***

The man moved through the house with authority; he noticed with satisfaction that none of the men looked him in directly in the eye. *Good, they're learning some respect.* He'd just left the room they were holding Elizabeth Endicott in. It was a shame she couldn't see his point of view. Attempting to explain to her why she was there, why her aunt would be dead soon, had seemed pointless. She didn't want to understand. The woman had actually had the temerity to attempt to attack him! What was wrong with these people? Why couldn't they see what Midnight Chevalier was doing?

He walked through the house, hearing Elizabeth Endicott's screams. The girl should have just repented for her disgusting, filthy relationship with that lesbian. If she had, his men wouldn't have had to teach her a lesson she wouldn't soon forget. These people just needed to wake up. They were depraved and foolish and needed to be eradicated before they did more damage. She'd stared at him with what he knew was false bravado.

***

"Fuck, where is she?" Cat said, pacing. "Blue, put the pictures back up. Let me look at them again." After running down every lead they had on the plates that Cat had seen, they were still nowhere. Cat's frustration level was through the roof.

Christian nodded, glancing at Stevie. She shook her head slowly. They were all feeling like it was hopeless at that point. It had been five hours since the failed attempts to find Elizabeth.

Cat sat down in the chair Christian vacated for her. She scrolled through each picture slowly, back and forth, praying for something, anything. Her mind couldn't stay away from the mental picture of Elizabeth tied to a bed somewhere, beaten, or hurt, or worse... All she could picture was the house she'd been held in. Then something clicked.

"Nob Hill," she said, scrolling back to the original pictures and addresses. "Nob Hill, damn it!" she exclaimed, moving to stand. "That's where she is." She pointed to the address.

"That's major upper class," Jeanie said to Cat, shaking her head, her look sympathetic. They were all tired and very discouraged.

"Exactly!" Cat said. "So was the house I was being held in, remember? Midnight thought that was weird." She looked to Kevin, who was turning the possibilities over in his mind. "She's there, Mace, I know it," Cat said, her tone sure.

Kevin nodded. "Okay, let's mount up. We'll go for some surveillance and hit it if we need to."

"What about a warrant?" Donovan asked.

"Fuck the warrant," Cat said. "If they have her, I'm getting her back."

The members of Rogue Squadron exchanged glances, then shrugged, knowing they had to back Cat up on this.

A half hour later, they were parked in two SUVs a block from the house. Donovan and Kevin did some reconnaissance. They came back looking confident.

"It's possible," Donovan said.

"For a nice house, on a nice day, most of the shades are down," Kevin said. "Especially in that back room there." He pointed to the back of the house, which was visible from the street.

Cat nodded. "Let's try a knock and talk and see where we go."

Jeanie got out of the car. She wore civilian clothes, to act as the decoy. She had her gun at her back.

"Be careful," Donovan told her, leaning down to kiss her on the lips.

Jeanie walked up to the house and knocked on the door, waiting patiently for someone to answer, looking for all intents and purposes like she was selling something—right down to the clipboard she'd picked up from the front desk at the hotel.

The door opened, and a man stood in the doorway.

"Good afternoon, sir," Jeanie said, smiling brightly. "I'm in the neighborhood today to give assessments on dual-paned vinyl windows. Would you be interested in a free estimate?"

When the man hesitated, Jeanie went on undaunted.

"You have a lovely house here," she said, moving to look inside. "Lots of windows. I'm sure, though, that your energy bills must be outrageous. These old windows let in far too much of a draft..." She went on talking, even as she leaned past the man to peer inside, pointing out areas in which he could save money.

"So," she said, smiling, "what do you say? anna give a girl a break, let me give you a free estimate? I'm sure it would be worth your time."

The man looked back at her, obviously moved by her looks, rather than her speech—he'd been staring down her shirt, purposely low cut, most of the time.

"Well," he said, reaching up to scratch his chin, unknowingly baring a very definite prison tattoo, and the fact that the heel of his hand had blood on it, "I can't really do it today, honey." He winked at her. "But maybe you can come back tomorrow."

"Sure," she said, smiling happily. "I can do that. What time would be good for you?"

"Say one thirty?" he said, licking his lips.

"I'll be here," she said, smiling again. "Thank you so much." Her eyes flicked behind him again, then back at him. "I'll see you tomorrow."

"Great," he said, his grin lascivious.

Jeanie turned and walked down the stairs; he watched her the entire time. When she got back to the SUV, she tossed the clipboard in the back and grabbed her bulletproof vest marked with POLICE and the Department of Justice patch.

"Definitely," she said, nodding.

The team started getting ready.

"I saw two men, plus the tree trunk that answered the door," she said, not mentioning the blood she'd seen on his hand, knowing it would only upset Cat. "I didn't see weapons, but my guy stood like he was packing, so let's assume yes."

Donovan nodded. "Okay, Blue—you, Stevie, Mace, and Cat take the back door. Jeanie and me will take the front. They won't be expecting much from the back. Blue, you're on shotgun. Let's go."

The operation took minutes. Christian heard Donovan's knock and notice, and kicked the back door open at the precise time Donovan kicked open the front. There were shots fired, and general mayhem ensued. Amidst gunfire, Cat and Kevin made their way through and got to the back bedroom they thought Elizabeth was in. Cat stood back, kicking the door open, while Kevin covered her. She pulled back out of the doorway, then spun back into it in a crouch, her gun at the ready.

She was stunned at what she saw. Elizabeth was on the bed; there was blood, too much of it, around her. She was bloody and bruised. Cat was sure she was going to be sick. Fortunately there was no one in the room with Elizabeth, because Cat couldn't see anything but the woman she loved on the bed, almost dead.

"Mace!" Cat yelled. "In here, now!"

Kevin moved into the doorway as Cat strode to the bed, dropping to her knees next to it. Kevin kept watch, glancing at Cat, then back out into the hallway.

Cat reached out and touched Elizabeth's cheek, cut and bleeding.

"Bet?" Cat queried softly, tears in her eyes, her lips trembling.

Reaching up, Cat touched Elizabeth's neck, feeling for a pulse, her hands shaking terribly.

"Bet?" she said again, her voice louder this time.

Elizabeth stirred, opening her eyes, although they were mere slits because they were so swollen.

"Cat?" Elizabeth said, her voice full of wonder.

"I got you baby," Cat said, moving to stand. "We're getting you out of here. You'll be okay."

Cat strode to the door, taking over for Kevin. Kevin holstered his weapon and walked to the bed, picking Elizabeth up in his arms as carefully as he could. It didn't matter—she'd passed out again by that time. Cat covered him as he strode out of the back of the house and down the back stairs. Everything had quieted by then. As soon as Cat was out of the house she was calling in the paramedics.

***

Two hours later, Cat and Susan were at the hospital, waiting for word on Elizabeth. Meanwhile, Rogue Squadron was turning the house upside down looking for clues as to where Rick and Mikeyla were being kept. Whoever had planned this was hiding their tracks well. Dave called Joe to report in about finding Elizabeth and give him the rundown on what little they had to go on.

"Don't bother checking anything that points toward the slums," Dave said. "This isn't about money. Our enemies have resources, and they're not using cheap muscle either. The guys we took down were expensively hired mercenaries."

"Fuck," Joe said. "Things are going to hell here too."

"What d'ya mean?"

"Midnight and Tiny have both spiked mysterious fevers. They're getting worse, not better," Joe said, sounding tense. "The doctors can't figure out what's going on. The gunshot wounds were minor. They should be awake and fine by now, and they're not. We gotta find these guys, Dave, or they just might win this time."

"Jesus," Dave breathed, shaking his head. "How's K?"

"She's better, but even she's not recovering as fast as they said she should be. She wasn't able to give us much, though—they blindsided her. What we did get is that Rick called Kana at the airport and was ranting about how this could happen and how they could let Midnight get shot. Kana told him Midnight was fine and handed Midnight the phone. Apparently the signal was cutting out so Midnight

298

headed for the front doors of the terminal to get a better signal. That's when she was hit. This was well coordinated, Dave, and I'm not liking the direction it's going in."

"I'm with you on that," Dave said, his voice low. "We'll keep looking, man. We're running down who owns this place and their associations. I'll call you as soon as I have something."

"Got it," Joe said. "Be careful."

"You too."

***

Cat stood outside the building, chain-smoking, leaning against the glass. They were waiting for word on Elizabeth's condition. Inside, Susan was on the phone. She'd already called her mother when they knew Elizabeth had been kidnaped, so Deborah was already on her way to San Francisco. Susan was letting her know that they had found Elizabeth and which hospital they were at. Deborah told her she'd be there in two hours.

When the doctor came to talk to Susan, Cat saw him and walked inside. She hovered nearby, watching the man closely.

"She's been brutalized," the doctor said. "She was raped repeatedly. There was a lot of internal damage, bleeding, bruising and tearing. She's also got various external bruises and abrasions. We've managed to control the bleeding, and she's resting comfortably now."

"Is she going to be alright?" Susan asked, her cultured English accent sounding far too calm.

"She's going to need time to heal," the doctor said, "but eventually she'll be good as new, at least physically."

Susan nodded, looking unhappy. "When can we see her?"

"You can go in now, if you'd like. She's down the hall, room 145," he said, pointing. "She's been sedated, so she won't be very lucid at this point."

Cat had already turned on her heel and was striding toward the room.

"Thank you, doctor," Susan said, watching Cat's retreating back.

Cat opened the door to the hospital room. Elizabeth was lying in the bed, her eyes closed. Stepping over to the bed, Cat searched Elizabeth's face, her look pained. As she watched, Elizabeth slowly opened her eyes.

"Cat?" she said softly, her voice full of wonder, as if she couldn't believe Cat was really there.

Cat took Elizabeth's hand in hers, holding it gently.

"You're… here?" Elizabeth stammered, her voice a mere whisper.

Cat squeezed her hand. "I'm here, babe."

"You… came for me?"

"I'll always come for you," Cat said, feeling very affected by everything suddenly.

She'd been running on pure adrenaline all day. To have it turn out like this, with Elizabeth brutalized while Cat was chasing her tail looking for her. *If I'd thought about the house sooner…* was all Cat could think. It made her sick.

"I… didn't…" Elizabeth began, but it was obvious she was struggling to stay awake.

"Didn't what, Bet?" Cat asked softly.

"I didn't… I… couldn't…"

"Couldn't what?"

"Repent," Elizabeth gasped out, then she was unconscious again.

Cat stared down at Elizabeth, unable to understand what she'd just said.

"Repent?" Cat repeated.

"What?" Susan asked as she entered the room.

"Bet just said she didn't repent," Cat said, perplexed.

"What did she mean by that?"

"I have no idea."

Susan sat down in the chair next to the bed where her sister lay, her eyes on Elizabeth. Cat leaned against the wall for a while, then went back outside to smoke. It was a bad end to a long day.

***

Mikeyla Debenshire had never been as afraid as she was at that moment. She'd seen her father shot; she'd seen that man kick him in the head. Was her father dead? He wasn't moving, just lying on the floor where he'd fallen, *bleeding*. That was the thought that kept going through Mikeyla's head—he was bleeding. He could be lying there bleeding to death, and she couldn't do anything to help him.

Of course she'd seen it all; they'd made her watch. They had sat her in a chair in front of the monitor for the camera in the room Rick was in. She'd heard and seen everything. Screaming when the man had shot her father. In her head she kept thinking this wasn't really happening. These people weren't real; this was all make-believe somehow. But it was real. Her mother had been shot, twice. Tiny Ako had been shot—they'd shown her the morning paper. And now they'd shot her father too. Was she next? She didn't know, but somehow she felt surprisingly calm about her own possible death.

She thought about Nick, her boyfriend, how he had no idea where she was or what was happening. He was up in Los Angeles in college. She kept looking back at the monitor, hoping to see her father move. He couldn't be dead. There was no hope of her mother coming to the rescue. Midnight was lying in the hospital, possibly dying. The papers had reported that Midnight had been shot twice and that although the gunshot wounds hadn't been serious, Midnight had spiked a mysterious fever that had doctors baffled.

The man who'd shown Mikeyla the paper had smiled gleefully. "It's a fever that will kill her, slowly and painfully."

"Why are you doing this?" Mikeyla had asked.

"Because your mother is the worst kind of politician. She's a menace, and she needs to be stopped."

Mikeyla hadn't answered, only looking back at the monitor again. She sensed that this man was crazy. He had a maniacal air about him. He'd already mentioned things like what a depraved family she had. How her cousin was disgusting with her penchant for women. He'd gone on to criticize Midnight's use of Joe Sinclair to help her with her "program"; he'd said that Joe and Midnight were lovers and they were laughing at the citizens of California as they fornicated everywhere at the state's expense. He'd said they all needed to be put down like dogs in heat. It had terrified Mikeyla—was he after all of them? All of the people she loved?

Sitting there for hours, Mikeyla listened to the people around her. They all agreed readily with everything he said. She'd seen three other men since being brought into the room. Whenever the dark-haired man had gone on one of his tangents, the others nodded and agreed. At one point, one man had made a comment, a leering comment about wanting to see the "two lesbos makin' it." The dark-haired man had turned on him, viciously punching him in the face. The man who'd made the comment, although twice the size of the dark-haired man, had shrunk from the man's anger, apologizing profusely.

Three hours after she'd seen Rick shot, she saw her father move his head. She watched, praying he'd keep moving. He did—she watched him sit up, touching the blood at his stomach, grimace then look around him again. Slowly, he got up off the floor and sat down on the bed, wincing as he did. Mikeyla felt the pain written on his face. She could also see that he was feeling extremely dejected. She took a deep breath and blew it out slowly, knowing she needed to do something to help.

"May I take my father some water?" she asked quietly. They were the first words she'd spoken since being brought there. Her voice was respectful, the way she'd heard the other men speak.

The dark-haired man looked at her, his surprise evident.

"A young lady with manners…" he mused. "And so concerned about her father."

"Shouldn't a child always be respectful of her elders?" Mikeyla asked, her tone subservient, as she knew he'd want it to be.

"Yes, a child always should be," he said, sounding pleased. He snapped his fingers. "Let her take him some water."

Roy Jacobs eyed the beautiful strawberry-blonde. She was young, yeah, but did that really matter? She was one hot little number, and he had every intention of fucking her before this whole deal was over. To that end, he was the one who volunteered to take her in to her daddy.

In the kitchen, he stood by while she filled the cup he'd given her. He checked out her ass while she bent to do so. She didn't think he noticed the surreptitious glance she cast in his direction, but he did. At this point, however, his ego was still smarting a bit from the smacking he'd taken from the boss in front of her. It wasn't like Roy to take shit like that from anyone. He'd killed men for a lot less. But the amount of money this guy was paying… They'd all agreed he was the boss, no matter what. So, that's what it amounted to. They were his minions, and they did what they were told. Which also meant bowing to his bullshit theories and thoughts.

Personally, Roy thought the AG was one hot broad, and the man they had in the room in the lower part of the house was a damned lucky one. Business was business, however, so killing Rick Debenshire was necessary. They were holding him and the girl right now for insurance. Mikeyla Debenshire was going to die too; the boss thought it necessary to "exterminate" the entire family. So Roy figured before he killed her, he'd nail her first, but not yet. He could wait.

Mikeyla glanced over her shoulder to see if the big man was watching her. She saw the gun on his hip and suspected from the way he moved that he was an expert with it, so she wasn't foolish enough to try anything. She just wanted to assure her father that she was okay, so he wouldn't worry or give up hope. It wasn't much, but she hoped somehow it would help her father get through this.

The big man, with tattoos and an earring in one ear, escorted her downstairs. He stayed close to her, so much so that Mikeyla felt her skin crawl a bit. She'd caught his lecherous stare and wasn't naive enough to think that he couldn't rape her if he chose to. Her only hope was that the man who seemed to be running things wouldn't allow that. Mikeyla had every intention of playing up the innocent-girl part. She didn't know if it would help in the end, but she sensed that it was what the man in charge saw as appropriate. She'd heard enough stories from her parents and extended family to know that sometimes it was better to play along with your captors than fight them. She'd seen graphically what fighting these men got her father. If pretending to be what they thought ideal would help her and her father, and maybe her mother too, Mikeyla intended to do it.

Rick looked up when the door to the room opened, and he thought he'd pass out from the relief flooding his veins. There stood Mikeyla—from what he could see, totally unharmed. She was carrying a cup and walked toward him, her eyes intent on his as if she was trying to communicate something. The man behind her stood in the doorway, blocking the only way out.

"I've brought you water," Mikeyla said evenly. "I thought you might need some."

Rick narrowed his eyes slightly, noting the style of her speech. It was totally different from the way his daughter usually spoke. Looking her over, he could see that she was trembling. He was fairly sure it was because she was desperate to throw herself into his arms. She was terrified; he could see that in her eyes too.

"Yes," Rick said, taking the cup from her. "Thank you."

He took a drink and then looked at her. "Are you alright? They haven't hurt you?"

"No, they haven't hurt me," Mikeyla said, purposely not answering the first question, which told Rick that she was not alright.

"We'll get out of this, Keyl," Rick said, wanting to reassure her. He found himself aching to take her in his arms, but he somehow knew that wasn't what she wanted him to do. Something wasn't right here, but he didn't know what.

"I'm sure that we will, Father," she said. "I think that we just need to do what he wants."

Again Rick hesitated. Something in her eyes was trying to convey something, but he wasn't sure what. If she was a cop he'd know, but this was his daughter, his little girl. She wasn't used to this kind of thing; she wasn't used to being held captive. Was this guy brainwashing her? The thought hit him and made him ill suddenly. No, that couldn't be… But Mikeyla had been kept out of danger her entire life;

she had no idea how to respond to violence. Rick and Midnight had seen to it that it wasn't part of her life. After the time she'd seen her mother lying in a pool of her own blood, they'd made that pact with themselves and each other—never again. Now Rick worried that in not ever having been exposed to this kind of trauma, not even having heard about it, Mikeyla was wholly unprepared. It scared him more now that she didn't seem to have a scratch on her. What was this guy doing?

"Mikeyla…" Rick began.

The big man stepped into the room and took Mikeyla's arm. "Time to go," he said.

Rick wanted to knock the guy out, grab Mikeyla and run, but he knew that was hopeless. So he could only watch as his daughter was led out of the room. He consoled himself with the fact that she was okay. It nagged at him, however, that she seemed so strange. Something wasn't right; he just didn't know what it was. It was likely to drive him crazy.

***

Mikeyla was led to a room and given food and water. She fell asleep shortly after that. When she woke in the morning, she wondered if the food had been drugged, because she felt extremely fatigued all of a sudden. She walked into the small bathroom located within the room and looked in the medicine cabinet. There was nothing in it, nor in the cabinet under the sink. She splashed cold water on her face and then looked in the mirror. Her long hair was in one braid down her back, the way she slept with it all the time. She was grateful for that. Using some water, she smoothed the sides of her hair down; the cold water on her scalp seemed to help lift the fog, so she wet it some more.

She went over to one of the windows and moved the blind aside, looking out. They were on the beach. She was fairly sure it was La Jolla. Remotely, she wondered how far she was from her Uncle Joe's house. Joe and Randy lived on the beach. She heard the door behind her being unlocked, and she moved away from the window, fairly sure that they wouldn't want her looking outside.

The dark-haired man stepped inside the room to see her sitting primly in a chair. He sat down on the bed, across from where she sat. His eyes searched her face. Mikeyla made a point of not looking away from him, knowing it wouldn't be what he wanted.

"I hope you understand that what I'm doing is very necessary," he said finally.

"Necessary?" she said quietly.

"Yes. What your mother has done to this state with her disgusting views and lack of morals is absolutely reprehensible. She needed to be stopped."

Mikeyla nodded, looking as though she was trying to understand. "But isn't killing wrong too?" she asked, her tone still respectful.

The man smiled sadly. "My dear child, you do not understand. This isn't killing in the sense of murder. It is simply a revolution. And in a revolution, people die—it's part of the cost."

Again Mikeyla nodded. "What will happen to me?"

The man looked thoughtfully at her. "I have seen in you some redeeming qualities," he said in a superior tone. "So perhaps, if you prove yourself, I will spare you. It is not, after all, your fault that your parents have such horrible morals. They came from gangs, for heaven's sake—it's no wonder they're jaded. But you, you seem to have remained untouched."

"How would I prove myself?" Mikeyla asked, her voice hopeful now.

"We'll see," he said, standing up. "Let me think about it."

Mikeyla nodded, her hands in her lap and her head down.

***

Sierra caught a taxi from San Diego International Airport to the hospital. She hoped that Kashena wasn't going to be angry with her for coming down, but she couldn't stand the thought of no one believing Kashena's visions. Sierra knew that Kashena could be very valuable in finding out who had tried to kill Midnight, Tiny and Kana—it was too important to ignore. When she arrived at the hospital, she explained to the information desk who she was, showing her credentials. She was directed to the proper floor. Seeing the press stationed near the elevators, Sierra opted for taking the stairs.

As she stepped out of the stairwell, she looked around to get her bearings, then headed in the direction of Midnight Chevalier's room; she knew Kashena would be there. Sierra was dressed very casually in jeans, T-shirt and tennis shoes, her hair pulled back in a ponytail. She'd wanted to remain unnoticeable to the press. When she rounded a corner, she ran right into a security officer and almost knocked him down. His reaction was to grab her shoulders. Out of sheer terrified instinct, Sierra put her hands to the man's chest and shoved him, struggling to get away. In her mind, she realized she was overreacting—Jason's assault on her was too recent in her mind. She tried to pull back and apologize, but now the guard was on the attack.

The guard was thinking that Sierra could be someone sent to finish off Midnight Chevalier—he'd already heard that there was still a police officer missing. Maybe this was his chance to score a few points with San Diego PD! As he did his best to control the woman struggling in his arms, she screamed out "Kashena!" He had no idea what that meant, but as far as he was concerned, it was probably some kind of battle cry. He redoubled his efforts to contain the woman.

Suddenly a voice said, "Let her go."

He was surprised to hear someone behind him. He turned his head to look at Kana. In his surprise, he took his hands off Sierra momentarily; he didn't expect the attack that came from his other side.

A blonde-haired fury grabbed him by two handfuls of his uniform shirt, and he was slammed into the wall next to the door he'd just been guarding. He could feel his feet dangling as he stared into Kashena's face, which was contorted in barely controlled rage.

"If you ever manhandle a woman like that in my presence again, especially her" she said, letting go of one handful of shirt to point at Sierra, her other hand still supporting the man's weight, "I'll take you apart piece by piece. You got it?" she asked, her voice low and threatening.

The guard wasn't sure if she even noticed him nodding, but he was suddenly dropped, and he struggled to stay on his feet. The woman turned her back on him and addressed the other woman, so he carefully eased away, stepping closer to the door.

"I think we're pretty clear on that, aren't we, officer?" Kana, who had stepped into the doorway, asked pointedly.

"Yes, ma'am," the guard said, fairly intimidated at that point.

Kana looked back at Kashena, a smile curling her lips slightly. Then she looked at Sierra.

"Good to see you again, Chief Deputy Youngblood," Kana said, smiling at the smaller woman.

"I'm glad to hear you're okay, Special Agent in Charge Sorbinno," Sierra said, smiling too.

"Palani," Kana said, putting her arm around Palani, "this is Sierra Youngblood. She's Midnight's Chief Deputy Attorney General in charge of the criminal division, and Kashena's girlfriend."

Palani smiled at Sierra, noting the way Kashena's eyes widened slightly at the way Kana had introduced Sierra.

"It's very nice to meet you," Palani said, extending her hand to Sierra.

"I'm sorry it's under such horrendous conditions," Sierra said sadly. She looked to Kashena. "How is Midnight doing?"

"Worse, not better," Kashena said, her voice pained.

Sierra pressed her lips together, very worried about the dynamic Attorney General.

"Kana, you need to lie back down," Palani said, noting the way Kana's hands were shaking.

Kana nodded. "Kashena, let me know if there's any change."

"I will," Kashena said.

Sierra and Kashena walked back toward Midnight's room. Sebastian stood to one side of the door, nodding to Sierra as they walked up.

"Good to see you, Deputy Youngblood," he said.

"Hi, Sebastian," Sierra said, smiling.

"Missed her, huh?" Sebastian said.

"And then some."

Sebastian smiled. "Kash, why don't you take a break and go grab something to eat?"

Kashena narrowed her eyes at him, knowing that he was trying to give her time with Sierra. Sebastian only grinned unrepentantly.

"I'll bring you something," Kashena said, nodding.

"A blonde would be nice."

"Tramp," Kashena said under her breath.

"And?"

"And nothing. That was it," Kashena said.

Sebastian grinned. "See you in a bit."

***

An hour and a half later, Kyle Masterson had been "set straight" on Kashena's mental state. He'd also been informed that it was never wise to discount something simply because he himself didn't either believe in or understand it.

Kyle rocked back on his heels when approached by the small woman. She introduced herself, and he quickly found that her stature had absolutely no relation to either her determination or her clout. He was fairly sure she didn't understand his amused grin, since she found it necessary to remind him of the use of psychics in a great many police cases, but she truly reminded him of Midnight. It was obvious that Midnight was putting women like herself in power at the Attorney General's office. He knew he should have known that, but it was amusing, if not a bit off-putting, to have it in his face suddenly.

"So, what exactly would you require, Chief Deputy Attorney General Youngblood?" Kyle queried when she'd finished with her diatribe.

"A police sketch artist," she said, not lightening up a bit. "Kashena Marshal has likely seen the man behind all of this in her vision, and we'd like to find out who he is as soon as possible. Locating him may be key in finding a way to save the AG."

"I'll contact someone in my department right away," Kyle said.

"Good," Sierra said, her dark eyes staring up into his. "Thank you, Chief Masterson."

***

Mikeyla stared open mouthed at the man for a full minute.

"You want me to what?" she asked.

"I need proof of your resolve to change your future."

"But you want me to shoot someone?" Mikeyla asked, sounding afraid.

"Yes," he said as he pulled out a gun and handed it to her. "That one has no bullets in it for now."

Mikeyla looked at the gun as if it were a foreign object.

"Surely you've seen a gun before," he said. "Both your parents are law enforcement."

"Yes, but I was never allowed to handle their guns. I don't even know how to shoot a gun."

"It's very simple. You hold it like this," he said, demonstrating. "And you squeeze the trigger."

Mikeyla looked up at him wide eyed, but then nodded, swallowing convulsively.

"Okay," she said. "Who do I have to shoot?"

The man smiled, his eyes glittering evilly. "Your father."

Mikeyla's eyes widened further. "B-But…" she stammered, "isn't that a sin? To kill your own father?"

"Not when your father is as depraved as he is," the man answered. "He's gone along with everything your mother has done—he has to die too, Mikeyla, or else our revolution will be stopped. People will make him into a victim when your mother dies, and we can't have that. He can't be a hero to them; he has to be gone, just like her." His eyes narrowed. "I'm sparing your life, Mikeyla. Certainly you can understand that I need to trust that you want to change who you will become?"

Mikeyla took a deep breath. "I can't be who they meant me to be," she said with resolve. "I have to be a better human being."

"And this," the man said, handing her the gun again, "will prove to me that you really want that."

Mikeyla nodded slowly.

"I'll give you some time to think about this." He gave her a fatherly look. "It would be such a shame to kill you," he said wistfully.

He turned and left the room.

Mikeyla sat down on her bed, her eyes on the gun, her head down.

CHAPTER 14

He was no fool—he knew that Mikeyla Debenshire may have been a consummate actress and merely seeking to save her own skin. Children weren't very loyal these days, sadly. The way he saw it, if she did as she was asked, this would be the final nail in Midnight Chevalier-Debenshire's coffin. Her own daughter killing her husband. And if Mikeyla Debenshire has only pretended obedience simply to save herself, he'd have no qualms about killing her too. If she was sincere, perhaps he could use her. There were still others associated with the Debenshires that needed to die.

Unfortunately some of the fools he'd hired had failed him. Those lesbians should have been dead! So should Samantha Cobb! At least the inept fool sent to kill her was killed by her bodyguard. No evidence left behind, no one to interrogate. The woman was a fraud; she didn't deserve to practice civil law. Either way, it was a mild distraction, that bodyguard being shot. The plan to kill these people hadn't worked the way he'd planned. The lesbian cop should have died when they had her; now she'd come back to ruin his plans for Elizabeth Endicott? How had they found that house? It was in no way connected to any crime. His friend at the San Francisco Attorney General's office was a fine upstanding citizen. His friend had no idea why he'd wanted to use his house while he was in Europe for a month. But now that was ruined too! He'd get to them—he'd get to them all. But first, Rick Debenshire needed to look into the eyes of his own daughter as she killed him.

"So what have you come up with?" Sierra asked as she walked up to where Kashena and the sketch artist were sitting.

"Just about done," the sketch artist said as she made some final marks.

When she turned the sketch book around, Kashena nodded, and Sierra gasped.

"Oh my God, Kashena, I know him!" Sierra exclaimed.

"What?" Kashena asked, as Joe's and Kyle's heads snapped around in their direction. They strode over to them.

"You what?" Joe asked.

"I know him," Sierra repeated. "He was a Chief Deputy Attorney General in charge of the civil division—his name is Johnathan Weiskoff. Midnight made a point of getting rid of him," Sierra said, worried. "He was crazy. At least that's what I've heard. Very maniacal about his domain and civil rights and all that. A lot of people have said he's the type to go postal some day…"

"Lovely," Joe said, nodding. "Well, he's not going postal—he's doing much more damage than that." He looked at Kyle. "Let's run him."

An hour later they had details on Mr. Weiskoff—he owned a house in La Jolla. Joe got Rogue Squadron, who'd flown back in that morning, to suit up for a raid. He also asked Kashena to assist them. Sebastian and Kyle stayed behind at the hospital to keep an eye on things, just in case there was another attack on Kana, Tiny or Midnight. Sierra stayed behind too, with Sebastian keeping an eye on her.

Kana joined the team as they headed down the hall.

"Where do you think you're going?" Joe asked.

"With you," Kana said, still adjusting the straps to her vest.

"K, you're still not full strength," Joe said gently.

"Fuck full strength," Kana said, narrowing her eyes. "I owe this sonofabitch. Midnight's my responsibility. He fucked with that."

Joe nodded, knowing that a freight train couldn't stop Kana at that point. He almost felt sorry for Johnathan Weiskoff if Kana got ahold of him. Almost.

***

Rick was starting to feel sick again. He knew it was from the blood loss. He felt lightheaded and extremely woozy. But there was a sense of dread growing. It had been well over twenty-four hours since he and Mikeyla had disappeared—he guessed it was getting closer to forty-eight. He hadn't seen Mikeyla again since she'd brought him water. No one had brought him anything since then. He was getting edgy. Getting up to pace again, he shoved aside the feeling of nausea that hit him. *Gotta stay alert*, he told himself firmly. Now was not the time to lose it.

He heard the door to the room open, and he spun around to see who it was. A wave of dizziness hit him due to the fast movement. Putting his hand out, he steadied himself on the footboard of the bed. Looking over at the door again, he saw Mikeyla standing there, with the dark-haired man who had shot him behind her.

"Go on," the man said encouragingly.

Rick looked at Mikeyla, seeing the stoic look on her face, the look of resolve. Glancing down, he was stunned to see a gun in her hand. It was a semi-automatic pistol. His eyes widened. Rick knew there was no way this man would have given Mikeyla a gun unless it was for his own purposes. That purpose became quite clear a moment later. Mikeyla stepped toward him, raising her arm, the gun in her hand. Rick stepped to the side, circling her slightly; her eyes tracked him, as did her arm. She moved around to get a better bead on him.

"Keyl… what are you doing?" Rick asked, shocked.

"I'm sorry," she said, shaking her head.

"Don't be sorry," Rick snapped. "Just put the fucking gun down."

"I can't," she said, moving again as Rick circled closer to the door. "I'm sorry, Daddy."

Johnathan Weiskoff smiled triumphantly as he saw Mikeyla's finger tighten on the trigger of the gun. But he was stunned when the gun actually fired. He'd put the safety on—he wasn't stupid enough to hand her a gun that she could actually fire. The impact of the bullet, however, didn't hit Rick Debenshire as it should have. It slammed into Johnathan's chest. He died a moment later, sinking to the floor with the most surprised look on his face.

"Keyl?" Rick asked, shocked at what had just happened.

"Just like Uncle Joe taught me," Mikeyla crowed. "The red dot means it's hot," she said, pointing to the safety, "and *always* hit what you aim for." The last part was said with venom.

Rick stared open mouthed at his daughter. She'd fooled this man into thinking she would be willing to shoot her own father. She'd also obviously fooled him into thinking she knew nothing about guns. Joe Sinclair, an expert marksman, had taken care of that issue over a year ago.

Before Rick had a chance to comment on this astounding turn of events, they heard feet running down the stairs toward the room they were in.

"Give me the gun," Rick said, holding out his hand.

Mikeyla clicked the safety back on and tossed it to him. Rick released the safety and moved behind the bed.

"Get down, and stay low," he said.

Mikeyla did exactly as her father told her. She saw Rick wince and noticed that he shook his head a few times to clear it, but then the door was thrown open. Rick ducked behind the bed, then went up and squeezed off two shots. The man, the one who'd brought Mikeyla into the room the first time, dodged to the side of the door just in time. Pulling his own weapon, he fired back. Rick ducked again, gesturing for Mikeyla to get lower. She lay down on her side, watching the other man's feet from under the bed. She saw a second pair of feet appear just as Rick was going up to fire again.

"Daddy! There's another one!" she yelled.

Rick narrowly missed getting hit as he ducked back down.

"Fuck," Rick gritted out, knowing they were pinned down. He was damned if he and his daughter were going to die this way.

Thinking fast, he looked under the bed—there was a pillow under there that had fallen the night before. He reached for it and tossed it across the floor to draw the men's fire. It worked. Standing up, Rick fired three times, hitting the second man in the chest. Rick dropped to the floor as the first man turned his weapon back on him. There was a hail of gunfire, then silence. Rick waited two beats, then fired four more shots, hitting the other man in the leg. The man dove for cover. Rick waited, listening. He heard the distinct sound of a jam being cleared, or an attempt to do so. He heard the man cuss as he tossed aside the weapon. Rick stood up, taking a chance that the man didn't have a backup weapon, and walked toward the door, pointing the pistol at the other guy.

The man looked up and stood with lightning-fast speed, pulling out a knife and charging Rick. Rick squeezed the trigger of the gun, but the slide locked back in place, indicating that the weapon was empty. It was a low-capacity, non-law-enforcement gun—it only had ten rounds instead of the fourteen Rick was used to having. Throwing the gun aside just as the man hit him, Rick did his best to stay on his feet. It was no use—the man was almost twice Rick's size and weighed at least a hundred pounds more. Rick was all lean muscle, not bulk; what he had going for him was speed and agility. It was that agility that got Rick out from under the man before they hit the floor. Rick managed to get back on his feet before the guy got up, and Rick kicked him in the stomach. The man rolled away, covering his side, and amazingly rolled to his feet.

Both men crouched in fighter's stances. Rick's deep blue eyes were watchful. The man still had his knife, and Rick refused to be killed by way of hunting knife. The man circled; Rick kept equal distance between them, making sure he was out of arm's reach.

"Your boss is dead!" Mikeyla cried, pointing to the dark-haired man lying on the floor. "You can just let us go now."

Roy gave her a lascivious wink. "Not till I'm done with you, sweetheart," he said, his tone leering. "See, you're my bonus on this job. Nailing your sweet ass."

"You aren't going to touch her," Rick said in a deadly voice.

"Wanna bet me?" Roy asked confidently.

"With my life."

"Well, that's doable." Roy stepped forward.

Rick kicked him, knocking the knife out of his hands. He'd been waiting for the man to do just what he'd done. Rick followed up the kick with a punch in the face. Roy staggered but didn't go down. Rick winced, knowing he was too close now. A moment later, Roy grabbed him and threw him against the nearest wall. Rick sank to the floor as Mikeyla screamed. It was her scream that kept Rick from passing out. Roy, assuming Rick was out cold, turned to Mikeyla, who was cowering in the corner.

Roy took a step forward, reaching down to grab her. He didn't see Rick get to his feet, but he did hear the blade of the hunting knife scrape the floor as Rick picked it up. Roy turned, ready to fight Rick some more, amazed that the much smaller man could withstand what he had so far. With the lightning speed that had kept him alive for many years, Rick spun in his still-crouched position, driving the blade in and up, putting as much force as he could behind the plunge.

Rick had to do his best to stagger out of the way to keep Roy's body from falling on him. Not taking the time to see if the man was dead, Rick put his hand out to his daughter. Mikeyla grabbed it, and they both moved toward the door.

"There's one more, Daddy," Mikeyla said.

Rick shook his head, trying to clear it, gritting his teeth to focus and not give in to the idea of passing out, as his body kept trying to get him to do. He looked at the body of the first man he'd shot. He reached down and found the gun the man had dropped. Depressing the magazine release, Rick checked to see how many bullets were left. Two—*fuck!* If the third man was as big as the first two, these were going to have to be well placed shots. The gun was a nine millimeter; it didn't have much knockdown power. The men they were dealing with were huge, so it took a lot to stop them. Moving as best he could, Rick kept Mikeyla behind him, always aware that she would need cover. At the stairs, Rick had Mikeyla wait below, hiding under the cover of the stairs. As Rick was making his way up, the door at the top of the stairs was flung open, and a hail of gunfire followed it.

Rick threw himself over the side of the stairs; since he was halfway up, he fell four feet, landing hard on his side. It took everything he had to roll out of the line of fire. The man above wasn't messing with nine millimeters—he had a MAC-10 and was spraying gunfire everywhere in hopes of hitting Rick. Obviously the man had seen what had happened in the room via the camera, and he wasn't taking any chances.

Rick knew they were pinned down, and he had no idea how much ammunition the man had. Just as he was trying to determine what he could do, Rick heard a crash from up above, and the gunfire stopped. Not moving, unwilling to see if it was some kind of ploy to draw him out, Rick waited and listened.

Rick was stunned when he heard an English-accented voice yell, "Drop it, or I'll drop you," from what seemed like it would be the front door.

The man above clearly didn't realize who he was dealing with— Joe Sinclair could hit a man from one hundred and fifty yards if necessary. The man must have made a move, because the next thing Rick and Mikeyla heard was a single gunshot. The third man came tumbling down the stairs, dead with one shot to the head.

"Never fuck with Joe," Rick said, grinning as he moved out of his cover.

"Too right," Joe said from above him on the stairs. "You okay, man?"

Rick shrugged as he put his hand out to Mikeyla. "Only one new hole," he said, "and a new respect for my daughter and former rangemaster." He winked at Mikeyla.

"Huh?" Joe asked.

"I'll explain later," Rick said as he and Mikeyla headed up the stairs. "Is Midnight okay?"

Joe hesitated, which told Rick everything in one instant.

"I need to get to her," Rick said in a no-nonsense tone.

Joe nodded. "There's a car outside. Have them take you to the hospital—you need looking at anyway."

Rick was already heading for the door, Mikeyla's hand still in his.

***

Kana, Kashena and Rogue Squadron were securing the rest of the house. Kana encountered the bodies in the room downstairs. Rolling one body over, she thought it looked like the man in the sketch.

"Kash!" she yelled, knowing Kashena was just down the hall checking out another room.

Kashena appeared almost instantly. "Ma'am?"

Kana pointed to the body on the floor. "That him?"

Kashena nodded. "Guess we're not going to get any information out of him," she said matter-of-factly.

Kana gave her a pointed look. "Is there anything else you can tell us?"

Kashena looked back at Kana, surprised. She hadn't realized that Kana knew about the visions. News traveled fast.

Kashena closed her eyes, recalling the pictures that had flashed in her head.

"The word that I saw," Kashena said, her eyes still closed, "it's handwritten… There are words around it—they're blurred, but there are a lot of words. Like a journal." She opened her eyes.

"His bedroom," Kana said, thinking out loud.

Kashena nodded.

They made their way through the house, locating the master bedroom on the second floor. The two of them searched the room, dumping out drawers and looking through everything. Joe joined the search, telling Dave and his crew to check the other rooms for journals of any sort.

They were getting frustrated. Kashena was starting to wonder if she'd been mistaken—maybe it wasn't a journal, maybe. Anger welled up inside her. *Why send me the damned visions if you're not going to help me figure them out?* She slammed her fist into a picture on the wall, and it caved in around a knob.

"SAC Sorbinno!" Kashena exclaimed.

"God, Kash, call me Kana already, damn it," Kana said as she walked over to where Kashena was taking down the picture from the wall.

"I'll work on it," Kashena said, staring at the wall safe.

"Odds are they're in there," Joe said, walking up behind the two women.

"Call a locksmith," Kana said.

Kashena got on the phone immediately.

***

Rick and Mikeyla rode to the hospital in an ambulance. The paramedics checked him over and made sure the bleeding from the gunshot wound was stopped. "You'll need to see the doctor for this," the young paramedic told him.

"After I see my wife," Rick told him in a no-nonsense tone.

Once at the hospital, Rick insisted on checking on Midnight before he'd be seen. Mikeyla followed her father, as worried as he looked about her mother. They were directed to the third floor, ICU. Rick's humor didn't improve when he was stopped getting off the elevator by a young rookie.

"I'm sorry, sir, this floor is restricted at this time," the young man said, holding his hands up as he blocked their way.

"Get the fuck out of my way before I beat the shit out of you," Rick growled.

"Sir," said the young officer, his look becoming stern, "I have to ask you to leave."

"Captain Richard Debenshire," Rick said. "Does that mean anything to you?"

"Uh," the young man said, not sure but thinking that did sound really familiar.

"Midnight's my wife, you idiot," Rick said, moving toward the young man. When the man didn't step out of the way, Rick took him down with a well placed foot behind his knee.

The officer hit the floor with a thud. "Never let a suspect get that close," Rick said over his shoulder as he strode down the hallway.

The officer got up and was about to follow him when Chief Kyle Masterson walked up. "I wouldn't," Kyle said from behind the young man. "Rick doesn't take confrontation too well when he's worried about his wife. He might kill you before you realize who he is."

The young cadet snapped to attention at seeing who was talking to him. "But, sir, I was just doing as I was told."

"I know," Kyle said, "and Rick was doing what he needed to do. He's right—never let a suspect get that close to you," he said with a wink, then proceeded quickly down the hallway after Rick and Mikeyla.

The cadet stared after the chief, open mouthed.

Kyle caught up to Rick and Mikeyla. Sebastian was forestalling them.

"Rick," Kyle called as he saw Rick tense. "Don't."

Rick's head snapped around to look at Kyle.

"That's Sebastian Bach, from Midnight's Sacramento team. He won't go down as easily as that cadet did. Let's save what blood you have left. Bach, this is Rick Debenshire, Midnight's husband, and her daughter, Mikeyla." Kyle walked over, hugged Mikeyla and extended his hand to Rick. "Good to see you two are in relatively good shape."

"Where's Ricardo?" Rick had worried about that while they were being held—had they found his son too?

"He's safe," Kyle said. "Marie and he are staying at my place, with two officers at the house until they're cleared to bring him here."

"Great, thanks, Kyle," Rick said gratefully.

Kyle's cell phone rang then; he answered it. It was Joe, telling him they were calling in a locksmith to open a safe in Weiskoff's house.

"Weiskoff is dead," Joe told Kyle.

"Damn," Kyle said. "Okay, well keep me posted."

He hung up, looking at Rick.

"What?" Rick asked.

"The man behind all of this is dead," Kyle said. "We were hoping to get some information out of him."

"Who?" Rick asked, glancing at Mikeyla.

Kyle pulled the picture out of his pocket and handed it to Rick. Rick unfolded it and grimaced.

"We're the reason he's dead," Rick said.

"You?"

"Me," Mikeyla said.

Kyle looked at her, shocked.

"She learned a few things from Joe," Rick said.

Kyle looked a bit alarmed. "I'll be sure to let Nick know," he said, winking at Mikeyla.

"So, what's going on?" Rick asked. "What happened to Midnight?"

"She was shot twice," Kyle said. "Tiny took one round. We thought they were minor—no major arteries hit, no major damage.

325

Now they've both come up with fevers that the doctors can't seem to break no matter what they try."

"Oh God," Mikeyla said, sounding terrified. "That's what he said, Daddy. He said Mom was going to die a slow, painful death from a fever."

Rick and Kyle exchanged a look. This wasn't a good sign. If Weiskoff purposely gave Midnight the fever, he'd know that it could kill her.

"Joe, Kana, Kashena and Rogue Squadron are tearing his house apart right now, looking for some clue as to what the bullets were tainted with. Whatever it was, it dissipated on impact. We got nothing off the bullets."

Rick nodded, knowing they were racing against time on this.

"I need to see her," Rick said, his voice shaking with the emotions running through his mind.

Kyle blew his breath out. "Mikeyla, you stay out here with me," Kyle said, putting his hand on her shoulder.

Rick looked at Kyle sharply, and then he realized that Kyle was trying to protect Mikeyla from a sight he didn't think she'd want to see. Even knowing that didn't prepare Rick for what he saw when he walked into the hospital room. Midnight looked like she'd been severely beaten. Her skin was darkly discolored in a number of places, including the side of her face. He felt like he was going to be sick, seeing his wife so gravely ill. Standing right next to the bed, Rick took her hand gently in his, noting the discoloration on her hand as well.

"Babe," he said softly, his lips next to her ear, "I don't know if you can hear me, but you gotta fight this. The sonofabitch that did this is dead. Don't let him take you with him, Night. I love you. Please fight." Hi voice broke on the last word.

Rick sat in the hospital room for a while. Finally one of the doctors came in.

"Are you Mr. Debenshire?"

"Yes," Rick said.

The doctor looked at Midnight, then back at Rick.

"I wish we were able to do more," the doctor said sincerely, "but this fever is eluding every attempt we make."

"What is this?" Rick asked, touching the dark, bruise-like discoloration on Midnight's cheek.

"She's bleeding internally," the doctor said. "It's a symptom of a viral hemorrhagic fever. We just don't know what strain, so we have no way of curing it."

"Jesus, isn't that like Ebola?" Rick asked, aghast at the thought.

"It's like that, yes, but it's a different strain. None of the usual antiviral drugs are working to break the fever."

"So what happens if you can't cure her?"

The doctor looked at Rick. "She'll get worse. She's likely to be delirious, have seizures, her whole nervous system will fail, her kidneys will fail…" The doctor's voice trailed off as he saw Rick pale.

"She's going to die," Rick said, devastated.

"If we don't find a cure, yes."

Rick nodded, doing his best to recover his composure. His eyes went to Midnight, his fingers smoothing gently over her hand. The doctor watched him for a minute, his heart going out to this man. It was very obvious that Rick Debenshire loved his wife as much as everyone who'd seen anything about their love affair believed he did. There were no cameras here, no limelight, just a man devastated over the possibility of losing his wife.

The doctor left the room, silently praying for a miracle.

It took some cajoling, but Rick finally allowed the doctors to take a look at his gunshot wound. They managed to get the bullet out with a quick minor surgery. Fortunately, the wound was easily packed and bandaged up, and Rick resumed his position at Midnight's bedside.

***

The safe door popped open, and the locksmith had to practically leap out of the way as Kana and Kashena descended on the contents. Books, at least twenty of them, leather-bound journals.

"Jesus, how are we going to read all of these?" Kana asked.

"We'll all take one," Joe said. "Let's get back to the hospital."

Grabbing the journals, they headed for the door. Rogue Squadron joined them. Everyone took a journal and started reading while Joe drove them all back.

Joe called Kyle from the Escalade, telling him they'd found Weiskoff's journals and that they were searching them for any clues about what he'd given Midnight and Tiny.

"How are they?" Joe asked.

"Midnight's getting worse," Kyle said. "Tiny is the same, maybe because he was only hit with one dose, I don't know. Either way, they're both dead if we don't find a cure."

"We'll find one," Joe assured. "I don't care what experts we have to fly in here. Do me a favor," Joe said, his tone changing slightly. "Get some of your lab boys to the hospital. I want them on hand if we need help finding a cure or understanding some technical crap."

"You got it," Kyle said.

***

In another room in the hospital, Jessica sat, her hand in her husband's huge one.

"Nathanial Ako, you better be listening to me," she told him, tears in her eyes. "I love you, and I'll be damned if I'm going to lose you now. Forget it, pal—you're not getting out of getting me pregnant that easily," she said, a sad smile on her face.

She'd been talking to him for hours. Her voice was hoarse. Everyone had come by to check on her and Tiny. She'd been told they were trying desperately to find a cure to whatever was causing the fever that was killing him. Jessica knew they were doing everything in their power to help. She only prayed it would be soon enough. His fever had worsened in the last hour. She'd heard that Midnight's fever was much worse. She'd had a seizure earlier and was bleeding internally. Silently, Jessica prayed that both Midnight and Tiny would come out of this.

Gripping Tiny's hand tighter, she thought about their last conversation. They were arguing about her wanting to get pregnant. He was, as always, very calm.

"I won't do it, Jessica," he said, not for the first time, even in that argument. "I won't endanger your life."

"It won't!" she exclaimed. "Your mother gave birth to five boys your size, and it didn't kill her."

"My mother is twice your size, Jessica," he replied calmly.

"Not twice my size," Jessica growled. "That would make her over ten feet tall."

"You know what I meant, honey."

"I want a baby, Nathanial."

"We'll adopt."

"I want your baby, Nathanial."

Tiny simply shook his head, continuing to pack his suitcase to leave the next morning.

They went to bed. She was angry at him for his obstinance on this issue. It was a long-standing feud between them. When he put his hand on her waist to hold her, she pushed it off, letting her anger push him away. Tiny, as always, said nothing, simply lying behind her in their bed. It was his way—he would never raise his voice to her. He certainly would never raise his hand to her. He respected her in ways no man had ever respected her before. He loved her beyond anything she'd ever experienced. She just didn't understand his immovable stance on the baby issue.

The next morning, when he climbed out of bed at 3 a.m., he quietly went about getting showered and dressed. When he was ready to leave, he kneeled next to the bed, on the side she was facing.

"I love you," he said softly, "and if anything happened to you giving birth to my child, I'd never live again. I'm sorry for being selfish, but I love you too much to lose you." He kissed her softly on the cheek.

Jessica had lain there not saying a word. She'd heard him sigh softly, then get up and leave the room, carrying his suitcase. She'd warred with herself about going after him, but she'd told herself that if she ran after him, it would only assure him that he'd won this round. No, she couldn't do that. She wanted a baby; he was just being ridiculous about this. He'd have to see that eventually.

He'd been shot that morning, and now he was lying there possibly dying. Jessica felt that she was dying inside too. *Please, God, hurry and find a cure.*

***

"Fuck!" Joe yelled, throwing the journal that he'd been skimming across the room.

He glanced at the rest of the group, who'd looked up from what they were reading. "There's nothing in that one." he said, gesturing to the book lying on the floor across the room.

"I would hope not," Christian murmured. Rogue Squadron had gotten back to the hospital about the same time as Joe and the team had returned with the books. They were all reading one of the journals.

Stevie elbowed him. "Don't start."

Christian nodded, knowing what she meant. Joe was on edge right now—they all were. The last thing they needed was a fight. They were getting nowhere fast, and it was frustrating them all. Midnight was getting worse; Tiny was starting to show signs of internal bleeding. Tiny and Midnight were dying, and they were reading the rantings of a lunatic. They confirmed that both the attack that had wounded Sebastian and the attack on Cat were engineered. It was also confirmed that Johnathan Weiskoff had meant to kill not only Cat, but Elizabeth as well. He also wanted Kana dead for their "depraved" lifestyle.

"Dumbass deserves to be dead," Kana muttered when that part was brought out.

"If he wasn't I'd kill him again," Mikeyla said darkly.

Everyone looked up, surprised by Mikeyla's statement. Rick had told them all that Mikeyla had been the one to shoot Weiskoff, beating him at his own game. They'd all congratulated her on an excellent shot.

"And the perfect first target," Christian had said, his voice a growl.

Everyone had agreed with him.

"Okay, what do we know for sure?" Joe asked, standing up and pacing.

"We know that the fever is caused by a virus called Korologos," Christian said.

"It's not spread person to person," Donovan put in.

"And he had several versions of it," Dave said.

Kashena's head snapped up. "What?" she asked. She'd been involved in reading a volume that was dated over two months before.

"He had several versions of the virus," Donovan repeated, flipping back through the pages of the journal he'd been reading. "He talks about several tries to get it right. He tested it on rats, and determined how long it would take to kill them, then upped the strength and dosage. He mixed the virus with something called… Dimpraline, some kind of—"

"That's it!" Kashena said. "That's the word I saw!"

"It is?" Kyle asked, looking over at her.

"That's it," Kashena said, standing up and starting to pace, glancing at Donovan, "What is it?"

"It's some kind of solution that he used to tame the virus a bit, so it would take longer to work. He wanted it to be a slow painful death," Donovan said, grimacing as he realized that was exactly what was happening.

"Slow and painful…" Kashena said. Her mind was telling her she was close.

"He tested it on rats?" Sierra asked. "How did he know how much to use on a human?"

"He could have calculated based on the size of rats in proportion to humans," Jay Mark said. He was from the crime lab.

"Or he could have tested it on a human…" Kashena said, her voice trailing off as she looked over at Sierra.

Sierra's look was perplexed.

"What?" Joe asked, knowing something was catching on here.

"How are things like anti-venom made?" Kashena asked Jay, wanting to confirm her theory before she got too excited.

"In the case of snake bites, it's made from the blood of an animal immunized against the venom," Jay said.

"Okay, so they have the cure for it in their bloodstream?"

"Yes, essentially," Jay said. "But in the case of this virus, the AG and Mr. Ako haven't been cured yet. So they cannot provide the anti-venom."

"But I can," Kashena said, her tone sure.

"What?" Joe asked, sounding shocked and excited at the same time.

"The fever…" Sierra said, realizing what Kashena was talking about.

Kashena nodded, then looked over at Joe and Kyle. "He tested it on me," she said, pulling up the sleeve of her shirt, showing the thin red scar on her arm. "From the scratch I mysteriously received in the Los Angeles airport. The one I received right before I came down with a very bad fever."

"One that didn't break for four days, and only then with the help of a healer," Sebastian put in.

"Healer?" Kyle asked.

"An Indian healer," Kashena explained.

"Our doctors," Sierra told them.

Jay Mark looked at both women, his face hopeful. "I think you might be right."

"Kashena Marshal, can we borrow some of your blood?" Kyle asked.

"Take whatever you need," Kashena said seriously. "I swore to protect her with my life. If I can save her with my blood, I'm more than happy to."

It took a lot of blood, and Kashena was feeling lightheaded by the time they managed to get the serum so that Jay was happy with it. Sierra fed her orange juice to keep her strength up. Every time Sierra suggested that they allow Kashena to rest, it was Kashena who refused.

"We don't have time, Sierra," Kashena said, her tone as lifeless as her face.

***

Rick was thinking along the same lines as he paced back and forth in Midnight's room. At one point he glanced over at her still form and was shocked when he saw blood seeping from one eye.

"God, no!" he yelled, striding over to her and taking her hand. "Midnight! You have to stay with me, babe. Please don't go..." His voice broke as tears welled up in his throat. "I can't live without you, Night, I can't. Please hold on."

Midnight started to writhe then; the delirium the doctor had talked about had come and gone and come back again. She gasped, writhed, whispered things, often Rick's name. He did everything he could to soothe her, but she was beyond hearing him. After a couple of minutes she calmed again.

"Midnight, please, please hold on," he said, holding her hand and stroking her face with his other hand. "I can't lose you, not like this. I won't let you slip away from me like this. Damn it!" he yelled in frustration. He put his lips to her ear. "I love you, Midnight. I can't breathe without you. Please don't leave me."

Mikeyla stood in the doorway, brought there by Rick's original shout. She'd stood watching her father fall apart, tears running down her cheeks at the words he said. Knowing your parents loved each other was one thing; hearing your extremely strong and daunting father losing all composure at the thought of losing your mother was another. She remembered back to when she was twelve—they had thought Midnight was dead, killed by the car bomb that had destroyed her classic Corvette. Rick had been devastated then, but he hadn't had Midnight there to beg her to stay with him. At twelve Mikeyla hadn't been able to totally grasp what it meant for her father to lose Midnight. Now she understood it, and it tore her heart out to hear him.

"Daddy?" she said from the doorway.

Rick turned around, continuing to block her view of her mother's face.

"Keyl, you shouldn't be in here." Rick said, his tone solemn.

"Is the fever contagious?"

"We don't think so," Rick said, "but…"

"But you could be in here catching it if it is," Mikeyla said sadly. It was another testament to her father's devotion to her mother—he didn't care if it killed him, as long as he was with her.

"Daddy, I want to see her," Mikeyla said softly.

"Keyl…" Rick shook his head. "This isn't how I want you to remember your mother."

"Daddy, I'm not a child anymore," she told him. "I know that she's sick, and I know what this hemorrhagic fever can do. I want a chance to tell her I love her too," she said, tears in her eyes again.

Rick took a deep breath and nodded. Mikeyla walked into the room, and Rick stepped aside. Mikeyla gasped when she saw the blood seeping from her mother's eye.

"Oh, Daddy..." she whispered, understanding now what had him so upset.

Rick put his hands on her shoulders as he saw her tremble.

Mikeyla nodded, resolving herself to do this. She took her mother's hand.

"Mom, Daddy's right, you can't leave us. We still need you. I still need you. I love you, Mom," she said, tears streaming down her cheeks. "Daddy, Ricky and me need you here with us. Please don't go, please."

"Rick," Joe called from the doorway. He winced at the glance of Midnight he got; it was more than he could handle at this point. "We've got something. The doctor is preparing it now, so hold tight."

Rick nodded, silently praying it was in time.

***

It had been five hours since they'd given Midnight the antiviral serum they'd created with antibodies from Kashena's blood. Rick was asleep, his hand on Midnight's, his head on his arm next to their hands.

Midnight woke slowly, feeling like she was coming out of a very deep sleep. She moved her head slightly; it felt like a lead weight. Glancing down, she saw exactly what she knew she'd see: her husband. She smiled softly. She wasn't sure what had happened this time, but she did know that whenever she woke up in a hospital, Rick was right there with her. And she knew she was in a hospital—she knew the smell too well. In the business they were in, you spent way too much time in hospitals, either for yourself or for someone you cared about.

336

So what had happened this time? Midnight wondered. Reaching down, careful not to disturb the IV in her left hand, the one Rick was holding, she touched where there were bandages. There were two different places. Closing her eyes, Midnight tried to think back to what she remembered last.

They were at the airport. Rick called. He was upset about something, going on about a hospital. The signal cut out; she tried to get a better signal... Things got fuzzy from there. She searched and searched her mind for the details, but she couldn't think of them.

As if Rick sensed her agitated thoughts, he stirred, lifting his head.

Rick didn't think he'd ever see a more wonderful sight in his life. Midnight was awake and, as usual, deep in thought. He smiled brilliantly, feeling so relieved it almost made him sick. His wife was back.

Midnight turned her head to look at him. "So what happened this time?" she asked, her voice a hoarse whisper.

Rick grinned. She had her usual sense of humor about her too. "Oh, you know, the usual—people getting shot, people almost dying." His words were light, but Midnight could see that he was very serious.

"Who? Who almost died? Is everyone okay?" she asked, worried instantly.

"You, Midnight, you almost died. We almost lost you," he said, "and Tiny too, but he's okay, and so are you, thank God."

Midnight breathed a sigh of relief. She'd been more worried for one of her people almost dying than herself.

"What about Kana?" she asked.

"She's fine too," Rick assured her. "Everyone is going to be just fine."

"Everyone?" Midnight repeated, knowing there was more to this than he was telling her.

Rick stood up, leaning down to kiss her gently on the lips. "Get your strength back and I'll tell you all about it," he said, smiling. "For now, I'm going to go let everyone know you're awake and better."

Midnight's brow furrowed. "What happened to you?" she asked, seeing the fading but still evident bruises on his face.

"Oh, you know," he said, shrugging nonchalantly. "New hole, wrecked car, the usual."

"Rick…"

"I'm fine, Night," he said. "I'll explain everything later. You need to rest for now."

Midnight stared at him, obviously debating arguing with him. She didn't like being kept in the dark. To head her off, he kissed her again, his hand gently cupping her face.

"I love you more than my own life," he whispered to her when their lips parted, his eyes staring down into hers.

"And I you," Midnight replied softly.

Rick smiled down at her, then turned and left the room. Midnight heard the cheer go up a minute later. She smiled to herself, shaking her head as she closed her eyes. She definitely had a loud family.

***

Elizabeth spent four days in the hospital. For the first two she was in and out of consciousness, and often woke with nightmares, but Cat was there for her every time.

"So, when are they releasing Elizabeth?" Sable asked. They were lying in bed in Sable's hotel room. Cat had come back to the room to get some sleep, as she'd done the previous days.

"Tomorrow," Cat said. "It looks like I'm going to drive her back down to San Diego."

"Drive?" Sable asked.

"Yeah, the doctors don't think she should fly just yet. Something about the pressure or something, plus she's feeling really self-conscious about the bruises and stuff that haven't healed yet."

Sable did her best to clamp down on the jealousy that surged through her. Cat was going to chauffeur her ex-girlfriend, the one she was still in love with, back down to San Diego. Lovely.

Cat saw the flash of jealousy in Sable's eyes and waited for the comments to begin. To Sable's credit, she said nothing. For that Cat rewarded her with a lovemaking session that left them both exhausted the next morning.

The next day, Cat picked Elizabeth up from the hotel, settling her in the passenger seat of the Cayenne. They talked a bit; eventually Elizabeth asked the question she'd been wanting to ask for days.

"Are you in love with her?" Elizabeth asked.

Cat turned over the question in her head. So many things had happened; too many things had changed. She noticed that Elizabeth was looking at her. She finally just shook her head.

"I'm not in love with anyone anymore," Cat said, feeling the weight of what she'd just said.

"Including me," Elizabeth said sadly.

Cat couldn't help but feel annoyed. Elizabeth was so good at playing the victim. "You made your own choices, Elizabeth."

"I made a mistake, Catalina."

"And mistakes have consequences too," Cat replied, refusing to be drawn into another sad play about Elizabeth's choices in life.

"I know that," Elizabeth snapped. "It sent you running to someone else. Is she so much better?" she asked, her lip trembling.

Cat pulled herself up short. This was not a discussion she wanted to have right now.

"Bet, look," she said, feeling the need to just let things lie. She reached over and touched Elizabeth's hand, "I don't want to talk about this, okay? Not now. Things are too hard at the moment. Can't we just not, for now?"

Cat was relieved when Elizabeth blew her breath out in a sigh and nodded slowly. "You're right," she said. "I'm sorry. You've been so wonderful about all of this, and I need to just…" She shrugged, looking back out the window.

They were silent for a while. Finally Elizabeth made a comment about the music Cat was listening to, and they talked easily for a while. The rest of the drive was without incident.

Two months after being shot twice in cold blood, Attorney General Midnight Chevalier testified against the men accused in her attack. These men are being charged as accomplices to Johnathan Weiskoff, the mastermind behind a series of attacks on both personnel and family members of Attorney General Chevalier. Weiskoff was reportedly shot and killed during a fight with Chevalier's people. The men are being charged with seven counts of attempted murder, five of those attempts on peace officers. One of the attempts was on Attorney General Chevalier's husband; two of the non-peace-officer attempts were on AG Chevalier's daughter and niece. Other attempts were on officers in AG Chevalier's current or previous employ.

While all are said to be recuperating well, Attorney General Chevalier condemns the attacks as having been personally motivated rather than political. Midnight Chevalier is quoted as saying, "If you bring the fight to my home, be prepared for a war." That's exactly what Weiskoff and his accomplices found out. Journals written by the deceased Weiskoff were submitted into evidence. It is expected that all four men arrested will be found guilty, as the evidence against them is overwhelming.

Special Agent Supervisor Kashena Windwalker-Marshal is being hailed as the agent who cracked the case and found Weiskoff's journals. She's also being credited with assisting in the saving of Midnight Chevalier's life. When asked, Kashena Marshal declined to comment, saying only that she was doing her job. Kashena Marshal is a member of Attorney General Chevalier's security detail. Special Agent in Charge Kana Sorbinno was quoted as saying, 'Marshal is the reason Midnight Chevalier is alive today. Midnight's family will never forget that.' Midnight Chevalier herself stated that "Kashena Marshal is the kind of person I trust with my life for a reason."

Things in the Attorney General's office are, as always, busy and moving onward. Midnight Chevalier is coming back from this latest string of events as she always does, with more strength and determination than this state has seen in any politician in its history. California has never encountered a politician like Ms. Chevalier. Then again, that's why this reporter voted for her.

EPILOGUE

Six Months Later

Sebastian lay in his bed; he was just drifting off to sleep when he heard a light knock on the doorjamb of his bedroom door. Opening his eyes, he looked toward the door.

"Hey, Sam," he said, grinning. "What're you doing here?"

"Just came to see how you're doing," she said, smiling as she walked over to the bed.

He didn't bother to sit, just looked up at her. "Bad day?"

"It had its moments."

"Come here," he said, patting the bed next to where he lay.

She shrugged out of her jacket, kicked off her shoes and lay down next to him. His arm went around her as she snuggled close.

"So, tell me about the moments," he said, his voice warm and comforting next to her ear.

Samantha proceeded to tell him about the issues that had come up at the office that day. She was adjusting to the change in her assignment. Changing over to public rights had been a good decision, but things were a bit different for her now. She liked what she was doing, but that didn't make it easier sometimes. Sebastian had, as always, been her sounding board for any and all misgivings she had about herself or the job.

"Sounds to me like you just need to brush up on your Bill of Rights etiquette," he said.

"I know," she said with a smile. "Don't start in on me."

Sebastian chuckled. Samantha laughed softly too.

"You know," she said conversationally, "this isn't exactly what I thought would happen between us."

Sebastian looked back at her for few seconds, then nodded slowly.

"You also knew I wasn't a one-woman kind of guy," he said quietly.

"Yes, I did know that," she agreed, smiling. "I guess I just hoped I could be that one woman who could keep you."

"You wouldn't want to keep me, Sam. For all the changes you've had in your opinion of me, above all you still can't relate to me easily. I'm not really your type."

"How can you say that?" she asked, curious about his point of view, as she always was.

"You need someone on the same intellectual level as you."

"You're by no means inferior to me intellectually, Sebastian," she said, surprised.

"No," he said, "but my intellect is based on something totally different than yours. It makes us very different people. While we're compatible on a casual level, something deeper just isn't in the cards for us."

Samantha nodded, trying to understand. "You need someone wilder than you, don't you?"

Sebastian grinned in spite of himself. "I hadn't really thought about it that way, but I probably need someone who's had as much or more real-life experience than me, yeah."

"You get bored easily."

His mouth dropped open at such a bald statement, but then he laughed. "I guess you could say that."

Samantha nodded again. "I think I knew that all along. But I can't say I don't enjoy being around you still."

"I'm easier to take in small doses, babe," he said, winking at her.

Samantha laughed. "That's what Kash says too."

"Oh-ho!" he said, giving her a shocked look. "That was low."

Samantha grinned impishly at his disgruntled look. "Payback," she said, poking him in the chest.

"Uh-huh," he murmured. He narrowed his ocean-green eyes at her, then he leaned forward and kissed her lips softly. "You're not sleeping well again, are you?"

She sighed. "Not the last couple of days, no. The divorce should be final tomorrow. I guess I'm still keeping my fingers crossed that Jeffrey doesn't suddenly try to pull a rabbit out of his hat, you know?"

"Sleep here tonight," he said, pulling her closer. "That way I know you'll sleep."

She looked up at him, her blue eyes sparkling. "Do we have to sleep the whole time?" she asked suggestively.

Sebastian smiled, his eyes sparkling too. "No, that's not a requirement. But you better plan to call in sick tomorrow."

"I already have the day off."

"Then I better plan to call in sick tomorrow."

"Yes, you better," she said, moving to kiss him.

His arms wrapped around her, and she forgot everything for a while. They slept late into the next morning, after making love for hours. It was far from the relationship she'd thought she'd have with Sebastian Bach, but it was definitely exciting.

***

Rick turned over and was awake instantly. Midnight wasn't in bed. Sitting up, he noted that the bathroom light was on.

"Night?"

"Yeah?" she answered as she walked out of the bathroom, turning off the light.

Rick lay back as she got into bed next to him. "Headache again?"

"Yeah," she sighed, settling against him as his arms wrapped around her.

"Should they be lasting this long?"

Midnight shrugged. "The doctor said it could take quite a while to get back to normal, babe."

He nodded, looking unhappy.

"Look," she said, touching her finger to his lips, as if trying to quell his thoughts, "it's a lot better than being dead."

"That's not funny."

Midnight rolled her eyes. "I wasn't trying to be funny, Rick. The fact of the matter is, I got off without too much recovery from all that. I'm trying to point out the bright side here."

"Well, stop it," he said stubbornly.

Midnight grinned. "If you don't stop it, Richard, I'm calling your mother."

"You wouldn't dare," he said, a grin of his own starting.

"Try me."

He leaned in and kissed her lips. Pulling back, he looked into her eyes. "I love you."

"And I love you," she replied, staring up at him. "We made it through, Rick. We always do, we always will."

He nodded, wanting to believe her, and praying she was right.

"It's us, babe." Midnight touched his cheek. "It's what we do, who we are."

"Yeah, who we are that makes people hate us so much they want to kill us."

"We're passionate about what we do," Midnight replied. "We don't let anyone tell us we're wrong. That kind of passion breeds contempt sometimes. I'd like to think we're appreciated by more people than we're hated by."

"I'm sure we are," Rick said, then sighed. "It would just be nice if the people that appreciated us had more money than the nutcases that hate us."

Midnight laughed at that. "Yeah, that would be nice for a change. Although you have to say we've received a lot of support from the music industry."

"Yeah, cause BJ Sparks wants your body," Rick said, smirking.

"Hey!" she said, poking him playfully. "I think he appreciates much more than my body, thank you very much."

Rick laughed, dodging her attempts to poke him.

"Speaking of BJ," Midnight said, narrowing her eyes at him, "you make your deal with him yet?"

Rick's eyes lit up as he grinned like a schoolboy. "Yup, we are now the proud owners of a 1965 Shelby GT500."

"Oh Lord," Midnight said. "How much did you end up settling on for the price? Or do I even want to know?"

Rick pressed his lips together, looking at the ceiling like a guilty child. "You probably don't want to know."

"You went six figures, didn't you?"

Rick winced, then looked down at her, his face schooled in an innocent expression. "Well, yes, but—"

"Richard Joshua Debenshire, you paid more than a hundred thousand dollars for a car?" she exclaimed.

"Well, yeah, but—"

"Oh, you are so in the dog house…"

"He went one hundred even, though. That car is worth well over one fifty."

"I don't care," she said, shaking her head. "Men and cars…"

"Hey, now," he said. "Don't you have a classic Corvette sitting in the garage?"

"Yes, but I'm betting it didn't cost you a hundred thousand."

"Close," Rick said matter-of-factly.

Midnight's mouth dropped open. "It only cost me thirty-eight thousand for my first one."

"You bought it from a retiring cop, didn't you?"

"Yeah."

"I bought it from someone who knew what they had," he said, winking at her.

Again her mouth dropped open, then she closed it and sighed. "Okay, you win."

He grinned, accepting her defeat. He knew she hadn't been mad at him about the amount of money. She never questioned him about what he spent his trust fund on; as far as she was concerned that was his money to do with whatever he chose. It was just appalling to her that they were driving such expensive cars. She was a kid who grew up on the streets—$100,000 cars were for rich people. No matter how much money she made, no matter how much money Rick was worth, it didn't matter; she didn't consider herself rich by any means.

Going from working as the Chief of San Diego Police Department to being Attorney General had increased her pay by a couple thousand dollars a month. Rick had gone from being a lieutenant to a captain, so his pay had increased as well. Rick's trust fund, through skillful investing by his father and the Debenshire accountant, was in the millions now. But to Midnight, however, they still weren't rich. Rick knew she simply resisted the idea that his money belonged to her as well—it was Midnight's way. He loved her for that. She wasn't about money; she was about doing things to make a difference.

"So when does Kana go on leave for the wedding?" Rick asked, changing the subject smoothly.

"Today was her last day," Midnight said. "Rick, she's so tense it's not even funny."

"I'll bet," Rick said, smiling. "She's our last hold-out, last one of us to get married."

"True," Midnight said. "I think she's just worried about Palani's parents."

"I thought they approved of the marriage."

"Well, I guess they gave their blessing, but it was under pretty tense circumstances. Palani's older brother had just attacked Kana."

"Oh yeah," Rick said. "He's not coming to the wedding, is he?"

"For his sake, I hope not."

Rick grinned. Palani's older brother Sampson, the man responsible for Palani's fall down a flight of stairs that had caused her miscarriage, may be big, but Kana's family was a lot more dangerous than he could ever be. If he was foolhardy enough to come to the wedding, he'd be wise to keep his comments to himself and watch his step.

***

Tiny was lying on the couch, lazily flipping through the channels on the television. At six foot five, even though he was half sitting up his feet dangled over the end of the sofa. Jessica walked into the kitchen, carrying a grocery bag. She was quiet so she was able to observe her husband without him noticing for a little bit. She smiled to herself. He looked like a traditional Samoan, wearing jean pants that cut off just below the knee and no shirt. The top half of his pe'a tattoo showed above the waistline of his shorts. It was incredible, this deeply etched tattoo of black markings against his dark skin.

Jessica had asked him about the tattoo the first time they'd made love. It was impossible to miss, covering a good portion of his body. The tattoo began just below his knees on both legs and spiraled up, covering his skin to well past his waist. It was an extremely intricate design, with lines and shapes etched in black. Tiny had patiently explained to her that in Samoan culture this tattoo, called the pe'a, illustrated the transition of the Samoan male from childhood into adulthood. The tattoo had taken three days and was extremely painful to have done. He'd explained the different parts to her—the va'a, which represented immediate family genealogy, and the aso laiti, which translated to "small lines" and meant his mother's and father's families. He also explained that this tattoo was not accomplished with a needle, like normal tattoos, but was done by a "tufuga ta tatau," a tribal tattooist, with bone chisels and ink.

It had both surprised and impressed Jessica that this man was so deeply connected with his culture. It was one of the things she loved most about him—his sense of tradition, honor and loyalty. He was a true Samoan man. One she loved very much. She knew there was nothing he wouldn't do for her. If she asked him to, he'd lay down his life for her. It was something that made her understand the deep commitment he had made to her. Traditional Samoans didn't take marriage lightly, so they would only marry when they found the person they believed to be their soulmate. Tiny had told her that she was indeed the other half of his soul, and she believed that. She was ever surprised by the gentle, sweet man that he was; he never ceased to amaze her.

Tiny sensed her standing behind him and glanced back. He got up immediately, moving to assist her.

"I'm fine," she said, setting the bag down, knowing he always felt it was his responsibility to do any lifting.

"Are there more?"

"Yes, but—"

"I'll get them," he said, smiling down at her.

"Okay," she said, sighing. She knew it was futile to ever try to handle something in their home herself. If it involved manual labor, he expected to do it.

Ten minutes later she had all the groceries put away.

"Go back to relaxing," she told him, pushing him toward the couch.

"You're home now."

She smiled up at him. "You can't relax when I'm home?"

He canted his head to the side. "I can relax with you," he said warmly.

"You can indeed," she said. "Do you want some iced tea? I made some this morning."

"Of course."

She poured them both some iced tea, then walked over to the couch where he stood waiting for her. She was accustomed to his genteel ways, so it never struck her as strange anymore, but it had taken a lot of getting used to in the beginning. He never sat before she did; he always pulled her chair out, opened doors for her, stood when she entered a room. Nathanial Sarani Ako was a gentleman from the tips of his toes to the top of his head. It was astounding, considering he'd been a gang member when he'd met Midnight Chevalier and joined her task force almost thirty years ago. Midnight had told Jessica that even when he'd been fresh out of the gang, he'd always treated her with the utmost respect. "He was like no gang member I'd ever met," Midnight had said.

In truth, he was like no man Jessica had ever met. Her law enforcement family, which included three brothers, her father and her mother, adored Tiny. They'd liked him from the moment they met him. He took very good care of Jessica, and that's what they all wanted for her. She and Tiny were scheduled to leave for Sacramento the day after Kana's wedding to visit her family. Jessica wanted a chance to tell them that they were finally going to start a family of their own.

Tiny sat back down on the couch, and Jessica sat down between his legs, leaning back against his chest as he wrapped one strong muscled arm gently around her waist. They watched TV together for a while, then at one point she turned around to look up at him. As always, his dark eyes met hers directly.

"Nathan," she began softly, "I have something I need to tell you."
"Yes?"

She bit her lip, nervous for a moment. "I'm pregnant."

His mouth opened, but no words came out. His shock was evident—he blinked a few times, as if trying to process what she'd just said. He started to say something a couple of times, but then stopped.

"I don't understand," he said finally, looking flabbergasted.

"Well," she said, "apparently after we decided to get pregnant, my body decided to go ahead and really do it."

"But I thought we'd have more time…"

"Nathan, it's fine. We still have a few months to plan. Don't worry."

Tiny took a deep breath and expelled it slowly. It was obvious he was trying to rein in his concern.

"I'll be fine," she told him, running her fingernail over one of the lines on his tattoo, her head down.

He touched her cheek, making her look up at him. She was stunned to see a glazing of tears in his eyes.

"If anything ever happened to you," he said seriously, "I couldn't go on. I can't lose you, Jessica."

"You won't lose me, Nathan," she assured him, putting her hands up to cup his face. "I promise you. I'm going to be strong, healthy and extremely fat. You'll get so tired of dealing with me, you'll just want me to hurry up and have the baby."

"Never," he said, shaking his head. "I'll never get tired of you."

Jessica smiled. He was always very serious when it came to his feelings about her.

"How about me and ten screaming children?" she teased.

"Ten?" he asked, the beginnings of a grin on his lips.

"Two?"

"Let's see how one goes first," he said, his tone lightening now.

"Deal," she said, smiling at him.

"So now we tell your parents you're pregnant instead?"

"Oh yes," she said. "I could barely wait to tell you."

"How long have you known?"

"Since this morning at my appointment."

"You didn't tell me you had a doctor's appointment," he chided.

"Because then I'd have to explain why, and I didn't want to freak you out for no reason, honey."

Tiny looked at her for a long moment, then nodded, accepting her reason for deceiving him. It was rare that they didn't tell each other everything, so he knew she'd been honestly trying to save him worry. In truth, he appreciated that; he would have worried no end. She was his entire life—she meant everything to him. The idea of something happening to her, even with the remote chance of complications in childbirth, scared him to death.

"So, how pregnant are you?" he asked.

"Two months," she said, smiling.

"So in seven months, I'm going to be a father?"

"In seven months you're going to be a father," she confirmed.

He nodded slowly, his mind obviously already churning over the idea.

Jessica wrapped her arms around his neck, reaching up to kiss his lips softly. "You'll be a wonderful father, Nathan, just as you're a wonderful husband."

In response he wrapped his arms around her, careful, as always, not to hug her too tight, but holding her close as a way of thanking her for her words. They spent the rest of the afternoon discussing details about a nursery in their three-bedroom house, as well as some ideas for baby names. It was a nice day.

***

The wedding between Kana and Palani took place on a beautiful day. Kana was handsome in a Dolce & Gabbana suit that Palani had had custom made for her. Palani's dress was in the style of a traditional sarong, but that was where the similarities ended. The sarong was made out of ivory silk mingled with silken lace. It molded Palani's perfect shape and flowed down to her ankles. She wore delicate ivory silk sandals that laced up her slender ankles. Her hair was a cloud of silken black curls, her flowered wreath a mixture of ivory roses and small purple orchids, with ribbons of ivory and tiny orchids trailing down to mix with her waist-length hair. As their friends and family watched, they said their vows and exchanged rings.

The ceremony ended with the priestess saying, "May you create a home that surrounds your family and friends with warmth, laughter and love. Pili olua e, moku ka pawa o ke ao—you two are now one; the darkness is past."

There were sighs and smiles from the group. Then the whooping, cheering and catcalls started as Kana took Palani in her arms, kissing her deeply, her hand gently cupping Palani's face.

Later at the reception, Kana and Palani were toasted and thoroughly enjoyed themselves. After many of the guests had gone home, the Gang still remained, willing to stay until Kana and Palani were ready to call it a night. It was 2 a.m. by the time they decided it was about time to do a final toast.

"What should we toast to?" Tiny asked, grinning.

"People have been toasting us all night," Kana said, shaking her head. She was sitting on a chair she'd turned around, her arms resting on the back. Her suit jacket was on the back of the chair, and the sleeves of her white shirt were rolled up on her forearms.

"True," Palani agreed. Her feet were bare, her dress pulled up to her knees. Her flowered wreath was on the table next to her. She sat on a chair next to Kana, her feet resting in Kana's lap.

"So, let's think of something else," Joe said with a grin.

"We never think of anything else," Dave complained.

"Yeah, we have to toast to something that even Rick isn't in anymore," Spider said.

Rick smiled. "Quit yer bitchin'."

"We toast it because it's what brought us together," Kana said.

"Not us," Christian added.

"No, Midnight did that," Stevie said, winking at her husband.

"You owe her for that," Donovan told Christian.

"I'll owe you somethin'," Christian countered, smirking.

"Boys…" Jeanie put in, rolling her eyes.

Midnight shook her head. The family didn't change much, just seemed to get bigger and bigger. Kashena Marshal and Sierra were sitting with the group, still obviously getting used to the banter that went on.

"Look, we just survived yet another attack on this family," Midnight said. "As far as I'm concerned we can toast to that."

"Or the fact that Mikeyla is now officially part of the adult table?" Dave said, winking at Mikeyla.

"Or the fact that we have a psychic in the group now," Kana added, inclining her head to Kashena.

"Or the fact that I'm going to be a father in seven months," Tiny added casually.

"What!?" was the official response of the group.

"I'm pregnant," Jessica said, smiling.

A cheer went up from the group then, and everyone congratulated Tiny and hugged Jessica.

"Well that didn't take long." Kana grinned at Tiny.

"We'll see if you're next," Tiny said, making a face at Kana.

"Not me." Kana shook her head. "That's Palani's job."

"Well, you'll be the one in the waiting room like me," Tiny said.

"I'll be in the delivery room, thank you very much," Kana said. "I'm not a puss when it comes to this stuff."

Rick rolled his eyes. "We'll be picking Tiny up off the floor."

"I recall picking your ass up off the floor too," Joe said.

"That was different," Rick said.

"You passed out cold when you saw the blood."

"There's going to be blood?" Tiny asked, paling.

Everyone laughed, as Jessica patted his hand.

"Don't worry, babe. I don't expect you to be anywhere near the delivery room."

"We'll be there," Midnight said.

"The girls, that is," Stevie said.

"The boys can wait outside," Cat said.

"Always on the outside looking in," Elizabeth said, grinning.

Kana laughed. "True enough."

"Wasn't there supposed to be a toast in here somewhere?" Spider asked, looking tired.

"Getting old, huh?" Dave asked.

"Bite me," Spider said.

"Let's not start that, boys." Midnight raised her glass. "To FORS."

"To FORS!"

The end of the *Midknight Blue* series

You can find more information about the author and series here:
www.sherrylhancock.com
www.facebook.com/SherrylDHancock
www.vulpine-press.com/midknight-blue-series

Also by Sherryl D. Hancock:

The *WeHo* series follows a group of women from Los Angeles as they navigate the ups and downs of love, life, work, and everything in between.
www.vulpine-press.com/we-ho

The *Wild Irish Silence* series. Escape into the world of BJ Sparks and discover how he went from the small-town boy to the world-famous rock star.
www.vulpine-press.com/wild-irish-silence-series